friction 3

best gay erotic fiction

edited by jesse grant
and austin foxxe

 alyson books
los angeles | new york

MANUFACTURED IN THE UNITED STATES OF AMERICA

THIS TRADE PAPERBACK ORIGINAL IS PUBLISHED BY ALYSON PUBLICATIONS,
P.O. BOX 4371, LOS ANGELES, CALIFORNIA 90078-4371
DISTRIBUTION IN THE UNITED KINGDOM BY
TURNAROUND PUBLISHER SERVICES LTD.,
UNIT 3 OLYMPIA TRADING ESTATE, COBURG ROAD, WOOD GREEN,
LONDON N22 6TZ ENGLAND.

FIRST EDITION: FEBRUARY 2000

00 01 02 03 04 a 10 9 8 7 6 5 4 3 2 1

ISBN 1-55583-535-X

LIBRARY OF CONGRESS CATALOGING-IN-PUBLICATION DATA
APPLICATION IN PROGRESS

CREDITS
FOR A LISTING OF PUBLISHING CREDITS FOR EACH ARTICLE, REFER TO THE "ABOUT
  THE MAGAZINES" SECTION AT THE END OF THIS BOOK.
COVER DESIGN BY CHRISTOPHER HARRITY.
COVER PHOTOGRAPHY BY BODY IMAGE PRODUCTIONS.

Contents

Preface

Hi guys! Welcome to the third volume in the *Friction, Best Gay Erotic Fiction* series. I'll keep this preface short; I know you're anxious to get to the good stuff. As you probably know by now, this series collects the best erotic stories that have appeared in gay magazines in the preceding year. This year, my coeditor, Austin Foxxe, and I have selected a wide variety of stories—everything from "wonder bread" to hardcore bikers to gritty detectives to punk rockers. We hope you enjoy reading this collection as much as we enjoyed putting it together. Austin and I would like to give a special thank you to our friend Alan Mills for pointing us toward a number of excellent stories.

Jesse Grant
Los Angeles
December 1999

Now and Then
Dale Chase

I don't understand the time warp, I just enjoy it. The professor tells me to stay the hell out of it, but he says this while he's got his dick up my ass, and anything said during a fuck doesn't count, at least not to me. So I indulge myself, so to speak, because there are things I like better about then as opposed to now although then and now sort of lose their context on these particular trips.

It's really more place than time, these voyages, even though I know time alters place. The result is always an unfamiliarity that in itself finally becomes familiar. I awaken from a state just this side of sleep to find myself somewhere so far beyond beyond that I feel a kind of weightlessness, then a gradual settling, like coming back down to earth when I've never left. And then I take in the sights, which are always remarkable.

I've learned not to ask exactly when I've landed and if where isn't apparent I don't ask that either. Questions are a giveaway, at least those kinds of questions, so I just try to blend in.

I've taken maybe a dozen time trips, and the professor knows it—how I'm not sure. I wonder if I'm leaving some kind of snail-trail or maybe come-trail because, you see, I'm travelling strictly for the fucks.

"If you'd gather a bit of scientific data," the professor says during one of his tirades, "I wouldn't mind so much. But all you're doing is coming in another millennium. It's such a waste."

"They don't think so."

He shakes his head and huffs, almost endearing with his genius pout. I sidle up behind him and grope his crotch, and he doesn't stop me. "And I won't have you fucking in three different millennia," he says, pushing into my hand. "There have to be limits!" I unzip his fly and fish out his dick, and he goes quiet. He always does.

I won't call all this a problem because I'm having too much fun. Situation is more accurate because I genuinely adore the professor, this 50-year-old scientist-stud who took a mere lab techie under his wing and into his bed. I already had a crush on him so everything was quite welcome and he's a great fuck, don't get me wrong. It's just that when I tried out the time warp in his absence things got complicated and now there's this issue between us. Come spread out over three millennia. What a kick.

"You're too bright for your own good," the professor says as I suck his dick. We're in the lab, me just back from my latest jaunt, ass full of future-come, and the professor starts thrusting into my mouth. I suck his long shaft, tongue cradling him until he's fully primed. He's talking the whole time, telling me it's not real out there, that I have to remember it's a warp, that I haven't really *gone* anywhere. I keep sucking. Listening and sucking.

"You'll have to give me a full report," he says as I pull back to play with his fat knob. The professor is well endowed, mind and body, and I like to handle his big cock as much as he likes to stick it up my ass. "I hope you made at least *some* scientific observations this time," he adds. And then he pulls out and slips on a condom—he carries them in his labcoat—while I strip. He mounts me from behind as I grip a table, and I savor the feel of that hose snaking up into my rectum.

The professor is never urgent. As with his scientific inquiries, he fucks methodically and I enjoy the ride. My own cock is just the opposite, and I last about three strokes before squirting cream all over the table. The professor pauses, peers over my shoulder, and murmurs his approval. He always saves my jism. I don't know what he does with it, but I like the idea.

He resumes his fuck and we settle into an easy rhythm, and then he says, "Tell me about your trip." As much as he dislikes my little runaway adventures, he still gets charged at the idea of future fucking.

"I'm not sure they're people," I tell him. "But then I've run into that before. Maybe by the fourth millennium human beings have superseded themselves. Anyway, they look human, of course, only better. It was the same as always about where, a lab but empty looking, as if they don't need *devices.* I didn't ask—"

"But you should!" the professor shouts, ramming his dick into my ass for emphasis. "One or two questions could bring me so much."

I give it a second and he resumes his stroke, hands on my hips, cock steadily thrusting. I continue; I'm getting to be an expert at giving reports while taking a prick up the backside. "So I'm in this lab alone but I don't hang around. Outside it's beautiful, there's a kind of serenity in the air, almost like it's part of the air, like the air has been drugged. Some kind of natural high."

The professor starts fucking madly at this, over-excited at such a discovery. He's squealing now, and I know he wants information as much as he wants to come. He gets off on all kinds of things. "I keep taking these deep breaths," I continue, "because the air is so sweet but not in a scented kind of way. It's what it *does* to you, and I realize I'm getting a hard-on from just breathing. Just from air. And then I wonder if it does this to everyone, if they're all walking around with stiff dicks or is it just us newcomers who are overwhelmed." I start laughing now because I've made a pun. The professor isn't interested, he's almost there now, but I won't give up. "New*comer*!" I say. "Get it?"

He doesn't acknowledge my attempt at humor. The fuck has taken him over and he's very unprofessorlike as his dick squirts its load. "Fucking shit!" he cries. "Oh, fuck it, oh God, yes, fuck it! Fuck! Fuck! Fuck!"

I grip the table as he slams into me, stopping my narrative to listen. I love it when he gets dirty. "Fuck! Fuck! Fuck!" he shouts, and I know each fuck is a pulse of come. I savor the idea of his highly educated dick spewing cream like us commoners, never mind science or millennia or anything. "Fuck," he says one final time before slumping against me. I squeeze my muscle and he groans. "You don't need the future do you, Jason?"

"Need? No, of course not. I have everything here." I nuzzle back into him, give it a second, then add, "But the lure of adventure is very powerful."

He yanks his dick out of me and storms to the bathroom, wounded yet again. I've reminded him so many times that I'm faithful in *this* world, but that never seems enough for him. It's become a sore point and yet I can usually get around it. Geniuses are such babies about life and sex and all the good stuff.

I purposely don't put on my pants because I know he'll want to hear the full narrative of my journey and also that he likes it best when I stretch out on the corner sofa and play with my dick as I tell it. I settle there now and wait.

He ignores me at first, acting professorlike, capital P-h-fucking-D, acting as if he's never stuck his cock up a techie's ass or any ass for that matter. I ignore him back and he glances at me as if I'm just some kid masturbating in a corner but after a few minutes at his desk he settles into the old leather armchair opposite me. He adjusts his cock and says, "Tell me more." He's got a notepad on the arm of the chair; he writes down the non-sex parts, eager for clues about the future in the crumbs I bring him. I keep telling him *he* should go, but I think he's afraid of what he's found.

"The atmosphere," he prompts. "How did it affect you as time passed, aside from the hard-on?"

"I don't think time passes there. It all seemed stopped in some way, like maybe they found the right moment and just kept it. But maybe not. It was just a feeling I got."

The professor gives me an exaggerated sigh. "You've got to be more observant, Jason. If you're going to keep sneaking into the warp without permission, without guidance, the least you can do is maintain a minimal level of scientific inquiry."

I go silent and look down at my prick instead of him. It's starting to fill and I wag and squeeze until he says, very softly, "Go on."

"So I've got this hard-on and it feels urgent, like I might just come with no hands any second, and...oh, wait, did I mention I'm naked? Sorry, didn't mean to leave that out, but it was so natural. So it's all very smooth outside, clear, fresh, with that great air. No buildings even though I was just in one, but I've learned things like that happen, things come and go. Oh, man, another pun, get it? *Come* and go?"

The professor frowns. My dick is hard now because it knows where we're headed. "Go on," the professor says.

"So there are trees and lawns, everything soft. No concrete, no streets or sidewalks, and then I see this kind of meadow, and there they are, these people if that is what they really are. And I just walk right in among them because I look like them or them me. I mean we're all naked, we're all blond, and we've all got major boners."

"Jason," the professor snaps and I look up at a scowl. "You're not making this up, are you? It's a bit much."

"It's the fucking future!" I say, ticked off that he doesn't believe me, which makes me work my dick even harder. Juice starts running out my slot and down my hand. "And maybe they're not so uptight," I add, mustering all the indignance possible with a cock in my hand.

He considers this, then says, "I just don't want to be manipulated. If this is simply one of your little masturbation plays please tell me as I have better things to do."

He doesn't, of course, at least not in my book. Science will always lose out to a good dickoff. "It's real," I say. "Honest to God."

"Very well."

I close my eyes and stroke my cock as I continue. "At first I think there's really no difference between them and me. They don't say anything but hands are all over me, warm hands, too warm. That's the first clue, like they're artificially heated and it's a notch too high. One is pulling my cock—did I say they're all gorgeous, young, firm, smooth, tanned?—and the rest are watching. It's like it's all kind of ceremonial, like they know I'm from somewhere else, but boy it feels a lot more than that and I'm still sucking in that drugged air and it's starting to feel like it's going into my prick and my ass, and then it's like I'm sort of oozing, my whole body about to dissolve into a pool of come. And they *know* it. They smile and this guy playing with my dick starts fondling my balls and then another is behind me sticking a finger up my ass and it feels *sweet*, there's no other way to describe it, not a tasting kind of sweet but still sweet. Honest to God. And I feel some kind of lube, warm and so smooth, and God I love even that, and then, when I'm so ready I'm about to scream, the crowd parts and up steps this guy who must be the king or something because his cock is about a foot long and they're all kind of bowing to it. I just stare at it and suddenly I can *feel* it in my mouth even though he's 10 feet away. He's aimed at me and he's like this Greek god, so handsome, curly blond hair, perfect features, incredible blue eyes, red mouth, and pecs I want to climb on and down below a bush of yellow silk and then that missile. And I want him to fuck me so bad I start to wiggle because there is still a finger up my ass and the guy is still playing with my cock.

"The Greek god smiles as if he gets the message and they lower me to this thick lawn and it's cool and warm all at once. I'm on my back now and I don't have to do anything. They pull my legs up so my ass is positioned perfectly, sort of hanging there, and a guy even pulls open my cheeks and I feel this kind of air-enema go up me, as if they're blowing the channel clean, and *that* feels good, everything does. And then...."

I couldn't go on. I was working my prick and about to come, and I looked over at the professor who had his hand at his crotch, rubbing himself as he watched me. His look was a sort of scolding lust that I'd seen before. And then I'm going over, juice shooting up onto my belly as I pump my meat. I'm thinking of the Greek god and what he's going to do to me, and it makes the climax keep on going, as if part of him is still in me. When I'm finally done, breathing hard, limp dick in hand, the professor simply says, "And?"

"Gimme a second," I say, knowing I have to lie here with come all over me because he'll want to harvest it, as he says. But first the future.

"All right," I say finally and as I picture it, it starts to feel real and it doesn't matter that I've just emptied my balls. My cock twitches and my nuts start to swell. I take a deep breath and continue. "So I'm sort of hanging there in their arms, ass up, and he's there at my hole which has been cleaned and I know he's clean as well, it's like he's telling me in some way, and then he sticks his dick in me."

I stop the narrative for the initial few strokes because they are truly other-worldly and the professor clears his throat because he doesn't want me going off so totally. Going off, all right. My prick is getting hard again. I can't believe this.

"So the guy, the Greek god," I say, "fucks me." I'm afraid to tell much more because I don't want to hurt the professor and yet I know he wants to know while at the same time he hates it. But never mind all that because my ass feels like the whole other world is going up into my bowels, so warm it feels like a creature all its own, so sweet I think I'm salivating. Jesus, I am. I swallow and I have to grab my dick because I'm so ready, so already ready. I'd call it an out-of-body experience if it wasn't so *in-body*.

"Tell me what you're feeling right now, Jason," the professor says. "You're turning a shade of pink that's a bit beyond human."

I hadn't noticed but now I look down. I'm a sort of magenta color, hot pink without the hot, cool looking except underneath I'm saturated with heat. And all the while I can feel the Greek god's cock up my rectum and come is boiling in my balls and those balls are straining my sac. "Tell me," the professor says, leaning toward me now. His look is something between sexually excited and scientifically excited, which is so very much the professor, the only guy who could mix the two and *enjoy* it. "Tell me about the fuck," he says. "I know he's doing you right now so give me details, please. It appears this particular fuck has transcended the time warp and we haven't experienced that before."

I'm looking at my genius mentor, my teacher, employer, the man I admire more than any on earth, and as I do I'm feeling that dick pumping in and out of me and I can't really find words. My mouth is open, my eyes are fixed, sort of lost to the moment. I see the Greek god instead of the professor; I stare at his hard nipples and wish I could suck on one. I'm stroking my prick while all this plays inside me and outside me, and then I feel the Greek god start to come. He doesn't go frantic like we do and he doesn't make a sound; his cock just sort of does things on its own, contracting and shooting stream after stream, recoiling inside me like a repeating rifle. The come is hot and it goes up me in gushers, in waves, and I feel myself filling. There's an urgency now, I'm reaching capacity, and it gives the fuck a kind of sweet agony that pushes me over and I come like never before. As cream pulses out my slot I wonder if it's even mine, there is so much, and when I finally stop, which seems like minutes later, my stomach is awash in jism. The professor runs a finger through it because it's a gorgeous sky blue and has a scent—not a smell. He sniffs it, runs a fingerful by my nose. "Remarkable," he says. "You've brought me quite a treat. Our first sample from the future." He leans over and kisses my cheek. "You don't have to tell me any more."

I lie still while he scoops all the blue come into a beaker. My skin is now its usual human pale pink and I'm having trouble remembering the Greek god or his fuck. I can feel it getting away and it scares me. I tell this to the professor.

"The fourth millennium seems to have control over the warp," he says, all professorial now which is what I want, "and I suspect the inhabitants might not appreciate our intrusion. They've allowed you a bit of recall as a sort of consolation, but they essentially want you to forget them. A privacy issue, most likely." He comes over and sits beside me and fondles my tired prick.

"Why won't you tell the world that you've discovered a time warp?" I ask him for what must be the hundredth time. He's never answered me before, but he does now. "They'd all want to go," he says a bit sadly. "Who could resist such freedom?" His hand gently traces my cockhead. "Promise me you'll stay here from now on. No more warp trips."

"I promise."

He kisses me and my tongue meets his; I feel his breath against my own. And then he takes his beaker of blue come to his worktable and begins to prepare slides. I think about the promise I've made him and how I make it after each trip. He knows it won't be kept.

Ready
R.J. March

B y the time Kevin and Billy reached Cape Cod, they had broken up. They hadn't really known each other long, and neither was particularly impressed by the strange twist this vacation had taken.

"I think it's a good idea," Kevin said. He'd been skeptical all along—it hadn't seemed the best idea, the two of them as a couple, from the start. (They'd seemed rather mismatched, in his opinion, but the sex was fucking awesome.) And so the breakup seemed justifiable until he started calculating the cost of it, what with the vacation and all: a house for the week, rental car, souvenirs—he'd gotten off cheaper in the past. "So, we're going to go through with this?" he asked, just to be sure.

"The trip or the divorce?" Billy asked facetiously.

Kevin laughed. "Both" he said.

Billy looked at him for a moment—looked *into* him, it felt like—before answering. Kevin had to force himself to keep an eye on the road.

"We're amiable, aren't we?" Billy asked. "I mean, it's not like we hate each other, right?"

Kevin shook his head.

"We just want different things," Billy continued. "I think we can still have fun. What do you think?"

Kevin turned his head and nodded. *I hope so,* he thought to himself, wanting to smile.

They rode in silence for a while, Kevin driving and then playing with the radio, searching for a good song, as Billy looked out his window at a landscape that was becoming less and less dense. The thing Kevin hated about road trips—or maybe this was actually one of those love-hate relationships, like the one he'd just ended—was the boners he'd get. What was it about being in a car that made him want to play with himself? He glanced over at Billy's legs, the hem of his silky basketball shorts raised high, sunlit, and he felt a moment of remorse—*Was that why I loved him,* he asked himself—*his thighs?* It hadn't been love, though-not in the real sense of the word. It wasn't consuming or anything like that. He knew consuming—he'd been there. He put his hand out the window and let the rush of air drag it back. He opened his hand and felt as though he were holding something wild and light. But still, he had the hard-on of a lifetime, sticking up like a telephone pole planted firmly in the crotch of his pants.

He looked over at Billy again, this time to see if he'd noticed his sudden burden. Of course, he hadn't. He was too busy looking out the window, cruising every man they happened to pass. *It would have been nice to have rented a convertible,* he was thinking, but he probably would have gotten a terrible burn, anticipating what fate had in store for him in the week to come.

He looked at himself in the rearview mirror, furtively, not wanting to be caught by Billy, whom he'd always considered a bit vain. Of course, the boy had every right to adore himself-physically, he was well put together, lanky, casually muscled. But his eyes—that was what had drawn Kevin to him from the start—those green eyes and their crowd of black lashes, his sensually shaped brows, all seen in a nanosecond, Kevin running the last of a five-mile race and Billy handing out cups of water, standing in the sun like some sort of…angel. He regretted the word, but there was none better to fit how he looked at that moment, holding out the plastic cup, wearing baggy basketball shorts and a red-trimmed V-neck T-shirt (like he was wearing now—turned out it was something of a uniform for the boy). Everything stilled, and Kevin ran in slow motion toward the dark-haired youth, who held out the cup to him like wine, like elixir, and he took it from him, and their hands met roughly, and the boy said to him in a voice like a man's, "Way to go."

What he saw, getting back to his own reflection, was the gray in his hair, a multitude of gray that seemed untimely, unkind, and unnecessary at this point in his life. He wasn't yet 35, so what was the point? he wondered. He didn't feel mature enough to warrant anything that marked maturity so pointedly. He realized that sort of thing was relative—he had an aunt who went silver-haired in high school; that was the story, anyway-and besides, it didn't really mean anything.

But it caused him to look sideways at Billy, whose hair was coal-black, like glistening tar, when he overdid the gel. He loved—the word nearly made him wince; not anymore did he *love*—the way Billy's scalp shined so whitely through the black bristles of his hair when it was cut like it was now, close to the sides and back of his head. It was longer now than it had been on that day in July when Kevin had run through the crowded streets of Brewerton, begrudgingly admiring the hilly terrain he'd failed to notice when he'd driven the course the week before. He sought the boy out afterward, panting, the muscles in his legs already starting to stiffen. He searched the crowd until he'd found him. He was eating a hot dog. He got himself a cold drink, lingering, following the boy, who, on closer inspection, was more into his 20s, Kevin decided, than he'd originally figured. He got himself close enough and finally into the boy's field of vision, close enough to be noticed, close enough for the boy to say, "Hey, it's you! How'd you do?"

"Just over 30," he answered, walking up to the boy with his hands on his hips, pleased with himself for the first time that day—both for his time and for the fact that Billy had remembered him. The boy—maybe he should say *man* or *guy*, but *boy* just fit—was wearing a name tag: WILLIAM, VOLUNTEER. "Is William your first name or your last?"

The boy blinked.

"Huh?"

"Nothing," Kevin said, the dumb joke aborted.

They'd fallen into Billy's unmade bed quickly—too quickly, Kevin thought now and at the time too, tasting the beer on Billy's mouth and saying to himself, *This is a bit early*—but Billy's motto that week was "Carpe diem" or "Carpe whatever tickles your fancy," and Billy was feeling rather ticklish that day, which was why he brought Kevin to the houseboat where he lived during the summer, docked at his uncle's marina. He'd tossed him onto the tousled sheets and drawn the blinds, pulling off Kevin's running shorts, fumbling with the laces of his shoes until he was frustrated by the intricate knot Kevin had tied earlier that day. "Your feet," he said, almost breathlessly. "I want to see your feet."

"They're ugly," Kevin said, grimacing. "They're callused, ugly feet."

Billy pulled off his own T-shirt, revealing a nearly smooth torso. His nipples were small but defiant the way they jutted out, with a fringe of hair, and a dark line rose up out of his shorts and into the dimple of his navel. Kevin struggled to shake off the shackle of his ankle-bound shorts, and Billy knelt on the bed.

"I like your place," Kevin said. "I could use a shower, though—I stink."

Billy put his nose close to Kevin's chest. "You smell fine," he said, drawing his tongue up against the fine spread of hair that grew across his pecs. "You taste fine too."

"But still—" Kevin said, squirming.

"We could swim," Billy offered.

"We could," Kevin said.

"Now?" Billy asked, looking down at the moist package of Kevin's groin, his underwear a sodden mixture of sweat and precome.

"Why not?" Kevin replied.

They walked down to the fuel pumps. The sun was just setting, and the effects of the beers they'd had at the Oyster Shuck—"A typo?" Kevin asked. "No," Billy answered, "a tool"—were on the wane as well, but Billy had yet to lose the boner he'd sprouted at the sight of Kevin's bared feet: bony, well-used toes, long and articulate, with trimmed nails and hardened tips. He possessed high arches, a network of blue snaking veins and a dusting of hair across the tops. The feet, Billy theorized, were the windows to the prick. He walked ahead, keeping an eye out for his uncle, who could at any moment pop out of nowhere and commandeer Billy and his new friend into the bacon-smelling front room of his house by the lake, regaling them with interminable stories about the second World War and how he'd accidentally slept through Pearl Harbor. He wouldn't have minded a can of Old Milwaukee, though.

The pumps were the best place to swim because the water was deep, the channel cleared for some of the bigger boats that sailed Oneida Lake and berthed at Dickson's Happy Harbor, which sounded to Kevin like some sort of funny campground rather than a marina. It turned out that the place was home for more than Billy; Kevin met Billy's neighbors the next morning, stepping out onto the back deck (they'd had occasion to "meet" Kevin the night before, Kevin a self-avowed "noisy fuck" who didn't realize how easily voices carried across the water) to admire the sunrise. "Morning," they said narrowly, an elderly man and woman, minding their fishing poles and cups of coffee.

They jumped into the dark lake like boys, with flailing arms and running feet. They splashed each other and flirted underwater, and Billy put his foot between Kevin's legs. They hid against the pilings and kissed, Billy looking up, waiting for the sudden appearance of his uncle.

"What's that?" Kevin asked, pointing to a zig-zag on the water's surface.

Billy looked. "It's probably just a snake," he said.

Kevin swam to the ladder.

"They're really more afraid of you," Billy said.

"I don't think so," Kevin replied, scrambling up onto the dock.

In the houseboat Billy had Kevin lie on his back on the bed. He knelt at Kevin's feet, placing them on either thigh, and he massaged Kevin's legs, his fingers kneading the long muscles of thighs, inching closer to the hairy inert sack that lay between them. Although his balls rested heavy, his dick was anything but motionless. It hopped across his belly like a teased dog on a leash, leaving a sticky trail of drool everywhere it went. Kevin grabbed the rammy thing in his fist, holding it like a stick, and brought Billy's mouth to the head. "Nice," he breathed, as Billy took it all into his mouth with one swallow, his throat constricting around the glans. He jimmied his hands under Kevin's buttocks and squeezed them until Kevin gasped.

Kevin held onto Billy's head and fucked his mouth, and—rolling him over, never leaving the hot orifice—he did push-ups into it. Billy was unchokable—born without a gag reflex, he explained the next morning—and could have deep-throated Kevin all night long, if that's what Kevin had wanted, but Kevin had other things in mind. He pulled himself out of Billy with an audible pop and went to work on Billy's own tool of trade. It was a formidable handful, squat and blunt like a schoolyard bully, and it tested the elasticity limits of Kevin's lips. *Imagine getting plugged by that,* Kevin thought, not that he would ever, unable even to imagine it, because he was born, he would later explain, with a very strong fuck reflex—"I can barely tolerate a finger," he told Billy down the road, a confession that would play a part in the relationship's unfortunate and untimely demise, as Billy was as avid a top as he was a bottom.

On this night, however, Billy was content to be porked—more than content. He was determined to enjoy the night on his back, feet planted on the low-hanging ceiling of the bunk, Kevin well-placed between his thighs, filling up Billy's hungry asshole with his hard dick. He spread his legs wide, inviting Kevin softly to go hard at it, encouraging him with savage tit play. He cupped Kevin's pumping ass and played in the culvert between his muscled cheeks, just touching the tightened bud of Kevin's hole, sending him into a fury of fucking. Kevin lifted himself up on his toes and plowed into Billy, making the boy grimace, his mouth frozen in a silent wail. He wanted to stop, to draw it out, prolong what was turning into a beautiful fuck, but he was locked into it now, thrusting toward the end, his skin sticking to Billy's skin, his cock sucking out Billy's insides, withdrawing to make the hole puff air, only to slam back in and make Billy grunt.

"Fuck," Billy said quietly. He sent a flying stream of come between them.

Kevin gripped Billy's ankles and strove into the soft heat, pressure building behind his balls, which had tightened and taken on the appearance of a brain, thanks to the shave he'd done that morning. He opened his mouth to express delight, and Billy bolted up and shoved a thick tongue into it, and Kevin mewed, capped off like that, his cock leaving the buttery hole and unloading a wild spray of semen.

The drive now taking its toll, they stopped at a restaurant and ate a quiet meal. It was almost 5 o'clock, and they were nearly there, almost in Hyannis, where they'd rented a house for the week. The real estate agent had said it was a cottage, and it definitely had looked cottage-like in the fax they'd received, but in all actuality it had the appearance of an overgrown tool shed in somebody's grandmother's backyard, according to Billy, who would have preferred the amenities of a hotel with a balcony and a swimming pool and a bar downstairs. Still, it was nice inside, however small, and suited Kevin and did not disgust Billy, who surveyed the cottage with a buyer's eye. "It's cute," he said. "It's Martha Stewart-y. I like it. Let's make some pot-au-feu."

They unpacked. The bedroom was small, most of the space taken up by the iron bed. Billy sat on the double mattress, testing its give, and sank deeply. "We'll be hunchbacks by the end of the week," he said.

Kevin liked the matelassé spread and the celadon-colored sheets and the way the curtains were pulled back from the windows and draped over simple hooks. He sat down on the bed and leaned into Billy's back, forgetting for a moment that they were no longer intimate. He inched away from the stiffness that had crept into Billy's body and closed his eyes, thinking that it was going to be a long week and not that easy to ignore the siren's song that Billy's body unwittingly emitted. Kevin covered his eyes with his forearm, tired from the drive, and fell fast asleep.

He awoke from a dream that seemed to be continuing into his waking state—Billy on his knees between Kevin's legs, his mouth covering the whole of Kevin's engorged prick. Billy pushed his lips into the feathery brush of Kevin's pubes, his hands roaming the contours of his chest, fingering his nubby nipples. Whatever their status, the one thing Billy couldn't resist was a sleeping Kevin. He'd deftly undressed his ex and coaxed him into a state of arousal in a matter of two seconds—*he was like a sexual pickpocket,* Kevin was thinking, still feigning sleep, going so far as to fake a little snore, watching through half-closed eyes the bob of Billy's head. *Amazing,* he thought, feeling a bubble of orgasm rise up from his testicles and spread across his stomach. It smacked him between the eyes, and he stretched his legs out, making the muscles of his thighs taut, and Billy chugged down a swallow or two of Kevin's baby juice.

"I wish you wouldn't call it that," Billy said later on.

"Why?" Kevin asked, smiling. He'd had one more beer than usual and was feeling tart, if not exactly bitter. He was upset, in his state of slight inebriation, to be bereft of the finest man in town. "In this town, anyway," he'd said—there was that tartness—and then he brought up Billy's "chugging the baby-juice cocktail."

"Is that really necessary?" Billy said, glancing up and down the bar.

Kevin smiled. "That's the vehicle, though, the medium," he said, "the stuff babies come from."

"You always do that," Billy said, pushing his drink away from him. "You're always trying to teach me something I already know. You think you're fucking Jean Brodie."

"Fucking her? I don't even know her," Kevin said into his beer.

"You are an asshole," Billy said, getting up.

Back at the cottage, which Kevin could think of only in quotes now, there was a little sitting room that barely contained a weak-looking wicker settee. Billy grabbed an extra blanket and the pillow from his side of the bed and tried to make a bunk for himself on the settee. Kevin watched him carefully arrange himself on the cramped cushion.

"You don't have to do this," he said quietly. The light from the bedroom shone on Billy's face, which he'd shut down for the night. His lashes, dense and black, rested on his cheeks and turned Kevin to mush. He went over to the rickety wicker sofa and squatted beside Billy, putting his hand on the man's shoulder. "Come to bed," he whispered. He uncovered Billy then, and the boy opened his eyes.

"You're not going to pick me up, are you?" he asked.

"Well, I was thinking about it," Kevin answered.

"Don't you have a hernia or something like that?"

"You think I'm old," Kevin said, leaning back on his haunches.

"Well, you think I'm immature," Billy replied.

"You hate me."

"I hate wicker," Billy said. Then he smiled broadly. "We're in love again," he said sweetly.

He let himself be picked up and later said that it was the sexiest thing anyone had ever done to him. "If I'd known that, I would have done it a long time ago," Kevin said.

In bed their bodies met in the center of the rutted mattress. Billy ducked his head under the covers and put his mouth on Kevin's chest, lapping around and around the left nipple, bringing the little thing up hard. He licked down Kevin's hair trail to the bush that lay at the base of his cock, also up and hard, and worked his tongue into it. He moved himself, snaking down under the sheet that covered them and got himself turned around, his head burrowing Kevin's crotch. Kevin twisted, arching his back, and offered his rear end to Billy, who obviously had not gotten enough to eat at dinner.

"What's with you and this sudden turn of events?" he heard the covered boy say.

"I'm not sure," Kevin said. "I won't be sure until it happens."

"Happens? Do you mean as in 'Going to happen'? "

"I think so," Kevin said.

"Wow," Billy said, sitting up, ghostlike.

Billy offered some advice and did his best to make Kevin's transition from *unfuckable* to *easy lay* as easy as possible.

"Relax," he intoned, pressing his smallest finger into the well-lubricated pucker of Kevin's anus. He stroked the small of Kevin's back.

"Easy, easy-easy-easy," Kevin panted, nearly hyperventilating.

"I think we have issues here that go beyond my capabilities," Billy said. "I think you need ass therapy."

"I'm doing fine. I'm doing fine," Kevin breathed. "Just go on to the next finger and keep quiet."

"I'm trying to keep your mind off your troubles," Billy said, slowly withdrawing his pinkie and replacing it with his middle finger out of spite.

"Christ almighty," Kevin said, and his ass cheeks clenched with a ferocity that cracked Billy's knuckle.

"Take it easy," Billy snapped.

"You do the same," Kevin snapped back, "and I know that's not your ring finger either."

It might have taken an hour, maybe a little more, but at 1 A.M. Kevin announced his readiness. "I really think I'm going to like this," he said, grinning, straddling Billy, who did his best to disguise a yawn as an expression of excitedness. After getting Kevin to explore himself with his own finger, to feel for and find "that little ball" that becomes stimulated—"It'll harden right before you come," Billy explained; "I know that much," Kevin griped, his left arm underneath him—he advised that Kevin opt for the man-on-top position. "You get to control the whole thing," he said brightly.

At the first touch of Billy's thick-headed prick, Kevin balked. "I'm really not ready, not ready, definitely not ready."

"Oh, shut up and take it like a man," Billy bitched.

"It's like a fucking can or something," Kevin said. "You can't take a can like a man. Can't you do something to make the end pointier?"

"Are you fucking serious?"

"It hurts. Take it out."

"It's not in," Billy said, his voice taking on an edge.

"Maybe this isn't such a good idea after all," Kevin said, trying not to let himself rest on Billy's hips.

"Yeah," Billy said, wiggling his body out from under Kevin, who stayed squatting precariously on the precipice of the mattress.

"Just where do you think you're going?" Kevin asked.

"Back to bed," Billy replied from the sitting room, trying to make himself comfortable on the settee again.

Kevin nudged Billy awake. "I'm really ready this time," he said. Billy opened one eye. "I am not," he said simply.

Kevin grabbed the boy's arm. "Please," he said. "You've got to now. I really am ready." He put his hand under the blanket, finding Billy's nowsoft but greased-up cock. He tugged a few times and put his mouth on Billy's, his lips sticky with sleep. Billy put his arms around him, opening his mouth, accepting Kevin's probing tongue. His cock responded as well, growing in Kevin's grip, thickening enough to make Kevin swallow hard, becoming limblike.

Kevin took a deep breath and some of Billy's as well and got himself on top of him. He took hold of the bully between Billy's legs and gripped it firmly, positioning his fanny so that the head touched the pinched opening. He let his hips drop and felt the first inch enter him. And then he felt the hole blossom, opening like the aperture of a camera, as fast as that, and the head slipped in. He didn't say what he wanted to say, which was "Oh." It hurt, some, but not nearly as much as he'd expected it to. He felt the slow slide of Billy's exceptionally fat shaft, his ass lips rasping, and he pinched on his own nipples, turning them sharply, the equivalent of bullet-biting, he guessed. When he'd taken the whole thing, the whole big fat goddamned motherfucking thing, he took a deep breath. "See," he said, "I told you I could do it."

Billy put his hands on Kevin's hips. "Ride me," he said.

"Ride you," Kevin said, biting the inside of his lips. He twisted his tits one last time and lifted his ass, and Billy's cock swizzled his insides. "It's...excellent," he said through clenched teeth.

And then, all of a sudden, it was excellent—well, maybe not all of a sudden. It took quite a few squats for Kevin to get used to Billy's circumference, but after that Kevin was jockeying Billy's beer can, bopping on it like a bronco buster, hooting and hollering and giving Billy cause to blush even—the things he said, begging for it loudly, proudly, wanting more, more, more!

"The neighbors," Billy reminded him quietly.

"Fuck them," Kevin answered. "We're on vacation."

And so it happened that Kevin and Billy enjoyed their trip to Hyannis, known forever thereafter to Kevin as *Hi, anus.*

Gorgeous Tits
by Roddy Martin

Harvard was lounging on his patio—robe more off than on, pectorals brushed by creamy brown shadows. He stretched and you could see all the way down his hip. I knew what kind of day this would be.

I went to buy my wife sweet nothings.

I first glimpsed the florist through his shop window. Well, I glimpsed his thigh. He had his boot on a crate. The thigh was burnt umber and shapely. Ding! I hurried inside.

The man himself had clear, savvy eyes. He wore cut-off overalls that went down to here and up to there. I stood gaping. The collarbone! The hollow at the base of his throat! And moving lower... "You're late," he purred.

"Late?"

"You're not my 11 o'clock? Oh. Never mind. What can I get you?"

"I'd like a dozen yellow roses."

He went in the cooler, bent over the blooms. You could see the side of his pec, a flash of underarm. It wasn't enough.

"How's this?" he asked, coming out.

"Beautiful."

"Likewise. You want" —his voice dropped an octave— "long stems."

"The longer the better."

"Baby's breath?"

"Oh, yes."

Holding my gaze, he unhooked his suspender straps. The bib fell foreword. What gorgeous tits! I had to fondle them, mash them, taste every inch.

"Whoa." Him dragging me by the belt to a back room. He undid his hip snaps, which left the overalls barely hanging. Now I could worship the pert nipples, the way muscle glided to muscle.

"You just gonna stand there?" he asked.

"Un huh." I dived for his chest. He grabbed my head. He arched his back and went, "Uh!"

This was what I lived for.

Panting, he stretched out on a table covered with green floral wrap. Off came the overalls, leaving him naked except for boots, socks, and garden gloves. His cock was big and black, straight up. I pulled up a stool and swallowed until it jabbed the back of my throat.

Only then did I realize that the shop was a front for some type of high-class, illegal fuck pad, and that the roses might cost $200.

"Don't you," he gasped. "Don't you want to get comfortable?"

"Oh no. I'm married. I've got to be good."

"You call this good?"

"Don't you?" I shoved two fingers up his butt. Zing, found his prostate and he moaned. I've always loved pleasuring a guy while I played with his tits, and the florist's were—"Oooh!" From some angles, you might have wished his nipples were a quarter of an inch rounder, but on the whole, the package was A-minus, at the very least.

Presently his balls got high and his breathing labored. "Oh, I'm close."

The bell in the shop rang. "Hello?" called a baritone voice. Possibly the real 11 o'clock. Or the cops.

"Don't stop," the florist panted. I was frigging him now. A handful.

"Hello? Anyone here?"

"You stop, you die…Oh! Oh! Oh!" The florist shot all over his chest. It pooled there, looking gorgeous. I sprinkled it with yellow petals.

As you may have guessed, windows were my friends.

Ever seen one frame a topless guy with his arms folded, biceps tight against pecs? Or a bottomless guy? He seems twice as naked, peeling a tee-shirt over his abs. Such was my great fantasy, to see Harvard on a water bed that way, while the wave machine makes wave after wave after….

OK.

Once the swelling subsided, I caught the uptown train at Christopher. Across from me stood a Spanish boy with lithe arms and cute little biceps. His tee was baggy, but a portfolio strap crossed his heart. You could see what he had, for sure. He was so sweet and innocent. I wanted to spank him.

By Penn Station the car was SRO. I found this hip in my face. It looked shipshape in taupe pleats. I bet the guy's chest was that way too. His shirt clung like a milk mustache.

He smiled and lifted a brow. My eye traveled back down, watched something stiffen and stir. Slipping off a loafer, I rolled my toe around his anklebone. He flopped his tie aside, undid his collar, and the next button and the next. He glanced left. He glanced right. He flashed a pec.

How I wished I was wearing a butt-plug.

This incident reminded me of a man my mother dated when I was 18. I went to his apartment after they broke up—ostensibly as a go-between, but in truth to practice techniques from *How to Land in the Feathers (with Practically Anyone)!*

Steven appeared to be dressing for a date. He was a brisk, tailored optometrist. His slacks worked butt magic. His shoulders strained his expensive undershirt. I cooed, "You don't mind my Coming?"

"Quite the opposite."

"So, no Hard Feelings?"

"None."

"Why do Hard Feelings make us Come Again and Again…to a bad End?"

"Don't try to con me," he said evenly, rolling deodorant in a virile underarm. "I know that seduction routine." Still, he let me sit on his lap and suck his tits.

I arrived at the foundation where my wife works 12-hour days, something I need not do. I'm kept, baby. Kept, kept!

You probably wonder about the roses. You think, "Her birthday, and he's acting like a wretch." Not so! We want to make a baby. When we conceive, Daddy-O's going to give us a fuckload of cash. True, my behavior with the florist was inappropriate, but most people wouldn't call it adulterous.

Raised my sperm count, didn't it?

In the foundation building, glass elevators scale a vast atrium. Elevator boys wear ties and navy jackets. Mine that day was angel-faced, round-eyed, and sensuously dark. "New here?' I asked.

"Yes, sir. Nice roses."

"Nice uniform."

We passed seven, eight, nine floors. I scanned them all. Once in this very shaft I happened to witness an assignation involving the most beautiful pair of—

The elevator ground to a halt.

"What's wrong?"

"I don't know." The elevator boy hovered by the control panel with a vague air of premeditation. "Might be here a while. I hope you don't mind"—adorable stammer—"tight places."

"Rather enjoy them."

"Isn't it getting kind of warm, sir?"

(Yes well. The truth is, I can land in the feathers with practically anyone.)

I tossed his jacket on the floor, groped him through his immaculate cotton shirt—one of my favorite things, by the way, along with scoop tanks, open collars, bathrobes, strategically cupped hands, and all types of underwear.

"You're built like a football player," I said, opening his fly. "Go to college?"

"Rutgers."

His cock was thick and ready. I started unbuttoning his shirt from the bottom up. "What major?

"Social work."

"Sexy. Tell me, has a man ever done social work on your tits?"

"Ah!"

Thought he'd come all over me. Stepping back, I crunched my wife's roses and felt a pang. After all, I made certain promises when I married her. But she must have known they'd be tough to keep, and I'd be house-bound soon enough, with a little boy or a little girl and Daddy-O's $4,000,000, which we could then double and triple. Our brokers had explained this.

Only we had to conceive, like fast. Because…trust me, it's complex.

I set to work on the elevator boy from behind. Pants-humped his butterfly buns. Felt up his obliques, his violin-shaped abdominal crest, the ridge that bisected it. Yes! Great abs meant great tits.

I knew his would be. I was foaming at the mouth.

I thrust my pelvis, pinned his to the glass. Forced him to fuck it, 10 and a half stories high. His shirt slipped down. White cloth, brown skin. Drove me wild. I bit his shoulder.

My fingers brushed the bottom curves of his pecs. Felt so good, I grabbed. I kneaded. Oooo! Wide, smooth, nipples low on the muscle. I was like, Wanna come, wanna come. Ah, ah! I want to come!

"Oh sir!" cried the elevator boy.

Close call. I slumped, panting.

The elevator boy's virility rolled down the pane. It dawned on me that if we could see out, others could see in.

Sticky. Ick. Dripping down.

Time to regroup.

The way things were going, I skipped over to 8th Avenue for lubricant and a cheap butt plug. The bookstore clerk was atypically handsome. He caressed my palm with $1.75 change. "Would you like a bag? Or should I insert that for you?"

"Please." I dropped my pants....

By now it was 4 o'clock. Times Square evangelists were out, exhorting the brothers. "Do you suck up to the white man and the white woman?"

Not unless they have gorgeous tits.

I took the #9 down to the flower hook shop, where I found the florist clad in cap and leather harness. I said, "I need another dozen yellow... Did I interrupt something?"

From behind the counter arose a john with a studded belt in his teeth.

"I can't think of a snappy bon mot," said the florist. He looked at the john, who nodded. They advanced hungrily. "11 o'clock, meet 5:30."

I shouldn't. I couldn't. I had to get home, make dinner, wash the guys off my skin... 5:30 grabbed his shirttail and pulled it up. I thought maybe I'd stay a few minutes.

He was a *Playgirl* "Real Man of the Month" type. You know, 30ish WASP in upscale shoes. Nice abs, though. Nice pecs. Too much hair. Overall effect was B-plus, but I could raise that. I produced the clippers I carried for such occasions.

5:30's eyes grew wide. "Oh, no. No way." I switched on the instrument. Its buzz cut the air.

Somewhat later—

"Not the bush! Not the bush!"

"Just going to shape it." Buzz. The clippers bit into the wiry hairs, forming puffs that floated onto the florist's head. He didn't care. He knelt with foam and razor, shaving 5:30's nuts.

I left 5:30 a quarter of an inch.

"My cock's bigger," he exclaimed, staring in amazement. "My cock's 20% bigger." He swung it thigh to thigh.

I also left him a dusting on his chest, for accent. Vast improvement, brought out the lines. Now I could watch his beef-red tits rub against the florist's brown ones.

(You might think me a solipsist with a fetish, but I know this is passing phase.)

"Want me to go down?" the florist asked, addressing his client but looking at me.

"Yeah."

Watching those pillow lips slide instilled a desire to have them for myself. I knelt beside the florist. "Let him have it," gasped 5:30. "Let him suck it."

We took turns. Sucked fast, slow, lazy, macho. Did lollipops, corkscrews. 5:30 didn't know the florist and I were showing off, teasing each other, closer and closer. Our mouths met on the tip of the cock and I kissed him, put my heart into it.

"How do you feel?" he asked.

"Great, man. Real good."

He reclined. I swallowed. I felt 5:30's hands on my basket, on my hard-on. I felt his mouth on my balls. I let the daisy wheel spin....

When I spun out of the wheel like a roulette ball, there was a righteous cock in my mouth. Biggest I ever. I didn't care who it belonged to. I was about to come, and from the taste of it, about to swallow a forbidden, unsafe load. I got a mental picture of $4,000,000 in a sack with wings, flying out the window.

I opened my eyes. The cock was mine.

The florist stood fucking 5:30's tits, the most potent sex act in the world. "Fuck him, baby," I growled, zipping up as best I could.

Cocks are potent. Pecs are potent.

"Fuck him, he's a whore. The john's the one who's a whore... Baby, I'm getting fucked too." Not the actual case, but if you say it, it's so. And I knew how to work a butt plug. I have great suction. I squeezed it. I squeezed and squeezed.

Oops.

Took me 15 minutes to dig it out.

Afterward I took baby steps to the street. Anything more definite would have meant a case of wham pants. Not that you could tell the difference, with all the precome.

We'd conceive tonight, no problem.

I tumbled into a cab on 7th Ave. "Hey!" Someone grabbed the car. "Mind if I share?" My eye took in the cut-offs, the massive thighs, the chest.

"You are most welcome."

Ten minutes later I was prostrate in the body-builder's lair, drooling as his ass gyrated. Down came the cut-offs, up went the tank-top. His waist was narrow, his back broad and bronze. Whipping a sleeveless flannel shirt over it, he spun front.

Sweet voyeuristic torture! The round inner pecs. The flat stomach, the flat navel. The cock solid enough to provide ballast for tits whose masculine fullness I could but imagine.

"Oh baby," I groaned. "Masturbate for me."

He rolled his hips and worked it, two-fisted. Inflation—who'd have thought? Despite its heft, his was a blood cock. "Lick my boot," he said, sticking it in my face. I licked. I didn't care, barely noticed when he tied a jimmy on his shaft with both of my shoelaces.

And yanked off my pants.

Of course, when the first inch popped my bubble, then I noticed. "Ouch, ouch, ouch!"

"Fuckin' take it."

"Ahhh."

He hit a spot—that spot—again and again. My blood turned to buttered rum. "Harder," I gasped.

"Shut up." He knew how to build.

There was a mirror. I saw his butt pump. I saw his Adam's apple, the veins in his biceps. I had to see the rest! I reached for his shirt. He grabbed my wrists and held them over my head. Struggle as I might, there was nothing I could do but watch his shirt as it slid, thrust by thrust by thrust thrust thrust. Until—

"I love your tits! Oh, I love your tits!"

My wife left a message, "Be home late." Good. I thought I'd unspool with a soak and my hidden stash of non-explicit but outlandishly erotic soft-core gay videos. Those Czechoslovakian boys look great without shirts.

Harvard was out again, lounging in a very full red thong. He squeezed it, slipped his hand… I ran for binoculars.

What a show. I could feel a fresh $4,000,000 spawn in my testicles. Presently Harvard reached for his cordless. My phone jangled.

"You're watching." His voice was low and hot. "I can feel it. You watch often."

"Well, you have gorgeous tits."

"Hold that thought."

He went inside. I could see him bending in silhouette, presumably skimming the thong off. I was so excited I couldn't breathe. Then the cops came and dragged me away for invasion of privacy.

The Hot Nine at 9:00
by Derek Kemp

Iknew it was him the moment I heard his voice. I was dialing through
stations on my car radio when, out of nowhere, there he was. He said,
"Let me hear you beg for it," and that was enough for me. It was like something out of a dream, like déjà vu. My cheeks suddenly flashed hot, and
my cock started to swell in my pants. I closed my eyes and tried to focus
on his demand: Let me hear you beg for it. I sucked my tongue and tasted
a plea forming there but didn't put voice to it. I knew he couldn't hear me.

Almost immediately a young girl took up his request. She whined
"Please, Max," and I instantly hated her. Her voice was high-pitched and
annoying, her plea pathetic. I thought she should have had to work harder
to win whatever prize Max was giving away, but Max let her off easy.
"Please what?" he gently teased her. She started whimpering, "Please, Max,
I'd do anything to win those concert tickets." She put extra emphasis on
the word *anything,* but I didn't think she had a clue what that might mean
to a guy like Max. "Oh, really?" Max purred suggestively. "Are you sure
about that? *Anything?*" The heavy hint of sex in his voice gave me the
vapors, but the girl seemed utterly insulted by his dallying. "Yes, anything,"
she defiantly declared; she wanted those tickets no matter what it cost her.
Fortunately for her, Max was smart enough not to test her limits. "Well,
don't sweat," he said. "This one's easy. All you have to do is tell me what
station is your choice for the hottest hits." Like a cheerleader, the girl suddenly perked up. "Ninety-nine, K-POW," she said enthusiastically, with
the station's call letters coming out at as one word. *Kapow!* Like in a comic
book. *Biff! Thwack! Kapow!* Her fizzy answer was immediately followed by
a sharp crack of thunder, then a canned station-ID tag. Kinda gimmicky,
I thought, but also easy to remember.

As Max went on to introduce the next song, I picked up my new cell phone (a freebie from my latest employer) and dialed the number for local information. When the operator came on, I turned down the volume on the radio and asked her for K-POW's number. She gave me two options: the station's office number or its request line. I figured it would be easier to reach Max on the request line, so I chose that one. But every time I tried the number during the next few minutes, I got a busy signal. It was exasperating. I started wondering if I should have asked for the station's office number as well when I noticed a gas station's glowing neon sign about a quarter mile up the road. Surely they would have a phone book I could borrow, I thought, but when I got there the kid sulking behind the counter said, "Sorry, somebody stole our phone book."

I was briefly disappointed by such a ludicrous theft, then it hit me: The kid behind the counter was drumming his fingers to the beat of a familiar song. It was the song Max had started playing when I first pulled into the gas station's lot. So I asked the kid, "Is this K-POW you're listening to?"

He nodded his head eagerly: "I listen to it all the time." Even better, when I told him I was trying to find the station, he said, "That's easy. I know how to get there. It's not far from here, maybe 20 minutes or so." I quickly scribbled down the directions on the back of a paper bag, then hastily left to resume my quest.

When I got back to the car, Max was on the air plugging the Hot Nine at 9:00, K-POW's nightly countdown show. "There's not much time left," he warned his listeners. "If you want to hear your favorite song tonight, you've got to call me and get your request in." I looked at the clock. The digital readout said 8:27. "Yeah, right," I mumbled to myself, "like anybody could get through." Still, I picked up the cell phone and hit redial again. To my surprise the line started ringing, but Max didn't answer right away. He left me hanging for a good 20 minutes—plenty of time to think back to the night we first met.

That was at least 10 years ago. I was 18 years old at the time; Max was about 30, maybe 35. We met one weekend night at a roadside rest area on the highway between the state university and my parents' house. A college freshman, I was on my way home to visit Mom and Dad when the urge to take a piss suddenly came over me. I stopped at the rest area with nothing more than relieving my bladder in mind. I was naive then; I had no idea how cruisy rest areas can be. As a matter of fact, I didn't even know then what the word *cruising* meant, but Max clearly did. From the moment I walked through the door, he had his eyes on me. When I first noticed him he was standing in front of the state highway map and had this screwed-up look on his face like, *Can you help me, man? I'm lost.* But I couldn't stop; my bladder felt like it was going to burst. I quickly scanned the room to see if there was anyone else who could help him. The place appeared to be deserted. I was the only other person there, so I tilted my head at him and gave him a signal to follow me into the bathroom. I figured I could give him directions while I was standing there peeing. Nice, huh? Completely innocent? Little did I know, he had something other than directions in mind.

Almost from the moment I pulled my dick out, I felt him standing uncomfortably close to me, just behind me. For a brief, panicky moment, I thought, *Oh shit, he's got a gun. He's going to mug me.* But then I turned around. Instead of a gun he had his dick in his hand, and it was huge. He tugged on it slowly and pointed its dribbling eye at me. For a long moment I just stood there, slack-jawed, staring at it, thinking, *My God.* But then reality sank in. I realized we were in a public building. This was insane. I didn't want to get caught by someone or possibly even arrested, so I turned my back to him and tried to focus on peeing. *Just do it,* I tried to tell myself, *just piss and then run for your life.* But I couldn't piss. I was too nervous and deliriously scared.

Sensing my distress, the man finally spoke. "Looks like you've got a problem there," he said, his voice low and gravelly.

I shook my head stupidly and stammered "N-n-no." I almost wished I could crawl down the urinal drain and disappear.

Then he smiled at me; I could feel it, warm and kind, against the back of my neck. He said, "Just relax, pal," and his voice was so friendly, so soothing; it felt like fingertips pressing against my spine. Then he started humming, or murmuring, really: "Hmm…mmm." I closed my eyes and concentrated on the slow cadence of his breathing, those subtle *mmms,* then my dick twitched, and suddenly I was pissing. It came out in a torrent, hot and seemingly unending. When it finally stopped, my shoulders slumped; I felt weakened. The man behind me whistled. "Holy shit, kid," he said. "You been holding that back for days?"

Again I slumped and leaned back a little. The man put a hand up to steady me, and the heat of that first touch dissolved any further reluctance I had to turn around and face him again. He was handsome, I thought, in a rugged, older-man sort of way. He was tall and well built, with dark hair and scruffy stubble. Our eyes locked—his wet, gray eyes were utterly mesmerizing—and he lured my gaze down to his dick, which was enormous. I'm not kidding. It was at least nine inches and obscenely thick—a work of art. He gave it a few proud strokes, then asked, "You ever seen a dick like this?" My mouth watered; I shook my head. His stroking—long, languorous squeezes from base to tip—made me think of a cake decorator squeezing a tube of frosting, which in turn reminded me of my father, a closet cake decorator himself. How many times had he let me eat the frosting right out of the tubes? It was our little secret. My father would always warn me, "Don't let your mother know I let you do that." My mother didn't approve of him indulging me with sugary treats, but that never held my father back, and I absolutely loved him for it. My father was the first man I ever fell in love with—not sexually, just the idea of him, a generous man. After him there was Mr. Thompson, my ninth-grade gym teacher. Then a long string of muscular high school jocks. But over the years I'd never acted on any of those desires. I'd been too frightened. I was still a virgin.

My stranger—that's what I called him for 10 years, until I heard the girl on the radio call him Max—asked me, "You ever sucked dick before?" I thought about how I'd only thought about it, and gulped: "No." His question frightened me, so I took a small, reflexive step backward. "Well, there's always a first time," he said and stepped forward, pursuing me. Again I stepped back—one, two, three steps—and bumped into a stall. I looked back to see what I'd run into. "Not here," my stranger said. "Somebody might come in." As if I'd been trying to find us cover! I opened my mouth to protest, but he put a finger to my lips and pushed it in a little. I licked the tip and tasted the saltiness of him. Then he pulled it out and said, "Follow me." He reached down and stuffed his dick back in his pants, then walked out the door.

For a moment I was gripped by panic. *Don't do it,* the reasonable side of my brain tried to tell me, *just run to your car and head for home.* But the taste of his finger lingered tantalizingly on my tongue. It tasted like a promise of more where that came from. And my dick was hard; I didn't even notice until I had to struggle to push it back in my pants. I knew I was starving for some kind of experience, some lightning-rod moment that would change my life and push me out of the closet. This had to be it. I took a deep breath and zipped up my pants. Then I walked through the door and followed him outside.

I half-expected my stranger to lure me into his car, to drive me somewhere private, like his apartment or a motel, but instead he walked across the parking lot and waded into a small, lushly wooded area that lay on the other side. He disappeared into the brush like a phantom, so I quickened my pace and honed in on the spot where he'd vanished. Although it was dark, I had no trouble finding him. A narrow, well-worn path guided me through the foliage to a large open space where my stranger stood waiting for me. He seemed to know the place well.

Shaking with nerves, I tried to be funny. "You come here often?"

"Often enough," he responded. "Now, why don't you get on your knees." For a brief moment I didn't know what to do. My throat tingled, and I lost my sense of equilibrium. I couldn't help wondering, *Is it safe for me to be here with this man?* But it suddenly hit me: I wasn't scared of him; his anonymity was actually a turn-on. The only fear I had was of getting caught.

"*Shh,*" I whispered, admonishing him. "Someone's going to hear us." I got down on my knees.

He seemed startled by my silly rebuke, but didn't pay it much mind. He just stared at me, then slowly his scowl softened into a dirty smirk. He stepped in front of me, his crotch in my face. "You want this?" he asked. "You want this dick?"

That close to him, I could smell the saltiness of his flesh. "Yes," I hungrily moaned, my voice husky with desire. I leaned forward and nipped at the fabric of his jeans, then licked it and felt the thick pulse of life pounding beneath.

He tilted my head back. "Let me hear you beg for it."

Almost choking on my own desire, I managed to sputter, "P-p-please."

Playfully, he stepped back a few paces and crooked a finger at me. He wanted me to come after him.

Like a baby going for its bottle, I started crawling. "Let me suck it," I moaned. "Please. Let me suck that cock." I licked my lips and started growling. I felt like an animal driven by instinctual lust.

After a few more steps back, he stopped and sighed. "Fine," he said, feigning reluctance. He was a masterful tease. "Maybe just a taste."

With my lips just inches away from him, he pulled down his zipper. Oh, how I remember that sound, the staccato chatter of metal teeth. He pulled out his dick and rubbed my face with it, and that surprised me. My cheeks tingled, and I could feel the blush. My entire body erupted with gooseflesh. I stuck my tongue out to catch a taste of his dick, and when it finally skidded across my tongue, it was not enough. My taste buds sprang to attention, demanding more. I chased his dick, struggling to get my lips around it. When I caught it in my mouth, I started sucking. I worked my tongue over and under it but refused to let it go. I was afraid he wouldn't let me have it back. I tongued the shaft and tickled the head, tasted his pre-come. I swallowed and drooled and gave my stranger the best blow job I could muster.

When he suddenly came I was reminded of my pissing. His load seemed unending, bloating my gut. I swallowed every drop, but still it wasn't enough. I wanted more. I wanted him to fuck me. My asshole twitched with need. But it wasn't to be.

Out of the blue we heard a sudden squawk, a cop car's siren-a highway patrolman. He must have seen our cars in the rest area's parking lot and gotten suspicious when he didn't find anybody inside.

In a panic I jumped up and worried aloud, "Oh shit. What do we do?" I pictured myself in a police station trying to explain things to my parents. But my stranger was calm. "Don't worry," he said, and casually zipped up. Then I heard the crackle and honk of a nearby walkie-talkie. The cop was coming up the path. Frantic, I looked at the trees around us, trying to find some place to run, but my stranger put a hand on my shoulder. "Be quiet," he whispered. "Don't say a word." Then he reached into his jacket pocket and pulled out a length of chain. Just as the cop discovered our hiding place, my stranger started making kissing noises. Smooch, smooch, "Here, Dolly," he called and crouched down, as if he were calling a dog.

The cop sneered in disbelief. "You fellas lost?"

My stranger shook his head. "Just my dog, officer. This guy here was helping me try to find her."

The cop rolled his eyes at us. "That so?"

"Yep," my stranger confirmed, then turned back to the trees and clapped his hands. "C'mon, Dolly," he whined, "I haven't got all night."

To, I think, everyone's surprise, there was a sudden jingling noise and a rustle of leaves, then a tiny yip. A moment later a small puppy came charging out of the bushes. "Dolly!" my stranger said, beaming as he scooped up the dog in his arms. "You bad dog," he baby-talked to her as he scratched her under the chin. "Daddy better not get a ticket for you being off your leash."

The "daddy" part set me off. I started laughing; I couldn't help it. A trained dog? Both the cop and my stranger looked at me. My stranger looked panicked; the cop just looked amused. He smiled at me, "Looks like you're off the hook." But I didn't take his hint. I just stood there look-ing dumb. Then, a bit more forcefully, he insisted, "You can be on your way now." In other words, dismissed. I knew from the look on his face he had something other than a simple slap on the wrist in mind for my stranger, but I felt powerless to help. "Thanks," I said, wishing I could come up with something to get my stranger out of there, but my mind was a blank. Finally I turned around and skulked off, but before I was out of earshot I called over my shoulder, "I'm glad you found your dog, mister." I didn't know his name. What a fucking shame. "Thanks, kid," he called back, and that was it. A legend was born. My sexual die was cast.

Needless to say, I spent the next several years making many unnecessary trips home to visit my parents. Every time I did I stopped at that rest area and walked down that same well-worn path, hoping that maybe I might find my stranger waiting there to fuck me. But I never did. I finally gave up looking for him after a few years. I graduated from college and moved away, ran through a series of jobs, then I got the call for a job in Max's hometown. Again, it required a move to a new state, a new place I didn't know, but I didn't mind. I've planted very few roots in my life; I'm not a sentimental guy. But that man—my stranger, Max—is one of the few things I've ever regretted leaving behind.

"Ninety-nine, K-POW," a voice said from the receiver.

Bolting up, I pressed the cell phone to my ear. "Max?" I asked, just to make sure; I hadn't been listening closely. Was it him?

"Yeah, this is Max," he said, a little impatiently. "Do you want to make a request?"

I didn't hesitate. "Yeah, Max, I want you to fuck me."

"Uh—" he started to say, then paused.

"I'll even beg for it."

Finally he said, "Listen, I don't know who you are—"

"How's Dolly?" I interrupted.

"What?" he asked. "Who?"

"Dolly," I said, "your dog. Is she still alive? I haven't seen her in ten years."

For a long moment the man was silent. I started worrying that he might hang up on me. What if it wasn't him? What if I'd made a mistake? Then he asked, "Who is this? Do I know you?"

As casually as possible, I answered him, "You'll see. I'm an old friend." Then I hung up. A quarter mile ahead of me the aerial warning lights on

K-POW's transmitting tower blinked like a Morse-code beacon. It seemed to be saying, Come and get it. I hit the gas.

Max remembered me right away when he opened the station's door to let me inside. "You're the guy I almost got caught with by that cop," he said without prompting, and I was heartened by his remembering that night. Still feeling bold, I quickly asked him, "Are we alone?"

Max looked over his shoulder, as if to make sure there wasn't anyone there, then nodded confidently. "No cops tonight."

"Good," I said, and lunged forward to kiss him. He hadn't changed much over the years, aside from getting a little grayer, which actually turned me on. He was still a model of pure masculinity—muscular and strong, butch and fit. He was so completely a man, it drove me wild.

To my delight he met my kiss with equal fervor, then steered me back into his studio control booth. When we finally came up for air, he put a finger up to his lips and instructed me to be quiet, then flicked on his microphone and introduced a song. While he did that I scanned the machinery, marvelling at the multitude of knobs, switches and flashing meters. I looked at the walls, which were covered with promotional posters and glossy photographs. On the back of the door there was a collage of Polaroids, all identified with hand-markered captions. Most showed K-POW staffers with touring musicians, but in the middle was a shot of Max with his dog. The caption read "Max and Dalí—Partners in Crime," and that made me laugh.

Max came up behind me and embraced me around my waist. "What's so funny?" he asked, pulling me close. I pointed at the photograph: "Dalí's a he?" Over the dog's white nose was a dramatic Daliesque wisp of black mustache; the name made sense. Max nuzzled against the back of my neck and growled, "Mm-hmm." I was instantly reminded of the night we first met, when he stood behind me at that urinal, murmuring "Mmm" to help me pee.

"I thought it was Dolly," I said, and arched my back against his hard body, "like Dolly Parton." Max chuckled. He pushed away from me and said, "Oh, man, you're cute. I want to fuck you right now, but I have to work." I pouted suggestively and that seemed to inspire him.

In a blur of motion he set to work, utterly amazing me with his technical prowess. From the moment I knocked on the door to K-POW's studios to the start of the Hot Nine at 9:00, Max had about five minutes to get everything carted up and ready for broadcast. In that brief window of time, he gathered up the top nine CDs and stacked them in descending order, then went back to the phones and recorded various listeners announcing each song. By the time he shoved the cartridge in for number nine and pressed play, I already had his fat dick in my mouth.

Max leaned back in his battered vinyl swivel chair, the soundboard controls an arm's length away. I was kneeling on the floor between his legs, almost hidden beneath the soundboard desk. It seemed like I was hiding, trying to conceal myself and the sexual act I was performing, and that only helped to make the experience seem more naughty, more furtive, like our first adventure in the woods—except that this time there wasn't much chance of our being caught.

Still, my heart was beating like stuttering drumbeat. I felt so wicked. A tear on the arm of Max's swivel chair was held together with a shiny bumper sticker, and the logo read 5in. it took me a moment to equate 5in with "sin." *Ah, yes,* I thought, feeling debauched. *No doubt about it.* I inhaled deeply, and the fragrance of Max's sweaty pubic hair filled my nostrils. The salty taste of his flesh overwhelmed my senses until I felt light-headed, my brain popping fizzily like a freshly opened bottle of champagne. I couldn't get enough of Max, of his cock. I gorged myself on it as if it were a long-lost family recipe, found now, years later. It tasted sensational.

Then Max leaned forward an inch or two and pushed in the cartridge for number 8. I heard a teenager recite the song's title, then Max pressed play. A swollen drumbeat thudded around the room and seemed to fill it. I felt compressed by it, felt Max's abdomen pushing down on the top of my head as he slowly turned down the volume a bit, but I never let his cock fall out of my mouth. It was a prize, all mine. I didn't want to let it go.

Max leaned back and put his hard, strong hands on my head. He guided me down, down, down. I sucked and swallowed, and let him control me like a maestro conducting an orchestra. He twined his fingers in my hair and pulled me up. "Lick my balls," he instructed, and for once I felt no anxiety in letting his cock go. I obeyed him, basting his ball sac with saliva. A moment or two later, he let go of my hair with one hand and turned his chair a bit; I followed. He reached out and strained to shove in the cartridge introducing number 7. Again a teenager's voice filled the air, but I paid no attention to it; it sounded like white noise to me. The number 7 song followed, then, a few minutes later, a prerecorded string of commercial breaks, followed by number 6. Max managed each cartridge and CD like a magician, with a minimum of motion—sleight of hand. He stayed put, letting me do what I was clearly meant to do, and only lifted his hips once when I reached up to pull his jeans off. Then Max spread his legs and arched his ass up so I could have easier access to his humid asshole.

For this, I got off my knees. I crouched down so my butt rested on my heels. I held onto the chair with one hand and used the other to probe Max's hole. Each time I pulled a finger out, I sucked on it greedily, then I leaned forward and wiggled my tongue deep inside of him. Max groaned with satisfaction and writhed in his chair. He had to struggle to pop in the cartridge introducing number 5.

As the song waned and Max leaned forward to segue into number 4, I stood up to shuck off my clothes. I pulled my shirt over my head and Max let out another satisfied murmur. I looked at him as I slowly kicked off my shoes and stepped out of my chinos. Max was leaning back in his swivel chair again, naked from the waist down, his dick standing up, hard in his lap. He gave it a few lascivious strokes, then reached up to slowly thumb open the buttons on his shirt. He pulled it off, and I felt myself suddenly grow harder watching the muscles in his shoulders and arms flex as he dropped it to the floor. Then he leaned back again and motioned me forward. He pointed at the digital timer on the number 4 CD. "I've got two minutes and 37 seconds before I have to introduce the next batch of commercials," he said. "Get over here so I can get a quick taste of that dick of yours."

I quickly obeyed. I stepped up beside Max and he leaned over the arm of his chair and instantly swallowed my dick—every inch of it. I lifted my hips forward, then shifted back on my heels. I slowly fucked his mouth, even though there were only seconds left before he had to say, "And now a word from our sponsors." His tongue and cheeks languorously caressed the shaft of my dick like a warm, gentle sleeve, and my whole body shook from the pleasure of it. It was a struggle for me to say on my feet.

Then it was over. Max suddenly let go of my dick and pulled his microphone toward him. He flicked a switch and babbled in DJ-speak. I didn't hear a word of it. I kept my eyes closed and let my imagination keep going. Then his hands were on me, exploring every inch of my skin. He tweaked my nipples and felt the taut musculature of my neck. His fingers roamed down my back, as he counted aloud, backwards—"Nine, eight, seven, six, five, four, three, two, one"—and then his fingers were digging between my ass cheeks. I bent forward and let him explore the throbbing heart of me. I don't know when he did it; somewhere along the line Max reached back and popped in the cartridge for number 3, then he was back in my ass, digging and stretching, moaning huskily, "Yeah, what a nice, tight hole. I can't wait to get inside of you."

I felt my heart lodge itself in my throat. I would have begged him, "Now, now," but Max was already a step ahead of me. Reaching back again, he popped in the cartridge for number 2, then grabbed me by the hips and guided me down onto his lap. He pulled me back so we were facing the same way. As his cock head nudged its way between the twin mounds of my ass checks, I felt my asshole clench tight in protest, then suddenly give way. Max blew out hot puffs of air as I slowly slid down the length of his massive dick; I felt his warm breath pelting my back as if he were trying to melt my spine and turn my body into jelly, a more accommodating fit for his massive cock. Then it was done; I had him inside of me, all nine inches. I started to ride him, slowly, eagerly, up and down like a horny carousel horse.

The swivel chair squeaked under us and groaned in protest. It rolled on its casters—back, back, back—until Max put his feet down and inched us forward again. Number 1 was coming up, and we were too far away from the desk. Then it was time. Max stood up, moving me with him. His cock never fell out. He bent me over the desk and pulled the mic toward him.

"OK, folks," he said. "You've been waiting for it, now here it is." And then he pushed in the final cartridge. Another giddy teenager announced the number 1 song, a sweeping love ballad from the current box-office champ, and then Max started the CD. Over the opening strains of the song, Max said, "And after that, stay tuned to K-POW for Dr. Sex." I let out a guffaw; Max's body tensed. "Thanks for listening," he blurted. "This is Max Bundy. I'll see you tomorrow night." Then he flicked off the microphone and playfully swatted me on the ass. "You little brat," he chided me.

I laughed again. "Dr. Sex?"

"It's a national call-in show," he said, "for sex advice. Maybe we should call him and see what he says about sexual partners who don't take sex seriously."

I stood up and reached back to cradle his head in my hands. I turned my head so he could suck on my tongue, then when our lips parted, I said, "I seriously want you to fuck me."

Max needed no other prodding. Placing a palm against my back, he bent me over again, then started pummeling my ass. I watched the little lights on his console blink and imagined them as seismographic meters measuring his powerful thrusts into my ass. My tender hole felt raw and utterly used; his cock was like a rigid piston. The light meters were all blinking maniacally now, so I reached out and turned up the volume knob I'd seen him turn down only minutes before. The ballad was now in full swing, its orchestral swells and dramatic vocals filling the room. I closed my eyes and constructed a mental picture of the music, an animated crescendo, vividly colorful and luridly throbbing, and as it reached its climax, Max did as well.

Pulling out of me, he hosed my thighs with thick blasts of come, then I came too. I pointed my dick down and heard the splatter of liquid as it rained down on the floor.

Max slumped back in his chair and pulled me down in his lap again, this time so we could face each other. He kissed me hard, tugging on my tongue and chewing on my lips, then he suddenly pulled back and said, "Hey, you didn't tell me your name."

"No, I didn't," I said, grinning at him impishly, "just think of me as your stranger." And I left it at that.

Firebomber: Cigar Sarge
Jack Fritscher

In the night world, men exist
who will do to you what you want.

Sarge is hot. Really good-looking. You offer him a cigar. He takes the box slowly. He pulls the cigar out slower. Long. Fat. Brown. Wrapper crinkles. Cigar is soft inside cellophane. Sarge tears wrapper deliberately with his strong teeth. Feels cigar. Smells good. Aroma. Wets lips. Inserts first one end of cigar. Then other. Licks it smooth and wet. Taste feels sharp on his tongue.

You kneel between his spread thighs. Look up to watch him reach into his fatigue pocket for a match. Cigar locks in his teeth. Poised. Wet. You wait for the moment. Incredible moment. When a man strikes fire. Lifts it to his face. Match in one hand. Cigar in other. You watch his face. You know the taste of a cigar lingering in a thick moustache.

Sarge rubs his hand across his crotch. Your mouth burrows down into his fatigues. Your eyes look up into his face. Instead of lighting the cigar, he holds the match. He stares straight into your eyes. The butt of stogie juts square from his mouth. Surrounded by moist lips. Locked tight in his teeth. The match burns. Sarge gives the cigar another slow, long lick. He clenches it hard. Your hand moves faster in anticipation of the moment the match will touch the tip. When deep blue smoke will rise from the hot, red coal.

Sarge touches the match to the cigar. Burn point. Smoke curls. Fills his mouth. Rises in a rich blue halo around his face and close-cropped hair. He pulls on it. Easy. Smooth. The tip glows hot. Red. A burning coal. A weapon.

You kneel adoring between his legs. Worshiping cock. Worshiping his face. The cigar smoke is his incense. Is your incense. The cigar is a thick cock. Wet. Hot. Burning. Commanding in his face. He exhales the smoke down on you. Spews smoke down on you. The smoke has volume. The smoke is thicker than popper. The taste in your mouth is better than you imagined. The smoke lifts you higher. He puffs. He puffs. He puffs and between his thighs you sniff the smoke he exhales. You snort the aroma.

You go down on him. Your eyes never leave his mouth. His cock is in your mouth. You pull your lips out. To the head of the dick. It's your trick. You know it. He knows it. It's your signal. You want him to hit his cigar and hold its heat. Hot against the back of your neck. To force your mouth buried root-deep on his dick. The back of your neck carries faint erotic marks of past cigar-sucks. You want his heat. You want his fire. You want his come. You want the wet splash and the hot burn. You want the smell of cigar in his hair and moustache. You want the smell of his sweat. You worship his mouth. His prick.

You strip off your shirt. You drop your jeans. You hold your mouth open wide, estimating measure of his cock. Your wide wet oval of mouth goes down on his cigar butt smoking in his mouth. He puffs it heavy and hard. You wrap your mouth wide around the burning tip of cigar. You inhale the smoke billowing from his mouth, curling up and out of his hard-bitten teeth. Again in perfect balance. Sarge on the cigar's wet end. You on the hot. Cigar-locked together like two men fucking. One up the ass of the other: the fucker orders the fucked not to move, not to dare even flex his ass or the cock buried hilt deep will shoot despite the fucker's warning. Two men on one cigar. Smoke shared. His eyes roll back in his head. Close to your face. Down the length of hot cigar. You see all.

You feel him piss. Warm. Wet. All over your belly. You worship his face. His mouth. His cigar. His cock. His body. His energy sears you more than a match to a rich dark Havana.

Your eyes beg him. Your empty mouth pulling back from his cigar-mouth begs him. Your hands frame a small area on your belly, above your cock.

He looks at the space like a firebomber over target.

You need him. For once finally you need him to do it. Your eyes say he must. Please. Your face shows your need. Please. Your hard cock shows your commitment. Please. His own meat hardens. More. With three last stoking puffs on the butt in his mouth. You need it. He wants it. Again a balance. Control between you both. Consent. Mutual understanding. You need what he can give. He likes what you can offer.

Sarge pulls his cigar stub from his mouth. Your hands milk his cock. Pull his meat. His hand lowers the glowing tip to your groin. Your eyes lock together. Your eyes beg him. Your dick moves fast in your one hand. His cock moves fast in your other. His thick arm, cigar butt curled into the palm of his hand, moves down between your moving arms. The glowing tip is inches away from your belly. Three inches. Two. You can feel the heat from the tip moving warm toward your skin.

The energy locks totally between the two of you. Perfect partners. His eyes search your eyes one last time. Never has any man so totally offered what you so totally need.

A shadow falls heavy across his eyes. It says NOW.

His fist with the burning cigar butt moves in for that last body-inch and holds. The pleasure. The pain. His heat pours into your belly. Contact: the briefest second. A tick of pain. Seared. You come. Now. You come. His face moves in to yours. An inch away. You rock. Jerk your cock. Worship him. Think of him. Together you separate. His hand moves away from your belly. Your belly moves away from his hand. He keeps his eyes locked into yours. Balance.

Sarge tucks his dick toward your groin. He licks his hand. He shoves his cigar back between his teeth. Locks it down. He pumps his hard greasy cock over your red-spotted belly. He pumps his dick hard. Until the smoke, filling his mouth, his nose, his chest, fills your mouth, your nose, your chest. Until in the blue haze around the pair of your faces, his cock comes wet and hotter than any cigar, shooting healing seed, salving juice over the loving brand that will all too soon fade to a light lover's mark. Made by him. Made by this man. Made by this toker. This taker. To carry hidden and secret for the rest of your life.

Somewhere out there, Sarge waits for you.

Because you know what Sarge has and Sarge knows what you need.

Basic Training
Michael Cavanaugh

"All aboard!" the conductor called. I turned to Elizabeth. She was wearing her best dress, and her hair was all frizzed across the front. "You be sure and write whenever you have a chance," she said, smiling uncertainly.

"Uh…yeah. Sure thing." I'd known Elizabeth practically forever. We grew up on adjoining farms and had made the transition from playmates to sweethearts without giving it much thought.

I had always known we were expected to marry someday, although I couldn't quite picture it. I still thought of her as a pal, and I wasn't really sure what she thought anymore.

"Well…'bye." She leaned toward me and closed her eyes. I looked up and down the platform. Other guys were kissing the girls who had come along to bid them farewell. I leaned forward and kissed her forehead, and those frizzy curls tickled my lips. I wiped my mouth on my sleeve, then boarded the train as it began to pull out of the station. By the time I stowed my gear and found a seat, the depot was no longer in sight. I heaved a sigh and settled back into the cushions.

"Sorry!" The train lurched on uneven track just as I pulled open the bathroom door. I pitched forward against a tall, dark-haired guy built solidly enough to break my fall. I started to beat a hasty retreat, but the door slammed shut behind me.

"Come on in!" the guy boomed in a resonant baritone. "I ain't having any luck. Maybe hearing someone else cut loose will prime the pump." I wasn't used to having folks invite me to join them in the bathroom, but then, I was from the sticks and figured there were lots of things I wasn't used to.

He moved aside, and I unzipped my fly. I felt self-conscious about exposing myself in front of another guy like that, but I really had to piss. I stared straight ahead, careful not to look at him, but I couldn't help seeing our reflections in the small mirror angled over the sink in the corner. He was good-looking, his hair slicked back, his swarthy face shadowed with stubble. He was big—all in his chest and shoulders, not his belly—and taller than I was by about four inches. A pale scar split the bushy black brow above his left eye and continued across the curve of his cheek. He caught me looking and grinned at me.

I looked away quickly. I was having a little trouble getting started myself, despite my bursting bladder. I took a deep breath, and finally the stream began to flow. I settled my shoulders and leaned slightly forward. As I did, my eyes shifted to the mirror again. The guy was looking down intently. I couldn't help it—I looked down as well.

"Damn!" I tried to bite down on the word, but it was too late. Sticking out of the man's fly was the biggest dick I'd ever seen—not that I'd seen all that many. It was as hard as a rock, the thick shaft laced with purple veins, the crimson head all swollen and shiny. "Uh…I'm sorry," I stammered.

"Hell, man, don't be embarrassed. I'm the one can't control the frigging thing."

"I'm not embarrassed," I lied, damn near pissing down my leg in my hurry to finish up.

"Your face is as red as the head of your dick," he retorted. I looked up at him, ready to be mad. Then he winked at me, and I started laughing. It was at that moment that Vic Angelotti and I became buddies.

I was glad because I needed a buddy. I grew up in the deep country, and the biggest crowd I'd ever been in was at the county fair where I went to show livestock. Now here I was in Uncle Sam's army with thousands of other guys. Fort Bennett was bursting at the seams with men training to go overseas and beat the shit out of the Nazis. Vic helped me get through all the induction stuff, and then, lucky for me, we got assigned to the same barracks. Vic snagged a top bunk beside a window and got me the upper right next to him. Seemed like anything Vic wanted, he went after it and got it. The man could talk an egg out of its shell. Hell, he even managed to get on the good side of our drill sergeant. No matter what came his way, Vic made sure I got a part of it too. He was a real pal.

I'd grown up bucking hay bales and hauling hundred-pound sacks of grain to the feedlot, so I didn't mind all the drilling and the calisthenics.

As long as I was busy, I was happy. It was the nights, late, after lights-out, that got to me.

I wasn't so much lonely as I was hard up. Believe me, I wasn't the only one. The barracks always smelled like jack-off and sweat, no matter how much scrubbing and washing the men did. The floors were clean, and the windows sparkled, but the place still smelled like horny men. And it was no wonder—almost every man in the place whacked off every night of the week. Right after lights out you would start to hear heavy breathing, groans, and the creaking of springs. I was intimidated at first, but I got used to it quick enough and joined in, adding my own moans to the chorus and the smell of my jism to the air.

The first couple of weeks, I kept my eyes closed while I was beating off, but curiosity finally got the better of me, and I started watching. My daddy used to take me night-hunting with him because my eyes were so sharp in the dark. The barracks was bright at night compared to the forest, so I could see most of what was going on around me. About 90% of it was just blankets billowing up and down, which I ignored. It was the other 10% that could get pretty interesting.

There were two guys about halfway down on the opposite side of the barracks, side by side in upper bunks, like Vic and me. The redhead was built real solid, and his blond buddy was tall and slender with a face as pretty as a girl's. They both spent their waking hours bragging about all the pussy they had plugged, but at night they would lie in their bunks, buck naked, staring at each other while they jerked off. The redhead would flex his big muscles, and the blond would squirm around like he was tied down on an anthill. When they got ready they would roll right to the edge of their bunks and shoot come across on each other. Afterward they would lie there and eat each other's jizz, smacking their lips like it tasted really good. It was crazy, for certain.

Most of the other guys just lay there and did themselves with their eyes closed, pumping till they shot a load. Some of them shot a little, some came a lot. After a while I got to feeling guilty about spying and quit watching—well, almost. The one guy I couldn't seem to quit watching was Vic. He never opened his eyes while he was working himself over, so he never knew what I was up to. Besides, with him I never got to feeling guilty enough to make me quit.

Vic was the total opposite of me. I was strong but lean. You could see my muscles shifting under my smooth, pale skin when I flexed, but they didn't really bulge or look huge. With Vic it was like everything was exaggerated. When he flexed his arms, his biceps rose up in big veiny mounds of muscle the size of softballs. His chest was a thick slab of sculpted flesh jutting out above a belly that was ridged like a washboard. He was hairy too, from the top of his head to the tops of his feet.

When he was jerking off, he was usually turned slightly toward me on his right side, working his dick with his left hand while he fingered his balls with his right. Vic's dick was even bigger than I'd thought that first day on the train. When it was soft it hung heavy, reaching for his knees. When it was hard, it thrust up out of his pubes like a club, the fat head backed up with a shaft like a battering ram. It was long enough so that he could grab it with both hands and still leave the knob sticking out in the clear.

Vic always started out slow and easy, stroking the shaft, rubbing his thumb over the snout, squeezing tightly around the base of his piece till every vein bulged. After it was stiff for a while, he would start milking it, pumping out drops of sticky ooze that ran down the shaft, making little trails as shiny as moonlight on water.

After Vic got his bone all nice and slippery, he would really start pumping it. I watched, beating my own meat, my fist keeping time with his. I could pretty much tell how he was doing by looking at his balls. His balls usually hung low and loose, but when he was jerking, his hairy bag would start to shrink, pulling his nuts up tight against his fist. The man's nuts took a hell of a pounding every night, but it never slowed him down till the bitter end.

Whenever Vic got ready to go off, it seemed like I was ready too. I could see the hairs on his sweat-streaked body bristling and smell the pungent odor rising out of his groin. By then the barracks would be full of jack-off, but Vic's smell was easy to pick out for some reason. Don't know why—it just was. It was bittersweet and nutty, tinged with his sweat. He would whimper, and his muscles would knot, and his narrow hips would rise off the thin mattress of his bunk. His big cock would start jerking in his hand, then he would let fly with a fountain of gooey white come. He always did three or four big shots, never letting go of his crank till he had pumped the hardness right out of it.

Once he was done he would lie there panting, his body limp, his dick on top of the trail of silky hairs that split his belly in half. That's when I'd come, watching him, his chest rising and falling, covered with his own juice. His face would be turned toward me, but his eyes would be closed, so he couldn't see me blow my wad and smear it all over my chest and belly, looking at him the whole time. I never stopped looking till I dropped off to sleep. I couldn't seem to help it. Must have had something to do with all those guys cooped up together and the smell of the place.

"Let's go, Sammy!" Vic grabbed my arm and pulled me off the bus. We were in town on a pass, our first since basic training ended. I was excited about it, mainly because I was tired of the obstacle course and parade grounds at Fort Bennett. We grabbed a burger at a cheap café, then walked across the street to a dark bar for a beer. We started drinking with some guys from the base, and it wasn't long before we were feeling no pain.

"Let's go to Gina's," Rafe Gomez suggested, poking Vic in the ribs with his elbow. "Give them babes a little bit of heaven. Hell, man, one look at the hose on you, maybe they'll give us all a high-volume discount." Vic shook his head, but the others took up the chant, and the next thing I knew I was standing in the parlor of a whorehouse for the first time in my life.

I was scared shitless. Elizabeth and I had made out, but we had never gone all the way. Touching her didn't make my dick hard. It just made me nervous. I watched guys disappearing up the stairs with different women. Before long I was the only man left in the parlor.

"Come on, Sammy." Vic stepped back into the room, put a hand on my shoulder, and propelled me out into the hallway.

"Hey, Vic, I'm not so—"

"I got it all taken care of, buddy." Vic winked at me and squeezed my shoulder. I followed him upstairs to a door on the third floor. Vic knocked. I stood there sweating, my stomach in a knot.

"Come on in, boys." A tall blond with big tits motioned us into the room. She looked me up and down, then turned to Vic. "I definitely see what you mean, buddy. You look real tasty, sweetie," she told me, caressing my cheek. "Have a drink, you two. I'll be back in a bit." She smiled and left the room, closing the door behind her.

"Beer?" Vic handed me a cold bottle. "Meter's running, buddy. Better strip down." He started unbuttoning his shirt. By the time I'd taken two swigs of beer, he was stark naked.

Seeing Vic here, alone with me in a small, dimly lit room, was different from seeing him naked in the showers or on his bunk at night. He was so damn big that he seemed to fill the room. I was backed up against the door, and he was at the foot of the bed, his weight on his right foot, his left leg cocked at an angle. Every muscle in his body looked like it was flexed. I felt insignificant.

"Hey, soldier, what's the matter?" Vic took a step toward me. I could smell him. My nostrils quivered. I looked down. His cock, still hanging against his furry thigh, was huge. I suddenly realized that I wanted to touch it. The thought terrified me. What was wrong with me?

"I…I think I should go, Vic," I stammered. "I'm not really into this."

"Looks to me like you're into it," he murmured, taking another step toward me. He was so close I could see the individual hairs feathering up over his collar bones. His knee bumped mine.

"I don't know what's happening."

"Maybe not, soldier, but your body does." I felt his hand against my thigh, then his strong, warm fingers squeezed my hard-on through my uniform trousers. My dick flexed against his palm. I started to speak, but Vic dropped to his knees, and there was nothing more to be said.

"You need a blow job, soldier. You need it bad." I looked down at Vic's brush-cut head, his broad shoulders slabbed with thick muscle, not quite sure I believed what I was seeing. He unbuckled my belt, popped the button at my waistband, unzipped my fly, and stuck his hand through the gaping slit in my boxers. My cock lurched out and skidded under his chin, the tender skin scraping against the rough stubble of his beard. I groaned, but not from any pain. He pushed forward, pressing his chin hard against me, rubbing it from side to side. I almost fell down.

He leaned back just a little, looked up at me, winked, and started down on me. When his lips touched my knob, my cock snapped up and slapped me in the gut. Vic hooked a finger around the base and pointed it back in his direction. His long pink tongue flickered out of his mouth and curled around the shaft. I grabbed his shoulders, my fingers digging into the muscle. I could feel his hot breath on my dick, my balls, the inside of my thighs.

I watched in disbelief as my dick disappeared into his mouth until his forehead was tight against my belly. I felt his tongue on me, and his lips, and the soft insides of his cheeks. His head pulled away until his teeth snagged the rim of my crown. He sucked my dick head till the head on my shoulders was spinning, his tongue lashing back and forth on the swollen bulb. Just when I felt I was going to explode, he lunged forward, burying me deep in his tight, hot throat.

I felt him swallow, heard the soft slurping sounds he was making as he nursed on my dick like a hungry calf. He had my balls in his hand, squeezing them gently, rubbing a finger back and forth on the hard ridge between my legs. His other hand had worked its way up under my shirt and he was pinching my tits. *Who would ever have thought they were connected to my dick?* My knees gave way, pressing hard into his big chest. Vic grunted and sucked harder. I whimpered and began to shoot, filling his mouth with my load. He swallowed it, still sucking long after I was drained dry.

He leaned back, hands braced behind him, cock thrusting up from between his thick thighs. He licked his lips and grinned at me. "Would you suck a buddy off, soldier?" he asked, his voice hoarse. I sank to my knees in front of him, watching his prick as it loomed closer and closer. I took a deep breath, smelling the leak that was drooling out of his piss hole, his balls drawn up against his shaft in a big furry knot, the heat rising off of him.

I touched his cock, stroking the broad back tentatively, like it was some kind of exotic animal. Then I gripped it in my hand and felt his pulse pounding against my palm. I licked it and tasted the salty goo that spilled out onto my tongue. I opened my mouth wide and lowered my head. "That's it, soldier," he moaned. "That's it."

I gagged at first, backed off, and tried again. I got the huge head wedged firmly in my mouth and started jacking him, pumping my fist up and down the entire length of the thick shaft. Vic was groaning, his big body trembling as I began bobbing my head up and down. His knob plugged my throat, then went beyond until I was kissing my knuckles halfway down the shaft.

"Jesus, soldier, I'm gonna—" He never got the sentence finished, but his meaning was clear enough. His prick swelled and flexed, and hot, thick jism hit the back of my throat. I choked and then swallowed just as he pumped out another burst of ball juice. My mouth was flooded with more of his thick, warm cream. It drooled out of the corners of my mouth and ran down his cock shaft. I held on through it all, gulping his pungent load until he was drained, then I licked the sticky remains off his cock and his balls.

By this time my prick was rock-hard again. Vic saw it and hauled me to my feet. He pulled me over onto the bed and stripped me naked. We spent the rest of the night sucking each other's balls hollow. The woman who had left us alone that night reappeared the next morning in time to escort us down the stairs to meet with our buddies, arms around our shoulders, smiling like she'd had the lay of her life. Hell, Vic and I both paid her the going rate for nothing, so she had good reason to be smiling.

The guys asked how it went, and I admitted that I'd had my cherry popped that night. The guys cheered and agreed that my basic training was now complete, although Vic just looked at me, winked, and shook his head. I've got a funny feeling that he still knows something I don't.

Hot Shave and a Haircut
Lance Rush

He strode into the barber shop sporting the Daddy of Colossal Afros! A big curly bush that rivaled Linc Hayes of The Mod Squad! Hello? All that hair distracted me. But then, as I really checked him, my attitude and cock were like: "Solid!" The man standing in my shop was fine as a midnight's FUCK! Tall, dark, tantalizingly buffed in black jeans so tight they looked possessed by long, lean thighs. I gazed at this dude's protruding package and wondered what kind of sexual contraband was he smuggling behind that zipper? This man took my imagination and rammed it firmly against his outsized crotch. Still, it was almost closing time when he asked, "You free? Folks say I could use a makeover. But hell, I'll settle for getting my head shaved."

His words purred in a velvet echo, resonating in my fevered brain. I think I said, "Yes. I'm free," but I can't be sure. I was too busy falling into the sex of his face. My gaze raced from his bushy caterpillar brow to the hard bone cliffs of his cheeks to the slow rafts of his full, moist lips. He was so hot, even his dark cocoa skin had a slow burn about it.

He sauntered to my chair, and I wrapped a barber's cape around his neck. I broke out the wide-toothed electric clippers first. The thick clumps began cascading. Clipping his hair became a bonding experience. I touched his face, jaw, neck. I brushed the curls from his wide shoulders. Then, smoothing warm lather on his head, I traced his ears. As the blade skated along his skull, I smelled his manscent, wiped his sweat. We shared a powerful silence, a trust that when our ritual was over, he'd emerge looking, feeling better. Then I witnessed what our closeness had done. He'd turned the thin material shrouding his lap into a tent—and that tent was high and dancing!

"My name's Derrick," he said.

"Hey, Derrick. I'm Malik."

"Malik? That's Arabic, right? You mean…?"

"Yes, Derrick, I'm a Brother. Biracial, but still a Brother," I said. His tent pitched a bit higher!

"Oh. OK. I wasn't sure. Thought maybe you were Latino," he shrugged.

Suddenly we could relate, and we started to kick it. I found out all kinds of personal shit, on the sly. Could be he was feeling out which way I leaned, because he started revealing all this intimate stuff like how there was no better sex than the "sweet tight sensation" of getting his dick sucked!

"Guess every man digs it, right? But see, I got a real big joint, and not too many can take it all the way down. Know what I'm sayin?" he confided, holding, stroking that bozack down his thigh. Shit! I heard and FELT what he was saying! Before it was over, my dick was hard as a fucking Chinese Math test! As I slowly finished him off, my hands held the mold of his head longer than necessary. His dome had this hot and shiny appeal, like a big ole good-looking charismatic dick! And I was into it, for real. I mean, I was giving that smooth naked skull a serious handjob!

"How's it feel?" he asked.

"Like butta!" I nearly sobbed. "You look good, man. Real good. Damn good!"

"Well it feels like sandpaper running all down my back. Mind if I wash up?" he asked, rising slowly from my chair, a Congo cobra in the front of his pants.

"Yeah. Sure. Bet. The bathroom's down the hall and to the left."

The place has a full bathroom. He disappeared and left me standing there with a bone the size of a small black Cadillac, knowing he and that naked dick were just a few feet away. My mind rewound to that sly way he had of introducing the size of his johnson into the conversation: "Got a real big joint, and not too many can take it all the way down." Sounded like a real big challenge. I had thoughts of bouncing my buckwild ass in there with him, dropping to my knees, and sucking down that mysterious 'zack Hoover Deluxe style! But that wouldn't be cool!

Just then, as if on cue, I heard, "Yo! Yo! Malik!" bellowing in an echo from down the hall.

"Yeah? What's up?" I yelled, compelled to follow his voice and my dick into the bathroom.

"You got a problem in here, man! Better check it out!"

Oh shit! What was it? Stopped up toilet? A flood? What? I dashed into the john expecting to find some plumbing catastrophe. But all I saw was Derrick, in the raw, and the view was so hot it's ridiculous!

"What is it? What's the problem?" I asked.

Derrick slides open the glass, and says, "This!"

His nakedness made my dick stand up and scream! My eyes swept over the chocolate succulence of him, across his ripped, glistening chest and along those Extra Large sable nipples. The six-pack looked tight, firm, lickable. And shit! OH DAMN! He didn't lie about that dick! I'm talking about a long-hanging, Massively Thick, Scare-the-Horses type DICK! It was encased in a dense cola black skin! He seized the turgid organ by the hairs of its nappy thatch and said, "I think this here is the problem. It's way too hairy down here. Don't you think?"

But I couldn't think for the huge, hypnotic, uncut bone dangling beneath that woolly, wet thatch!

"C'mon, help a Brother out! The place is closed. Why don't you grab a blade and shave down there for me? Yeah, I know it's kind of kinky, but I'll make it worth your while!" he said in a purr. "I'm starting to like this clean-cut look, and I was thinking, why stop at the head? Why not just go all the way!" And every word took on a deeply wet, sexually charged edge!

Shave it? Hell! I wanted rip that woolly afro from his crotch with my fucking teeth, just to get to his dick! Briar bush aside, I swear, bar none, Derrick had about the biggest hanging cock I'd seen in years! As it half-hung and half-projected from his fist, the massive dong's helmet seemed to draw me closer to him, to it, like a fucking magnet. My knees were weakening. The pull of lust surged through my balls, lifting my dick up and out, bringing on a wicked, nearly nine-inch bulge that Derrick couldn't help but notice! Grinning, he began soaping his hair-nest. Did I imagined it, or did Derrick's long deep cola-skinned dick JUMP?

In a flash, I grabbed a can of shaving cream, wanting to slab it on his region manually—lather him up the right way! But in case I'd read the situation wrong, I handed it to Derrick and retrieved a razor. When I turned back, my eyes drank in the sight of puffy white froth, billowing all around a long, viciously thick, angling cock! Hell! I almost shot off!

"Step over to the edge of the tub and roll a rubber on it," I told him as I sat on the side

Derrick slid on a safe, for protection's sake. He put hands on hips and his rubberized prick suspended just over my forehead, nuts swinging down like fur and leather pendulums.

"You ready for this?" I asked.

"Go for it, dude," he said. "Just be careful! Don't wanna lose these jewels!" he warned.

With a steady, if sweaty hand, I let the blade glide through the lather, holding onto one strong thigh for support. I traced, then skated along the sides of his furry crotch, taking away great nappy tufts with each sweep. Derrick held his hardening prick downward and the schlong pulsed several inches below his burly nuts. With intense concentration, I drew the blade up, then down, as fresh dark skin surfaced. Skin he probably haven't seen since the onslaught of puberty! In a few hot minutes he was spanking clean of hair and his dangling hose looked even longer than before!

"Now the balls!" he said. "Don't forget those nuts!"

The blade inched precariously along his drooping bangers as I, not wanting to nick those flawless orbs, moved very slowly. I could see by the perspiration beading on his thighs that he was nervous!

"Uh, er, look Derrick. I'll have to hold your balls if you want this done right," I told him.

"Yo! Grab what you need to, Brother!" he said. "I trust you!"

Bet! I cupped his nuts and went to work! My razor skirted a trail through the foam, erasing all traces of his thick man-forest. I sweated my way between his spreading legs. He held the swelling tube vertically up his belly giving perfect access to the thick ringlets dotting his full, jizz-heavy sac. The razor was full of Derrick's curly tangles. Figured I'd use it as beat-off fodder when he was long gone. I almost didn't want this shave to end, but finally he stood ripped and dangling before me, hairless and hot! I couldn't believe he was the same Brother who'd strode into the shop an hour before looking like a Woolly Mammoth! Now he was completely bald, head to big prick!

"Thanks, dude! You're all right! I appreciate this. Feel like a new man, now!" he said.

As I turned to place the razor in the sink, I heard Derrick ask the horny question: "You ever jerk your dick in here, man?" I could feel his eyes on my ass.

I didn't turn, just kept cleaning up, pretending I hadn't heard the question. But he was insistent.

"I said, you ever jerk your dick in here?"

"All the time. Especially when no one's around," I confessed.

I heard him shut off the water. It got so quiet, my ears were tuned to his breaths. Then he said, "Get naked, man. Let me see how you do it."

PAYDIRT! Now was his chance to get a look at his barber! With my back turned, I pulled off my sweat-soaked shirt. I let him see the shoulders, the delts, the traps—weight-trained and sculpted into a perfect V-shape. I loosened my belt, running my hands along my 30-inch waist, then to the slopes of my ass. I pulled my pants down, inch by inch, giving him a view of my taut caramel globes, the cheeks etched and rounded by years of biking and countless hours on a StairMaster. Finally naked, I turned to find him soaping his cock with long, slow, lazy strokes.

"Damn! Got some size on you, too!" he said, surveying my hard, nearly nine-inch rod. "Look at that! You're kinda large!" he grinned. But when I looked down at him, his cock was even longer! A BIG WET FUCKING PIECE OF EBONY HORSE MEAT! He skinned it back, and shit! DAMN! Dick must've been ten, eleven inches at least! It was still encased in rubber, but throbbing as he urged, "C'mon! Let's stroke these big motherfuckers till they shoot!" Then, pulling his johnson up his belly, he let it slap hard to his dampened thigh. As I stepped into the shower, beads of soap and water whipped off it. I wished it was his come. He scooped his cock and balls, shaking and jacking them simultaneously. I stroked my shaft's base, running my hand up slowly to its juicing head. Derrick spread his muscular legs and began showing off, pinching his skin at the reservoir tip and wiggling his whole dark dong like a slippery eel! Then he took that long brown log in both hands, beating it, flogging it, making it SNAP! Slowly I began to fuck my fist, bending my knees and bucking my ass as I did. Derrick snaked his hand around and grabbed my wet cheeks.

"Can you take a finger?" he hissed. Before I answered, he a jabbed a long digit up my chute!

Shit! I felt my knees buckle from the jolt, and I found myself a breath away from his ripe sable nipples. I latched on, twisted one, and his body jumped from the pleasure. Shit, yes!

Now we were finally touching each other! His finger prodded up my ass as I moved in to suckle his sweet man tit. He shivered, banging his big hard dick to my belly. Oh! I ground my upturned cockhead on the smooth skin of his shaved crotch, getting off on its naked feel! That thick finger started motioning, deeper, jabbing, stabbing, making my heated asshole even hotter! He slid it out and slowly moved me from his nipples, down his pounding belly to his looming dick. Breathless, my lips snatched the wide head up in a gobble. He groaned! Man! Even rubber-clad Derrick's cock was delicious! Echoes of soap and sweat rode along my slick tongue. He pushed. I grabbed his wet bubble ass, guided the globes, and led him into my motion.

"Oh, damn! Suck my dick! Oh yes! Suck my big dick, baby!" he sighed as my lips swam down the dark length of it. I could feel his every throbbing vein pumping as it aimed towards my gullet. It was such a long, hot, meaty motherfucker. I had to know what a dick this size felt like in its entirety. Opening extra wide, I battled to cram the whole fucking mass down my throat. I took a deep breath, lunged down. My horny mouth enclosed the full rod, but only for an instant!

"Oh! Aw! Shit yes! Damn man! No one's ever done that before!" he sighed as my cheeks bloated around him. Pulling back, I gasped, then went for more. Flexing my throat, I burrowed down the long stifling shaft, burying the tip of my nose in raw pubic skin! Oh! He pumped, gagging me but good! Yet the clutch of my throat seemed to set him off! Derrick groaned, pulling the long, vein-jagged tube from the depths of my sucking throat. Suddenly the wet dong POPPED free. The enormous cap was a bubbling brown hue. I just knew it was about to erupt!

"AW! AWSHITBABY! Now you did it! I'm…gonna …shoot! Shooting, shooting, SHIT!" He whipped off the safe as the first rope dashed a wild white streak from his pisshole! Oh! Then the fucker just went off, spitting, spurting, spraying this vat of ivory slop like there was no stopping it. He leaned against the shower wall, cock still sputtering, leaking come down his thigh. His fine hairless body heaved and pitched, torso coated with a sheen of water and sweat. I gripped his long jutting dick, squeezing the last bits of jism out the wide, sticky slit.

It was still fidgeting as I drew back its skin to admire it. The long, slick mahogany tube curved up. I bent. It wavered as I kissed the warm, pulsating shaft of this HUGE, fucking beautiful prick!

"You, you're so hot, baby! Do you fuck, or get fucked?" he asked between panting.

"Both," I said. "But I don't think I want—"

"Good! I want you to FUCK MY ASS!" he said boldly, turning around and spreading his globes to reveal a tight, blackberry hole and his long dark dick dangling several inches below it.

Hell! I was almost relieved that he took it in the ass, judging by the size of that pulsing pole between his legs! Stepping out of the shower, I quickly grabbed a towel, wrapped it around me, and went into the salon to pull down the shades. As I pivoted back, there he was, looking like wet chocolate, his dick full, turgid, and slapping thigh to thigh as he walked! Staring intently at my lifting dong, he fell before it. Derrick's tongue shot out, wickedly teasing, licking my shaft. OH! The touch of his spinning tongue was electric! His dagger-like dick stood straight up. I clutched tight to his shaved head as he swirled and suctioned me deeper and deeper! Then he pulled back and dove down with this insanely loud slurp until his hot lips kissed the pubic bone!

"Oh! Shit! That's enough! Easy! EASY DERRICK! Gonna have a throat full of cream if you keep that horny shit up!" I warned. And I was serious!

He rose and I cranked the handle on the Barber's Chair, lowering it into a reclining position. I slid a rubber down my pulsing boner.

"Why don't you sit down first, and I'll get on top," he suggested. "That way you can fuck my ass and stroke this big dick all at once."

"Cool," I said. I lay back in the chair, prick jutting high and hard as he climbed aboard, legs over armrests. He held my cock, easing it slowly through the puckered rim of his fuckhole! OOOH! That sudden clamp of tightness enclosed me! The moist anal eye slowly swallowed my dickcap, then my throbbing shaft, squeezing it in a narrow snatch of skin! I felt every muscle in his stretching anus constrict and grip me as he whispered, "Yes! Aw shit yes! Don't move!"

He lowered down my boom, bringing on more intensity as his long dick flopped hot to my belly! Even through rubber, the heat of his ass was an inferno! The head of his cock a fire poker!

He rose, fell, grunted. "Oh shit!" Slowly he churned down and wiggled, forcing every fraction of my swollen dick deep up his grasping gut. I laid back and let my pole flex inside his hungry tunnel! Shit! He was so deep and vise tight! The glide and clasp of his ass was already milking me. His anal grip was firm, and with each descent his heavy prick slapped down with a THWACK! It kept growing harder, longer, till the fucker was thrusting clear up my chest! As I pulled his erect nipples, his rhythm increased. I jacked his long dick in one hand and squeezed his black poking nip with the other. Sweating, he threw back his newly bald head and swooned!

I switched on the hot lather machine. In seconds, the cream was nice and warm to the touch. Then I slapped a fistful along his dick, working it up his hard, sliding shaft as he groaned, "Yeah! Oh yeah! Ah! Aww!

Mmmm! Yeah! I like that! Put some down below, too!"

I applied the heated foam to the base of my shaft and swathed the edges of his impaled hole. When he slid down and swerved, OH! Long, trembling howls echoed from both of us! The heated sensation was so strong, but I still had a few good primal bucks left in me! My savage hips flew up and slammed his ass! The warm foam had me humping, jabbing his writhing cavern like a man on fire!

"FUCK! FUCK!" he cried! Suddenly, the long hard dick sliding in my lathered hand erupted! Come wads jumped from his piss slit in high, exploding bursts, vaulting, pelting my chest and neck! He swirled with a crazed speed as his jism rained white-hot sparks on my skin. The clutch of his ass rocking, rolling on my prick compelled me to shoot! "AW SHIT! HERE I GO!" I cried. Latching onto his nipples, I unleashed a growl as my cream catapulted in wild blasts into the rubber. I felt it riveting against the spastic walls of his colon as our bodies jittered violently! A come-soaked, lather-coated Derrick smiled a hot, sweaty grin and planted a big wet one on my burning lips.

"Damn, man! That was one hot fuck! Too much! Now, how much do I owe you," he panted.

"Let's see. Shave and a haircut, 25 bucks. The suck and fuck, well, that was on the house!"

Knowing Johnny
Bob Vickery

The single bulb that lights up the hallway is broken, and I have to negotiate my way to Rico's apartment by trailing my fingers against the wall, counting the doors. In the dark the smells of the place seem a lot stronger: boiled cabbage, mildew, old piss. Heavy-metal music blasts from one of the doors I pass, and I get a sickly sweet whiff of crack. Fucking junkies. I can hear loud voices arguing in the apartment across the hallway, then the sound of furniture breaking. Rico's apartment is the next one down. I grope my way to it and knock on the door.

I stand there for a minute, waiting. "Who's there?" a voice finally asks from inside.

"Open up, Rico," I say. "It's me, Al."

I hear the sounds of bolts being drawn back. The door opens an inch, still chained, and Rico's eye peers at me through the crack. He closes the door, undoes the chain, and opens it wide this time. "Get in," he growls. I slip in, and Rico bolts the door behind me. The room is small: an unmade bed, a beat-up dresser, a table by the window. The kid Rico told me about on the phone is sitting at the table, looking scared and trying not to show it. It's quieter in here than in the hall, even with the sounds of traffic coming in from the window. I can faintly hear above our heads the clicking of writer-god's keyboard.

I keep my eyes trained on the kid. I take in the shaggy blond hair, the strong jaw, the lean body. "Where'd you find him?" I ask Rico, without turning my head.

"Out on the street, hustling," Rico says. "I convinced him he could do better with a little management." Rico walks into my line of sight. "He tells me he's 18." Of course, writer-god has Rico say that to keep the censors happy.

"What's your name?" I ask the kid.

"Johnny," he says. There's a slight quiver in his voice.

"Did Rico rough you up?" Rico stirs, but I silence him with a gesture. "Did he force you up here?" Again, writer-god is having me ask this for the sake of the fucking censors. If there's coercion, the story won't sell.

Johnny shakes his head. "No," he says. "I wanted to go with him. Rico told me about you. I thought maybe you could help me." His voice is steadier now, firmer. But the wideness of his dark eyes still gives away his fear.

"How good are you at taking orders?"

Johnny licks his lips and swallows. "Real good," he says.

This is the first sex scene of the story. Writer-god usually limits it to oral only, saving butt fucking for the end-of-story finale. "Stand up," I say. Johnny climbs to his feet. "I want you to come over here and suck my dick."

Johnny's eyes flicker toward Rico and then back at me again. He shifts his weight to his other foot but doesn't move. He seems to be weighing his options. "OK," he finally says. He walks over to me and drops to his knees. His hands are all businesslike as they unbuckle my belt, pull my zipper down, and tug my jeans and boxers down below my knees. I keep my face stony, but my dick gives away my excitement. It springs up and swings heavily in front of Johnny's face. Johnny drinks it in with his eyes. "You've got a beautiful dick," he says.

"Just skip the commentary," I reply.

Johnny leans forward and nuzzles his face into my balls. I feel his tongue licking them, rolling them around in his mouth, sucking on them. He slides his tongue up the shaft of my dick and then circles the cock head with it. I stand there with my hands on my hips. Rico stands behind the boy, watching. His dick juts out of his open fly, and he's stroking it slowly.

Johnny's lips nibble their way down my meaty shaft (all our shafts are "meaty"; writer-god won't let us in the story without a crank at least eight inches long, and thick, always thick, topped with "flared heads" or "fleshy knobs" or "heads the size and color of small plums"). When Johnny's mouth finally makes it to the base of my stiff cock, he starts bobbing his head, sucking me off with a measured, easy tempo. He wraps one hand around my balls and tugs them gently as his other hand squeezes my left nipple. I close my eyes and let the sensations he's creating throughout my body ripple over me.

Rico comes up next to me and yanks his jeans down. He strokes his dick with one hand while his other hand slides under my shirt and tugs at the flesh of my torso. I reach over and cup his balls, feeling their heft, how they spill out onto my palm so nicely. I lean over, and we kiss, Rico slipping his tongue deep into my mouth. Rico lets go of his dick and Johnny wraps his hand around it, peeling the foreskin back, revealing the fleshy little fist of Rico's cock head (another favorite phrase of writer-god). He takes my dick out of his mouth, sucks on Rico's for a while, and then comes back to me. I spit in my hand and wrap it around Rico's thick, hard cock, sliding it up and down the shaft. Rico lets out a long sigh. He starts pumping his hips, fucking my fist in quick, staccato thrusts. Johnny pries apart my ass cheeks and worms a finger up my bung hole, never breaking his cocksucking stride. I lose my cool, giving off a long, trailing groan. Johnny pushes against my prostate, and I groan louder. I whip my dick out of his mouth just as the first stream of spunk squirts out, slamming against Johnny's face. My body spasms as my load continues to pump out, splattering against his cheeks, his closed eyes, his mouth. Rico groans, and I feel his dick pulse in my hand. Johnny turns his head to receive this second spermy shower, and soon Rico's jizz is mingling with mine in sluggish drops. Rico bends down and licks Johnny's face and neck clean, dragging his tongue along the contours of the boy's features. The clicking sound of writer-god's keyboard gets faster and then suddenly stops.

We all look up. "Do you think he's done?" Rico finally asks.

"With the scene, maybe," I say. "He still has to finish the story."

Johnny climbs to his feet and looks around the room. "Christ, what a dump. I hope we don't have to stay here long."

Rico laughs. "Hell, this is fuckin' swank compared to where I was before." He starts pulling up his pants. "Writer-god had me lying on some teahouse floor with a bunch of guys shooting their loads on me. Then he just left me there, stuck in that stinking piss hole." He looks around. "I just wish there was a TV here."

I offer a handkerchief to Johnny. "Here," I say. "Rico missed a few drops." Johnny takes it and wipes the last of my load off his face. I pull out a deck of cards from my jacket pocket and sit down at the table. "Poker, anyone?"

There are only two chairs, so Rico has to sit on the edge of the bed. We start with five-card stud. "It's no fun unless you play for money," Johnny grouses.

I shrug. "I don't have any money. Do you?"

Rico grins. "We could always play for sex." We all laugh. As if we don't already get nothing but that from each other. Johnny finds matchsticks in the drawer of the dresser, and we divvy them out.

I deal the first hand. "So what have you been up to, Johnny?" I ask. Johnny and I have worked together more times than I can remember. I've fucked him in locker rooms, in the back seats of cars, in alleys, on secluded beaches—once in the torch of the Statue of Liberty. Johnny is always "the kid" in writer-god's stories, sometimes going by the name Billy, sometimes Eddy or Andy, always a name that ends in "y." I look at him across the table, feeling the old frustration. For all the hot sex we've had together, I hardly know the guy. No conversation, no snuggling together under the sheets, just fade to black and then the cycle starts all over again.

"Oh, I was in a great place last story," Johnny said, laughing. "I was a street hustler in Cozumel who hooked up with an American tourist. You know him—it was Cutter."

"Shit," Rico mutters. I glance at him, but he keeps his eyes focused on his cards. Cutter's a stock character writer-god uses for his more upscale stories, usually about some married man straying to the other side or a well-heeled gay yuppie. I've worked with him a couple of times. Rico and I both think he's got his head up his ass.

"Did you have a good time?" I ask.

"Oh, yeah, it was great fun," Johnny says. I look for sarcasm, but his smile seems sincere. "After writer-god wrapped up the fuck scene on the beach, we just hung out there—sunbathing, snorkeling, collecting shells— the whole tourist thing." Johnny nods at the room around us. "Until I wound up here."

"I'm sorry you're disappointed," I say.

Johnny grins. "Who said anything about being disappointed?" He looks across the table at me and winks. My throat tightens.

"Hey, are you guys going to flap your jaws or play cards?" Rico asks. He throws three cards down on the table, and I deal him three more. But the wheels are turning in my head. Writer-god usually writes several stories at the same time. I glance at Rico, who's sorting through his cards. Rico's all right, but I wouldn't mind it if writer-god suddenly pulled him for another story and left Johnny and me alone.

Johnny drops two cards on the table, and I deal him two more. I keep what I have. Rico starts the betting off with five matchsticks. Johnny throws in his five matchsticks and raises five more. "Which one of your past scenes would you most like to go back to?" I ask Johnny. "If you had a choice."

Johnny grins and shakes his head. "You'll just laugh."

"No, I won't, I promise." I throw in the ten matchsticks and raise another ten.

"It was a college story," Johnny says. "Writer-god had me gang-fucked in the UC Berkeley library by the college football team. After he wrapped up the story, he didn't use me for weeks. I got to hang out there all that time doing nothing but reading." He glances at me. "Have you ever read the poem "Leaves Of Grass," Al? Or any of Robert Frost's poems?"

I don't laugh, like I promised, but I do smile. "When would I read poetry?" I say. "Between blow jobs in a back alley?"

Johnny gives a rueful smile and shrugs. "That's my point. I hardly ever get to spend time in places where I can improve my fuckin' mind."

Rico sees my ten matchsticks and calls. We show our hands. Johnny's got a pair of eights, Rico two pairs, aces and fives. I win with a straight, jack high. I gather up my winnings and deal us all new hands. Rico leans back on the bed and stretches. "I wouldn't mind going back to the story where I was a ranger in Yosemite," he says. "I ended up fucking these back-packers."

I open my mouth to comment, when I feel my feet begin to tingle. I know only too well what that means. "So long, guys," I barely have time to say. "I'm off to another story."

There's a knock on the door, and then Old Bert sticks his head in. "I got the lad here for you, Captain," he says. "Just like you told me to." He knows better than to give me a wink, but his mouth curves up into a randy leer. I can hear the rest of the crew fighting over the *Magdalena*'s spoils.

"Bring him in," I say gruffly. I'm lying on the bed that belonged to the *Magdalena*'s former captain. Since we've tossed him overboard with a slit throat, I don't think he'll be needing it anymore.

Old Bert opens the door wider, pushes the *Magdalena*'s cabin boy in, and closes the door behind him. The lad stumbles forward and then straightens up to face me. His dark eyes glare at me, but I can see the fear in them as well. *So Johnny's in this story too,* I think. Poor Rico, stuck in that room by himself. The boy stands in the middle of the cabin, his hands at his side, head lowered, waiting.

"Do you speak English?" I ask him.

He nods, his eyes still trained to the floor.

"Look at me, lad," I say. He raises his eyes again. My gaze sweeps down his wiry, muscular body and then back to his face again. "What's your name?" I ask.

"Juan Francisco Tomas Santiago, sir," he says. His voice is barely audible.

"That's quite a mouthful for such a young lad," I say. "I shall call you 'Johnny.' " There's a moment of silence. I can faintly hear the clicking of writer-god's keyboard. I've never been in a period story; writer-god usually confines me to slums and back alleys.

The heat of the tropical sun pours into the cabin, and I feel my head grow light from it. I lie back in the captain's bed, my eyes traveling up Johnny's body: There's a coltish quality to his muscular young body that makes my dick swell. Johnny watches silently, his eyes now never leaving my face.

"Get naked," I say.

The blood rushes to Johnny's face, and he shifts his weight to his other foot. *Writer-god should watch that little bit of business he always has Johnny do,* I think. *It's getting repetitious.* Slowly, hesitantly, he unbuttons his shirt and lets it fall to the floor. His torso is as smooth and dark as polished driftwood, the muscles beautifully chiseled. Johnny slips off his shoes, pulls his breeches down and steps out of them. He stands naked at the foot of the bed, his hands at his sides, his cock lying heavily against his thigh. His face is as pure as any angel's, but he's got a devil's dick: red, fleshy, roped with blue veins. In the stifling heat his balls lie as low and heavy as tree-ripened fruit. "Turn around," I say.

Johnny turns around. His ass is pretty, high and firm. My dick swells to full hardness. Johnny ends his rotation and faces me.

"Well, come over here, lad," I say, smiling slyly, "and give me a reason why I shouldn't just slit your throat and toss you overboard."

Johnny stands where he is, head bowed but with his hands curled into fists. "Aye, Johnny," I say. "Is it coaxing you want instead of threats?" I sit up in the bed. "Please do an old sea dog a favor, lad," I say in exaggerated politeness, "and come join me in my bed."

Johnny looks me in the eye, still saying nothing. His mouth curls up into the faintest smile. He crosses the small room and climbs into bed with me. I wrap my arms around him and kiss him, and he kisses back, lightly at first, then with greater force, slipping his tongue into my mouth. I pull him tightly against me. I wrap my hand around both our dicks and start stroking them slowly. Johnny reaches down and cups my balls in his hand. "Tell me, lad," I whisper in his ear. "Have you ever been buggered before?"

"Yes, sir," Johnny whispers. "Many times." I don't doubt it. A lad as handsome as Johnny would be fair game on any ship.

There's a jar of pomade on the table next to the bed. I reach over and scoop out a heavy dollop. "Well, maybe I can still teach you a few new tricks," I say, as I work my hand into his ass crack and begin greasing up his hole. I slip a finger in, and the muscles of Johnny's ass clamp around it tightly. I push deeper in, and Johnny's body stirs. "Do you want more of the same, lad?" I growl.

Johnny nods his head. "If you please, sir," he says.

"Well, since you asked so politely...," I laugh. I grease up my dick with the pomade and hoist Johnny's legs over my shoulders. Johnny takes my dick in his hand and guides it to the pucker of his asshole. I push with my hips, and my dick slides inside him, Johnny thrusting his hips up to meet me. As I start pumping his ass, Johnny meets me stroke for stroke, moving his body in rhythm with mine, squeezing his ass muscles tight with every thrust of my cock.

I laugh from surprise and pleasure. "Aye, Johnny," I say. "Ye're a lusty young buck. I can see that clearly enough. And ye've learned your buggery lessons well." *This is the first story where I've fucked without condoms,* I think. *Sweet Jesus, it feels good!*

I continue plowing Johnny's ass with long, slow strokes. A groan escapes from his lips, and I grin fiercely. "That's right, Johnny," I say. "Sing for me. I want to play you like a mandolin." *Where is writer-god coming up with this fucking dialogue?* I wonder. I thrust savagely until my dick is full inside him and then churn my hips. Johnny groans, louder. I bend down and kiss him, and he returns my kiss passionately, thrusting his tongue into my mouth. As I skewer Johnny, he reaches up and runs his hands across my body, twisting my nipples hard. He wraps his legs around me and rolls over on top. We're drenched with sweat, and our bodies thrust together and separate with slapping noises. I wrap Johnny in my arms, and we roll again, falling off the bed onto the deck below.

I pin Johnny's arms down and plunge my cock deep inside him. Johnny cries out. "Do you want me to stop, lad?" I ask.

"No, sir," Johnny groans.

I thrust again, and again Johnny cries out. I can hear the pirates brawling outside. They're probably drunk by now on the *Magdalena's* cargo of spirits. "Louder, Johnny," I snarl.

"Don't stop, sir!" he cries out.

"That's better," I grunt. I wrap my arms around him and press him tightly. My sweaty torso slides and squirms against him as I pump my dick in and out of his ass. A groan escapes from Johnny's lips. I thrust again, and he groans again. Johnny reaches down and squeezes my balls. They're pulled up tight, ready to shoot. He presses down hard between them, and my body shudders violently as the first of the orgasm is released. I throw back my head and bellow as my dick gushes my jism deep into his ass. Load after load of it pulses out, and I thrash against Johnny. After what seems like an eternity, the last of the spasms end, and I collapse on top of him.

I push myself up again. "Climb up on my chest, Johnny," I say, "and splatter my face with your load."

Johnny seems only too happy to oblige. He swings his leg over and straddles me. I look up at him, at the tight muscular body, at Johnny's handsome face, at the hand sliding up and down the thick shaft of his dick. "Aye, there you go, lad," I mutter. "Make your dick squirt for me." I reach up and twist Johnny's left nipple.

I feel Johnny's body shudder, and he raises his face to the ceiling and cries out. A load of jism gushes from his dick and splatters against my face. Another load follows, and then another. By the time Johnny's done, my face is festooned with the ropy strands of his wad. He bends down and licks it off tenderly, and I kiss him, pulling my body tight against his.

Writer-god's keyboard is suddenly silent. We wait expectantly for it to start up again, finish the story, but nothing happens. I look up at Johnny, and we both burst out laughing. "Do you believe that fucking dialogue?" I say. I twist my face into comic fierceness. "Aye, Johnny," I growl. "You're a lusty young buck. How 'bout letting me bugger your ass?"

Johnny laughs again. He climbs off me and helps me to my feet. We hunt for our clothes strewn all around and pull them back on. I feel like I'm dressing for a costume ball. I look at Johnny appraisingly as he tucks his shirt into his breeches. "You look really good as a Spanish cabin boy," I say. "It suits you."

Johnny raises his eyebrows. "You're not putting the make on me, are you, Al?"

I have to laugh at that. "Right. Like I don't get enough sex from you as it is." Still, I'm feeling light and playful now that I'm alone with Johnny. I look around. The cabin is cramped, and a glance out the porthole shows nothing but sea and sky. The deck beneath our feet rolls gently with the movement of the waves. The tropical heat makes the small room feel like a sauna. I jump onto the bed and pat the empty side next to me. "Hop back in," I say to Johnny. "Let's just relax for a while. Maybe talk."

Johnny joins me on the bed, stretching his legs out and placing his hands behind his head. My heart is beating hard, and when I notice this I almost laugh. I've forgotten how many times I've fucked Johnny in how many countless stories, and yet I'm actually feeling nervous. I cautiously wrap my arm around Johnny's shoulders, and he snuggles against me. "This is nice," he says.

"I've been wanting to do this for a long time," I say. "All we do is fuck. We never talk."

Johnny looks up at my face, his eyes amused. "What do you want to talk about, Al?"

I think for a long time. The only subjects I can come up with are back alleys, docks, and quarter booths in the backs of porno bookstores. I'm struck by a sudden thought. "Tell me about the poems you read in the UC-Berkeley library," I say.

"Do you want to hear one?" Johnny asks, grinning.

"Sure." I nestle back against the pillows, my eyes trained on him.

Johnny pulls himself up to a sitting position and turns to face me. He clears his throat and begins.

"In Xanadu did Kubla Khan
A stately pleasure dome decree
Where Alph, the sacred river ran
Through caverns measureless to man
Down to a sunless sea."

Johnny squeezes his eyes in concentration for a second and then looks at me apologetically. "I don't remember much more. Just the last few lines:

"His flashing eyes! His floating hair!
Weave a circle 'round him thrice
And close your eyes in holy dread
For he on honeydew has fed,
And drunk the milk of Paradise."

He looks down at me. "Sorry, that's all I know."

I shake my head. "I don't get it." Johnny shrugs, but doesn't say anything. "I mean, who would name a river Alph? And who ever heard of hair floating?"

"I don't know," Johnny says, laughing. "I didn't write the damn poem." He lies back down in the bed, burrowing back into my arms. "Just let the words create the pictures."

We lay in the bed together, Johnny's body pressed against mine. My arm lightly strokes his shoulder. I can smell the fresh sweat of his body, feel the heat of his skin flow into me. "This is so nice," I say, half to Johnny, half to myself. Johnny says nothing, just lays his hand on my thigh and squeezes it. I close my eyes.

My feet start to tingle. "Fuck!" I cry out. I look up at the ceiling. "Writer-god, you bastard! Can't you give me a just few fucking minutes of peace!" The tingling spreads up my body, and the ship's cabin fades out, along with Johnny.

I got Nash taking point 20 meters in front of the squad, and Myers and Benchly behind us working the radio, keeping the com line open with the base. The others are in different positions waiting for orders. That leaves me alone, with the kid, Jamison. Earlier reconnaissance reports indicated enemy movement about five clicks north of the base, working its way toward us, but fuck, that was hours ago, and Charley could be anywhere. I look around. We're on elevated ground, with good cover, and I don't anticipate any action for hours; our best bet is to lie low and hope Charley walks into our ambush.

I crawl over to Jamison. "How you doing, son?" I whisper.

Jamison looks back at me, his eyes wide, his mouth set in a tight line. He's a green recruit, just assigned to the squad, and this is his first combat action. He still wears the look of someone trying to wake up from a bad dream. "All right, I guess, Sarge," he says.

I put my gun down and sit down beside him. "It's a hell of a business, ain't it?"

Jamison grins, and I feel my throat tighten. I've been sporting a hard-on for the kid since he was first assigned to the squad. "What's your name?" I ask. "I mean, what do you go by?"

Jamison looks at me, and a little crackle of energy shoots between us. "Johnny," he says.

I put my hand on his thigh and squeeze. I'm risking court-martial, but I'm sick and tired of this fucking war; I may be dog meat tomorrow. I bend down and plant my mouth over Johnny's. He doesn't hesitate for a moment; it's like he's been waiting for me to get the ball rolling. He kisses me back, pushing his tongue almost down my throat.

Johnny, I think, *one of these days, between stories, we'll get that chance just to hang out, to talk, to get to know each other a little.* I've got to believe it will happen. I look into Johnny's eyes, and for a moment I think he can read my thoughts. He gives a tiny smile and nods, a gesture out of character for the story.

As writer-god's keyboard clicks away, I reach down, unzip Johnny's fly and pull out his thick, hard cock.

Gustavo
T. Hitman

The story begins on a warm, windy night, Sutter's Butte in Northern California. I sense right away this story will be different, special, by the warmth of the air after two weeks when El Nino has pounded my new home state, sense it as the sun begins to set, and the flat landscape outside Yuba City glows golden-red on the drive to the sprawling farm at the bottom of the hills. At the moment the story actually begins, I feel what can only be butterflies taking flight in my stomach, try to blame it on too much coffee that morning, stress from work, and most likely the fact that less than a week has passed since the break-up with my girl became final.

The back story is: My name's Lawrence, Larry to my friends, and somehow I've lucked out and been promoted to a staff position in Sutter County reporting on the sports beat, local/amateur and Northern California pro. Five days a week, I see my name in print with the rest of the jocks I get to write about. Only major thing I can gripe about is that my girlfriend walked two days after my 22nd birthday. I haven't been in California long; nine months, almost to the day. But most of that time's been spent working, taking in games, drinking coffee, and trying not to feel lonely or lost as I carve out something of a career on my way to bigger, better things.

"You work too much," the voice in the passenger seat grouses. "Relax, man. Take a break. We ain't here to work tonight."

I realize I've been talking out loud about the job again as we get closer to the farm, passing huge stands of walnut, peach, and fig trees. The man to my right is Tony. He sells ads for the newspaper, is my age, probably the only reason we hang out together. It's because of him I'm here, blinded by the beauty of the countryside—I can't believe how beautiful this place is! I'm not a romantic. At least, I don't think I am.

"Sorry," I placate, look into the rearview mirror and see my eyes, green and sad, covered by black shades. Hair looks good. Clean-shaven and trendy in my black linen jacket over white t-shirt, jeans, deck shoes, no socks. Tony's wearing a pair of shorts that show off his decent, hairy legs, white ankle socks, expensive sneakers, T-shirt, shades, and a ball cap. He looks ready to party with this friend of his who's back from the service, on leave for one more week before shipping out to Europe. Me—I could use a party, but I don't look like it. It's a party full of strangers, and all I can think about are deadlines, interviews, more deadlines, anything to fill the silence of my apartment now that she's gone.

"Turn left. Here," Tony says.

I turn. We drive higher, and the trees gradually thin out. Enormous sculpted gardens of marigolds and dahlias spell out the words AQUINO FARM, the letters growing on the hillside to welcome visitors to the family's palatial house. It's a large white Victorian surrounded by rose gardens, with bright yellow awnings over each window. The farmhouse sits right at the base of the butte; a large deck extends out over the lawn. I see bodies moving about on the deck, and smoke from a grill. Suddenly, the air is full of enticing aromas and deep male laughter. Strangers or not, I'm excited.

I park my jeep beside a fleet of Beemers, sport trucks, and 4 x 4s. "This guy's pretty popular," I say.

Tony's half out of the truck before I even come to a full stop. "Tavo's the best."

"Gustavo," I mumble under my breath. His name has a strange poetry about it. It resonates in my mind as we crunch up the gravel drive onto the path that will lead to the front door. What I already know about Gustavo Aquino is that he's a year younger than me, a full-blooded Chicano who was the Number-One lady-killer in Tony's high school, star of both the baseball and football teams, a total jock who totally p.o.'ed his parents by going into the Marines instead of college. Tony's told me that Gustavo's parents got fat by having the farm, over a thousand acres of producing land, and one of the best reputations on the West Coast. As Tony and I reach the front door, I have to stop, turn, catch the breathtaking view of the slopes, the flowers. I haven't yet downed one beer, but I already feel drunk. The door opens.

"Tony!" It's a handsome, dark-skinned man with a mustache who answers the door. He's Miguel, Gustavo's older brother, one of the foremen in charge of the pickers who work the farm. We are welcomed into the house, and quickly I'm introduced. I shake Miguel's hand and notice how rough and strong his grip is—I know he's done his share of harvesting, too. Soon after that, I'm lost in a sea of strangers. Tony disappears into the bare chests, T-shirts, and all-guy company drinking beer and eating nachos, grilled hamburgers, tamales, and burritos, while a driving Spanish beat infuses the air from big speakers in the corners of the large main room.

I make my way to the kitchen. The sink is full of ice, Mexican beer, and whole limes. Two kegs sit on the counters along with more food—chips, salsa, fruit. There are big bowls filled with giant peaches. I'm sure they came from the farm. Like the outside of the house, the inside reminds me of a modern villa, elegant, but with a feel of culture and history thanks to the paintings on the wall, the expensive furniture, the money that no doubt went into throwing this party.

A few guys tip their heads up, recognizing me, but not stopping to talk. They're about my age, though most are dressed like Tony in shorts, sneakers, sandals, ball-caps. I hear some dude talking baseball between swigs of beer. I figure I'll join the conversation, talk sports, so I go for a beer—Mexican, of course—only when I turn around, the huddle has disbursed. I'm alone again, overdressed, wondering what the hell I'm doing up here on this hill, and why I'm so full of gloom when I should be laughing like everybody else.

I make my way through the crowd, catch sight of Tony talking with Gustavo's brother, the orchard foreman. Through the big room, beyond all these strangers, I find myself standing at the open atrium doors, staring out at the big deck I'd seen from the drive with its view of Sutter's Butte. The sun is perched right on the mountains, almost blinding in intensity. The air is intoxicating and smells like the farm—trees and flowers stretching as far as the eye can see. Time seems to draw out as I stand here, for this is a magical, beautiful place.

Way too beautiful for such a hard-ass like me.

I'm staring into the light, blinded by its brilliance, but I feel somebody move up beside me, causing my arms to break in goose-flesh despite my jacket and the warmth of the setting sun. When I turn, tipping my head only slightly, the effects of having stared at the sun too long linger a moment longer. The man who's come up beside me—his features remain embossed with a nimbus of light. I blink rapidly to clear my eyes. He slowly takes form, though I begin to realize he's more than just some guy dressed in a white T-shirt and perfect-fitting blue jeans. Still blinded, I glance down, catch sight of what I think at first are perfect bare feet with long, flat toes capped by shiny black hairs. I soon recognize that he's wearing sandals, holding a bottle of Mexican beer in his strong-looking hands.

"Beautiful, isn't it?" A warm, deep voice with the barest trace of an accent pulls my focus back up. The illusion caused by the sun continues to put spots in front of my vision, but for the first time in a long time, this jaded, wounded sports writer can honestly say he's speechless.

"Real beautiful," I say, my voice barely above the whisper line. I'm aware that I've been staring, but more confusing than the fact I'm standing there with my mouth open is the rush of icy-hot panic that flushes through me when the stars burn down and I'm able to see him clearly.

He has dark brown eyes, a square jaw. He is clean-shaven, but sprouts the shadow of a goatee just around his chin, no mustache. He's wearing a pair of glasses; they are far from geeky, and lend his incredible good looks an innocent, intelligent quality. But it's his hair that gives him away. He's got a military buzz-cut, and it makes the rest of him look like he's been through some serious basic training. He's six solid feet of walking wet dream.

"You must be the host," I yammer, extending my free hand.

"Gustavo Aquino," he growls, shaking back. It's like being squeezed by a vice. Me, I'm certainly no wuss. However, even my best tough-guy handshake pales in comparison to his.

"I'm Lawrence," I say, still hoping to blame the rush of pins and needles up my arm on the pressure of Gustavo's handshake, not something more, not the fact that I'm blown away by him for reasons I can't understand. "I'm a friend of Tony's."

"Welcome to the farm, Lawrence," he growls, releasing my hand, but moving right beside me at the edge of the deck. One more step and the two of us would fall down into the warmth and light of the butte. I'm about to tell him my friends call me Larry, only Gustavo drawls, "Lawrence. That's Lorenzo in Spanish."

I like his version much better.

Suddenly, it feels like I'm falling, only being next to Gustavo keeps me rooted to the spot. I'm confused, giddy, blinded. I have fallen. For Gustavo.

The party continues around us. Gustavo and I are sitting on two of the deck chairs that face the night falling purple-gray over Sutter's Butte.

"Tony told me about you," he says. "You're the dude who writes the sports page."

Each time Gustavo speaks, my insides ignite. I've been offered a hundred different things to eat in the last ten minutes; the butterflies won't let me sample even one. "Tony tells me you're the king of sports," I fire back. "Says you're one hell of a baseball player."

Gustavo's sexy mouth with its full lips curls into a grin. "Shortstop. I've got quick feet." My eyes are drawn down to Gustavo's feet where, true to his word, he gives me a quick, playful jab with his toes against my ankle. His feet are so perfect. I realize I'm staring again, just as I feel the itch constrained in my underwear become a burn, and I deflect back up, to his face. That doesn't help.

"You play football, too," I say.

"Used to," Gustavo sighs. "I hurt my lower back when I got sacked a few years ago. Didn't tell them that when I applied to the Marines—they would'a shit-canned me on the spot if they knew."

"I won't tell," I joke. "Why did you go into the service? From what I hear, you could have gone to any college, played sports, maybe gotten into the draft pool for the major leagues."

Gustavo shrugs. "A lot of guys enter the service because they want to get their lives in order. Me, I didn't know what I wanted to do with mine. I had too many options, so I chose this one." He takes a thoughtful pause. The Spanish-style music carries in the air, seeming to intensify the heaviness of his eyes behind those glasses. His mouth opens, as if to speak, but no words emerge.

"Did you find what you were looking for?" I blurt out.

Gustavo's eyes lock with mine. A melancholy smile replaces the grin on his face as he slowly shakes his head. Our eyes remain locked.

The music plays on over Sutter's Butte.

Saying nothing, Gustavo stands up, heaving out a deep bear-growl. "I'll be back," I hear him say, only the words don't really register as he walks away, disappearing into the crowd of bodies that have moved inside the house now that the moon has replaced the sun. Feeling stupid, feeling as if I've been jilted again, feeling more confused than I've ever felt in my life, I sit there, my mouth hanging open, sure the world would be a much better place if only a black hole would open up and swallow me into oblivion.

You should go now, a voice in my head keeps repeating. Go, run, back to your life before you actually start believing you care about this...other guy!

I look around for Tony, can't see him. Hell, he'll find his way back to Yuba City. I sit up, go to my feet, turn toward the door. Too many people block my escape. I'm ready to jump down off the deck, maybe break a bone, when I hear the shuffle of footsteps behind me. A rush of light moves up to my side, right at the edge of the deck where I'm contemplating jumping.

"I wanted to give you something, Lorenzo" he growls.

Gustavo's got a sexy, boyish grin on his face and is holding a hand behind his back.

I smile, too, flushed by this feeling I can't explain. "Yeah?"

Gustavo brings his hand up. He's holding one of those enormous peaches in his strong soldier's fingers. "We grow these here," he says. You can't just drink beer or you're going to get sick." He holds the peach right up to my lips. I decide to play things his way, taking a bite out of the warm, firm fruit. A crisp eruption of syrup splashes my face as I bite down, my mouth filling with the sweetest thing I have ever tasted. When I look, the juice runs down Gustavo's fingers. He leans in, I imagine, to take a bite, lick up the nectar, but he slips. Our mouths, both already full of sweet fruit, connect. Our lips brush.

Something ignites, warm and blinding, inside me.

Our next kiss happens after Gustavo tips his head toward the party to make sure no one is watching. I kiss back, knowing this is no more an accident than the first one.

I am on fire as we press together. The itchy-hot fullness of my cock in my jeans pushes against something else just as stiff in Gustavo's. We rub together, each tasting the summer fruit on the other's lips, but are driven apart suddenly by someone's loud burp, new voices just inside the house, near the patio, the sound of beer bottles clinking. We stand now at a safe distance from each other, two straight men who love sports, women, the good things life has to offer, but each knowing we love something else, have found something more.

I think I've gone insane.

I think I love Gustavo.

We sit on the edge of the deck, both of us barefoot now, my shoes, his sandals, lumped together in a pile, my suit coat discarded on a chair. Now in the full twilight, our white T-shirts glow in the dark.

My right foot brushes Gustavo's left; the itchy, electric feel of his toes rubbing against mine is strangely hypnotic. I tell Gustavo he has sexy feet.

He smiles from the compliment, then segues.

"You ever…," he says, pretending to balk. "You know, with another guy?"

I shake my head. "Only chicks. You?"

He doesn't answer right away, which means he has. "In the Marines," Gustavo eventually admits.

"Shit, I'm jealous," I sigh. "That's intense. Tell me about it."

"You really want to know?" I nod, grin. Truth is, my cock's so hard, I don't think it'd take much more to make me come. "It was my sergeant. Called me into his office. Locked the door. Told me he'd been watching my butt from the moment I stepped off the bus."

I let out a deep sigh in disbelief. "What happened?"

"Everything," he says, a cat-like, sexy smirk on his face. "He reached up, undid my belt, pulled out my dick, and sucked it better than anyone ever done it to me. Nobody sucks cock like another dude."

"I wouldn't know," I say, pumping my chest. But I'm too drawn to his handsomeness to remain cold for long. "But I'd like to," I whisper. He hears my pledge. The words burn in my memory, making me laugh, shake my head. "This beer's getting to me."

"Me, too," Gustavo chuckles. He stands up, looks around. The deck's still empty. Gustavo's brother and the rest of the guys are checking out a porn tape on the living room's wide-screen TV. Every now and then, a throaty moan from some woman getting fucked on video filters out into the warm night. I'm still sitting with my legs hanging down when Gustavo unzips his jeans. "Gotta take a piss."

He reaches into his boxer briefs. I look up, both horrified and hungry, as he pulls out his cock, letting it point half-hard over two fat, low-hanging balls covered in black fur. Hell, I've been in more locker rooms than I can shake my own dick at, and yeah, I've looked like every guy does. But I've never wanted to touch, to taste, another man's cock. Now, having Gustavo's is all I can think about.

His dick isn't huge, maybe a little more than six inches fully pumped, not that thick, lean and muscular like the rest of the handsome Marine it belongs to. But what makes my mouth water for the taste of nectar is the thick fold of foreskin that caps his cock. As I stare at it, and Gustavo realizes I'm staring, it fills out to the limit, rock-hard. Gustavo doesn't piss through his hard-on. He lets it hang a little longer in the moonlight, its head glowing silver and moist, the slit exposed out of its soft sock of cock skin.

"You can't piss through that," I joke, looking up to see the smile on his face.

"I know, *wapo*."

I quickly call up everything in my head I can remember from high school Spanish classes. *Wapo*. Handsome. Shit, I'm falling fast.

"You're the *wapo* hombre," I say, standing up beside Gustavo. It's not my intention, but the whole night feels like some kind of hallucination. There's no way I could have made such a connection like this; a guy like Gustavo just isn't supposed to exist, and I'm certainly not supposed to be putting my hands on his thighs, reaching around, sliding one hand over his balls, the other into his patch of coarse man-hair, groping down, taking hold of his cock. Gustavo groans when I put my hands over his and begin to jack his cock off, saying nothing. I go right up behind him, eager to feel that foreskin. I gently thumb its silky, slick texture. Gustavo releases his grip, whispers something in Spanish while I stroke his cock.

"*Te amo, mi amore....*"

Pressing my boner into his hard Marine's ass, I grip him, stroke one more time to feel the warmth and wetness of precome. I lose count, but a few hard jerks later, he shoots, some of it in the hand I'll lick clean, most of it down over the deck, raining nectar across the mountainside.

We stumble up the stairs. So many of the partygoers whose host I've monopolized are crashed or occupied. I see Tony with his dick out, sitting in the living room, oblivious to everything but the sex on the screen. I don't care. I only care about Gustavo. We reach his room. It's a big, normal boy's room—blue drapes, racing car wallpaper, posters of big league baseball teams, some super model in a bikini.

"*Te amo*, Lorenzo," Gustavo growls after locking the door, and we begin to tear off what clothes remain on our bodies. Soon, we are rolling on Gustavo's bed, kissing deeply, no fear of being discovered. The bed smells of Gustavo, like a trace of cologne and clean, athletic sex.

On instinct, we move into a 69, his warm, wet mouth engulfing my cock. While he sucks me off, I remember his words about men giving the best head, and I have to agree. The way he makes me feel—I can't recall the time before him, even though I know the bulk of my life existed mere hours before. I've never sucked cock, but now I have one in my mouth. Gustavo's cock. I lick his balls, reveling in the faint taste of sweat that lightly coats his sac, tonguing my way lower to his butt like I've been doing this all my life. I take my first taste of ass. It is bitter, addictive, and I lap my way to his crack, right to the moist, puckered hole and its ring of black hair. I'm hooked. I eat Gustavo deeply, so deeply he begins to moan. I feel his cock tense. When I look down, his face between my legs looks so happy. During this contemplative moment, he reaches into the nightstand drawer, pulling out a shiny metal packet.

"Fuck me," he moans.

It's strange to think, but ten minutes later, I'm the one flat on my back, begging for the same honor.

The Marine would honor me three more times before sunrise came to Sutter's Butte.

"Lorenzo," Gustavo growls in my ear, stroking my hair. He is still inside me, half-hard. "I'm leaving next week. They're sending my unit to Italy. From there, we're off to the Persian Gulf."

I try to swallow, only to nearly choke on the invisible knot that has suddenly cut off my breath.

"I know," I stutter. "When will you be back?"

"I don't know," he says flatly, his arms pulling me suddenly tighter against him. "It could be some time. A year. Maybe longer."

This is when it hits me hardest. "You can always go AWOL, hide under my bed," I joke, though the truth is I'm frozen, dying, despite Gustavo's warmth.

Gustavo's somber voice ends in a hearty laugh. "Lorenzo," he sighs, "I'd hide in it with you."

He tells me he'd found something he's always searched for, last night, with me. I tell him he will come home safely, home to Yuba City, Sutter's Butte, and the beauty of Aquino Farm. I tell him I will be waiting for his return.

"*Te amo, mi amore...*"

Peeping Tom
Sean Wolfe

I have to tell you I was less than thrilled with the prospect of my company transferring me to Denver from San Diego. I didn't want to leave my friends, my family, or my beaches, but it would be a big promotion for me if it worked out. So I had headed to Denver for a two-week trial period.

I was staying with my friend Paul during my visit. He lived in a high-rise just on the outskirts of downtown. It was so different from where I lived. I had a three-bedroom brick house with a yard, a two-car garage, an outdoor hot tub, and a state-of-the-art security system. Paul lived in a small two-bedroom apartment on the 15th floor of a plain white stucco building. His apartment had a tiny balcony, no garage, and a dead bolt.

Proving myself capable of a job I really wanted in a city I really didn't want to live in was proving exhausting. I worked ten to 12 hours a day and came home ready to sleep. My first week was finally over, and on Friday I walked in the door and headed straight for the shower. Paul had left town for the weekend, so I had the place to myself. A hot bath, a movie while curled up on the couch, and Chinese delivery would be just what the doctor ordered.

I used Paul's bathroom in the master bedroom since it had a tub and my guest bathroom only had a shower. I sat in the hot water for half an hour before deciding I was getting hungry and then got out to call for some chicken chow mein. I stepped into Paul's bedroom to dry off; the soft carpet in his room was much warmer than the cold tile in the bathroom. As I stood naked in his room drying my hair, I noticed that his bedroom curtains were open, and I walked over to close them.

Paul's complex is actually made up of two identical buildings, separated only by a small parking lot between them for those residents who wanted to pay an additional $40 a month for off-street parking. As I started to close the curtains, I noticed a man standing on his balcony directly across from me. It was dark outside, but there was a light on in the front room of the man's apartment, and he was silhouetted against it. He was shirtless and leaning against the wall of his balcony drinking a cup of something steaming. As I pulled the curtains closer together, the man raised his cup and turned to walk into his apartment. As he entered the front room, I saw his bare ass. He was completely naked!

He disappeared from sight for a couple of seconds as he turned the lights on brighter in his front room. When he came back into view, I could see him much more clearly. He was tall, about six feet or maybe more, and had light blond hair. He obviously spent a lot of time at the gym; his chest was hard and defined, his stomach hard and flat, his legs long and muscular. I felt my cock stir and remembered I was naked, my towel thrown carelessly over my shoulders. I started to wrap the towel around my waist, but my neighbor shook his head. I looked around the building to see if anyone else could see me. Satisfied that no one could, I dropped the towel to the floor but hid half of my body behind the curtains.

The man leaned against his sliding balcony door and smiled. He was gorgeous. He reached down and groped his cock with his hand. My dick was fully hard now and pulsed up and down as the blood rushed through it. My exhibitionist motioned for me to step from behind the curtains. I did so, slowly and shyly, as he stroked his cock to full hardness.

Even from this distance I could see that his cock was huge. He stroked it slowly and gently while he sipped on whatever he was drinking. I took my hard cock into my hands and imitated his movements. I didn't think I was that close to coming, but after only a few strokes of my hand, I felt my balls tighten and that familiar chill start at the base of my cock and work its way up my shaft. I was close.

I pulled my hand from my dick and leaned against the window as the man across the parking lot spread his legs wide and slid both his hands up and down his large pole. The glass was cold as I pressed my body against it. It cooled my hot dick and kept me from shooting a load immediately. I rubbed against the window for a few moments while my cock cooled down, watching my neighbor beat his meat.

After a few minutes of stroking his dick, the man walked over to the balcony wall and stood on what must have been a short stool so that he was standing about knee level at the top of the wall. I saw his strong, muscular legs flex as he stroked his big dick right out in the open. My heart started beating faster as I watched him speed up his pounding, and I felt my cock get harder and hotter again.

He leaned back, closed his eyes, and moved his hands from his cock just as the first blast of come shot out of his cock. It easily flew five feet from his dick and dropped 14 floors to the ground below. Several other shots of come spewed from his cock and landed everywhere: on the balcony, on the wall, at his feet.

I love more than anything seeing a man come, and that jizz shot sent me over the edge. I was still rubbing my cock against the window when he came, and my own load gushed out of my dick before I knew it. Five or six spurts of come flew from my cock and splashed against the window and dripped down my shaft in warm waves. It felt so good as I rubbed my cock in it and against the cold window.

I looked across the parking lot and saw my neighbor shaking the last drops of his load onto the floor of his balcony. He looked over at me, smiled, and then waved goodbye as he went inside his apartment and closed the curtains.

On Saturday I went out and bought a pair of binoculars. I needed to see what this guy looked like up close. I watched for him to appear periodically throughout the day, but didn't actually see him until 7 o'clock, just as the sun was going down. He walked out onto the balcony fully dressed and talking on the phone. I was standing behind the curtains and looking at him with my new binoculars.

He was even more beautiful than I had imagined. He looked to be in his early 30s. His light blond hair was short, neatly cut and brushed carelessly to the right side. He had bright blue eyes and short sideburns. A strong Roman nose accented his strong jawbones, and his mouth was extremely sexy: full pink lips that parted when he smiled to reveal perfect bone-white teeth. He had a short stubble on his face that tried unsuccessfully to hide a set of incredibly sexy dimples.

It was hard for me to breathe normally as I took in the beauty of this man. He was wearing a gray suit with a blue tie. I couldn't wait for him to start taking them off right there on the balcony in front of me. But I was to be disappointed that night. He disconnected the phone, looked right at Paul's bedroom window, and shrugged his shoulders as he pointed to the phone and lifted his hand to his mouth. Apparently he had a dinner date and was not going to perform for me.

Frustrated, I took another hot bath and curled up on the couch to watch an old black-and-white movie on television. I dozed off about halfway through the movie and must have slept for a couple of hours when the phone rang. I woke up groggily and looked at the clock above the entertainment center. It was 2:30 in the morning. Who would be calling at this hour?

"Hello," I answered the phone.

For a long moment there was no answer. Then, "Tomorrow night."

"What? Who is this?" I asked, still dazed from sleep.

"Tomorrow night around 7 o'clock. Don't disappoint me."

"Look," I said as I started to tell the caller that I was not Paul, but he hung up.

I grabbed my throw blanket from the couch, folded it, and put it in the hall closet as I stumbled to bed. I had known Paul about five years, but certainly didn't know all he was into or what he did in his free time. The caller was probably a friend of his who had plans with him tomorrow night and was calling to confirm their date. But I was too tired to think about that now. I crawled into bed and fell asleep almost immediately.

On Sunday I forced myself to get out of the house. It was a nice day for mid-March, sunny and blue-skied, with barely a hint of a breeze. I decided to hit the park. In Denver there is only one park as far as gay men are concerned: Cheeseman Park. An old city ordinance prohibiting nudity in public parks had been knocked down, and now the park was filled with lots of naked sun worshippers every Sunday afternoon there was even a hint of sun peeking through the clouds. Of course, it was mostly middle-aged balding men who walked around naked; the younger guys wouldn't be caught dead showing off their stuff in public. It was only 50-something degrees outside, and heaven forbid another cute young guy see them with their penises all shriveled. But it was fun watching the volleyball players, so I went.

When the clouds started approaching and the temperature dropped a few degrees, I decided to go shopping. I bought some clothes and a crystal angel for my collection back home and then headed back to Paul's place. Feeling only a little hungry, I made a light dinner of salad and fruit and ate while watching the news. At about 6 o'clock I ran another hot bath and soaked for an eternity.

I could see the window in Paul's room from the tub. The curtains were pulled back, so I had a good view of my friend's apartment across the lot. At about 6:45, I saw a light come on in the front room. I jumped out of the tub like I'd been electrocuted and grabbed the towel as I ran into the bedroom. I quickly dried my body as I ran back to my room to grab my binoculars and then ran back to the window in Paul's room.

The curtains to my exhibitionist's balcony window were closed, but I could see his silhouette behind them. He was taking off his clothes. I focused the binoculars on his balcony and reached down to fondle my cock as I waited for him to go out onto the balcony. I didn't have to wait long. In just a couple of minutes, the curtains parted and he stepped out onto the balcony. He was naked and drinking a beer.

I took a deep breath as I looked at the beauty of his face and body. With the binoculars I could see his nipples harden on his lightly hairy chest. My cock started to fatten as I followed the soft trail of hair down his stomach to his crotch. He was still soft, and his thick cock swung heavily as he shifted his weight to lean against the balcony door again as he had the first time I saw him.

I focused the binoculars on his face. He was clean-shaven, and his hair was brushed a little more neatly than yesterday. He had probably just gotten back from dinner or something. He smiled that perfect Adonis smile and winked at me. I blushed and put the binoculars down and pulled the curtains together. I tried to catch my breath for a moment and then realized how silly I had been. He knew I had been in the apartment since Friday, and he was definitely there for a reason too. I took a deep breath, pulled the curtains back, and picked up my binoculars.

He was still leaning against the door, as though he didn't have a care in the world, but now he was pulling on his long cock. It was halfway hard now, and I could see the large vein running the length of it. The skin looked so soft, and I imagined the sweet smell of his prick after a nice long shower. My own cock was fully hard now and throbbing as I wished I could taste his dick.

I watched as he carefully slid a metal cock ring on. First he slipped his balls through the large circle, then he squeezed his half-hard shaft through it and pulled the cock ring tight against the base of his prick. His big dick swelled to unbelievable length and thickness, and I saw the large vein pounding wildly against the silky skin of his shaft.

I tugged gently at my dick, loving the feel of the throbbing heat against my hand. When it's fully hard my dick is almost eight inches and about average thickness. But it is filled with veins that look like a road map coming to life when the veins are pulsing as they were then. I love to just hold my dick tightly in my hands when it's hard and just feel the hot blood pounding against my hand.

I jerked my meat slowly as I watched the man across from me do the same. He was pinching his nipples as he stroked his cock. I watched him do this for about five minutes. Then he turned and walked into his apartment. He was gone for about 30 seconds and came back holding a cucumber. He held it up for me to see and began licking and sucking it.

I was so caught up in the feel of my own throbbing hard-on and watching this sexy man try to deep-throat the large cucumber that I didn't hear the front door open. My hand was sliding steadily up and down my cock, and I was moaning sporadically when I felt a pair of arms wrap around my chest and stomach and a soft cock press against my ass cheeks.

I let out a startled gasp and dropped my binoculars as I turned around to see who was behind me.

Paul was standing there grinning.

"What are you doing here, Randy?" he asked as he looked past me out the window.

"I was just—"

"I know what you were doing," he said, and pushed me gently to my knees. "Here, take the real thing."

Paul was completely naked. I couldn't believe he had entered the apartment, seen me watching his neighbor, and stripped naked without my hearing him. His cock was still soft but starting to stir and thicken a little. He reached down and picked up my binoculars as I took his soft dick in my mouth. I licked around the head for a moment and then slowly sucked the shaft down to his balls. I felt his dick getting hard inside my mouth and kept sucking on it until it began to work its way deep into my throat.

Paul had an average-size dick, about seven inches long, but it was incredibly thick. It filled my throat, and I came up for air.

"You been having fun while I was gone?" he asked.

I blushed and looked him straight in the eye.

"Well, I'm glad," he said. "But now you'll have some real fun."

He pulled me to my feet and kissed me gently on the mouth. I was acutely aware the neighbor was seeing all this and began to get jittery.

"Don't worry about him. He likes to watch as much as you do," Paul said as he turned me around so that I was facing the window again.

The neighbor was smiling and rubbing the cucumber against his butt cheeks. He put it back in his mouth, sucked and licked on it some more, and then moved it back to his ass. Paul was rubbing his hard cock against my butt and playing with my dick, which had gone soft for a little while with the surprise, but was now almost fully hard again. He bent me over and knelt on his knees. I picked up the binoculars and watched the neighbor as he alternated sucking the cucumber and rubbing it along his ass crack.

I moaned loudly as I felt Paul's tongue tickle my asshole. He licked with short, jabbing movements around the pink hole for a minute or so and then slowly slid his tongue deep inside. I felt my sphincter grip his tongue with spastic movements and moaned as he pushed his tongue deeper inside me while he massaged my butt cheeks. He turned me around a little so his neighbor could see all the action and so I could also keep watching my new friend.

Paul stood up and walked to his nightstand, and I watched through the binoculars as the man swallowed half of the cucumber and pinched his nipple again. I could tell he was moaning just by the way he arched his body and closed his eyes as he sucked on the cucumber.

I could hear Paul behind me again, rolling a condom on his cock. A moment later I felt the thick head of his dick press against my puckered hole. He had left it slippery with his saliva, and his cock slid inside my hole easily as he gently pushed forward. I moaned deeply as his thick cock slid slowly inside my butt until his balls reached my ass cheeks.

"Oh, baby, your ass is so tight and warm," Paul said. "I'm going to come really quick."

"No," I said, "take it slow."

He moaned and started moving his cock in and out of my ass slowly. I looked up into the binoculars and saw the neighbor was working the cucumber slowly into his ass. He was watching Paul and me, and was matching Paul's stride beat for beat. I watched in amazement as more and more of the fat cucumber slid into the man's ass. I didn't think it possible, but by the time Paul was pounding my ass with a frantic pace, the guy across the lot from us had all but about two inches of the cucumber deep in his ass.

I felt Paul's dick get even thicker inside my hole as he fucked me. He was moaning loudly now, and I knew he was about to blow his load.

"Look at this guy," I told him, barely able to speak, since I was close to shooting myself.

He moaned even louder when he saw the huge cucumber buried deep in his neighbor's butt.

The man across the lot suddenly shoved the last two inches of the cucumber inside his ass and stood up. His butt had swallowed the fat intruder, and it was completely inside him. He jerked his huge cock frantically and leaned back with his eyes closed. I knew what that meant and was ready to shoot my load with him.

His come sprayed in every direction, huge thick jets of white covering the wall and chair in front of him. There must have been ten big shots in all. Paul saw it even without the aid of my binoculars and pulled his dick from my ass with another moan.

He ripped the condom from his cock just before the first of his come escaped. What seemed like a quart of hot cream poured from Paul's dick. Some of it dripped down the under part of his cock and onto his balls. A lot of it spurted a little and landed on my ass. He rubbed his still-hard cock in the come and rubbed it around my ass, humping my cheeks.

"Oh, man, I'm gonna blow," I moaned loudly.

Paul pulled me up and turned me around, falling to his knees as I turned. He moved my hand from my cock and swallowed about half of my dick in his mouth. I tried to pull out of his mouth before I shot, but he held on tightly.

My leg muscles tightened as the first wave of jizz blasted from my cock. I can't remember ever having such an intense orgasm, and Paul gulped as it hit the back of his throat. I felt him swallow twice, and the come was still shooting out of my shaft. A few drops escaped out his mouth and fell to the floor as he continued to suck me.

When I was drained of my load, we stood up and hugged each other.

"Wow," I said. "Are you OK with this?"

"Sure," he said, and waved at the man across the lot.

"You watch him often?"

"Yeah, you can say that. He'll be over in a couple of minutes. You can ask him yourself."

"What?" I asked, astonished.

"That's Tom. I've told you about him."

"Your boyfriend?"

Paul smiled and took my hand, and led me to his shower.

For Real
Dominic Santi

"No script?"

"Do whatever you want, Zak—whatever a couple of famous pornstars do together that everybody else only dreams about."

"That's not real specific." I drank the last of my soda and sighed—loudly. Marco was a good director. I liked working with him. But his brainstorms weren't always easy to understand when he was frustrated. At the moment, we were taking a break from filming a standard fuck flick. Marco was pacing a hole in the carpet, thwapping his clipboard against his thigh and complaining about his inability to cast The Right Couple for his next creative masterpiece. I was letting my dick rest and trying to figure out what the hell he was talking about.

In between his mutterings about "no fucking chemistry between them," I figured out that he'd been taping wannabe actors who'd answered his cattle call for "long-term couples willing to 'bare it all' living out their sexual fantasies for the camera." Apparently, the results had been less than stellar. Now, Marco was out of time. In fact, he was desperate enough that he was offering my partner and me a percentage, on top of our usual rates, if—big emphasis on the "if"—we could do a scene together hot enough for him to ditch the other footage he'd already shot.

The whole deal sounded too good to be true, which made me suspicious. Not that I didn't trust Marco. But I'd worked with him enough to know he always had a hidden agenda. I rolled the empty can in my hands until he finally slowed down enough for me to get a word in. Then I said, "I don't get it."

He stopped pacing and quirked an eyebrow at me.

"There's no script. We just have sex the way we do at home. If we do the scene hot enough, you pay us a bundle. What's the catch?"

"No catch, pal!" Marco grinned as he walked up next to me and slapped me on the back. "I film you and Jeff getting it on—you know, real porn-stars having real sex." He winked at me. "It's the ultimate voyeuristic fantasy! If you make the scenes really hot—bump up sales enough to justify the startup costs—I can use this as the pilot to open up a whole new line of candid videos. Your audience gets to jerk off watching, you get one helluva bonus, the studio gets rich. Everybody's happy."

Suddenly, Marco grabbed my shoulder and turned me around, narrowing his eyes as he looked at my butt. "What the fuck is this? Did that asshole give you a hickey just before a shoot? I'll kill him!"

"It's a bruise. The makeup must have worn off." I pulled away, batting my eyes innocently. "I got it when Jeff and I fell out of bed, fucking. Does that make you feel better?"

"Ouch. Kinky, though." He smirked, then his eyebrows narrowed. "You guys do that often?"

I could almost hear the wheels turning, and I did not want to go down that road. I tossed my empty can in the trash.

"Every day," I smiled. I didn't have the heart to tell Marco that after a long day of fucking for money, my boyfriend and I liked to relax at home. We read, worked out together, watched movies with plots—slept! Our private lives did not revolve around a social whirl of orgies and anonymous tricks in the bars of West Hollywood.

Not that Marco would have believed that. He snickered, turning away as he waved the gaffer over to him. "We'll talk more when we're done today." He paused. "But give me a teaser. What would John Doe on the street need to do to have a sex life as hot as yours?"

"Marry Jeff Evans," I grumbled. I grabbed my dick and started stroking, ignoring Marco's laughter as I walked out of the room to get ready for my next scene.

Jeff was due home from his latest European shoot in two weeks. I knew I'd be horny as hell for him by then. But I wasn't looking forward to Marco's little project. Even though I was half of an "internationally famous" pornstar couple, I relished my private time alone with my lover. To my way of thinking, we didn't get enough of it.

Other than the one-take "you-suck-me-I'll-suck-you" jail scene where we'd met, Jeff and I hadn't done any movies together. I worked mostly in the U.S. Popularizing cocksucking with condoms was my claim to fame.

Jeff worked more overseas. Having a thick, uncut, country cock—and being able to speak Czech as fluently as his never-adjusted-to-Omaha mother—gave him an instant in with American companies who were capitalizing on the burgeoning East European markets. Jeff looked Slavic. He could talk to his co-stars as well as to the director. And he had one fucking gorgeous body.

OK, so I'm biased. After five years together, Jeff's smile can still make my dick drool. Anybody watching a video of his can see how much he's enjoying himself. This is no straight man pretending to be gay. Jeff loves fucking ass. His beautifully tapered nine inches are thick as a beer can, and he's always hard. So, he's always cast as a top—even though he's so big it's sometimes difficult to find bottoms for his fuck scenes.

We get asked, often, what keeps us together. "You're both tops. Isn't it, you know, kind of pointless?"

Jeff's stock answer is "I married him for his mind." At which time he grabs my crotch and winks at our interrogators. His squeezing always has the expected result. It's a good thing I like being hard in public.

What he doesn't say is that when it's just the two of us, we bottom to each other. I'm as long as he is, though not as wide, and I'm cut. Directors love the way my wide-rimmed mushroom head looks popping in and out of lips and assholes. The definition stays clear even when I'm inside the rubber. The PR folks say that complements what they call my "chiseled Greek looks." I have to admit, my dick does look good—even more so on a wide-screen TV.

Jeff loves working that rim with his tongue. He gives a mean blowjob. I shoot geysers when he's doing me. OK, so I'm also in love with the guy. He's well-read, intelligent, prone to pulling practical jokes, and I've gotten used to sleeping with his prong poking me in the kidney all night. Besides, I love playing with his dick. His come tastes great, and he's got enough foreskin for the both of us.

That's what was going to be hard to explain to Marco—the skin part. At work, everyone we suck or fuck is always sheathed in latex. Jeff and I have both eroticized condoms to the point that just hearing a wrapper being torn open makes us stiff. But at home, we're body-fluid monogamous. A couple of years ago, after another round of negative tests, we'd decided that as long as we used latex with everyone else, every time—and as long as there were no accidents—we'd go skin to skin with each other.

I didn't know how that was going to fit into Marco's grand marketing plans. He was adamant that he wanted to film us on Jeff's first night back from Europe—before we'd had a chance to fuck. After several long and very expensive phone calls, Jeff and I decided ol' Marco was going to get exactly what he'd asked for. We'd burn that bed up with the hottest action our illustrious director had ever seen. And for our troubles, Jeff and I were going to walk away with the money we needed for the balloon payment on our condo.

On the day of the shoot, Marco was in his usual rush. "What kind of props do you need?"

Jeff snickered and rubbed his crotch, the sizable erection tenting the front of his robe. Despite his jetlag, after three weeks apart, we'd have been happy humping on the carpet.

"A couple towels, three or four pillows, some coconut massage oil," I answered, shrugging.

"I want a second sheet and a blanket at the bottom of the bed."

I raised my eyebrows at my hot and horny partner's requests, but Jeff just smiled and kept rubbing his crotch. I reached over to help him.

"You got it." The ever-efficient Marco snapped his fingers and somebody was on it. His crews are always good. "Condoms, lube, the standard kit will be on the nightstand."

Jeff and I sat on the edge of the bed, ignoring him and the flurry of activity around us as we turned our concentration to necking and stroking the erections poking out through each other's robes.

"Zak, Jeff...NOW, please!"

We came up for air, gasping as we made a pretense of composing ourselves. I kept my hand in Jeff's lap, though. I couldn't quite bring myself to let go of him. I'd missed him.

Marco grabbed a fresh cup of coffee from his latest twinkie assistant and kept right on talking, like he actually thought we were listening to him. "Do whatever you want—fuck, suck, jack off. Just make it hot. And stay on the bed so we don't have to screw around with the lights."

He looked away, wincing as he sipped the steaming liquid. "We'll do the voice-overs later, as well as specific questions about your relationship and so forth, based on the action. Don't worry about that now." He stopped and looked at us over the edge of his cup. "Unless you have questions, we'll start in 15 minutes."

When Jeff and I both shook our heads, Marco turned his attention back to the crew, and Jeff and I went off to finish getting ready. Marco assigned us each a minder, though, to ensure we didn't sneak off for a quickie somewhere. He wasn't going to let anybody disrupt his grand plans.

"Leave them alone! I will personally shoot anyone who interferes with what I expect to be record comeshots!"

Jeff and I knelt on the bed, facing each other, and handed our robes to the disappointed fluffers.

"Places everyone. Make me proud." Marco launched into his standard routine, and we were rolling. Jeff winked at me, giving my thigh a quick prod with that monster cock of his. I wiggled my eyebrows back at him. Then we took each other's hands and I let the techies' discussions fade away into the background. Just knowing they were there was all the encouragement my exhibitionist streak needed.

I was almost too worked up, though. I backed off until just my fingertips were touching Jeff's. Getting used to him again. Letting down my defenses. Letting him in. We didn't talk. Marco could damn well dub in music later.

Eventually, Jeff pulled my hand to his lips and sucked on my index finger, running the edges of his teeth sharply over my skin. When I shivered, he bit.

I don't know which of us moved first. One minute his mouth was hot and wet on my finger, the next we were kissing. I fell or he pushed me back on the bed—probably a little of both. Then we were rolling around on the sheets, groping blindly for each other, our dicks pressed together between us. I opened my mouth to breathe and sucked in his tongue.

"Damn, I missed you, Zak."

I shivered as he licked over my teeth.

"You are the hottest man on the face of this fucking earth!"

"Shut up and kiss me," I growled, shoving my tongue down his throat.

We were too turned on for refinements. When Jeff started licking my ear, I twisted around and latched onto a nipple. That had the expected result. My country boy threw me flat on my back and straddled me—his fat, juicy cock snuggling right up against my lips. He turned around and positioned himself over me, on his knees and elbows, his legs widespread so he could lower himself onto my face. Then Jeff pulled my legs up and back so he had access to everything he wanted. Marco always liked 69-ing. He was damn well going to get it today.

About two seconds later, I decided Marco was an idiot for not letting us come at least once before the cameras started rolling. My skin felt like it was reaching towards Jeff everywhere we touched. I fought not to shoot as he rubbed his face against my crotch. I gasped, wiggling as Jeff kissed the head of my dick. It was almost more than I could stand.

I tugged on his balls, trying to distract myself by licking his scent from them. It didn't help. It only made me want him more. His velvety shaft brushed against my cheek, teasing me. I opened my mouth. Using just my lips, I tugged his foreskin down over the slippery head. A drop of tangy juice oozed onto my tongue.

"Mmmm. You taste good," I whispered, carefully licking the sticky pre-come into my waiting mouth.

As my tongue swiped over his piss slit, Jeff cried out, bucking and gasping against me. In his next breath, with no warning at all, he sucked me deep into his throat.

I didn't expect it. I jerked back as my whole body convulsed. "Stop!" I gasped. "NOW! Fuck, man, I'm gonna shoot!"

"Camera 3, you better be getting this!"

Jeff froze, and I panted—ignoring Marco's comment and his muttering that we definitely hadn't given him enough footage yet. I clenched the muscles in my arms, concentrating on the details of the condo mortgage, on how nice Marco's clipboard would look shoved up his ass, trying to will myself back under control.

"Give me a second," I whispered.

"Whatever you say, lover." Jeff had taken his mouth off my dick, but he couldn't seem to quit touching me. Pretty soon, his hand moved to my perineum. He started stroking, gently at first, then more firmly, gradually moving down, touching, rubbing. He drooled spit onto me—lubing the way for his fingers. By the time I finally got my breathing halfway under control, Jeff was playing with my asshole. He kept my legs spread wide, so the cameras could catch the way he was stroking me—the slow, lazy, slippery circles.

When he slipped the tip of his finger into me, I moaned and gave it up. I knew right then how the rest of the scene was going to go. Jeff's fingers were talking directly to my asshole. I opened my mouth and took the tip of his cock between my lips—kissing him, working the soft, warm hood over the glistening head, tugging gently on his smooth, heavy balls. We were too far gone to go slowly. If Marco wanted more cinematic build-up, he could damn well edit it in later. Jeff lifted up, sliding his finger down my thigh. "Roll over, Zak."

I did. When I was on all fours over him, Jeff stuffed a pillow under his head. I spread my legs wide and dropped down until just the tip of my cock rested on his lips. I hoped the cameras were getting everything they needed, because I wasn't about to budge for anyone but Jeff. And he had me right where he wanted me. He put his hands on my hips and pulled me down towards him. Then his hands were on my asscheeks, massaging them, spreading them wider. My cock fell forward onto his neck as I felt the feather light touch of his breath caressing my asshole.

"Mmmm. This pretty pink pucker looks good, Zak. Real good."

I groaned, jumping at the first touch of his tongue. It was hot, it always is. He licked the edge of my crack, wetting skin that usually doesn't see daylight, especially not in my movies.

I nuzzled my cheek against his cock, kissing him, inhaling his scent. I wanted to let him know how much I appreciated his touch. Then I rested my face on his thigh, facing Camera 2, and focused all my attention on my asshole, just the way I knew Jeff wanted me to.

I didn't try to control my reactions. I'm not dignified in bed. Not in real life. I moaned as Jeff rimmed me. He licked up and down my crack. I gasped the way I always did when the tip of his tongue flicked over my asshole. I knew what was coming. I wiggled my ass at him, asking for it—begging. Loud and slutty. I didn't care who saw me. I hoped the cameras were catching every whorish grind for posterity.

Jeff stuffed spit up my hole. His fingers held me wide open, stretching my sphincter. Each touch of his tongue let him slip that much further in. My asslips fluttered, reaching back for him as he kissed and sucked. He licked further into me, caressing the inner skin, way inside, where the smooth surface was usually puckered tightly closed. With each step, he stretched me wider.

"You ready, babe?"

"Uh, huh," I gasped. I didn't care who heard the great pornstar's boyfriend calling him "babe." My ass was hungry.

"You know what I'm going to do." He sucked, hard, on the outside of my hole. "You ready?"

I shuddered, nodding against his cock, unable to speak.

"You taste so good, babe." He kissed my asshole. "Here it comes."

I yelled when his tongue sank into me. I mean, Jeff dug his hot, nasty tongue into my ass and he ate me. He tongue-fucked my hole until I was almost screaming. Harder, deeper, hotter, he spread my cheeks so far apart it felt like my skin was splitting. I pushed back against him, grunting, bearing down, opening my asshole to him as he slurped. I didn't care what I looked like. My asslips kissed his tongue like it was his cock.

I cried out as he pulled away. He pushed me over onto my back, still 69-ing, pressing his cock against my lips. I sucked him greedily into my mouth, inhaling the slippery, salty tang where the precome leaked out of his bunched foreskin.

"That's it, lover," he growled, thrusting into my mouth. His cock got longer, growing against my tongue. "Get it hard and get it wet. You know where it's going."

He was already like a rock, but I sucked, opening my jaw wider as his shaft thickened and stretched even further. His bared head was completely out of the foreskin now, the sensitive crown pressing against my tonsils, his cock filling my mouth. I breathed in through my nose, and as my lungs filled, Jeff thrust, gently, against the back of my throat. I tipped my head and opened to him, gagging as he slipped in deep. It was like trying to swallow a baseball bat. He shook—I love feeling him quiver, even when I'm suffocating. Then he pulled up and settled against me, his breath ragged, his cock resting above my mouth where I could play with it at my leisure—where the camera could catch every wet lick of me working the folds of his skin, sticking my tongue in his piss slit, sucking his low-hanging, smooth balls until they were pink and slippery.

In spite of his shivers, Jeff pulled my legs up and back. He braced his elbows on the bed, his biceps against the backs of my thighs. It was a perfect ass shot. I was spread wide and my hole was open. Virgin ground for Marco's cameras. I heard the click of the bottle cap, smelled the coconut. Then Jeff's oiled hands glided over my cheeks. He smoothed the side of his hand up and down my open crack, brushing over my hole, gradually concentrating on rubbing my hungry grasping sphincter. His fingers started stretching me.

"I want you nice and loose," he purred. "Show me how your boy pussy opens up for me."

"But Zak's a top!" Someone protested loudly in the background.

"Not today," Jeff snickered as he put one hand on each cheek. His index and middle fingers pulled me open. With each stroke, his fingers reached in further. He kept pulling, stretching me wider, until my whole world was my asshole. I groaned as he kissed the inside of my thigh, his finger once more sliding over my asslips.

"You like?" I could feel his smile as he breathed against my leg.

"Fuck, that feels good," I gasped, sucking hard on his monster dick, taking it as deep in my throat as I could.

He laughed, shivering as I swallowed against him. This time, when his finger went in, it dug deep. I groaned, long and loud, feeling the familiar jolt as he found what he was looking for.

"What have we here?" He rubbed again. I could hear the smirk in his voice. "Somebody wants his joyspot massaged?"

He pressed hard, and I cried out, an ooze of precome moving up my cocktube.

"Fuck, yeah, Jeff. Fuck, that feels good." I tried to arch against him. "Do it again, please!"

This time, his laugh gave me goosebumps. "I will, lover." I groaned as he rubbed, harder. "But I'm going to massage it with something designed specifically to make your slutty pussy purr."

He pulled his hand out. My nose twitched as the smell of coconut again filled the air. I jumped as I felt the nozzle against my asslips. His fingers pulled my asslips open, then the cool oil trickled into me, deep down into my hole, lubing it, getting it slippery wet.

"Jeez, man, that stuff is gonna wreck the rubber." The techie's voice sounded far away.

I was too far gone to even laugh. I sucked harder on Jeff's cock, getting it wetter, getting it stiffer for where it was going to go.

Jeff moved off me, his dick making a wet, plopping noise as it popped out of my mouth. He pressed the oil bottle into my hand. Then he was between my legs, lifting my thighs up and back, spreading them wide. I bent my knees and he pressed them back towards my shoulders, tipping my ass high in the air.

"You ready, babe?"

This time I did laugh. The head of Jeff's cock was pressed into my ass-cheek—hot, demanding. I squeezed a huge puddle of oil into my hand, slathered the slippery grease over his cock, stroking, getting him even harder. I dropped the bottle next to myself and positioned him against me, rubbing his dripping dickhead against my hungry, hungry hole.

"Jeez, man, what are they doing?"

"Somebody give them a condom!"

"Damn, Jeff's HUGE!"

Jeff grinned down at me. I smiled back. As we'd expected, our audience was shocked. My asslips fluttered against him, kissing him. I stroked his shaft, slicking the oil over him one more time, looking right into his hot, velvety eyes—velvety as his dick skin.

"Fuck me," I growled.

"Jesus, he's going in bareback!"

I don't know who said it. I didn't care. I cried out as Jeff's monster cock started crawling up my hole. They'd said to do it for real, and that's the way Jeff and I fucked each other—only each other. Bareback.

"Marco, do you see what they're doing? Fer crissakes, stop them!"

I gasped as Jeff pressed into me. It burned. Oh, god, it burned. It always did. Jeff's dick was so big and so thick and so fucking, fucking hard. I panted, keeping my mouth open, bearing down, willing myself to relax as my asslips stretched. I felt like I was being split in two. It hurt and it burned and, fuck, I wanted it.

"Damn, that's hot." Whoever said it was completely out of breath.

I knew we looked good. I lifted my head, watching Jeff impale me.

"I love watching my cock fill your hole." Jeff's words came out through gritted teeth. He was making himself go slowly, trying not to hurt me— trying not to come.

I gasped as he slid in another inch. My asslips stretched—thinner, tighter.

"That's it, lover. Loosen up and take it all." He gasped, shuddering, as the sound of his voice seemed to open my hole. "God, you feel good! Unh!"

My sphincter relaxed in a rush, and Jeff slid in to the hilt. I lay back down, taking deep breaths, willing my body not to shake, not to panic at the sheer size of the cock buried deep in my rectum.

"Easy lover." Jeff's thumbs stroked the backs of my thighs. He was breathing hard, holding himself still over me. "It'll be OK in a minute. I'm gonna make you feel so good."

The pain passed, slowly, the way I knew it would. Gradually I became aware of another pressure, of the hard cock nuzzling against my joyspot. Pressing precome out of me. I looked up at Jeff. His face was flushed, his shoulders and arms and chest glistening with sweat. My cock twitched at the sight of him. I felt the jolt all the way around my asshole.

"Do it, you prick." I clenched my rectal muscles around him. "Fuck my horny ass until I come."

Jeff grinned. He leaned over and kissed me, shoving his tongue deep in my mouth. I sucked, hard. My asslips kissed his cock, matching the rhythm of my mouth.

He closed his eyes and pulled back. His smile turned to a gasp, then to a grimace. "Damn, but you're tight."

The friction still burned, but at the same time it felt so good. So damn good. Then he was in again. And out. And in.

"You ready?" Jeff pressed hard, grinding his pelvis against me, his balls heavy against my asscheeks as he once more looked down into my eyes.

I grappled on the bed for the bottle, slathered oil on my hand. Then I grabbed ahold of my long, hard pornstar cock and growled up at my panting lover. "Show me what you've got, fucker."

"Asshole," he snapped.

I yelled as Jeff shoved into me. Then he started fucking me, wild and fierce, his balls slapping against me. I cried out each time he punched my joyspot. I could tell I wasn't going to last long. Each time he hit my prostate, I surged closer, my juices boiling, ready to erupt. Ready to explode. I jacked myself faster, trying to match Jeff's rhythm. With each stroke I pulled waves of pleasure through my ever-expanding dick.

"Gonna come," I gasped. I shuddered as my hand stroked up. "Fuck me. Harder." My balls pulled up, tight. "Fuck me—dammit, HARD!"

Jeff slammed his hips into me, punching into my joyspot—just the way I'd begged him to, just the way he knew I loved it. My hole clenched, hard and greedy. Then I howled as the orgasm washed over me. My dick and my prostate and my asshole became one continuous scream of pleasure. My come spurted out and I yelled until my throat hurt.

It was a helluva money shot. The wet splats landed on my chin and my neck and my tits. The last couple on my belly. Jeff ground his hips into me, twitching his dick inside me until I swear every drop of sperm in my balls shot out my cocktube. I shook like my bones were breaking.

I was totally wiped out. As my hand stilled, I looked up. Jeff was balanced over me, his arms shaking, his breath erratic, sweat dripping down onto me. His face was a mask of concentration as he arched his cock into me, prolonging my pleasure.

My arms trembled as I reached up and grabbed his tits. "I love you," I panted. I pinched, lightly. "You are one hot fuck."

Jeff gasped, his eyes glazing. We were the only ones in the world. My hole was raw and sore and stretched so loose it felt like it would never be tight again. I didn't care.

I smiled up at him, twisting the hard little nipples between my fingers. "Fuck me, lover."

Jeff's cry was incoherent as he started thrusting into me again, pounding toward his climax. His dick slurped in and out of me, wet and sloppy. I tried to tighten for him. I managed a light twitch before my muscles gave out. He felt it—he shivered.

His cock ravaged my asshole with fast, deep, full strokes. I tugged hard, rhythmically, on his tits. His breathing was so fast, I knew he was right on the edge. I lifted my hips, taking him as deep as I could, rocking back as he bottomed out, as his body stiffened.

"You fucker," I gasped, an evil laugh deep in my throat. He'd destroyed my hole. I was sore as hell and, damn, it felt good. I jerked hard on his nipples. "Do it!"

"Aargghh!" Jeff's roar almost deafened me. He buried himself balls deep, his whole body shuddering, his thick, hard cock pulsing, stretching, throbbing against my poor battered asslips.

"Get ready, this is gonna be one helluva shot…" This time I distinctly heard Marco's voice in the background mix. "When Jeff pulls out…"

"Um, it's too late, Marco."

"What?"

"Jeff just came up Zak's ass."

"What?! Nobody does that! Jesus H. Christ!"

"I'm not shittin' ya man, look! Jeff's whole ass is twitching."

"Jeff? Zak? Where's the come shot?"

"Man, I just came in my pants—and I'm straight!"

"Dammit! Where's my money shot? Zak? Jeff? Where's my fucking money shot?!"

Marco's curses degenerated into Italian. I tuned him out as Jeff collapsed on me. Jeff's breathing was ragged. He kissed me, clumsily missing my lips, then connecting. I lowered my legs and wrapped them around his waist, holding him to me in a ferocious bear hug.

Jeff pressed against me for a long time, his breathing slowly returning to normal. Finally he started to wiggle against me, his shoulders moving as he laughed into my neck.

"You liked?" He kept his voice low, just barely loud enough for me to hear.

I whispered back. "I'm gonna need diapers, you asshole. Damn, you're good."

He sucked on my neck. I could tell he was giving me a hickey.

"We gave them one helluva show."

When he could finally stop laughing, Jeff rolled off me, his dick pulling free with a loud plop. I reached down between my legs and felt my hole. It was puffy and sticky and about as well-used as a bottom boy's pussy can be. I knew it would be back to normal by morning—it always was. But for now, my butt positively purred.

Jeff grabbed the extra sheet and the blanket from the bottom of the bed and pulled them over us. Then he spooned himself up against my back and wrapped his arms around me. I clenched my butt muscles, enjoying the stretched feeling and the sticky, tacky pull of his drying come on my skin. The movement caused another trickle to leak out of my asshole and run down my leg. I shivered and pressed back against my lover, against his—for once—softly heavy cock.

"What are you two doing now?" Marco was beyond exasperation. He sounded genuinely perplexed. "What the fuck do you do for an encore?"

"We're rolling over and going to sleep," Jeff growled. "Just like in real life. Now shut up."

"Oh, fer crissakes!"

Something heavy hit the floor. It sounded like Marco's clipboard. Then somebody started laughing—a lot of somebodies.

I closed my eyes and smiled as Jeff's breathing deepened. I knew we'd be getting our percentage. Marco was too greedy not to use a scene like we'd just given him. Jeff started to purr. I drifted right behind him. Marco's video was going to be great. And Jeff and I were even getting paid to sleep.

Stripped of Inhibitions
Pierce Lloyd

I lived with Tim for a semester. It was an incredibly difficult semester. Not because of school; I was breezing through my classes. No, the difficulty lay in sharing a room with a god-like hunk and trying to keep my hands off my swollen dick. And it was none too easy keeping my hands off of his dick, either.

Many nights he'd go to sleep early, sprawled on top of his covers, clad only in tight white briefs. I would stay up late to do homework or surf the Internet, and my eyes would inevitably sneak over to his chiseled form. He had a baby face, which made his enormous chest seem even more out of place. He had rock-hard abs and a narrow waist, and his obliques—his "Apollo's Belt," in classical terms—etched deep lines that led beneath his clean white cotton sheath. On more than one occasion, I gazed lustfully on his sleeping form and wanted nothing more than to rip off his underwear and slurp greedily on his balls and cock.

His modesty was frustrating. It was as though Tim was teasing me with his amazing body, but was too shy to reveal himself all the way. So I fantasized about his cock, which he always kept hidden, even changing his underwear in the shower stall instead of in our room. Sometimes I envisioned his erect cock as big and menacing; sometimes I pictured it as small and cute. But I never got a chance to see it.

As it was, we were pretty good friends. Tim was a fun guy who enjoyed his beer, but never seemed to gain an ounce. Since we were close and I had few friends, I sometimes felt an urge to tell him how I felt about him—or at least that I was gay. But he was always talking about women, and I never could figure out quite how he'd react. I was only a sophomore in college, and I wasn't yet ready to come out to everyone in my life.

At the end of the first semester that year, Tim moved out to live off-campus with a friend. I ended up having the whole dorm room to myself. That was nice, but I missed Tim.

A few weeks into the spring semester, I bumped into Tim at the library. "Dude!" he yelled, grabbing my hand. A nearby student, studying, shushed him. "How're things?" he went on, more quietly.

"Things are good," I said, noticing that he held my hand an extra instant before letting go. *Why do I notice these meaningless things?* I wondered. *Why torture myself?*

"What have you been doing with yourself?" I asked nonchalantly. "I haven't seen you around much."

"I got this new job," he whispered, "making, like, so much money."

"Really? Where do you work?"

"I'm a male stripper now."

I was taken aback. "Really?" I managed to say.

"Yeah. Dude, we've got so much to catch up on. You free later?"

"Sure," I said, not caring if I had plans or not.

"So your new job…," I said as we munched on pizza.

"It's the easiest money I've ever made. All I do is, I go on a Friday night or a Saturday night, I dance around a little, take off my clothes, and I get at least 100 bucks."

"All your clothes?" I asked, truly fascinated.

He smiled mischievously. "Sometimes, if the mood is right."

I wanted to ask, "So when can I see you perform?" I settled on, "So how did you land this job?"

"It was just dumb luck, I guess. This exotic-dance service in town used to just provide female strippers for parties, but they were always getting requests for men. So they hired a few. There are three of us now, and we can barely keep up. I found out from Tina, this girl who sits in front of me in chemistry. She's a dancer too, and she told me I had a good body and should apply."

"Wow. I never knew that was a business."

"Yeah. It's great. I make at least $100 for the dance, and then I usually make anywhere from $20 to $200 in tips. Sometimes I do two dances a night."

Suddenly, his face lit up. "Dude! You'd be perfect. You're just the type they're looking for."

"What? Me?"

"Yeah. You've got a good body. You haven't gone downhill since last semester, have you?"

I bristled. "Of course not."

"Then you should apply. It'd be great. We could do big parties together, get felt up by tons of hot chicks...."

It didn't really sound like my cup of tea.

Tim stood up and pulled me to my feet. "Come here." He led me to the bathroom, then locked the door with the two of us inside.

What's he doing? I wondered.

"Take off your shirt," he ordered. Confused, I did as I was told.

"Perfect. See? You've got great pecs. Women love pecs."

I looked down at my chest. While the work I'd been doing had begun to show, I wasn't really at Tim's level yet. Still, I had to admit I looked pretty good.

"I don't know if I'm comfortable with the whole thing."

"Aw, dude," he whined, sounding like the sitcom best friend trying to talk his chum into some crazy shenanigan. "Tracy says a lot of guys worry that their dick is too small, but most guys are just fine. They aren't expecting porn stars." He reached for my pants.

"What the hell are you doing?" I said as I mentally willed him to go further. He unbuttoned my fly.

"I'm checking you out. I'll bet your dick is bigger than mine," he said. He yanked my underwear to my knees, and I stood before him in all my glory. He checked me out for maybe two seconds.

"See?" he said. "You're plenty big. I'll give them your number, OK?"

"Uh, OK," I said, pulling up my pants. "But you've got to help me with the tricks of the trade."

"Absolutely, buddy. Rule number one, trim your bush."

We both laughed hysterically at that one.

My "interview" wasn't nearly as seedy as I'd expected—or hoped. I was asked a few questions, looked up and down, and hired.

My first job wasn't nearly as seedy as I expected, either. It was some woman's 40th birthday, and her friends were determined to embarrass her. I stripped from jeans and a dress shirt down to my briefs, then did a teasing dance as I stripped to my G-string. The birthday girl turned bright red, and when my 20 minutes were up, I left—no nudity, but a $100 fee and $30 in tips just for shaking my butt. All in all, I guess it was a pretty good job.

I was at the agency picking up my check with Tim when the secretary got a call. She said "Uh-huh, uh-huh" a few times and then put the caller on hold.

"I got a party on the 25th," she said, chewing her gum. "They want two guys."

"We'll take it!" Tim chimed.

"It's an all-male party," she said.

Tim shrugged. "I got no problem with that." He looked at me.

"Fine," I said, secretly wondering, *What if I see somebody I know?*

I needn't have worried. The party was on the outskirts of town and consisted of 15 older men, all slightly bearish. I had never met any of them before.

Tim whispered to me after we had walked in the door, "The secret to dancing for guys is to pretend you really enjoy it." I nodded.

We took turns. Tim did his striptease first, with a dance song blaring on the stereo. He looked like a regular college student, in flannel shirt and khakis. He stripped these off to reveal boxer briefs, then peeled off the boxer briefs until he was wearing only a skimpy blue G-string. He lowered the G-string enough to reveal his pubic hair, then did a final bump and grind as the song ended.

"Your turn, partner!" he yelled to me and then turned to one of the men who was seated on a large sectional sofa. "Mind if I sit on your lap?" The man smiled as Tim straddled his knee.

I did my dance, pleased at the cheers I got when I took off my pants and again when I pulled off my boxers to reveal my red G-string. Wanting to be creative, instead of showing my bush, I turned around and flashed my ass. I got some scattered applause.

When I finished I looked to see what Tim wanted to do next. I hoped he would take the first step and get completely naked.

Instead, Tim was still sitting on one of the men on the couch, but he had at least five different guys feeling his body. Tim just closed his eyes and lay back as the partygoers massaged his chest and legs.

I realized that there was a whole group of men on the sofa staring at Tim, but sitting too far away to reach him. I walked over and planted myself on top of two of them. They took my cue and began to run their hands along my muscles, one guy even discreetly kneading my ass.

I looked over at Tim. One of the guys had a $10 bill out and was sliding it down Tim's chest. He pushed it past Tim's stomach and then down into his G-string. My eyes widened as he reached down into the well-filled pouch and fondled Tim's cock. Tim only moaned with pleasure. Within seconds two more hands were inside his underwear, feeling him up. Tim responded by pulling his G-string to his knees, freeing his hard, circumcised cock. It looked to be a hefty six or seven inches.

Suddenly, I felt a hand gripping my already-hard member. Then another and another found their way into my G-string, which was soon being pulled off my legs and unceremoniously thrown onto the floor.

Completely bare-assed now, I looked over to see Tim watching me. He smiled to show his approval of my compromising situation as a hand wrapped around his cock. Although heavy, hairy men typically are not my type, watching the horny daddies pet and stroke my friend was indescribably erotic.

After a few moments Tim stood up. Still naked, he walked over to me, his stiff dick swinging in front of him, and took my hand, pulling me off the couch and onto my feet.

"Well, that's our show," he said. There was a chorus of disappointment. "At least, that was the first half of our show. We can stay and do a second act if you want."

I stared at Tim dumbly. *Second act? What was he talking about?*

"What do you guys do for an encore?" asked the guy who was throwing the party.

"For an extra 100 bucks, my partner and I will do anything to each other you'd care to see." As if to prove his point, he put his arm around my waist and pulled me close to him.

As a few of the men pooled their money, he whispered in my ear, "So, are you up for it?"

I whispered back. "I didn't know you were into this."

"Dude," he said, "you can't tell me you haven't felt something between us these past few weeks."

"I have," I said. "I didn't realize you felt it too."

He pulled me closer, embracing me. "Of course I did," he said. "I was just afraid to say anything. Now is our chance to relieve some of that tension." He grabbed my cock and began stroking it.

One of the guys handed Tim the money. Then he pointed to me.

"You," he said, "I want to see you suck his cock."

Tim sat down on the couch, and I obligingly put my head between his legs. I started to lick his dick head.

"Deep throat him!" one of the men shouted out. I did my best to get Tim's member into my mouth. Tim moaned as my head moved up and down between his legs.

"Rim him!" one guy yelled.

"Yeah," yelled another, "suck that asshole!"

Tim raised his butt to meet my lips, and I cautiously applied my tongue to his warm hole. To my surprise, it tasted almost sweet. His ass lips contracted involuntarily at the unfamiliar sensation of my tongue, but as I worked him over, he began to relax. He gasped in surprise when I shoved my tongue deep into his hole, then groaned with pleasure as I fucked him with my tongue.

I glanced around to see that almost all of the partygoers had their penises out and were stroking themselves as they watched Tim and I going at it.

"Put your dick in his ass!" someone yelled.

A few more voices chimed in, chanting, "Butt fuck! Butt fuck!"

Tim pulled my face toward his until we were eye to eye and my cock was just inches from his saliva-drenched anus.

He whispered in my ear, "I've never done this before."

"Is this how you want your first time to be?" I whispered back.

"Hell, yeah!" He winked at me.

I gently worked the head of my dick into his hole. He was tight, so it was with extreme care that I eased my shaft up his ass, inch by inch. Carefully, I pushed myself in to the hilt. One of the masturbating men lost control and shot his load all over my side. It dripped down onto Tim, who smiled and winked at the man.

"Are you taking it in all right?" I said to Tim.

He nodded and said. "Let's give 'em the show they deserve."

I started fucking Tim, slowly at first and then faster and faster, until I was slamming my balls against his ass. The expression on his face registered the pleasure he was feeling, and he never quit saying "Yeah" over and over.

I knew I couldn't take much more of this. After a few minutes I grunted and pulled my dick out. I grabbed my cock head, and the moment I touched it, I began spurting strands of thick white come onto Tim. There was a smattering of applause. Then Tim slid me down onto my back in one fluid motion.

"Turnabout is fair play," he said as he spread my legs wide and began sucking my cock while the partygoers looked on. After a minute or two, he moved down to lick my balls before pushing my legs up and leaning in to eat my ass, working his tongue into my hot hole. Another of the men ejaculated, this time onto Tim's back. I was amazed at how pleasurable getting rimmed is.

"Fuck him!" someone shouted. As Tim positioned his dick at my ass, I looked around at our audience. What a thrill, I realized, to have my body worshiped by this many men at one time.

After a brief bit of resistance, Tim's dick slid easily up my butt. He leaned in to kiss me, then started slamming his cock into me the way I had just done to him.

I allowed myself to enjoy the sensation. Our audience, realizing the show would soon be over, started pumping their cocks furiously, and Tim and I were soon awash in torrents of joy juice as each man shot his wad onto us.

I was impressed by Tim's staying power; he continued to fuck me like a rabbit for some time. *Will he come inside me?* I wondered. Finally, with a groan, Tim pulled his cock out and took it in his hand.

His semen hit me in the face at a surprising velocity, and we both grinned. Tim's come dripped onto my lips, and I licked it off, enjoying the flavor of my friend.

We embraced, naked, as the last of the onlookers deposited his sperm onto us.

The host of the party let us use his shower to wash all of the goo off us. (As a show of thanks, I let him grope my cock one last time before Tim and I went into the bathroom together.) I jumped into the shower first, letting the steaming water run down my body.

Tim poked his head into the shower.

"Buddy," he said, "that was the best fuck of my life." I pulled him by his penis into the shower.

"I wish all of my workdays ended like this," I said. "Do you think we'll ever get an assignment like this again?"

Tim, who had started soaping up my balls, leaned in to kiss me. "Someday, maybe."

He kissed me again. "I can promise you one thing," he said. "We're going to be spending a lot of time practicing our act."

He

Daddy Bob Allen writing as Lee Alan Ramsay

The man rolled over in the otherwise empty king-size bed. He was a man, and both he and the bed were big and empty. August desert heat infused the dark room, and though the windows were open, no breeze moved into the solid block of temple-pounding swelter. The man's temples were not the only aboriginal drums banging out rhythms in unison with his heart, the man's brow was not all that was moist with pungent male sweat.

He rolled his head toward the night stand and focused on the blue-green digital readout: 11:02. The ':' blinked incessantly to prove electronically that this was the proper hour. He wanted to sleep. But the blinking, blinking, blinking of the ':' added to the thunder of skin- and hide-covered drums. He did not have to move his huge hand down to his naked groin to confirm the major voice in the percussion section.

He teetered a moment longer on the cusp and he knew what he wanted. It would come to him in the smoke of dreams if he just willed himself to sleep. But that was only mind satisfaction; like masturbation, its fulfillment, its banking of the real fires would only be ephemeral, momentary, no actual cool water on the seething embers.

He came to full wakefulness, and it was time for him to get up off the white sheets. He pulled his great hairy bulk from the starched linen to the shower. Hot water from the polished tap overhead spilled and pressed the dark hair downward over the scalp and bulging sinews. He opened his mouth to the flushing stream and bathed himself, beginning and ending with the ritualistic cleansing of his engorged genitals.

He stepped from behind the plastic veils, pulled aside on clattering metal hooks, and dried his swarthy skin with fluffy towels, he was pink and gray and brown. He pulled on tight jeans, the worn pocket behind the zipper automatically shifted him to dress left. He slammed the door on the leather closet and chose a black T-shirt from the top dresser drawer. They that want leather will find it in my eyes, he thought sardonically.

He put on work boots and descended a staircase to garage level. Ah, the garage. Only half of it contained his Porsche. He mounted and pressed the proper buttons; the first opened the huge door to the street. How much of life is dictated by the pressing of buttons.

Shifting gears expertly he descended the planted hills in the roaring machine to the neon-flashing playground at the foot of the hills, hills shielded by expertly planted pines, pines and yucca around his affluently blinded home. Wielding the stick in his right hand he descended.

There was a bar. All people know bars, places where moods are altered and the folk either go wild with lies or tell the absolute truth. He had always been able to tell the difference. He parked and walked through the door like a new sheriff with a shiny star at his breast.

The store was smoky and yellow. There was pool and drinking. The scents of stale beer, misbegotten incense and sawdust flowed into his nostrils. Sawdust caved under his boot heels and the walls were decorated in cowboy memorabilia, harnesses, tracings, sickles, and horse hobbles. These mule skinners are delicate in their ways.

He walked to the bar and looked at the bartender; that was all that was needed to put a cold amber bottle in front of him. Then He looked about the room and He wanted to spend as little time as possible in this misbegotten marketplace. He was ultimately miffed that so few of his "peers" realized the difference between the talking and the doing of it.

In a few minutes a bulging Tide-bleached T-shirt slipped into position beside the He. "Can I buy you a beer, Sir?"

"Just bought one."

"Then maybe there's something else I can do for you tonight. That black hanky looks real."

"It's real."

The two males facing each other relaxed just a bit from their "OK Corral" posturing. The younger man in his white T-shirt moved a little closer. He lowered his tawny curled head, perhaps to draw in the scent of his potential mentor's breast. "I'm a little new at this," he whispered. "Please teach me."

"What would you like to learn?" asked the Master, as any Gypsy would explore a cold reading. He felt the fluids in his groin begin to move.

The man/boy looked up into the eyes of his protector, fawnish, innocent, vulnerable. "I'd like to belong."

"The breathtaking outrage of non-involvement," rumbled He. "So what have you read? What have you looked at on tape? What sort of dirty work do I have to undo?"

"It's all crap," said the boy. "I want the real thing."

"Do you, now?" He crossed his massive arms across his chest; the gesture was much louder than the murmured words.

"Is it OK if I'm afraid a little bit?"

"You'd better be afraid. Otherwise I'd have some questions about your sanity for openers." He began conjuring the great vortex, the grand imaginary tornado that sucked in the other man, the massive low pressure area that pulled the other soul into his sphere like inevitable isobars on a weather map. He breathed in and out, making sure the puffs of his mighty nostrils went directly into the shiny desert-colored curls below his face.

"Take a good look into the old brown eyes."

The young man raised his hairless, squarely masculine face and looked deep into the huge trickster god before him. After a tender moment the boy sighed. "It can't be faked and it can't be hidden, can it?"

"Nope."

After another eon of seconds, another sigh. "Teach me, Sir. I want to know your pain."

"What makes you think I'm going to hurt you?" huffed He.

The younger man did not hesitate. "Anything that's worth having hurts. Ask any mother."

He released a long low "Ooooo" sound from between his textured lips. Then He leaned into the young man's face and sealed the bargain with a moist kiss. For a moment the tongues played with each other like mating snails bringing their shells together. He disengaged. "Follow me."

He walked across the smoky room, not really caring whether the boy was indeed following. Then He heard the boy's shoes on the sawdusted boards, and a moment later on the sidewalk cement behind him. He unlocked the passenger door of the green sheet-metal bubble and opened the door to the boy. The boy folded his long Midwestern legs into the car like a praying mantis. He slid into the driver's cockpit and checked his blind spots through mirrors. The car cleared its throat.

The midnight traffic was sparkling and sluggish. He wielded the stick shift like a knight would manage a mace. "It'll take about ten minutes to get to my place. You'd better be naked by the time my garage door opens."

The boy leisurely untied his beige work boots and pulled them off. He was in no apparent hurry since the mentor had given him the full ten minutes. "Should I tease you, Sir?"

"Wouldn't be advisable."

With that the boy raised his butt off the car seat and slid off his tight jeans. A second gear shift appeared, long and throbbing, stiff and veined, assuming about the same angle as the one coming out of the floor of the German vehicle. The young man peeled off his socks and pulled the T-shirt over his head.

He glanced over at the lad, taking in the smooth tanned skin, the rather well-defined chest, not vulgar, not pumped, just defined precisely. He made sure the car was progressing safely and glanced again, this time taking in the tight waistline, firm abs and thick smooth thighs spread as wide as the confines of the passenger seat would allow. The boy's face and eyes remained locked forward. Again He mentally attended to the progress of the car, again He glanced back, this time at the center of the boy, his manhood, a wispy swatch of red-blond pubic hair visible momentarily in the glare of a flashing-past streetlight, and the shaft of flesh emerging from the nest, emerging and demanding in its hardness, casting moving shadows in the moving quartz halogen light. He reached over for the second gear shift and pumped it a few times. The boy went into small quivering spasms of pleasure, squirming, slightly squirming.

The Master snorted. "Pretty. Very pretty. Now, am I going to be able to get both you and the ego into the dungeon? Door's a little narrow."

The boy thought a moment. "Left the ego in the bar, Sir. I'll collect it on the way home…if I need it any more."

He snorted again, convinced now that He had made a rather spectacular choice.

The car made its way back up into the hills, back up to the camouflaged aerie in the planted hills. He pressed the button on the black box on the dash to open the garage door and the green Porsche slid silently into its niche. The machinery overhead hummed, and the door closed with a mighty thud, as if to punctuate the young man's state of being trapped.

He dismounted and spoke through the open driver's side door. "Out."

The boy scrambled out and gently shoved the door closed. Immediately the lad came to his teacher and went directly to his knees in front of the bear-like man. The boy buried his face in the bulging crotch and wrapped his arms almost desperately around the sturdy legs.

"Anyone tell you to do all that?" rumbled the He.

"No," mumbled the boy still in his Master's groin. "Maybe I should be punished."

"You think it's that easy, huh?" intoned the He. "What if I told you I don't need a reason to do what I do?"

The boy looked up with a weird amalgam of confusion and wonderment. "Teach me," the lad said in barely a whisper.

The He raised the boy to his feet by one wrist and with the other hand opened a door next to the driver's side window of the Porsche. The door led into an oblong room. He flipped a light switch and three very small amber bulbs lit up, barely revealing the black interior of the chamber. At one end of the room there was a jail cell; dominating the other end was a rack suspended on four square floor-to-ceiling pillars. Chains hung from the ceiling about the room and the walls were festooned with all manner of equipment: lashes, crops, weights, stretchers, paddles—the textured walls were solid with the toys of grown kinky men.

It took a moment for the boy to absorb the magnitude of the room he had just entered. Then the lad's eyes rolled back into his head and he gave out a long energized sigh. "I'm home," the boy pronounced almost tearfully.

With no wasted motion the He positioned the boy between two of the hanging chains and raised each arm to the height He wanted. He folded the boy's fingers around the chain where He wanted them and then He glared directly into the boy's eyes. The He said nothing, but the fixed and frowning stare said everything. He was certain now that the boy's hands would not release the chains even if the building caught fire. The boy was in bondage until the He released him with word or gesture. He positioned the boy's bony feet in the same manner, spread wide.

The boy gave out only one brief glance of bewilderment, then it was obvious from the resigned expression that the bondage was real. The boy strained slightly against the chains in his fists.

He stepped around the boy, his palm coursing over the smooth naked skin, flawless tanned skin stretched over powerful young muscles, the artist's canvas, blank and waiting for the Master's mark; blank paper for the Master to write his incantations. The boy's penis was still stiff; it had not relaxed in all the time the two had been together so far. The He reached for the organ and pumped it a few times as He had done in the car, but this time He could give full attention to his work. He rubbed the livid engorged head and the boy went into trembling spasms. He grabbed each cheek muscle in turn, holding on, squeezing it. Then He gathered up the testicles in his palm and massaged the sac, pulling until the lad winced slightly.

"Now then," said He, disengaging from the boy, stepping back in mock contemplation with his hand cupping his own chin. "What am I going to do with this naked young man I find in my chains tonight?" As if He had just chanced on the boy there, the He spoke. He licked his thumbs and began stroking the boy's dark nipples, rubbing them gently at first, gently but insistently with the moist thumbs.

The boy pushed his chest out within the limits of his tethers and groaned as the pressure on his nipples increased.

The He teased the boy's nipples, now stroking with moist thumbs, now pinching lightly, now pinching not so lightly, and all the time He gazed directly into the boy's eyes, gauging, watching, discerning the slightest change in the boy's demeanor, playing the lad like a well-tuned instrument, pushing, backing off, watching and playing.

If anything, the boy's male organ grew stiffer. As the boy squirmed lightly, the member flailed the holy air. The low-hung testicles jiggled about in their wrinkled sac, freed by well-parted thighs; the balls swayed and juggled. The boy pushed himself toward the He, pushed out, chest and body and mind, pushed toward the man before him, hungry for the man before him, hungry for the hands and the thumbs.

He disengaged his fingers from the lad's nipples and then slapped each pec lightly, then not so lightly. The cracking sounds of palm on naked flesh split the air. The boy began to slowly undulate in his chains like shafts of wheat before a prairie breeze. Swaying, the boy also moaned, long guttural moans of something akin to a thrilling death rattle. The boy's head rolled around slowly on his neck and the breeze over his vocal cords rattled louder as each slap grew louder and harder and louder, now not only on the pecs but on the belly—"Thy belly is like a pile of wheat…." And the louder and louder slaps continued, mounting slowly and slowly. Now to the spread-wide thighs and on the back, now to the juggling cheek meat, firm but lightly jiggling cheeks. And between the slaps the He drew his palm over the flesh, skin the color of honey and ripe wheat.

The boy's utter submission and continuing absolute submission began to surge into the He's being, little by little the scent of the boy's clean, smooth body began to invade his nostrils like pure amyl; slowly and slowly the He began to intoxicate himself on the boy's utter compliance, the lad's instinctive ability to sexify everything the He hurled at him. His breathing began to change the same as the boy's. He began to drool and breathe heavily and between the now-vicious slaps the He snailed his tongue over the flesh, skin the color of honey and ripe wheat. Now He savored the musky sweetness of the skin with his wide flowing tongue. He licked the pecs, He licked the naked spread-wide thighs, He licked the nests of hair in the pits of the arms and the boy went insane, thrashing in his chains, moaning louder than from the slaps.

The slaps continued, more on the belly, more on the cheeks, jiggling loaves of cheek meat. And the licking continued, from the secret place where the scrotum joins a man's body, the secret place in his groin where he joins his manhood, the snail tongue coursed its way slowly up the line where the leg joins the torso, up the crease where a man stands on his mobility, up the side of his belly. And the lad's moaning became monumental, the thrashing and hopeless quivering grew. The boy's body went taut and strained and the vocal cords tightened into strained silence for a moment, and then the boy thrashed and squealed. Riding the squeal like the perfect wave, the He drew the boy's penis into his mouth and drove it deep into his throat.

The boy went utterly mad. His young bony pelvis came helplessly forward, the low-pressure area sucked him helplessly forward, and the boy bellowed some trashy reference to the Almighty with his head back as far as his neck muscles would let it drop.

He knew the boy was his now. He felt the great shift in power, the monumental demonstration of who was Master and why. The He stood to his full height before the trembling and sweating lad, and the absence of any stimulation eventually got the boy's attention. The boy looked at his Master through watery eyes, through drooping lids, through a thin smile of admiration and respect.

The He pulled his T-shirt over his head revealing the thick bear-like body, bulging pec mounds, and the massive forests of black hair covering the bas-relief map. The boy's eyes rolled back into his head and he moaned anew. The boy pushed himself forward to be with the bulging Master, straining forward, the boy pushed himself toward skin-to-skin contact. The He drew back by centimeters just to remain teasingly out of reach and the boy begged with watery eyes.

Once the Master made it clear that contact would be on his terms, the He moved closer and the chests, one bulging and hairy, one smooth and defined, came together and the He pressed another kiss into the boy's mouth. The He's firm steady bulk stopped the boy's uncontrolled trembling, stopped the swaying and undulating. His mouth stopped the sighing. He sucked the boy's breath out of him; sucking on the boy's tongue, the He quieted the noise...for the moment.

He detached himself from the boy and without looking, without taking his eyes from the gaze contact with the boy's eyes, He reached out with his right hand, the right bicep bulging and bulging. The hand came back and in the gnarled, hairy, mighty fist was the handle of a cat, a cat with 20 strands the length of a man's forearm and the thick round handle slightly shorter.

The lad's eyes closed briefly, partly in dread, partly in resignation, partly in the same expression of being home that he had expressed the second he entered the room.

He drew the strands of the cat very slowly forward over the boy's shoulder and let the exciting tips trickle down the boy's chest, black trickling traces flowing down; these mule skinners are delicate in their ways. The He repeated the act on the other shoulder, this time the boy stretched his lips over and kissed the black rawhide, with a slow lick and a quick peck as the whip flowed slowly off his shoulder like black quicksilver flowing down.

The He stepped back, and then He made a very slow circle about the lad, like a spider spinning a devious web, spinning and circling, moving slowly and deliberately about the boy. Choosing the back first, the strands of his cat started pelting like a spring rain, softly but insistently. Stroking and pelting, getting the earth loosened up and ready for the agrarian's mighty plow, slowly and carefully getting the sod ready.

The He grew in bulk, grew in stature, grew in strength. Fed by the vital contact with the boy, the He grew. No one but the perfect Top knows the delicious thrill of the growing, the boldness, the strength and audacity that the perfect bottom hands his tormentor. No one but the perfect Top knows the thrill of perfect trust, and how that perfect trust can be used to send two men to S/M Nirvana. No one but the perfect Top can know how close to God two men can approach.

The He reached for his belt buckle and unfastened it. Then, with a vicious tormenting smirk He drew his fingers and palm down over the boy's face as one would close the eyes of a fresh corpse. The lad thrashed in his chains and bellowed. "No! Please don't blindfold me. Please! I'll do anything if you let me see you. Please." The boy was pleading and crying.

"You'll do anything, regardless," stated He, whispered forcefully into the boy's ear.

The whimpering subsided slowly. "Please let me see you...."

For the boy there was no time left, no time before the commencement of his catharsis, the great aboriginal awakening the boy had begged for in the bar, the bar covered with aboriginal wrought iron memorabilia from the prairie and the floor covered with sawdust. With tightly closed eyes, the boy braced his body like a young draft animal might do on his first day in the field.

The He took his jeans off, knowing the sounds of the tinkling belt buckle and the rush of denim on skin was exciting the boy beyond the lad's limits to contain himself. Yet He knew the boy would not open his eyes under any circumstances. The warm moist air engulfed the He's naked countenance, bulging hairy thighs and semi-engorged plantain-sized penis, the penis would slowly engorge itself the rest of the way as the next two hours unfolded. He pressed his naked body against the smooth tanned boyskin, unblemished, unmarked skin like a blank slate waiting for the shaman's incantations to be carefully and meticulously written.

The boy would feel it now; what had gone before was preamble, now the real poem. The lash strands sailed high into the holy air with a mighty whoosh and came down together into the small of the boy's back, and the boy went high into his tethers on trembling biceps, shrieking and sighing; his stiffened body went high and came down slowly before the next stroke.

The He never left skin-to-skin contact. He either kept his bulging hairy body pressed against the boy's skin or He kept his palm locked about some large muscle mass for contact, always contact; He never left the boy. Indeed it was through this contact that He not only read what was happening within the boy's quaking body, but it was also the means to take the journey with the lad, not send him on ahead, but go along with the boy. The galvanic signals sent through the lad's muscles and skin went directly into the cells of the He, and it was the happiest game of all.

The lash went on high again and came down again on the stretched skin of the boy's naked back. The lad stiffened and sucked in a quick harsh breath. The He could feel the boy's muscles stiffen and then relax.

He drew close and teased the boy's earlobe with the hot breath of his voice, whispered puffs of voice into the ear. "This is what you wanted, wasn't it?"

"Oh, yes, Daddy. Yes, Sir!" The boy spoke in quick gasps. "Please don't stop, Sir. Please."

"Do you trust me?"

"Yes, Sir. Yes, Sir."

"Daddy's gonna take you on a little trip. You ready for liftoff?"

The boy simply nodded his head quickly. Maybe it was the boy who suggested with his silence that not much more be said for the next stack of hours and indeed there was not much more said.

He began the long, slow pummeling of the boy's body. There was no rush to complete the act nor was there any need to exchange the cat in his hand for another of a different length and weight. The He simply adjusted the blows to the boy's skin with his arm, with his mind, with his heart.

And still He kept himself close to the boy, skin to skin, spirit to spirit. The lash had no rhythm to it—the He stroked when He felt like it, to no other man's drum beat than the demented one in his own psyche. The blows rained down on the boy's skin intermittently, when He felt like it, and in between there was caressing and skin rubbing skin and licking. The He's tongue coursed and snailed its way up the naked bony backbone and the boy reacted the same way as he had reacted moments earlier when the strands of the lash had caressed the same line of bone. The boy stiffened and heaved out great sighs of quivering delight. Pleasure and pain were bleeding into one; the He knew that because it happened all the time in this room, all the time.

With each thundering lash stroke the link between Daddy and boy grew stronger and more intense. The flash of energy exchange between the two intensified. Slowly, ever so slowly, the two souls were becoming one, linked and locked in the dynamic surge of sexual energy the He was unlocking from both of them. He had the mystical key that unlocked and unfettered the powers of the cosmos, the magic unfolded since the dawn of man in the ritual caves, in the jungles, and in the hearts and minds and groins of all those who went before us. He was the mighty shaman who could make the fiery magic happen, and He did it all with pain!

Stroke on top of lash stroke mounted on the boy's reddening skin. Now the chest, and the boy, still with his eyes tightly closed, pushed his boypecs out to the father, out to receive the delicious ecstasy of his initiation into the mysteries of the Brotherhood. Naked and trembling and probably still a little afraid, the lad pushed himself out with every ounce of energy he could muster, an energy pool that was waning as the lash strokes took their slow but mighty and inexorable toll on even the boy's reserve of youthful energy.

Now the cheeks, and the boy would shift his thrust backward, backward into the lash behind him. The whirring lash left its scarlet marks on the boy's cheeks, criss-crossed cheeks with red.

And now the back again. The back bone, the place that held the lad upright, the bones that had evolved over eons of time to be straight, now seemed to be turning to sponge because the boy was showing signs of not being able to stand upright that which was his birthright. The He was taking it away; little by agonizing little, the boy was weakening. And yet, the lad's fists clung to the overhead chains as if his life depended on the grip, and perhaps it did.

Harder now came the strokes, harder, and then a space of feather light taps and more caressing and licking and sucking, loving, slow and loving cock sucking, to drive the boy mad with the available spectrum of notes on the He's musical scale, to drive the boy on toward the incredible plateaus of S/M Nirvana, the places of intensity unknown to the timid, the ignorant, the intolerant. To drive the boy mad and bring the He along on the same surge toward utter madness.

At times He clung to the boy, his breathing changed as well as the boy's, his sweat mingled with the boy's and the two bodies at times writhed in unison to the pain and the pleasure and the agony and the relief. The lines between labeled and cubbyholed concepts were beginning to fuzz, to lose their powers to distinguish, just as the lines between the two dancing figures were beginning to fuzz. He grabbed the boy's tawny curls and pulled the head back for a kiss, a kiss delivered from behind with the He's massive hairy body pressed against the boy's back, their tongues traded places and massive noise pounded in both brains, temple against pounding sweaty temple the kiss was given by both.

The lash was raised again to surge on with its deadly work, on high the lash went again. And again it came down on the boy's skin, skin now afire with the welts of the black lash. No blood, the He didn't draw blood, that was not the meaning of the game. But the boy's skin was becoming hot to the touch, most of it raised and welted like some misbegotten living waffle iron.

The Master's rite surged on to its thundering conclusion. Blow after savage blow mounted on the boy's body, blow after blow, quickening now to staccato rhythms. The drums were quickening now, just as the boy's mind was quickening to the savage rites, just as the boy had quickened once before, long ago, encased in a watery womb, the boy had quickened for his mother—now he quickened for his father, and both mother and father felt the same twitching and quickening.

The He clenched his teeth for the finale, the last acts on the boy's body that would drive him to the point of unconsciousness, to the point of the keenest and most reverent awareness the boy would ever experience, the edge of the known world, the rim of the cosmos. The boy would know with a new kind of awareness how utterly huge the world he lived in really was, and He was there beside him sweating and straining and glowing just as the boy was fired and glowing.

The lash finished its divine tasks. Now leaving deep red marks with each mighty stroke, the lash and the Master's heavy arm bashed the lad onto one final plateau of ecstasy. The He knew there were none higher for the boy, not tonight. The lad slumped in his tethers, sobbing uncontrollably, yet not one syllable of stop came through the clenched teeth and the quivering lips, lips parched from shouting. The boy slumped sobbing but still the lad did not let go of the chains. He was fast to the chains as if the metal and his skin were one.

The He lifted the boy to standing and held him there; the He was sobbing too. The He held the boy close and the two breathed heavily for a long moment. The boy sobbed anew and perhaps the He sobbed anew, too. The moment of the loss of innocence is a sobbing moment, and maybe, just maybe, when father and uncles dragged a boy away from his mother and, in the savage aboriginal caves of our species' past, frightened the lad to turn him into a hunter, maybe, just maybe, father and uncles wore ugly masks not just to scare the boy, but to hide the tears.

The He released the boy's hands and feet with prying gestures, prying the boy's fingers off the chains and away from the imaginary shackles that had held the boy's ankles fast, ankles that had not moved from where the He had put them two hours earlier. The He scooped up the limp, tired lad and carried him through the dungeon door, through the garage, through the yellow kitchen of the house and up the stairs to the Master's bedroom. Though the lad's limbs were free, the He had not opened the boy's eyes, yet. The boy kept his eyes obediently shut and saw not garage, kitchen, stairs, or bedroom, not yet.

The He spread the boy out on the still-tortured bed clothing and stretched out beside the lad and held him in the huge arms. The boy, now breathing again, snuggled and purred against the hairy chest.

"Sir," came the pleading whisper from between the mighty pecs. "Sir, can I please look at you?"

The He reached into the drawer of the night stand and pulled out a wrapped condom. He put the packet into the boy's palm and then spoke. "Now, open your eyes and put that on me."

The boy's eyes popped open and it took only a fleeting moment for the lad to absorb the magnitude of the man he was with. The boy threw his arms around his benefactor, strong arms, yet arms dwarfed by the He's bulk. The boy set to his task and tore the packet open with his teeth, then carefully rolled the condom down the length of the Master's engorged shaft. Worshipping the organ, the boy sheathed it in rubber, worshipping and sighing, knowing what was about to happen.

When the organ was covered, the He gently pushed the boy onto his back and raised the boy's legs. This time the boy closed his eyes on his own. The youthful head deep in the pillow with closed eyes, perhaps because he would feel all he needed to feel without seeing.

The He reached into the night stand drawer for the tube of lubricant and liberally applied it to man and boy.

The He was already feeling the great pulse of ownership, the monumental surge of energy from one man to another as only men can know it. He would have the boy, and the boy would not mount one minuscule effort in resistance. The He pressed his body down on the lad gently, slowly, but inexorably.

The mighty organ entered the boy's body, and the boy went insane with the combination of pain and pleasure his benefactor had just taught him. The He did not know if this was a virgin or a veteran; it didn't matter, the boy belonged to him. He sank deep into the boy, and as the boy engulfed him, the He went into his own form of madness, the uncontrolled, flowing, smothering madness of ownership.

As He began to stroke, His body and mind centered and centered again. He did not lose sight of the boy, but the boy became a receptacle. The boy was real, human, but the boy was property as well. Owned. The He sank deeper into the lad's body and sank deeper into his uncontrolled chain reaction. Only the lead rods of orgasm would slow the reaction and that was moments off—until then the He would enjoy the slowly building rite of ownership.

The boy pushed himself up toward the Master, pushed his pelvis up and sank his bony knuckles into the soft pillows around him, grabbing handfuls of white sheet and squealing out his infinite delight of being owned.

There were no more words exchanged between the two, just a stack of long, sweaty moments, man in boy, boy engulfing man with equal desperation.

The He felt the mounting tickle in his groin, the signal that He was about to explode. He tried to drag the moment out more, to prolong the delicious mutual agony for man and boy out a little longer. He lost control and the gargantuan orgasm rent the air of the bedroom with searing explosive pleasure. The He quaked and pumped, pumped the last of his male juices into the boy, pumping and quaking until He slumped exhausted onto the boy's body and there, over the next few minutes, oriented himself to breathe again.

At length the He rolled to one side, withdrew his organ from the boy, peeled off the rubber and, after a quick toweling from a swaddling cloth of terry cloth in the night stand drawer, the He positioned the two for sleep. He embraced the lad, already sighing from sleepiness, and the two slept. Deep, satisfied sleep came to the He, and He was certain the boy was greeted in the realms of Morpheus equally well.

They slept.

In the morning the He stirred first. He looked down and the boy's mouth was pressed out of shape in the Black Forest of the He's chest hair. It was then the boy stirred too, perhaps sensing the changing of the breathing chest he was against. The pale blue eyes opened slowly, and over a thrilling moment the boy reconstructed where he was, and who he was. He looked up into the face of his mentor, the He, and whispered ever so reverently: "How do you like your eggs?"

Hunger Takes Over
Thom Wolf

My eyes met his as soon as I opened the door. He stood out in the crowd.

A dozen or so expectant faces turned toward me. For two seconds I had their undivided attention. I was not who they expected me to be, and the moment of adulation was over. They weren't interested in me, but they were not going to move aside to let me pass. I had to force my way through the crush of closely huddled shoulders. A couple of ladies in their 60s thrust souvenir programs beneath my nose.

"Would you sign these for us?"

They didn't really know who I was. I obliged them with hasty scrawls across my photograph at the back of the program.

"Is she coming out yet?" one of the two women asked.

"I have no idea."

They both smiled and thanked me before shoving their way back into the crowd to await the arrival of their favorite diva.

Although he stood in their ranks, he was not part of the crowd. I could see that he did not share their hunger for a rapid scribble and a sincere word from an aging star. He stepped toward me as I tried to leave.

"Could I have your autograph?" he asked. His voice was deep, older than I would have expected.

I smiled. "You can, but it won't be worth anything."

He did not smile. "That depends on what you measure as worth."

"I'm not a star in this show. I dance in the chorus."

"I know." He was standing close, I could feel the warmth of his body. "You also understudy the leading man."

"In four months he hasn't missed a single performance."

"I live in hope."

I opened his program and began to write.

"What's your name?"

"Jimmy."

As I wrote he stepped even nearer. His thigh brushed against mine. The pressure was light but deliberate. I could smell his scent. The fragrance of his body aroused me: sweat, cologne, and the sweet aroma of laundry softener. His chest was leaning against my arm as I wrote; faintly I could discern the masculine beat of his heart.

I gave him back his pen and program. We looked at each other and did not move. He was tall—an inch or two bigger than I am—and his body was lean. It was a warm night, and there was no need for a jacket. He wore a clingy red T-shirt and an old pair of faded jeans. I could see the hard points of his nipples. His eyes were dark liquid pools that could easily discern my desire.

We both understood one another.

We walked up the road together. The streets were quiet. We didn't have much to say. I slid my arm around his waist and drew him to me as we walked. The ass of his jeans was faded and worn. I could feel the heat of his buttocks through the thin fiber. He was not wearing underwear. Neither was I.

The night was young yet. We went to a nightclub. It was packed. We fought our way through the crowd and began to dance. We were crushed close together. We inhaled from a bottle of poppers and submitted to the heat. My blood pounded in my ears. The crotch of Jimmy's jeans was as worn as the ass, and I could discern every curve and contour of his cock through the faded denim. He rubbed up against me, grinding his hard dick against my own.

We could not talk above the music. We communicated through touch. We bumped and ground our two bodies, driven together by the frantic beats. Someone behind me tried to grab my ass, but I ignored him. My clothes were clinging to my body like a damp rag.

Jimmy moved closer. His mouth was open, and he pressed his lips to mine. He slipped his tongue into my mouth, and we shared saliva. His arms were around my shoulders. I unbuttoned the fly of his jeans and slipped my hands down the back. I cupped his ass; I dug in and lifted and crushed the hard flesh. He moved his hips in short circles between my cock and my hands. The front of his jeans was damp with precome.

I worked a finger into the crack of his ass and stuck it up his hole. There was no resistance to my intrusion. He kissed me with increased fervor, slipping his tongue into the recesses of my mouth. He dug his fingers into my hair, holding my face close.

I could smell the sex that was brewing between us. Very soon I would be replacing the fingers up his ass with my aching cock.

Jimmy's jeans were hanging down the back of his thighs, and his ass was exposed for anyone to see. I shoved my hand deep and lifted his body toward me. I pressed my lips to his ear. I kissed the generous lobe before sucking it into my mouth. He squirmed. I shoved my tongue into his ear, and he let out a gasp that could be heard well above the music.

"Let's find a corner," I said.

I hitched the seat of his jeans back up over his bare ass. He did not fasten the buttons but let them hang loose. As we shoved through the crowd, hands reached out toward us. Someone grabbed my tit; someone else found the throbbing bulge in my crotch. I shook them both aside.

We found a couch in a corner of the club. Jimmy lay down on the black upholstery. He lifted his ass and shrugged his jeans down his thighs. I lifted his legs one at a time and removed his shoes and jeans. I knelt on the floor between his thighs.

His cock was lying hard against his stomach. He had leaked a damp pool of precome onto his T-shirt. I started with his balls and a soft trail of kisses. His scrotum tightened and rolled lazily beneath my lips. His flesh was smooth, natural rather than shaven. The skin of his balls was two shades darker than the rest of his body. I licked up the seam of his sac, and the heavy nuts hung down on both sides of my tongue.

His body moved beneath me, and when the tip of my tongue slid up from his balls to the root of his cock, the throbbing organ jerked at my moist touch. I looked up to his face, and my eyes met his penetrating gaze.

"Do it," he mouthed.

I opened my mouth and closed my lips over his fleshy knob. His cock was swollen to the condition of a rock; there was not a centimeter of give in the tight skin. A beautiful clear pearl leaked from the tip of his purple jewel and mixed with my saliva. He lifted his ass from the couch and slipped his dick further into my mouth. I've never been much good at deep throating, but I gave his cock my best effort. Saliva oozed from the vacuum of my lips and dripped down the shaft of his organ. I held his balls in my palm. They were loose and wet.

A crowd had begun to form around us. No one spoke; they just watched. It was my second captive audience that night.

The taste of salt was now strong on my tongue. He was leaking precome furiously. I sucked and licked and swallowed. My fingers were wet, I stuck a couple in his asshole. That did it for him. The cock tensed between my lips, and his most precious secretion flowed into me. His spunk was hot and strong; I allowed it to ooze slowly to the back of my throat before swallowing. His asshole tightened around my finger.

He remained hard. I removed my fingers from his ass and quickly took off my pants. I took a rubber out of my back pocket and then tossed my jeans into an untidy heap on the floor beside me.

Jimmy rolled over on the sofa. He got down on his knees and rested his arms over the back. I looked at his perfect ass. His buttocks were firm and round, the texture of his flesh creamy and smooth. As he leaned forward, the crack parted, and I saw the small dusty brown hole. It was a flawless ass.

I had trouble getting the rubber down over my cock. My head was swollen like a huge bloated apricot, and my fingers were inefficient with haste. At last I fitted it securely. I tore open a sample of K-Y jelly and smeared the lubricant over myself. My cock trembled and pulsated at the slick caress of my fingers.

I planted a hand on the cheek of Jimmy's ass and spread him wide. He pressed back toward me, his asshole bulging like a hungry mouth. I spread the jelly over his hole and shoved a couple of fingers up inside him. He was hot and sticky; the strong muscle gripped my fingers. I pushed slowly in and out, fucking him with my hand. He grunted and moaned and pushed his ass back at me every time I withdrew.

I removed my fingers and stood up. I held my cock poised over his prone figure. I put it inside him. We sighed together, and I slipped into place. I felt the tight, powerful passage of his ass along every trembling inch of my cock. Someone behind me cheered. I started to fuck. His ass was relaxed, and I could slide back and forth without fearing I would hurt him. I held him by the waist, holding his perfect ass still while I controlled every movement. I was wholly aware of every sensation; my balls pressed against his underside as I buried myself in him.

The crowd around us was moving in closer. Someone came up behind me and put his arms around my chest. He unbuttoned my shirt and tossed it onto the floor beside my jeans.

"It's spoiling my view of your ass," the man said as he stepped back.

I had a good range of motion. My cock slipped out of Jimmy's asshole until only the bulbous head remained inside him, then I shoved in until I felt his buttocks press hard against my pelvis. We fucked hard, incited by the driving rhythm of the music and its erratic beat.

I shoved Jimmy's T-shirt up to his shoulders, exposing the graceful curve of his spine. I slid a hand beneath him and located an engorged nipple. I twisted the large nub between thumb and forefinger. Jimmy jerked his ass in a rapid reaction to the sensation. He arched his back and thrust his hips into me with increased vigor.

The sensations of my cock were exquisite. Every morsel of flesh throbbed as I sheathed myself in his ass. My hips were jerking frantically. My eyes were beginning to sting with the sweat of my exertion. A man stepped forward out of the crowd. He held an open bottle of poppers beneath my nose. I inhaled. In one rapid instant my pleasure was increased a hundredfold. My head and cock felt fit to burst. The man offered the bottle to Jimmy, and I fucked him even harder as he inhaled the potent fumes.

My stomach muscles clenched in excitement, and I came in spasms. My knees began to buckle beneath me, and my entire body went into rapture. I filled him with the aching length of my cock and allowed the hot milk to flow. A deep cry of satisfaction tore from my throat. I ejaculated one long, intense spurt after another. I leaned on Jimmy for support as my seed and my orgasm ebbed from me to him.

I removed my cock and sat down naked on the couch beside him. The leather stuck to my clammy ass. It felt good. I saw the faces of those who had gathered to watch. There were about 30 people standing there, and at least half of them held their cocks in their hands. My chest rose and fell as I took deep, rapid breaths.

I removed the rubber from my cock. Come dribbled from the sheath and spilled over the head of my dick. Although it had already begun to loose its color, the temperature of my come remained hot.

A man stepped forward from the crowd. He was blond and broad-shouldered, about 27 or 28. He got down on his knees in front of me and began to lick up the spunk from my cock. I remained hard.

Others began to move in fast. A young guy, dark, in his early 20s, already had a condom in place. His jeans were open; his hard cock and balls were framed by the parted flaps of denim. He stepped up behind Jimmy and slipped it to him, taking up my place in his ass.

The blond was devouring every drop of dying sperm; he held my pink shaft at the root and licked me clean. He opened his mouth wide over my head and sucked up the last pearls of come that continued to linger in my slit. My desire had not been satiated by the orgasm. The blond kept me turned on, I was horny and wanted more. I eased his head up from my cock.

"Take my ass," I told him.

He smiled, a hot smile, a voluptuous smile. I raised my knees up to my chest and lifted my splayed ass to the edge of the sofa. Now everybody could see what I had. My body held no more secrets from these strangers. Several men stepped closer. A couple made contact with my eyes, but most kept their gaze focused on my asshole. They stroked their hard cocks at different rates. As I watched, one of the guys let loose his load; it spurted from his circumcised cock head in long thin ropes. When he was done he shook his organ, displacing a lingering glob of come from the head. It fell to the floor. He did not put his dick away when he was done; he just left it there, hanging loose as he began to soften. He continued to watch me.

The blond pressed his mouth to my musky asshole. He gently kissed the smooth pucker. I felt his tongue slip inside me. My ass opened to take him. The sensation was wet and languid, tickling my sensitive flesh. I pulled my knees up higher and thrust more of my ass into his face. He held my hips and brought my ass to his mouth, eating me like a fruit.

Through half-lidded eyes I gazed at Jimmy. He was on his hands and knees just off to the side of me. His face was glazed with a veil of perspiration. His lips were parted, and he let out a series of gentle sighs. The dark boy was plowing hard into his ass; he was keen and enthusiastic. He came within a few minutes. Another man, this one older, was ready to take his place. As the boy removed his cock from Jimmy's ass, the man stuck his own, larger organ inside.

The blond had finished eating my ass. He stood up and unfastened his shirt and trousers. He had a long pink cock that he covered in a clear-skinned condom. He smiled as he wedged the tip of his dick into my muscle. I opened my arms, and he lay down on top of me. He had a fine dusting of dark blond hair across his chest. His nipples were hard and raw; they rubbed deliciously against my own as he began to jerk into me.

I tightened my ass around his long, pulsating shaft, massaging and gripping him. I encircled my arms around his back and held him tight, excited by the manly smell of him. He held me by the waist and lifted my ass up to his dick. I humped his cock hard and fast.

I felt his knees go limp for a second and his body tremble as he came. His cock jerked with the unburdening of his load. He climbed off me, and another man took his place. One after another they came. The faces became indistinct. I swung my body around so that my face lay under Jimmy's groin. As another man began to mount my ass, I took Jimmy's cock in my mouth and sucked him.

From my position beneath him I had a magnificent view of his splayed ass and the huge dick the was hammering into him. A massive pair of low-hanging balls slapped against his underside. Jimmy's cock tasted stronger than before. It wept a continuous flow of precome as he took a pounding from behind. I withdrew him from my mouth as I felt his organ tense. He sprayed my face and hair with a gargantuan load of strong-smelling come. I licked a gob from my top lip.

Strong hands took hold of my body and lifted me out from under Jimmy. The man who held me was enormous. He had already stripped naked and was sporting the biggest erection I had ever seen. He sat me up on the edge of the couch and began to kiss the come from my face. He worked his tongue in long, lazy circles around my eyes and nose, devouring every last glob of Jimmy's seed. I could smell the beer and come on his breath. I ran my hands through thick black hair.

I touched his body. He had huge, hard tits, dusted with a coarse layer of dark hair. His low-hung pecs were the size of dinner plates, and his nipples were at least two inches in diameter. I rolled the two hard stubs between my thumb and forefinger, pulling and teasing. I longed to have them in my mouth, to swirl my tongue around their throbbing points and hear him gasp.

When my face was clean of come, he lifted me up and turned me around so that I was face down on the hot leather surface of the couch; I inhaled sweat and sex. He shoved his fingers up my ass. I was loose and relaxed. His fingers were almost as big as some of the cocks that I had taken that night, but when he stuck his dick into me I immediately knew the difference. My loose, fuck-worn ass expanded further to accommodate the Goliath.

I was grateful to the kid who held a bottle of poppers beneath my nose; I inhaled the fumes and suddenly my ass had no problem taking in the monster cock. He leaned all the way up into my bowel; I experienced the pleasure and pain of a virgin asshole staked for the very first time. The hands around my waist were like shovels, and they held me rooted to his shaft.

He pulled his cock back. He pushed it forward.

I raised my head and looked toward Jimmy. The men had finished fucking him. His face was scarlet, and his whole body dripped with hard-earned sweat. He crawled across the couch and knelt before me. He smiled and kissed me softly on the lips. I opened my mouth, and the kiss deepened. He tasted of salt, sweat, and come.

My legs where shaking. The giant was pounding my ass with the kind of force only reserved for complete strangers. I pushed onto him, wanting all of him. Fucking him, fucking me. I gripped his cock, refusing to surrender him. Without touching my dick I felt the beginning of an orgasm. I held it back, but the effort was more than I was fit to sustain. If the man had not been holding tight onto my ass, I would have fallen over flat onto my face

I shot onto the black leather in long, white ropy spurts. I seemed to spout a gallon of my globby seed. I collapsed forward into Jimmy's arms, my heart thundering in my chest. I felt the man pull his cock out of my ass. He took off his condom and blew his come all over my back, managing to squirt it everywhere from my ass to my hair. I could feel the warmth raining down on me. He wiped his dick off on my bare ass.

About an hour or so later, I went with Jimmy to a café; it was time to feed a different kind of hunger. It was quiet, and we took a table in the window. Our clothes hung like damp rags on our tired bodies. The waitress came over, and we ordered coffee. We faced each other across the table.

Jimmy rested his hand on my knee and smiled. His face was burning as red as my asshole felt.

"So what happens next?" he asked softly.

I shrugged. "I'm tired. I have a show tomorrow. I need some rest. Do you want to come home with me?"

He squeezed my knee beneath the table. "Sure."

Just a Matter of Time
Jordan Baker

The office was dark, its gloom softened by slit rays of blue neon streaming through venetian blinds. By leaning forward a bit, Jimmy could barely see the object of his quest through the irregular space between "Robert Madigan" and "Private Investigator" on the glass door.

Madigan was near the window, slouched deep in an oversized wingback chair, with a pale amber glass and a near-empty bottle of Cutty Sark at his elbow. That was a bad sign. Madigan had a tendency to be a mean drunk. It was, unfortunately, one of his more endearing qualities.

Easing the knob clockwise, Jimmy managed to open the door with only a faint click to give away his presence. His sneakers—pale blue Keds of all things—allowed him to move silently across the threadbare carpet. Holding his breath, he crept closer to Madigan, his eyes resting lightly on the nape of the detective's neck.

Another step, then one more, he was within arm's reach now as he bounced the last step forward and shouted, "Boo."

"Hiya, Jimmy," Madigan said, without taking his eyes from the window. "If you weren't such a harmless fuck, that would have been a very stupid thing to do."

"What gave me away?" the younger man asked.

"You walk like a harmless man trying to be quiet and lethal," Madigan explained. "Problem is, a lethal man would have shot me from the door. No pro would've wasted that much time creeping across the room."

"You learn something new every day," Jimmy chuckled, letting his hands fall on Madigan's shoulders. Kneading the corded muscles, he sighed, "I take it things aren't going well."

"Not really," Madigan replied, his voice dead with boredom and hopelessness. "They killed Carl this morning…blew him up in his car. I suppose I'll be next. I was just going to wait here until the Grim Reaper arrived."

That was about as bad as it could get, Jimmy agreed, pressing his thumbs hard against the nape of his friend's neck and working the surrounding muscles with his fingers. Carl had only been a part-timer. If Tedesco's people had killed him, nobody was safe.

"Now what?"

Jimmy felt the older man's shoulders shrug beneath his hands. "You go home and I'll wait. I'm not in the mood for social intercourse."

"Who said anything about being social?" Jimmy grinned, pausing to press a pair of switches on his watch. "Besides, I only want five minutes of your time."

"Ummm…," Madigan sighed, allowing his head to fall back against the chair. Jimmy dragged his nails along the detective's scalp, admiring the slight change the neon rays caused in his short, sandy hair.

"Have you ever thought about how much time five minutes is?" Jimmy continued as he moved his palms inside the other man's shirt, smoothing his chest hair. "So much can change."

Robert felt himself becoming hard as Jimmy's manicured nails found his nipples and began tracing circles around them, twirling chest hair gently around his fingertips and then absentmindedly releasing it. "In five minutes?" he asked.

Leaning forward, Jimmy continued sliding his palms over the detective's torso, enjoying the feel of the hard, flat belly beneath his hands. Brushing Robert's ear with his lips, he breathed, "Uh-huh, you'd be amazed."

The detective arched his back, rising to meet his friend's lips. They sucked hungrily at each other's tongues as the younger man's fingers slipped inside the waistband of Madigan's slacks. A low moan escaped Madigan's throat as his lover's touch grazed the head of his swelling cock.

Madigan unconsciously raised his hips, thrusting his cock to meet Jimmy's hand. He could feel the younger man's palm flatten against his belly as Jimmy stretched his fingers. Madigan sighed contentedly as the second joint of Jimmy's fingers slid over the slit of his cock. His partner fell into a gentle, rhythmic pattern, rocking the heel of his palm against Madigan's pelvis, then drawing his fingers upward, cradling the top third of his cock as he squeezed.

"Maddening, isn't it?" Jimmy asked, his breath warm in Madigan's ear. Stretching his fingers again, he drew their tips along the underside of

Madigan's shaft as he whispered, "You feel like that orgasm is just...right...there...just beyond your reach."

A shiver ran through the detective's body as Jimmy's teeth closed softly over his earlobe, just as his fingertips found the sensitive ridge of the head. Straining, the detective arched his hips higher, trying in vain to slip more of his cock into the young man's hand.

"I wonder how long it's been?" Jimmy whispered, his tongue flicking against the detective's ear. "How close are we to being through? Thinking about that clock ticking down must be genuinely frustrating for you right now."

Shoving the chair back, Madigan lurched to his feet and turned to face Jimmy, pulling him close. Embracing, the two men ground their pelvises together, reveling in the pressure as tension mounted and heat grew between them...until the alarm sounded on Jimmy's watch.

"Sorry," Jimmy said, stepping away, "your time is up. Gotta admit, though, there was a huge improvement in your attitude in just five minutes."

Growling, Madigan pushed the younger man down into the chair. "Then let's see what changes in the next five minutes."

Flattening his palm against Jimmy's hard-on, Madigan massaged it through the heavy denim of his jeans. The pressure and the rough fabric sent shock waves of arousal into the pit of the younger man's stomach and he gasped with pleasure.

"I said your time's up," Jimmy laughed, pushing at Madigan's hands.

Grasping Jimmy's hands and pinning them to the arms of the chair, Robert looked deep into the green of the younger man's eyes and said, "But your turn's just beginning." Dropping his head, he bit the other man's cock through his jeans, roughly sawing back and forth along its length with his teeth.

"Fuck," Jimmy sighed, his body convulsing from the unexpected assault. "Give me a minute here."

"You've got less than five left, pal," Madigan growled. "See how it works?"

The pressure from Madigan's jaw was incredible, Jimmy thought. Without the denim to act as a buffer, he'd be raw from such treatment. But with the denim, he could feel the heat, the force of his partner's passion massaging the length of his dick. Realizing that the growing heat he felt against his cock came from Madigan's tongue, separated from his flesh by only a sixteenth of an inch of cotton, was almost enough to push him over the edge. Jimmy could feel the semen building up, its heat rising from his balls and journeying along the path to eruption.

Then Madigan pulled away, rocking back on his heels and grinning at the blond.

"I want to taste you," he said simply.

Fumbling with the button-fly, Jimmy worked to get his jeans undone as Robert fished a condom from his jacket and ripped the corner with his teeth. Jimmy almost came as cool latex unfurled along the length of his cock. Flashing a grin, Madigan said, "Wonder how much time you've got left?"

Then he dipped his head, taking most of Jimmy's nine inches into his mouth and working it with feverish intensity. Taking the young man as deeply as he could, Madigan pressed his tongue hard against the underside of his partner's cock and held it for what seemed an eternity before pulling back almost to the head and swirling his tongue around it. Then, he darted back down again.

Jimmy's hips began to buck as he drove his cock deeper and deeper into Madigan's mouth, probing for the back of his throat. A gasp escaped his lips when Madigan slid a hand under his ass, lightly tickling his balls. The sensation of Madigan's nails scraping the path below his testicles and upward between them to the base of his cock drove Jimmy crazy, and he found himself unable to hold back the rising tide of his orgasm.

Convulsing, he pumped his load into the condom, filling it with a seemingly endless flow of jism as Madigan took him deeper, clamping down hard with his mouth and tongue and holding Jimmy's erupting cock within his throat.

Jimmy was still lost in the flow of the orgasm when the alarm went off.

"Son of a bitch," he swore in mock anger as Robert rocked back on his heels, completely releasing his death grip on the younger man's prick. Standing, Madigan smiled, his crotch level with the young man's face.

"I guess we're finished," he grinned. "Unless you have some ideas on what to do with the next five minutes."

Quickly removing his own condom, Jimmy flicked it into the trash can with practiced ease, snapping the rubber like a slingshot.

Madigan was still fishing in his pocket for another condom when Jimmy ripped Madigan's slacks open, drawing the zipper down with his teeth as his hands fumbled with the detective's belt. Jimmy's face was soon nuzzled between Madigan's thighs, his tongue licking the underside of the guy's balls with long, sure strokes as his hands caressed the older man's ass. There was a definite sense of urgency in Madigan's touch as he tapped the condom wrapper against his partner's shoulder.

Grinning, Jimmy met his gaze. "In a hurry, huh? I thought you P.I. types were supposed to be slow and methodical."

Quickly, Jimmy rolled the rubber down the considerable length of Madigan's cock, pumping it a couple of times with his fist before enveloping the head of the detective's dick with his mouth. Madigan could feel Jimmy's mouth working as the boy tongued the condom in an effort to build up saliva. In the meantime, Jimmy shoved his jeans down below his hips.

"Now who's in a hurry?" Madigan chuckled as Jimmy stood, turning his back to the older man. Wrapping his arms around him, Madigan pulled Jimmy hard against him, enjoying the feel of his hard-on rubbing against the other man's ass. He began dry humping his dick along his partner's crack as he whispered in the boy's ear, "I believe I could finish like this."

"The hell you can," Jimmy swore, twisting his head back to meet the detective's lips with his own. "There's only one way this game is going to end, and we both know what that is."

Chuckling again, Madigan placed his hands on Jimmy's shoulders and pressed him firmly into a bending position. Sucking his own thumb momentarily, Madigan admired his partner's long, tapered waist and the firm curve of his ass before moving forward.

The detective stroked his spit-moistened thumb over the puckered star of his boy's asshole before slipping inside. Jimmy gasped and shook his head violently.

"Stop screwing around, Madigan," he groaned. "You know what you're supposed to be doing."

At those words, Madigan began rubbing his cock against the man's fuck-hole. Still damp from the combination of Jimmy's saliva and the condom's own mint-flavored lube, the head began to make progress through Jimmy's opening.

"Yessssss," Jimmy hissed.

Madigan hesitated slightly as he met with resistance. Then, slowly, inexorably, he increased the pressure, allowing the head of his cock to open the other man's ass. He could feel that last moment of resistance when it seemed almost as if his own cock would be driven back inside him, then he was through, caressed with that blissful emptiness that announced penetration even as Jimmy cried out in pleasure.

With that, Madigan began thrusting slowly, gently, taking his time as Jimmy got used to the feel, then gradually building in both tempo and force until he was pounding his pelvis against Jimmy's rear end, reveling in both the physical pleasure of the sex and the emotional joy of hearing his friend cry out in ecstasy as their lovemaking continued.

Madigan could feel the heat rising in his balls and knew he was close to coming when the younger man's alarm went off again.

"Don't you fucking dare," Jimmy hissed over his shoulder as Madigan hesitated.

"But, Jimmy," he joked. "It's your own rule. And without rules, we'd have anarchy."

Whether he chose to ignore Madigan or simply didn't here him, Jimmy began increasing the tempo of his own thrusts. The sudden burst of extra enthusiasm caught Madigan off guard, and he began coming, pumping spurt after spurt of semen into the condom as Jimmy collapsed across the desk.

His passion spent, Madigan fell back into his chair, the condom still wrapped around his rapidly deflating penis.

"Now what?" he asked, while struggling to catch his breath.

"How about I just shoot both you cocksuckers?" a new voice suggested.

Stiffening, both men turned to face the door as an armed man stepped from the shadows. His amusement was obvious, but the 9mm Glock pointing in their direction was deadly serious.

"I never figured you for it, Madigan," the gunman said. "Don't worry, though. It'll be our little secret."

"Damn. And I've worked so hard to build up my reputation as a tough, hard-boiled private eye," Madigan chuckled. "I take it you're not here to offer your condolences for Carl's untimely demise."

"If it's any consolation, he died well," the gunman shrugged. "I'll have to ask you to hand over any files you might have on my employer before I kill you."

"I'm afraid that's not going to be possible. We don't have enough time left."

"Take all the time you need," the gunman said, making himself comfortable on the edge of the desk. "I'm not in a hurry."

"But I am," Madigan smiled. "This is cutting into my time, and I only had five minutes to begin with."

"Huh?"

Stepping away from the desk, Jimmy explained, "It's a game. We were experimenting with how much difference five minutes can make in a man's life."

"Stop moving," the gunman snarled as Madigan took a step in the opposite direction. "There's no point in trying to flank me. I can see from here your friend isn't carrying a gun, Madigan. So don't try anything cute. I'm not about to let either one of you get within arm's length of me."

"Fine," Madigan answered. "I'll give you my gun right now."

Gingerly, he reached inside his coat and began freeing his Browning from its holster. Clicking the release, Madigan allowed the clip to fall harmlessly to the floor.

"See," he said, "I'm cooperating 100 percent. Now just do me one favor. I really don't want to die with my pants down. And I especially don't want the police photos to show me wearing a used condom. Let me get cleaned up before you kill me."

"Yeah, I guess that's a fair request, Madigan," the gunman replied. "You've always played square with me. I guess it's the least I can do."

Madigan began to reach for the condom when the gunman waived the pistol and snarled.

"Not so fast, Madigan. Let the kid take the condom off. There's less chance of you doing something clever that way."

"I'm not a kid," Jimmy snapped. "I'm 24 years old."

"Caught with his pants down and his dick leaking and he wants to argue about nicknames," the gunman said. "He's got balls. I'll give him that."

"Yeah," Madigan grinned. "That's what first drew me to him."

The younger man was gritting his teeth with frustration as Madigan and the gunman continued their discussion. "Hello," he said. "Remember me? I'm another person in the room."

"Oh, yeah," the gunman replied, motioning with his gun. "I remember you, kid. Now get the condom off your buddy."

Grumbling under his breath, Jimmy crossed the room and squatted in front of his partner.

"This really bites," he said.

"Don't sweat it, kid," Madigan said loudly, adding under his breath. "It's just a matter of time until we get a break."

Snapping his head up, Jimmy caught Madigan's eyes and realized the detective was amused. Madigan then allowed his glance to fall lightly on the condom before looking back toward the gunman.

With a grin, Jimmy caught on to the plan.

"When?" he mouthed.

In answer, Madigan glanced at his wristwatch.

"Well, I guess it's just a matter of time now," he said to the gunman. "Do you want to tell me why Tedesco ordered you to kill me and Carl?"

"I don't get paid to answer questions," the gunman said. "Or to ask them. Tedesco says kill you guys, I kill you guys. Period."

By this time, Jimmy had removed the condom and was crossing the room to the wastepaper basket as Madigan again moved a step in the opposite direction.

"Hey, I said don't spread out," the gunman barked at Madigan.

It was at that moment that Jimmy's watch alarm sounded again.

"What the...," the gunman said, shifting his gaze to Jimmy.

Things happened in a blur after that. With a practiced flick, Jimmy fired the condom across the room at the gunman's face. Howling in outrage, he backpedaled away from it...just in time to have the empty gun Madigan had thrown glance off his temple. His feet became tangled in the chair he'd backed into and he went down like a ton of bricks.

Madigan was on him before he could regain his composure and the gunman suddenly found himself tied to the chair with his own belt.

"You cost me my whole turn, you freaking weasel," Madigan snarled. "Now where were we?"

"Are you insane?" Jimmy blurted. "What about him?"

"I'll call the police in a few minutes and they'll come pick him up," Madigan said, as he fumbled with the mechanism on a wall mirror. "Then we'll give them a highly edited version of this videotape and they can go pick up Mr. Tedesco."

"You were taping us?" Jimmy said incredulously.

"Well, I was expecting him to try to kill me," Madigan grinned. "You trying to fuck me to death first was just a bonus track."

"You are insane," Jimmy repeated as Madigan slipped to his knees in front of him and pulled his jeans open again. "This is completely unacceptable."

"Just go with it," Robert said, teasing his cock back to life. "This'll only take a few minutes."

Crossing Thresholds
Alexander Welch

Chad drove his MG through the night as the wind and hard rain performed a steady dance on the windshield. The wipers were working, but the blades were in such poor condition that he considered simply turning them off. Keeping his senses tuned to the repetitive thump of the road markers, he focused his eyes on the taillights of the 18-wheeler he had followed for the last 50 miles or so. They served as a beacon of hope as he literally felt his way along the interstate.

He hadn't slept in 17 hours and had originally planned not to stop until he reached Charleston. The road began to bend and blur in his mind and eyes. Charleston was still several hours away. Would he be able to stay awake for a drive straight through? He thought not, bid the 18-wheeler a fond goodbye, and pulled into the exit lane for the oncoming rest area.

It was 3:20 A.M. The parking lot was deserted except for a Winnebago, a pickup truck with stickers that screamed redneck, and a bright yellow Z-28 Camaro.

Chad pulled in at the end the lot, just past the coffee and soda machines. The streetlight cast a soft shadow that would make it comfortable to sleep, yet left enough dim light to see by. He crawled out of the car, stretched, and headed toward the rest room.

Chad's nose quickly adapted to the mild odor of male urine floating just above that of ammonia-laced cleaning solution. Surprisingly, it was well lit, but otherwise it looked like a million other roadside rest rooms: cigarette butts floating in the toilet, piss trails on the lowered semicircle commodes, and a hollowed-out glory hole on the left stall, next to the only urinal in the room.

Chad bent slightly and looked down at the stall next to the urinal. True to form, a pair of loafers showed beneath the stall wall.

Chad had been on his own in many ways since the age of 16. He was thoroughly aware of many things in life, but hadn't been exposed to very much. He was straight, lived a rather conservative life, and seldom ventured far outside his general routine. With a 6-foot-2 swimmer-kickboxer's build, emerald-green eyes, and short-cropped blond hair, he never wanted for female companionship—a good thing, since Chad was constantly horny.

He headed for the other stall but discovered the toilet was not working and filled with all types of crap and paper debris. With slight caution but no real concern, he headed to the urinal and prepared to relieve himself.

Chad was not aware of the politically correct holding position when being viewed, so he simply placed his hands on his hips, allowing his cock to hang over the elastic waistband of his briefs. A heretofore unknown exhibitionist side of Chad began to emerge. He reached down and lowered the waistband farther, allowing the elastic to lift and rest behind his balls, leaving the sac to hang as well.

His admirer's feet began to tap their soles lightly against the cold floor. Chad assumed that this meant he was interested in what he saw. He leaned to the right, giving himself a better view of his inquisitive neighbor. He was amused and more curious than interested. The shoes were, as he suspected on first glance, Docksides, the original brand, and probably set the wearer back at least $95 to $100. The silver belt buckle that was hanging down was attached to what appeared to be genuine alligator. Was this a poor little rich boy slumming? Chad shifted his weight, exposing more of himself by standing back from the urinal. The stranger shifted his weight also and leaned closer to the hole, pressing his face snugly against the wall for the most advantageous view as Chad finished pissing and began shaking off the remaining droplets of urine.

Despite his intentions or awareness of what was actually taking place, Chad found himself enjoying this new ritual. Even as his hand began to fill with his own enlargement, his brain reminded him that he was straight and that there was a *guy* on the other side of the wall. Usually he would have finished his piss, murmured "faggot" or similar words, and gotten the hell out.

His admirer, noticing Chad's growth, shifted himself anxiously, lowering his head to the open hole and exposing his wet lips. They parted for his tongue to reach outside of them, trailing a layer of moisture around their exterior; not closing completely, they formed an entry point for pleasure. Chad went on automatic pilot as he turned toward the invitation with full erection and pressed himself through the hole, passing between the admirer's moist lips and down his waiting throat.

Chad seldom masturbated, and it had been a long time since his last sexual encounter, so the warm, moist mouth felt like heaven to his aching member. As he began to move his cock in and out of the willing orifice, he realized just how much he had missed mere human contact. He shifted his feet and his balance, getting into a smooth, rhythmic motion.

Chad let all thoughts and cares leave his mind and became totally absorbed in the soft sucking of the stranger, who seemed to ignite every sensitive inch of his cock. The room echoed with an occasional moan when Chad pushed himself hard against the dividing wall, shoving his belt buckle into his lower abdomen as his erection slid deeper into the throat that seemed to beg for more. The heat was intense, and the pressure building up in him was almost at the breaking point. The stranger must have sensed this also and closed his mouth, shielding the teeth with his lips, tightening his hold on Chad's cock while moving his tongue up and down the underside of the shaft and around the head.

Chad stepped up his motion, moving in and out of the hole, deeper with each thrust. The gentle moan he heard before was now turning into deep, guttural sounds as he slammed himself against the back of his receiver's mouth and down his throat. Chad admired the way he remained pressed against the hole, not backing off from the thrusting his face was enduring as it repeatedly received the protruding cock. He wondered what it would be like to bury his member up to the ball sac in the stranger's mouth, a *guy's mouth*, his brain reminded him. Just then he reached his limit. He thought he screamed deep down inside, but the sound escaped his lips and vibrated around the deserted rest room as his cock erupted on a downward stroke. The stranger held firm as Chad impaled him through the wall, burying himself deep within his throat. Chad couldn't move as he unloaded what felt like quarts of himself. The stranger met his force with the same level of intensity, massaging up and down the length of Chad's cock with his inner cheeks and tongue as he came.

As the flow ebbed and the onslaught subsided, the stranger lessened his suction grip and gently sucked the remaining juices. The action was soothing and comforting and caused Chad not to withdraw, even though he had nothing more to give. His rigid cock now simply hung, full and heavy, enjoying the aftermath attention.

The stranger did not encourage his departure. He seemed disappointed that the encounter was at an end and lingered, softly cleaning and soothing Chad's member as it receded to a withdrawn state. Chad slowly pulled himself from the hole. He leaned against the wall for a long moment. His entire body felt drained as he mentally prepared himself to go and find a comfortable way to curl up in his little car for a couple of sleep-filled hours. Then the door to the stall began to open.

Chad's first instinct was to dash out the door. This had been his first sexual experience with another guy, and he needed more time to evaluate how he really felt about it. The last thing he wanted was to be faced with a limp-wristed, swishy-hipped, lisping faggot who had taken his only remaining virginity. He wasn't blaming anyone, though, or going on a guilt trip; he had participated willingly and had a hell of a good time to boot. In fact, the mere fact that he had enjoyed himself so much was probably his only real concern. No girl had ever given him a blow job that was so good it made him scream. If nothing more, he thought, since he was basically trapped, he could at least be civil and say thank you, then get the hell out.

"Hi," Dalton opened. He realized the moment their eyes connected that this was a straight guy in shock. He brushed by him quickly, rinsed off his hands, and pulled down a couple of paper hand towels. "I'm Dalton," he continued; having dried his hands, he extended one to the stranger.

"Ah—" Chad hesitated, finally saying, "Hi, I'm Chad."

"Good to meet you, Chad," Dalton finished, returning a firm handshake.

Chad felt momentarily lost. Even though Dalton was probably in his late 20s compared to Chad's mid 30s, this guy could have been his dorm buddy, his science lab partner, or even his fraternity brother. He looked just like all the other jocks he played tennis and baseball with on weekends. Hell, he looked good enough to introduce to his sister. What the hell was he doing in a piss-smelling rest room giving blow jobs?

"Where're you headed?" Dalton ventured.

"Charleston."

"Well, it seems we've both got a couple of hours to go. I'm headed to James Island Park."

"Is that where you're from?" Chad inquired. For some reason he was comfortable conversing with this stranger—one who only moments ago, he reminded himself, was feasting on his cock.

"No. I'm from the Southwest, actually. I decided to get lost traveling around the country for a couple of weeks. You know," Dalton said, raising one eyebrow, "you really look tired. How long have you been driving?"

"Not long, really." Chad betrayed himself with a wide yawn before completing the sentence. "It's just that I've been up"—he glanced at his watch—"almost 18 hours. I spent eight of those finishing up a project at work before I left for vacation, so I'm burned out mentally as well as physically. I'm gonna die in my car for a couple of hours before I hit the road again." He turned and started walking slowly toward the door, totally unaware that he had slowed his movement to allow Dalton to depart with him.

Dalton was mesmerized by this stranger. Although Chad's intense green eyes were tired and bloodshot, they were also alive and alert. Dalton's original assumption that Chad was straight still seemed to be accurate. His comfortable conversation and relaxed eye contact made Dalton wonder if he had forgotten having had his cock sucked only moments ago, and damn well too, if he did say so himself. But now it seemed they were talking like two old friends chatting at a company picnic. Chad turned to leave and paused as if Dalton should naturally leave with him. Dalton had no quarrel with the implied gesture and quickly joined Chad on the porch.

"So what are you driving?"

Chad directed a simple smile at Dalton and pointed toward the MG under the soft light. The rain had stopped, and the car's emerald-green color shone under the streetlights.

"That's what you're going to sleep in?" Dalton realized how condescending his statement sounded, but only after it had departed his lips. He had immediately begun to formulate his apology when Chad broke into a deep, hearty laugh. He reached over with his right hand, placing it on Dalton's shoulder, and gave him a playful shove.

"Yes! You insensitive bastard," he responded. His road-tired face lit up like a Christmas tree with amusement. His dimples seemed to go right through his cheeks as his eyes took on the twinkle of a devilish 12-year-old. "And I suppose you're traveling in that big fucking condominium-size camper over there," he said, pointing to the large blue-and-white streamlined RV. Dalton saw the humor in Chad's face and decided he could give as good as he got.

"First of all, my parents were married—16 months before my oldest brother was born, I might add. So it is impossible for me to be a bastard; at least, impossible in the conventional definition of the word." He glanced over at Chad and saw the slightest hint of a smile forming, but he was on a roll and did not want to lose his train of thought. "Secondly, yes, I am in the, and I quote, 'fucking condominium-size' camper over there. If you watch your mouth and play your cards right, I just might let you stretch out on one of its full-size beds for the night rather than in your little 'speed racer' matchbox car." He ended his statement with a glare of friendly defiance that could not have been more perfectly timed. Chad became animated, and between bursts of laughter, he met Dalton's gaze with a grin of surrender.

"OK, you win that round," he conceded. "I throw in the towel." It amazed him how nice it felt to give in to Dalton. It was as if they were just meeting each other, playing the exploring games, teasing slightly without keeping score. These were games he played with girls, not guys. Something really weird was happening here, and he knew it, but it didn't stop him from following Dalton when he descended the porch steps and headed across the parking lot.

The camper was huge compared to most. It was comfortably cool outside, but Chad noticed the air conditioner was running. When questioned, Dalton explained that he enjoyed sleeping in colder temperatures with the covers pulled up—a habit that, Chad confessed, they shared. There was a well-stocked refrigerator and an equally well-stocked bar. The bathroom had a shower with an adjustable head. The dining table folded down to form a full-size bed with the two bench seats, and two full-size bunk beds were in the rear, with the lower one closer to queen-size. Following orders, Chad stepped out of his shoes and settled back on the bench seat while Dalton fixed him a drink.

"Hey, this is nice. What's in it?" Chad asked after taking the drink from Dalton and tasting its unique flavor.

"Vodka, orange juice, and peach schnapps, with just a touch of grenadine," Dalton beamed. "I'm glad you like it. I'm not too good at mixing drinks. Back in school, we had a guy in our fraternity who could make the most delicious drinks that would knock you on your ass in half an hour." Off the two went into detailed conversations, remembering fraternity drinking antics and dorm-room bar favorites.

In the middle of an hour of enjoyable conversation, Chad contentedly took another sip of his third drink, looked around the camper, and turned to Dalton. "Well, I have to tell you"—he looked up and flashed a low-beam version of his famous smile—"you sure know how to make a guy feel at home."

"Good," Dalton chimed in, "then there won't be a need for any discussion. You'll sleep here for a couple of hours instead of in your matchbox. Furthermore, you've been on the go for over a day, so you're also in need of a good hot shower. Get out of those clothes, wash up, and let's get a couple of hours sleep before the daylight hits us."

"Are you always this bossy?" Chad quizzed. The puzzled look on his face almost made Dalton hesitate, but only for a moment. He hadn't felt this good around anyone since Charlie, and with the lessons he had learned, he wasn't about to repeat his mistakes and roll over while another person walked out of his life. Not without a fight. Chad was too big to be intimidated and too intelligent to be hoodwinked, so he must be here because it was where he chose to be. Having given himself that sense of logic to hang on to, Dalton stood his ground.

"Yes, on issues where I know I'm right. We're both tired," he continued, "and it's obvious we sort of trust each other. Especially since we have already reached a sort of intimacy level. I have only been with one other man in my life, and—"

"Well, you were my first," Chad broke in.

"Really?" Dalton's look of amazement was obvious.

"Yes, really!" Chad repeated for emphasis. "I was a cherry boy before I met you."

Dalton hesitated for a moment, then broke into hysterical laughter, leaning over the table. Each time he seemed to compose himself and looked up at Chad, he would start up all over again. Despite his attempts to maintain a serious rapport, Chad found himself swept along with Dalton's antics, and soon the two of them were laughing until their sides hurt.

"Well, 'cherry boy,'" Dalton answered between giggles as he rose and went toward the door, "you get out of those jeans while I go and turn the backup generator on so you'll have plenty of hot water for the shower. It has a timer and will turn itself off automatically." With that said, he opened the door and disappeared, never considering the possibility that his directions would not be followed.

Chad sat somewhat dumbfounded. A short time ago he had pulled into a rest area for a couple of hours of rest. That's what rest areas are for, or so he thought. Some would say, in this day and age, that having his first gay sexual experience was not crossing a monumental threshold. But to sit, laugh, and enjoy the company of the guy who is currently carrying your sperm around in his stomach is not a normal threshold. At least, not a normal straight guy threshold. Was he too tired to comprehend what he was doing? That question seemed even more ridiculous for him to ask while he was sliding his jeans over his knees and pulling each leg free. The door of the camper reopened as his sweater was pulled halfway over his head. He just hoped it was Dalton returning and not a homicidal roadside murderer, since he now stood wearing only his socks and underwear. Second thoughts made him wonder if that was any safer.

The camper's shower proved to be more efficient than Chad had anticipated. The pressure was strong, and the water was hot. Better still, Dalton's supply of soap, shampoo, and conditioners was top of the line. Only when the water began to cool did Chad realize how long he had been inside. He turned off the flow, reached out the door, and grabbed the towel Dalton had left on the hook for him. He half-expected a comment from Dalton for staying under the water for so long, but not a word was heard. He finished drying off and reached out for his jeans on the back of the door to find they had been replaced by a pair of silk boxer shorts. He pulled them on. Perfect fit.

He stepped out of the bathroom into the main camper area to find the front end was completely darkened. Only the small glow of a night-light cast a shadow in the rear, so he headed toward it. The upper bunk had his clothes folded neatly on it, along with several sketch pads and what appeared to be art supplies. In the lower, queen-size bunk was Dalton. He was stretched out along the back of the bunk, leaving more than sufficient room for Chad to place all six feet of himself very comfortably.

Another threshold. Chad had never slept in a bed with another guy before. His sense of logic told him it was no different than when he had spent the night with a girl and not had sex. The air conditioner was definitely working well, and his still-damp body was beginning to take on a chill. Dalton seemed to be asleep, so Chad debated the issue only with himself. He could go and try to lower the dining-table bed, but he didn't have a blanket. And did it really matter? After all, this night wouldn't be a common topic of conversation. He didn't imagine he'd get to Charleston and say, "Hey, Max, how's it going? By the way, on the trip down I slept in a camper with a guy who gave me head in the rest room! So what's new with you?" No, he didn't imagine that was a possibility. "So what the hell am I afraid of?" He spoke to himself softly as he pulled back the covers and crawled into the bunk next to Dalton.

Had he been aware, Chad would have been surprised how quickly he fell into a deep sleep. Dalton also was somewhat surprised, but pleased nonetheless. He wasn't sure what he could have said to convince Chad to sleep with him instead of opting to sleep alone in one of the other bunks. So to avoid the confrontation, he chose to eliminate himself from the equation.

With his back to the room, it was hard to guess what was actually going on. For a moment he thought Chad might dress and leave. He had left his clothes folded in plain sight in case he chose to go. He hoped his mere lack of resistance would keep Chad from leaving. It appeared that this had worked, but a question remained in his mind: Did Chad crawl into his bed solely because he had no other options, or was he using the fact that no other option was convenient as an excuse to crawl into bed with him? It didn't really matter; he was there, and Dalton knew he would get no sleep at all. So he settled in a comfortable position and listened to Chad's deep, gentle breathing.

After a couple of hours, Chad fell into his usual sleep routine, established months ago while sharing his bed with Claudia. He rolled off his back onto his left side, draping his right arm across Claudia's midsection, drawing her body close to his. His hand, palm open, always rested flat against her stomach. His motion was as smooth and fluid as if rehearsed. Dalton did not move or offer any resistance. His composure was nearly shattered when Chad placed his lips gently against the back of his neck as he pulled him closer, fitting his ass snugly into Chad's silk-covered groin area. His breath felt warm against Dalton's neck and sent shivers down his back that caused his ass to twitch and tremble.

Traditionally, Dalton slept in the nude. Tonight was no exception. His ex-lover Charlie often would sneak over to Dalton's house and ease into his bedroom window. Once inside, he would strip, crawl gently into bed, and wake Dalton just before entering him. Many nights he had been pulled out of a deep sleep to discover Charlie's cock about to be wedged deep in his asshole, banging away. Dalton had taken to applying lubricant to himself just before going to bed to make the midnight intrusion go smoothly. Once again, tonight was no exception.

Chad felt comfortably at home in his state of slumber. The warm body next to his was, in his mind, of course, Claudia's. They had shared a bed for almost a year, sleeping each night in each other's arms. Claudia had an insatiable sexual appetite and often played with Chad's cock while he was asleep.

Dalton had no idea how to react to Chad's midnight actions. It was possible that Chad was still awake, even though Dalton had planned to let him get at least five hours of sleep before taking any action. Being cradled in Chad's arms was more than Dalton had dreamed of. Chad's muscular and hairy arm hung over Dalton, successfully pinning his own arm down to his side. With his butt firmly pressed against Chad's crotch, he could tell that his own cock was not the only one in the bunk that was growing in size. Chad was developing a hell of a hard-on. Maybe he wanted to explore some more but needed a little help to do so. Dalton slowly freed his pinned arm to reach around to Chad. Each movement or adjustment caused his ass to rub against Chad's crotch, and the effect was fast becoming more and more obvious, until Dalton could feel Chad's erection poking him in the lower back. The smooth fabric parted as gently as the waves, and Chad's cock escaped its silken cocoon. With an easy motion, Dalton gently pushed himself forward enough to slide his hand down between his ass and Chad's protruding cock. Hands trembling but steady on the mark, he guided the swollen cock to his eagerly inviting ass. His fingers gently stroked its massive size and coated the head and shaft with its own pre-come, oozing sticky and slick to the touch. As a surgeon gently guides a knife, Dalton placed the tip of Chad's slickened cock head over the entrance to his moist asshole and gently impaled himself on it. Inch by inch, his ass opened and swallowed Chad's cock. Dalton's warm inner walls enveloped the shaft and caressed it as it slid deeper and deeper inside him. Chad felt much larger than Dalton had anticipated, and he had to stop several times to control his breathing and himself. It felt as if the cock were extending itself up through his intestines into his stomach. It was then that Dalton's composure was shattered for the second time. Chad tightened his grip on Dalton's flat stomach and pulled him closer into his arms. Simultaneously, he flexed his hips and shoved the remaining third of his cock up into Dalton's unexpecting asshole. His shaft explored uncharted regions, until only his ball sac remained outside Dalton's ass canal.

Once Chad was nestled in comfortably with Claudia, or so he thought in his deep slumber, the old sexual reactions automatically kicked in. His first clue that he wasn't in Kansas anymore came from his sense of smell. Claudia wore a special perfume she had flown in from Paris. No other woman ever smelled like Claudia. It used to drive Chad crazy to smell it at night, but it was missing. The current scent was not unpleasant, but definitely not Claudia's. This conflict in his brain brought him further out of his peaceful yet aroused sleep state. He fully recognized where he was when Dalton gently lifted his arm. When the arm was raised and Chad felt no fleshy orbs of breast brushing against him, he realized what was happening. Obviously, in his sleep he had rolled over and cuddled his newly found bunkmate. Making matters even worse, he had awakened him with a raging hard-on stabbing him in the back. The proper thing to do, he decided, would be to just casually roll over to his other side. This would spare everyone's feelings. After all, he was asleep, or so assumed, and thus not accountable for his actions.

In the middle of his decision-making process, his bunkmate reached back and began to gently stroke his fingers over Chad's cock, spreading the sticky, smooth precome all over the head and shaft. To pull away now might be awkward, Chad rationalized. Besides, it felt great, and he felt himself getting harder as the massage continued. He closed his eyes and relaxed next to the warm body giving him so much pleasure.

Then it happened, and it took all that was in him to refrain from screaming. His cock was suddenly enveloped in a hot, wet canal whose walls seemed to come alive. He felt as if a form-fitting glove of warm water had been wrapped around his shaft as fingers along the tunnel caressed his cock head with just the right amount of pressure. He became lightheaded and was grateful he was lying down. He also became so sexually charged that he could not stand to remain motionless any longer. His right hand tightened flat against Dalton's stomach, and he pulled the tender body in closer to his. With the precision of a Swiss watch, he planted his feet against the bottom of the bunk and drove the rest of his cock forward, embedding it deep within his new buddy's ass. The idea that he was once again crossing a major threshold did not occur to him. An animalistic hunger had been awakened in him and taken over. He withdrew his cock three quarters of the way and returned it home with the artistry of a fencer thrusting with his sword. Each time he seemed to reach new depth. Chad rolled his weight forward and pinned Dalton beneath him on the bunk.

Once on his stomach, Chad, without speaking a word, placed his legs between Dalton's. Without withdrawing his cock in the slightest, he used his powerful legs to spread Dalton's the width of the bunk as he plowed his cock deep within his bowels. He leaned forward and began to nibble on Dalton's ears and kiss along the side of his face and neck, while sliding his rock-hard cock in and out of Dalton's ass with powerful strokes. At times he would slow his pace, withdraw his cock until only the head remained buried between Dalton's ass cheeks, then slowly slide the hard shaft up the canal, reaching underneath and lifting Dalton's ass to meet his strokes. Soon he quickened his pace and deepened his penetration.

As the point of no return neared, Chad reached under Dalton's arms with both hands and firmly gripped his shoulders, shoving Dalton farther into the corner while pulling himself farther up on and inside of him. Dalton's noises were no longer limited to occasional restrained murmurs. He could barely form words, but he made loud guttural sounds, pleading for Chad's continued fucking like a starving man begging for nourishment. The pleas spurred Chad to new heights. His passion seemed to take on a life of its own as he long-dicked the sweet round ass so eagerly offered to him. His hips moved in rhythm with the motion of his hard cock plowing up Dalton's ass; he felt such complete satisfaction that he couldn't have stopped if he wanted to, and he did not want to. Dalton was cornered, caught like a mouse in a trap, and getting the shit fucked out of him. Chad felt his cock become harder the more Dalton cooed and cheered him on. Dalton continued pushing his ass up to meet Chad's strokes, surrendering to the onslaught. Dalton screamed as he came without touching his own cock. Chad thought he would pop a nut over that alone. He tightened his grip on Dalton's shoulders and brought his hips higher up on Dalton's ass, allowing him to go in deeper. He placed his mouth next to Dalton's ear and whispered as his lips brushed over it, "I'm about to give you my load. Do you want it?"

Dalton was close to euphoric ecstasy. With Chad's big cock and energetic style of fucking, he was sure he had found Shangri-La. When Chad asked him if he wanted his load, he realized just how much he did not want the action to end.

"Do you want it?" Chad repeated, not missing a stroke as he intensified his action, shoving his cock in and out of Dalton's well-worn asshole.

"No," Dalton whispered through his tear-covered lips. "No, not yet. I don't want to stop yet."

Chad was surprised at the answer, but this had no effect on his physical need. He was on the brink of shooting his load into Dalton's tender ass, and nothing short of death was going to prevent that from happening.

"Sorry," Chad whispered. "You're so fucking hot, I can't hold back!" He shoved his face deep into the pillow beside Dalton's head as his hips buried his cock to the hilt up Dalton's ass. Dalton screamed as he felt the boiling-hot fluid flood his intestines. Chad screamed into the pillow with him, his body jerking violently as it emptied itself.

Afterward, Chad's body hung limp over Dalton's for what seemed like an eternity. Neither of them moved, long after their breathing had returned to normal and Chad's cock had receded, withdrawing itself from Dalton's ass. With no idea what to say, they lay silent until they surrendered to sleep, both drifting deep into slumber.

Chad awoke to the smell of bacon frying and the sound of soft jazz. It took him a few seconds to realize just where he was. It took half as much time to recall what he had done. He pulled the covers up over his head, hoping for a moment that they would magically transport him to the driver's seat of his little MG, where he would promptly engage the gears and then disappear. The more details that filled his memory, the more he was sure he did not want to acknowledge that he was awake and be forced to face his breakfast host. Unfortunately, the covers did not work magic, but the movement caught Dalton's eye.

"Good morning," he chimed before he actually made it to the back of the camper. He was radiant. One might say he had that "fresh-fucked glow." One might be right, but Chad wasn't ready to be the one to say it—or think it. *How can anyone be so damn cheerful in the morning?* Chad wondered. His attitude was making it harder for Chad to retain his aloofness and just slip out the door and away forever.

Dalton seemed to sense that Chad was having a difficult time dealing with all of this, so he reduced his sunniness to an acceptable level. He couldn't help feeling wonderful—sore, but wonderful.

"It's still early, but I know you must be hungry by now. I hope you're not a vegetarian. I cooked you a little breakfast to get started on. You've got a big day ahead of you, and we both have a couple of hours to drive yet. So get your lazy butt out of bed."

He made the last statement with the sunshine turned up just a little. Dalton didn't want Chad to have sufficient time to slip into the "regret" mode. Once he was there, guilt would catch up to him. At the risk of never seeing him again, Dalton knew he had to give Chad a wide berth and all the guilt-free space he could handle.

Chad was ready to get up, out, and on with his life. The fact that Dalton understood took a big weight off his shoulders, and besides, the bacon really did smell great.

Chad finished the breakfast of bacon, hash browns, eggs, and miniature pancakes as if he hadn't eaten for weeks. Surprisingly, he and Dalton talked about travel on the road, about work, about sports. Dalton heated up a couple of bakery-made blueberry muffins, and Chad sat through two cups of coffee finishing off his. Their conversation was excited and sometimes animated. Around them the rest area began to come alive, and Chad remembered that he was supposed to be on the road. Not ready to discuss either sexual episode, they had enjoyed the morning and successfully avoided bringing up the topic until Chad stood on the camper's steps, door open, saying his goodbye.

"Well," he began, "I suppose we probably won't see each other again, but thanks for your help." He started to add that he had had a good time, which was true, but decided that it might imply too much.

"You should never say never," was Dalton's only reply. Chad nodded his head, smiled and shut the camper door. He walked to his car with what appeared to be reluctant strides, but then, that could have just been Dalton's wishful thinking as he watched from the window. Realizing that, he turned away and started preparing for his own departure.

"Come on in," Max yelled from the deck. Chad pushed the screen door open and walked through the den to the back porch deck. "What the hell took you so fucking long? Wait, don't tell me! I bet you found yourself a nice piece of ass on the way here and stopped to do a little damage to it." Max slapped him on the shoulder and handed him a beer. "Mothers, lock up your daughters, Chad's on the prowl!"

Chad flashed his most convincing smile. "You must have a crystal fucking ball!" He hadn't expected Dalton's memory to occupy so much of his thinking for the last three hours. He was determined to take some immediate action before he began to actually miss him. His goal today was to get drunk with Max, watch lots of football, eat lots of food that wasn't good for him, and completely forget all the thresholds he had crossed in the last 24 hours.

"Hey, Max," Chad began, attempting to appear as casual as possible, "have you ever heard of James Island Park?"

"Yeah, sure," he answered, "it's just across the island connector from here, about 20 minutes away. Why, you thinking of doing a little camping out?"

"No reason, man," Chad slowly responded, reaching for his beer and sliding down comfortably into the La-Z-Boy. "Just asking."

Joe Pornstar
Alan Mills

A single white drop collects on the tip. I watch it, struggling to keep my eyelids from clamping shut. I concentrate, concentrate: Just hold back! And then, the sudden twitch of my pelvis, jizz rocketing upward in one long stream like Challenger '87, exploding mid-air, falling back to shower my stomach with seminal debris. I immediately think, this is exciting—me and this other guy, legs entwined, asses connected by a double-headed dildo, the sun on our naked skin, the two of us, on our backs, a couple of hot studs on a roof fourteen stories above Hollywood Boulevard.

I'd just delivered the come shot of my life. It was a perfect 10. I'd done everything right. Moved right. Tensed right. Groaned and moaned and swore right. Even my face gave a perfect expression at the moment of take off. I'm sure that I looked wracked and vulnerable, yet still totally a man, just like I'm supposed to. Now, it's up to the other guy. He strokes his cock quickly. It's smaller than mine. I lift my head and look at his face, saying with conviction, "Yeah, shoot that load, boy!"

"Oh yeah, oh yeah," he returns, his lashes shaking, his mouth gaping open. "Oh fuck, man, I'm gonna shoot my load, man." I know that rising in his pitch. "Oh fuck! Oh fuck!" It's happening. I grind my butt on the dildo, driving his end further up his ass.

"Yeah, shoot that load!"

He stops stroking, squeezes his cock with one hand, his nuts with the other. "Oh fuck!" He grunts, squeals, shakes all over, but nothing comes.

The shuddering stops, his body relaxes, and I just stare.

I stare, the cameras stare, the director can't take his next breath. I start to sit, eager to get the rubber out my ass. "Don't!" the director shouts. "Nobody moves until I get a come shot." He gestures to two cameramen.

"Take a break, but be ready."

"Carl—" I start.

"Joe, don't move."

"Oh God!"

"Joe, you were great. Now, just stay right there. It won't take long." Carl turns. "David...sweety..."

David's still panting. "I...I'm..." He's a cute kid, but I could kill him right now.

"Sssh... Honey, I need you to come for me."

David strokes his softening dick and opens his eyes. "I think I did come."

"Not really you didn't." I hear bitterness.

"I did, but...just...nothing came out."

"I know you have more in you. Take your time. We'll wait."

And that's that. David goes back to stroking his little prick. The camera guys back off. Carl goes to get a donut. The various stage hands and hangers-on pace nervously somewhere behind the lights. And, after having already been through eight hours of this crap, I'm stuck, flat on my back, while cold come drips down my sides even as a thick piece of unforgiving rubber cruelly rests about six inches up my worn-out gut. As far as I'm concerned, this is a pretty fucked up way to spend a Saturday, or don't you agree?

My life isn't always exactly as easy as many people imagine. Really, I don't ride in limousines that often, and I've only been taken to Europe a few times since becoming a star. Sure, that stuff's glamorous, and whenever I show up at a party or a club, it's a major event, but most of the time, through most of my days, my life gets fairly boring and is often almost unbearable.

I don't think I've ever stopped to ask myself why so many hustlers and adult video actors die young of drugs or AIDS or suicide. Now I think it's because dying young becomes the only thing left to do. At least, that way, the party never ends.

Carl was a porn star, too. Now, like other survivors, he directs and does almost too much crystal. Not quite too much. Just enough to be a major mess while still making lots of money. Of course, that's because he's one of the smart ones. But, he's one of the dumb ones too. It'll catch up with him, but for now, he's doing great. He owns his own company, distributes all over the country, and works overtime to promote his product in a rather noble attempt to rob more major porn studios of their spotlight. I have to say I admire that. I'd like to think that I could do the exact same thing, but I don't. Thoughts about aging annoy me too much. It's futile, but I enjoy fighting back.

There's too much in my life to worry about right now. Even as I lie here with a burning pink dildo snaking closer and closer to my heart, I worry about what my roommate's doing. I imagine going home to an empty apartment. Aaron's definitely gone unstable. But then, none of us age gracefully. It's to be expected We're all just too gay—us porn stars that is—even the straight ones. We are the quintessence of gay. For decades, we've defined sexuality despite ourselves. And aging just isn't part of that picture.

I don't have much to worry about. I'm still 24. I've been in the business for three years, and that's been enough to make me famous. I look great. I feel great. I could go on being fabulous for another five years, but that's not usually how things go. Even I know that.

It's too bad being in porn is such a taboo. This industry works so hard to create its own little world, with parties, awards, a tight tribe that works extra hard to make us feel OK. I wish it was acceptable to enter into a brief, lascivious career after high school, before going on to bigger but maybe not better things. It could be like the army. We could give scholarships and student loans. How cool would it have been if my guidance counselor saw my potential way back when?

Thinking about it now, I'd leave, if there was someplace else to go.

"How you doing, Joe?"
"Just fine."
I feel like the whole building is sitting up my ass. Carl must know this. Some questions just shouldn't be asked. I lift my head and look at David. His eyes are closed and he's stroking his tiny, half-hard dick with two fingers and his thumb.

I had a David of my own once. Years ago. We were really only supposed to be fucking around, but for me, it was something more. It blossomed the normal way: a few six packs, a Saturday night, David asking, "I wonder what getting head is like."
I'm all, "I don't know."
He's like, "Seth gets it all the time."

And so, after the appropriate amount of silence, David says, "You know, it's not a big deal. It's like sticking someone's finger in your mouth."

I stare at him like a camera. He's a jock. I feel the most intense friendship. I think of him as a buddy and often wonder why other guys don't care as much about their friends.

"I'd do it to you," he says, "if you did it for me."

"OK, Carl," says David, "I think I'm getting there."

Carl violently gestures to his cameras. Cameras, lighting, grips move into position. I close my eyes, the first dick of my life passing my lips, spreading musk across my tongue, all the way back.

I feel the dildo going deeper. David's squirming, shifting side to side, fighting to exhume his load, driving my end deeper, harder against my prostate.

I feel David coming, the dildo like a jackhammer, his hips bucking wildly, David coming down my throat, the bitter salt, me exploding a second time, a second big time, my sphincter feeling like it'll never close.

I don't usually just come when I'm working on videos, but the situation seems to demand it. Most of the time it's like acting. I force it to be something unnatural and shocking. That's why I get paid. It is, after all, called a money shot. More shot, more money. At least that's my way of thinking.

This second time, however, is a bit different. I do it with my eyes closed. I do it thinking of the past, not keeping my mind on the moment, on the holding back, the tensing and releasing on cue.

Looking down at the mess, I know I did good, but still, I feel a need to go home, Ohio. Back to Kent State. Back to David, if he's still there, not with Nancy, not hitched to her. That's naive. It's not how the world works. Carl throws me a towel and says, "Hey Joe, get cleaned up and I'll take you to dinner."

I know what he's doing. This means he's paying the stupid kid more, the flavor of the month, hot little bottom, blond hair, fresh face. The cameras have yet to satisfy their need.

I quickly decide to take Carl up on his offer. He'll offer fast times, I'll order calamari and swordfish, drink as much as I can, but not really eat. I'll make him pay the difference.

Of course, he invites David, gives David a bag—I try not to feel hurt.

It's all the kind of stuff you shouldn't take personally—drugs, sex, money. I set myself on "Don't care."

After a few drinks, I'm in the bathroom, filling a urinal with whiz. I'm fucked up in all sorts of ways, but not enough. I'm still connected to the world by a cord I want to cut, disgorging myself from the womb of reality, a crying fetus flinging myself into the great nothingness that has no sound.

See, better living through chemicals.

The door opens behind me, someone stepping into the small, brightly lit room. He moves next to me, about a foot back, to the toilet to my right. "Do you mind?" he asks softly.

"No," I say, "go ahead."

I hear the metal teeth gaping open, the metal clasp sliding down. I look over. He's a tall, broad, stud of a man. My chest tightens from the first sight of him, his fat, uncut cock still at the edge of my vision.

"Hey, you're—"

"Yeah," I say, zipping and walking to the door. I hear his piss fall, water collapsing into water, hormones rising inside hidden steam. I think of myself as a beast, sensing molecules in the breeze. I think of molecules moving, diffusing, forming compounds. It's indiscriminate, yet still makes sense.

I lock the door, a simple pushing of a tab. I move behind him, pressing close, taking his thick cock, his clean shaved sac cascading down my palm.

"You're fuckin' huge," I whisper as he continues to release.

"You too," he whispers back. "You're my favorite."

He's hard in my hand, so hard I just want to smack his cock against my face. "Don't mention it," I say, his piss trailing off. I squeeze the shaft, pump forward, shake, turn him around, his cock as the lead.

I descend to my knees, the smell of whiz still emanating from the bowl. I look right down his slit, piss still seeps from the end. I slap the meat against my cheek, rub it against my skin, feeling a light trickle drip down my neck.

I look up at him and lower his cock onto my tongue, the Eucharist. The bitter sting excites. I open my throat to it, submissive in the first moment, letting his cock enter me like the holy word. I suck on it, pull back until his foreskin is like gum between my teeth. I pump it in my fist, take one good look at its jaw-spreading size. I spit on it like it's life itself, spreading my spit across it with a fist. I spit again and notice, for the first time, a blazing tag along his fly reading Lucky You.

My mother still believes in signs. A tow truck or a bus. A street light flickering as she drives past. The stopping of a clock. I used to see them too, holding onto useless moments as if believing in preschool superstitions, the cracks in a sidewalk. But mother's signs were meaningless and inconsistent—omens undefined—and I tossed them all. But to this day, I think twice about a lot of things.

From my position on the tile floor, I look up at him. He grins. "I can't believe how hot this is," he says. "You look just like an angel."

I lower my mouth to his cock and cup my tongue under the head, lifting the weight with my chin. I lean forward, taking it all, the girth and length permeating my throat unnaturally. I feel plugged, shut up, picturing myself an angel, a cherub looking to Heaven, long lashes, pouty lips, cheeks overstuffed.

I lift myself up the expanse of his skin, letting my tongue enter the musky casing of his hard cock. I think I am a different kind of angel, a fallen angel at the feet of a fallen angel, a throne of corpses, me opening myself to tortures for sins for which I should permit forgiveness.

He grabs behind my neck and grips his nuts, his thumb hooked above his shaft. He fucks my face, not hard—steady—slow, deep. I moan around his flesh, spit dripping down my chin, drool rubbing all across my face.

"Oh God! Joe," he groans. "I always knew you'd be perfect."

And I think of him as alien, a divine figure who has watched me my whole life and is only now first meeting me. His love borders on obsession. I have always been his, but now, he has me.

Its pace increasing, his cock moves in time with hoarse breaths. I taste salt, like I'm swimming in the ocean. I think I'm a different kind of angel and I imagine myself painted by Caravaggio, light streaming down, the center of meaning not my serenity, but the lost passion on the forgiven man's face.

His cock escapes my throat. It is oblivion. I open to it, extending my tongue like in winter, catching snowflakes. Yes, it's all better living. His jizz strikes the roof of my mouth, behind my front teeth, falls on my taste buds, pours down my chin to the floor. My eyes closed, the vision taboo. All warmth. All chemicals. Jizz strikes my brow, slips through my lashes— I feel it clogging my nose.

I am without breath, without life, taken over by the seed of man's birth.

I lower my head, clasp my hands, and wipe spunk from off my face.

I stand. The emptied stud glances down at my crotch. "Aren't you?"

"No," I say. "I've got a shoot tomorrow, and I've already come three times today."

"Oh," he says. "I understand."

"Thanks, um, Joe," he says, flushing the toilet. I look in the mirror, water running, my hands cupping it, bringing purity to form. I'm still so high, I want to suck off someone else. If my ass weren't so sore, I'd get fucked, and fuck too. I'd go to sex clubs and fuck everything, the men, the holes between stalls. "When you come out, I'll get you a drink, OK?" he asks, stepping into the hall.

"That would be nice," I say, rubbing his come from my eyes.

David steps in. "Are you still in here? I just ran into—"

He stares at me, silenced. I look at myself, used, the impurity of flesh, drunk and fucked up. I look at myself, crying a soft chuckle, breathing in, needing to blow spunk from my nose. I look at myself, this total slut, this pathetic porn star, this unbelievable creature stolen from myth.

Second Chances
Grant Foster

I ducked into the men's room in the lobby to take a piss. I was supposed to use the employee can, but it was at the other end of the building, and I was too busy to make the pilgrimage. I hauled out my pecker and let fly in the urinal. As I was shaking the last drops off and tucking it back in, I heard a groan, then the distinctive sound of someone heaving. I looked up just as the stall door flew open and some poor bastard who'd spent too much time at the bar went down like a felled tree.

"Shit," I muttered, walking over to see what I could do to help. I had food coming up in the kitchen and drinks waiting at the bar, but I couldn't just ignore the man. I gripped his shoulder and rolled him over onto his back. It was Wade Talbot, former high school jock and stud-about-town, now playing the role of town drunk, dutiful husband, and lackey to his rich and powerful father-in-law, Randolph Madden.

"Hey, Billy." Wade opened his eyes. They were bloodshot and glassy. "I don't feel too good." He started gagging, and I hauled him back into the stall, holding his head as he puked his guts out. When he was done he passed out again. I cleaned him up and tried to revive him, but he was out of it. I carried him out of the toilet, dumped him on a couch in an empty conference room, loosened his tie, took off his shoes, and put a wastebasket beside him, just in case.

"Excuse me, Mr. Madden." Wade's father-in-law looked up at me and smiled vaguely. "It's Wade. He isn't feeling very well."

"He's dead drunk again," hissed Wade's blonde wife, Gloria. "Pardon me if I'm not surprised."

"For all I care, Wade can spend the night wallowing in his own vomit," Mr. Madden growled, rising from the table. "Give me the check, son. We're leaving." He paid, and the two of them left without Wade.

After I signed out I went to check on Wade. He was snoring, and I couldn't rouse him. I grabbed his shoes and carried him out to my battered old pickup. I got him propped up on the passenger side, but by the time I was out of the parking lot and on the highway, he had slumped over until his head was in my lap. "Dream on, Horton," I muttered, as Wade's warm breath penetrated the fabric of my trousers.

When I passed by the palatial Madden estate where Wade lived with his wife and her father, I noticed that the ornate wrought-iron gates were closed. I drove on to my turnoff, figuring it wouldn't make much difference to Wade's hangover whether he stayed in my humble digs or in Mr. Madden's elaborate pile of bricks.

He was still out cold when I pulled up beside my trailer, so I hauled him inside and dumped him unceremoniously on the bed. I began to undress him, partly because he looked uncomfortable trussed up in his tux, but mainly out of curiosity. As I removed the black onyx studs from his shirt, his once-familiar torso came into view. Ten years of heavy boozing and what was rumored to be a loveless marriage had done nothing to mar the perfection of Wade's physique. He remained the most gorgeous man I had ever laid eyes on. His sculpted pecs were capped by dark nipples poking through the silky fur that swirled around them. His belly was flat, split by a thin trail of chestnut hairs that stood up in defiant spikes around the hollow of his navel. His arms looked like those of a laborer, not a desk jockey.

I hung his shirt on a chair and unbuckled his belt. As I pulled his trousers down over his strong thighs, his distinctive scent assailed me, making my nostrils quiver. As always, he smelled of woodsy soap, overlaid with traces of sex. He still didn't wear underwear, I noticed. Wade had the biggest balls I'd ever seen. Nice cock too—hooded, thick, and veiny, and when fully erect stretching a bit over eight inches. I pulled off his socks and looked at him a little longer, then drew the sheet up over him. I grabbed a blanket, stripped out of my work clothes, and settled down on the couch in the living room.

I guess you're wondering how I know so much about Wade Talbot and his cock. Well, if you must know, Wade and I were lovers the summer after our senior year. We were both 18 and both very much in love. Or so I thought.

It was all Wade's doing, although I'd be a liar if I told you I hadn't thought about it. I, however, would never have had the nerve to do anything about my feelings. A poor kid with a jailbird for a father and a mother who turned the occasional trick to keep food on the table was the lowest of the low in small-town society. Wade, on the other hand, was at the top. Star athlete, senior class president, scholarship finalist, movie-star handsome—he had everything.

So why did he want me? Good question, not that I wasted much time thinking about it after it all began. The football team held practices throughout the summer after graduation so the players would still be in top form when they tried out for college teams as freshmen. We were in the locker room one night after practice, Wade as star quarterback of the football team, me scrubbing the mildew off the grout in the shower room to earn money to buy shoes. Practice ended, and the showers filled with guys, all of whom studiously ignored me while they washed up. I just focused on my scrubbing, imagining a future far away from this hick town and the people in it. As the minutes passed the noise from the locker room gradually died down. The door of the last locker clanged shut, and I was all alone again.

"Hey, Billy." I jumped up and spun around like I'd been goosed. It was Wade, gloriously naked, his thick curly hair matted down by his football helmet, the silky hairs on his tightly muscled body plastered against his tawny skin by his sweat.

"Wade." I blushed crimson under his steady gaze. In my confusion I dropped my scrub brush into the bucket of caustic cleanser, splashing it up into my eye. It burned like fire. I rubbed it with my dirty hands and only made it worse. Tears streamed down my face.

"Hold still, Billy." Wade was beside me in an instant. He turned on the shower and held my eye open, flushing away the chemicals with cool water. I was intensely aware of his hand against my cheek and of his thigh brushing mine. I could feel the heat of him through the cascade of water as his body pressed against mine, belly to belly, chest to chest.

He tilted my head out of the water, but he didn't let go of me. He stood there, looking at me. I saw water droplets glittering on his lashes, the black shadow of beard on his jaw and cheeks, the honey-colored irises of his eyes, the lush curve of his dusky lower lip. His face came closer. Our lips brushed. My heart almost burst.

"Billy," he murmured, his arms twining around me, his stiff cock pushing insistently against my belly. "You are so beautiful. So beautiful." This couldn't be true! He couldn't be here, saying this, caressing my back, his tongue flickering against my smooth skin as he slowly sank to his knees. I looked down at the top of his head, unable to move, watching as he unbuttoned my sodden cutoffs and pushed them down over my thighs.

My prick sprang up and clipped him on the jaw. He grabbed it and squeezed. His pink tongue flickered out and curled around the tip of my cock, burning the skin. My knob swelled, turning a dark crimson as it slid between his lips and into the soft wet heat of his mouth. I watched inch after inch of my dick disappear until Wade's forehead was tight against my belly and my prick was throbbing deep in his throat. My shoulders pressed against the tiles of the shower wall as water cascaded over my chest and belly, plastering Wade's hair against his skull. As the primal rhythms of sex took over, my hips started to pump.

"Jesus, Wade!" I gripped his shoulders and tried to push him away. He grunted and sucked my cock frantically. I bucked against him and began flooding his mouth with jism. It pumped out of me in a torrent, leaving me weak in the knees. Wade stood up abruptly, and my dick smacked against my belly, still oozing gobbets of thick white cream. He spit my seed into his palm and smiled at me, his lips glistening with my juice.

"Let me fuck you, Billy," he whispered. I nodded, too dazed to speak. If he'd asked to shoot me, my response would have been the same. He smeared my come on his jutting cock, hooked his arm behind my left knee, and pulled my leg up. "Grab the pipe," he instructed, glancing up at the shower spigot. I reached up, and my hands closed over the warm steel. He stepped closer, his cock sliding up under my balls. The blunt tip brushed against my asshole. He reached between my legs and pushed himself up into me, stretching my ass ring. It burned, and my muscles knotted against the intrusion, but I did nothing to stop him. He grabbed my right leg and pulled it off the floor. "Put your legs around me," he said. I locked them tight around his narrow hips. The movement spread my ass cheeks, and he drove deep into my bowels.

I moaned out loud, and Wade crammed his tongue into my mouth to silence me. As he fucked me the friction of his long fat prick quickly burned away any pain, replacing it with a pleasure so intense it frightened me. My limp dick grew hard again. He saw it and leaned against me, trapping it between the hard walls of our bellies.

I watched him fuck me, saw his body flush, the veins cabling across his muscular shoulders, his nipples tightening to thick points that stood out from the curve of his broad chest. He looked at me and grinned, then leaned down and bit my left tit, sinking his teeth into the swollen flesh. I jerked helplessly, my cock throbbing, every nerve in my body on fire. He rose up on his toes, thrusting his cock in me up to the hilt. He stopped, not moving except for the heaving of his chest and the flexing of his prick inside me. His eyes grew wide, his nostrils quivered; then he threw back his head and roared. I felt his dick jerk, and then the heat flooded me as he shot his load up my ass.

Once we had started, we couldn't get enough of each other. Almost every night Wade and I found some excuse to be together. It was bliss for me—and for him, judging by his eagerness. We did everything together, fucking and sucking in every combination that pleasure could devise. I never wanted it to end, but of course it did. One night we were together, taking turns fucking each other until dawn; the next, Wade was at a party announcing his engagement to Gloria Madden. The following week he had packed up and gone off to college, without explanations or goodbyes.

To hell with him, you say? Not that easy. Hey, I was in love with the guy. I was such a total wreck that I even thought about putting myself out of my misery. The only thing that stopped me was the hope that I might get another look at Wade's handsome face. The days went by, then the months and years, and Wade came back. He married Gloria and went into business with her father. Now I saw him at least three or four times a week at the club, sitting at the bar mostly, getting obliterated. He'd look at me sometimes, but he never talked to me unless I was taking his order in the dining room, which didn't really count.

I sat bolt upright, my heart racing. The report of the gun was still echoing from down by the lake. I jumped up off the couch and looked frantically around the bedroom. Wade's clothes were there, but he was gone. So was the rifle I kept propped up beside the bureau. I shouldn't have left it there, but a cougar had been prowling in the area, and I didn't want it to kill my chickens. I burst out of the trailer, buck naked.

"Wade!" I ran down to the lake. The moon was rising, its silver light shining on the water. The only sound I heard was a dog barking in the distance. "Wade!" Damn him. I loped along the shore, heading toward a grove of birches about 50 yards off to my right. "Wade Talbot! Answer me!"

I threaded through the trees, ignoring the branches that lashed against my bare body. I tore along, the blood pounding in my ears, terror rising in my throat.

"Unh!" I ran into him full-tilt, damn near knocking both of us down. He was as naked as I was, standing in a little clearing near the lake's edge. The gun was propped against a tree. Wade gripped my arms and steadied us. I looked at him, my chest heaving, relief and anger fighting for control of me. He met my gaze and grinned sheepishly.

"I'm afraid that cougar'll live to prowl another night," he chuckled. "Woke up and saw it sniffing around your chicken house. Thought I'd do you a favor."

"Next time, just shoot me. It'll be easier on my heart." In the moonlight he didn't look a day older than the last time we'd made love. His hands were hot against my skin. His scent was doing what it had always done to me. Wade moved—toward me, not away. I could feel the heat of his cock as it rubbed against my thigh. My dick began to rise at once, brushing the soft hairs on his leg.

"Wade, I—" He shut me up with a kiss. His hands trailed down my arms. He squeezed my hands, then embraced me. It was crazy, but he was still irresistible. I hugged back, my hands all over him, my tongue twining around his tongue, my prick pumping against his prick. It was as though all the intervening years had never been and we were love-struck teenagers again.

"Billy, put your dick in me. Fuck me, Billy. I want you to fuck me." His fingers curled around my cock, and he led me to the other side of the clearing. There was a long-fallen tree there, soft with moss. Wade knelt, straddled the log, and split the furry cheeks of his beautiful butt. I looked at him waiting for me to mount, his arms braced in front of him against the log, head bent, toes digging into the soft, moist earth. My cock throbbed like a tuning fork.

I lowered myself behind him and kissed his neck, his shoulders, the little triangle of fur at his tailbone. My hands on his thighs, I ducked my head lower, licked his crack, kissed the tightly puckered rosebud of his asshole. It fluttered against my lips, then gaped for me when I thrust my tongue into its hot, dark center. Wade groaned softly, and his thigh muscles swelled beneath my fingers.

I rose slowly, kissing his back, my hands moving from the tops of his thighs to their insides, then to the hot, hard stalk of his cock. I stroked it, pushing my thumb inside his foreskin as I pushed the head of my cock inside him. He leaned against me, head on my shoulder, his mouth on my throat. Wade scooted back, impaling himself, engulfing me in the sweetest heat I'd ever known.

I peered over his shoulder, watching his cock weep clear honey onto the moss as I began reacquainting myself with his body. I stroked his belly, tugging the hairs that split his abs. Still no fat there to mar the chiseled perfection. His pecs were fuller than I remembered, the hairs coating them denser, longer. His nipples were just as I remembered them, stiff points thrusting up from dark brown circles of flesh. When I pinched them his ass channel squeezed me tight, and his prick rose off the log, stretching till his knob emerged from its cowl of skin.

I pulled on his tits as I began fucking him, pumping in and out of him, my balls dragging against the silky moss. Wade groaned and raised his ass. My thighs slid under his, my belly pressed against his ass, my chest against his back as we began rocking out the rhythm of lust in the moonlit clearing.

"Jesus, Billy!" Wade gasped as I bucked hard. "I'm coming, Billy! I'm coming!" I grabbed his cock in both hands and pumped it. His body jerked as his orgasm hit. I felt hot jism gushing out of him, fell against him, pushed him down onto the log, and fucked him till I blew my hot spunk up his clutching hole.

Afterward, Wade put his arms around me and looked into my eyes. "I've missed you, Billy," he began softly. "That was the best—" I silenced him with a kiss, unwilling to listen to his lies.

The months passed, and I continued to see Wade only at the club, always distant, always polite. There was one thing different about him, however—he was never drunk. He would sit for hours, nursing a club soda, staring into space, looking unspeakably sad. Seeing him like that only made the ache in my heart worse. I had been in love with the man for over ten years, and our night in the clearing had done nothing to change that—unless an increase in my need for him could be considered a change.

I was working the night of Valentine's Day, giving in, as single people often do, to the pleas of coworkers who want to spend the time with loved ones. I didn't care—it would be a good night for tips, and I was used to being alone in crowds.

Or so I thought. When Wade came in with Gloria, all my feelings for him pressed heavily on my heart. He was gorgeous in his tux and snowy shirt. Gloria looked glamorous herself, although her sour expression wasn't much in keeping with the event. Terry, the hostess, seated them in my section, much to my dismay. I forced a smile and went to take their order.

Gloria ordered a cocktail, Wade his accustomed soda. "It's the new Wade Talbot," Gloria said sarcastically. "All health and sobriety, although I don't know what the point is. I'm sure not benefiting from it." I glared at her, then escaped before I said something to get me fired.

The dining room was packed, and I was too busy to think about anything but work until the dancing started. I cleared tables, served cocktails and champagne, then went into the waiter's station to fold napkins. The band played a succession of romantic favorites, and I sank deeper and deeper into a sloppy, sorry-for-myself depression. At midnight, when the lights were lowered and the bandleader called for every man to lead the love of his life out onto the dance floor, I threw down the napkin I was folding and stomped off.

I fled to the terrace overlooking the golf course. The music was muffled, but I could see dancing couples through the French doors. It was cold, and a light snow had begun to fall. I folded my arms over my chest and shivered as tears of self-pity overflowed my eyes.

"Billy." I spun around. Wade was behind me, smiling.

"What?" I sputtered.

"The man said I should ask you to dance. Billy Horton, will you dance with me?" I stood there for a moment in total shock, unable to believe what I'd just heard. Then I stepped into his open arms and pressed my cheek against his, no longer cold, swaying to the faint strains of the music in the love of my life's strong arms.

Smoker
Dale Chase

They were the new exiles. Drawn together by nothing more than their cigarette habit, they'd been forced outside when a law passed prohibiting smoking in the workplace. Similar groups had sprung up outside every office building in town, little mid-morning and mid-afternoon clusters of the disenfranchised.

I passed them when I crossed the courtyard for my morning latte and my afternoon soft drink. They were faceless for the most part, simply the sad little group beneath their private cloud, until someone new appeared in their midst.

I'd given up smoking long before the law went into effect and avoided smokers like most of the reformed, but when I saw this guy, cigarette balanced between long, delicate fingers, I wondered if it was poor form for a non-smoker to insinuate himself into the group. I stood looking out from the lobby and honestly considered taking up smoking again.

He was an incredible specimen who sent me on an erotic voyage with his loosely casual, almost neutral look, a benign disguise I was certain masked raw passion and a dick dangling to his knee. And the way he smoked: an extended suck, long pause to savor what he'd captured, then an exhale through lips drawn into a careful "O". I reached down to my throbbing prong and imagined it sliding into that hole.

I noticed he wasn't too involved with the others. Good newcomer that he was, he smiled and nodded, all the while sucking in, blowing out. I forgot about my soft drink.

In the men's room I came in about three strokes, so primed I needed only to free my dick and get a hand on it before I exploded. As I shot huge dollops of cream into the toilet, I envisioned that mouth and later on I bought a pack of cigarettes.

It was easy to join the group, cigarette the only admission. The next morning I lit up off to one side, then sidled in. Dizziness knocked me off balance for the first few seconds and while I knew it was a nicotine rush, I preferred to think it a prelude. My cock twitched agreement, and I sucked the smoke with new enthusiasm.

The guy was fine featured and blond, blue eyes, tiny gap between his front teeth. He nodded as I stepped into the circle and we stood opposite, eyes meeting too often to be casual. I can't remember what the other people looked like or if the day was warm or cold, I only know we connected from first glance, and that when he shifted his weight from one foot to the other it was to accommodate an erection. (I'd done the same thing seconds before.)

He grinned as I drew on my cigarette, and I knew he had me figured. When smokes dwindled, others checked their watches and hurried away, leaving us to stub out our cigarettes together.

"I'm Adair," he said, and the name caught me, piling onto all his other attributes.

"Carl," I replied. It sounded so blunt.

"How about lunch, Carl?"

"Great."

"Meet me here at noon." We lingered, eyes on one another, silent agreement that food would not be consumed.

The rest of the morning crawled along, and I found myself staring at the copier when a coworker nudged me. "You gonna copy that or what?"

"Sorry." I pressed the start button and heard the familiar click and whir.

"It's done," he said. "Jesus, where are you?"

I returned to my cubicle, but gave up trying to accomplish anything. Where was I? Sucking Adair's dick, probing his ass. I kept whispering his name over and over. Adair. I liked the feel of it on my tongue.

At quarter of twelve I was in the men's room combing my hair, straightening my tie, calming my erection. Nothing needed attention except my cock, but I wanted everything perfect. At noon I stepped out the front door where Adair waited. "Come on," he said, and I followed.

I'd worked in this building for four years and had never had sex on the premises, but realized, as I followed him across the courtyard, that I was about to. He was so sure of himself that I knew he was well-traveled, but that didn't matter. I didn't care if the world had fucked him so long as I got to. I followed him to the elevator and down into the underground parking garage, certain we were headed for his car, but I was wrong. We left the elevator, passed the main stairwell, and hurried to the far corner where he opened a door I'd scarcely noticed. Behind it lay a smaller stairwell dimly lit by a single bulb high on the wall. Adair closed the door behind us and dropped his pants all in one fluid motion.

His prick didn't go to his knee, but it might as well have. It was the longest I'd seen, dangling over an ample sac like a well-worn rope, neatly trimmed, knob darkening. He was only halfway hard, and I wondered if it might take more time for him to rise than us normally pronged guys.

I kneeled to lick the tip of this magnificent cock, then suck in as much of him as I could. He grew beneath my ministrations and when he was fully erect and jabbing my throat he pulled out. I looked up to see him gathering spit at his lips and realized this wasn't going to be what I'd expected. I'd anticipated my cock up his ass, but saw it was going to be the other way around, and, as much as I wanted to fuck him, I looked again at the snake before me, fully engorged and royally inflamed, and acquiesced. And once I'd decided to receive rather than give I couldn't wait to get this incredible dick up me. I shed my pants, bent at the waist, and presented myself to him, so eager now that I reached back and pulled my cheeks open in full display. He jammed a finger into me, lubing until I took hold of my own meat and began to work myself.

He applied a condom, then slid that gorgeous prick deep into my ass, and the effect was like none I'd ever experienced. No one had ever gone in so far, sliding up into my bowels until they throbbed in sweet agony. He allowed only seconds for me to acclimate, then began his fuck, driving his hose into me in strokes so lengthy I nearly screamed. God, he knew how to work that thing.

I was coming long before him, squirting cream onto the steps and squealing as his body slapped my cheeks and the enormous cock plowed my ass. I didn't want him ever to stop and I pushed back to let him know it, pounding against him, fleshy slap echoing through the stairwell.

When his come began to rise, his strokes became more determined, his whole body swaying forward to hit me with such force I had to reach out and anchor myself against the walls. He announced his climax with a half-growl half-squeal, slamming into me as I pictured juice squirting out his slot. I could see that hose turned on and it brought to mind bittersweet reflections of the enemas that had been a previous partner's favorite. But this wasn't some soapy fluid, it was come, it was milk rising from his balls and filling the sheath. I squeezed my muscle as I rode his dick, urging him on, and he dug his fingers into my hips, slamming home to the last drop. When he was finally spent he slumped forward and wrapped his arms around my chest. "Great lunch," he said.

I chuckled. "Yeah, but we'll be hungry in an hour."

"I could use a cigarette."

"Me too."

We dressed, retraced our path, and sat in the courtyard smoking for the remainder of the lunch hour. My stomach growled occasionally, but I ignored it, content to sit beside Adair as we inhaled our smokes.

"I have a confession," I told him. "I quit smoking a couple years ago. I only started again because I saw you out front."

"So I'm your downfall."

I pressed my thigh against his. "You better believe it."

When our cigarettes were gone I asked to see him after work.

"Can't."

"Why not?"

He sighed and looked past me. "I'm in a relationship. Long-term."

Everything in me stopped, and it must have showed because he added, "That doesn't mean we can't do lunches. Just no dinners."

"Tomorrow then?"

"Tomorrow."

On the way back to my office I added up the fucks. It was Wednesday, just two more, then a two-day dry spell, then five in a row. I could live with that, but later that day I was again caught drifting, this time with the phone ringing. When the receptionist put the call through a second time she bristled. "Where were you?"

That night I awoke with a raging hard-on, dreams of Adair so vivid I could taste him. As I worked my dick, I saw that my subconscious had done what I had not, gone up his ass, and as come erupted from my throbbing prick I could see myself mounting him while that cock of his dangled free. After this little solitary scenario, I enjoyed a good smoke.

In the stairwell the next afternoon we both dropped our pants, but before I could make a move, Adair had my cock in his mouth, doing me like I'd never been done. He received the same as he gave, going deep, taking every inch until I was banging his throat while his tongue hugged my shaft. He drove me to a complete frenzy, and I began to fuck madly, grabbing his head and reaming his mouth until my load began to rise. At the critical moment I pulled out, grabbed hold, and squirted streams of jism across his face.

Adair grinned and took all I had, then ran his finger down his cheek, gathered a gob, turned me around, and shoved it up my ass. I squirmed until he added a second digit and more of my juice. I was so high on the action all I could think of was getting him inside me, and I writhed on the finger fuck until he relented and pulled on a rubber.

Feeling his long rope slide up into my rectum erased any thoughts of my taking him, and I wriggled back, pulling him in to the root. He responded with long easy thrusts, as if he wanted this one to last, and I listened to our juicy slap as he gave me the end-all, be-all of fucks.

He picked up speed finally and I knew he was ready, a growl erupting as he went over, humping me like some insatiable rutting animal. It took him a long time to empty, and I hugged him with my muscle, holding onto a cock I wanted to own, a cock I wanted to stuff and mount and stick up my ass in perpetuity.

When he was done he pulled out and said, "I need a cigarette." I should have told him then what I wanted, that even though he had the cock of a lifetime I wanted my dick up his ass, but I stared down at that incredible sausage and said nothing.

Back in the courtyard with our smokes, the fuck seemed a million miles away. I asked him what kind of work he did and he said, "I'm a temp," as if that's all there was to it, and I was struck by an odd pang. Temporary was the last thing I wanted. "What kind?" I asked.

"Data entry, phones, whatever."

"But not permanent."

He paused so long I knew I was in trouble. "My partner is the one with the career and he gets transferred a lot, so I never take anything permanent."

I wanted to ask how long he'd been on this job, but didn't. Instead I blurted out, "I want to fuck you."

He paused, then said, "Makes no difference to me. I just assumed...." He took a long drag on his cigarette, then turned to face me. "Habit, I guess, getting my dick in wherever I can. You want it otherwise, it's my pleasure. But how about tomorrow we try somewhere new."

That night I rode him in my sleep, but the cock I had up his ass wasn't mine, it was his. I dreamed in long agonizing strokes and came prodigiously. In the morning my bed was a mess.

When I faced Adair in the little smoking group the next morning nothing was clear except the fact that I wanted him. While he sucked his cigarette I looked him up and down, thinking about getting *on* him, riding his ass while I held onto that prick of his.

"Follow me," he said at noon. He led me back into the building and unlocked a door off the lobby. The narrow room was filled walls of wiring, all kinds of switches, knobs, and dials. "The building's guts," he said as he secured the door behind us. I didn't ask how he'd managed a key in his brief tenure. I had a good idea, but didn't want to know.

He dropped his pants and I did the same, eyeing that long cock of his, still flaccid and so very inviting. "You sure?" he asked and I nodded. "Whatever," he said, turning around, kneeling, presenting himself to me. I opened a packet of lube and took my time greasing his hole, one finger, then two, and as he began to clench and squirm I pulled back, applied protection, took aim, and shoved in. For a second I kept still, savoring where I was, inside the coveted ass at long last.

When Adair wrapped his hand around his prick, mine went along and after a few seconds he let me have him all to myself, dick reaming his ass, hand on that salami of his which was absolutely the stiffest I'd ever encountered. It felt more pole than meat, and as I kept up a glorious stroke I couldn't believe this cock was the same one that had been inside me. It seemed like it had taken on a new life with the hand job, as if the feel of air or the grip of a palm changed its...what?...character. Can a prick have character? Or was it some nocturnal creature thrust into the light, warm and wet in its natural environment—the dark and steamy rectum—but rigid, on point out in the open. These thoughts swam through me as I kept up a rhythmic thrust, and I was soon overcome with a kind of sex-dementia, mind as fucked as ass. And then it all got away from me, the crazy cock went starkers, come began to churn, and I went verbal, telling him what his ass felt like from the inside, what the cock-mole in there was snorting, what was squirting from its snout. The creature was drowning up there, cranking out ecstasy while it blissfully succumbed, and then, as if my scenario was just the topper he needed, Adair grabbed my hand and doubled the pace, squeezing mightily as he erupted. As my own climax subsided I looked over his shoulder to see what had always been trapped inside a rubber, great long streams shooting out that magnificent cock until an impressive puddle glazed the floor. "Holy shit," he said afterward. I hugged him from behind as my dick slid out of him. "Here, here," I seconded.

Back in the courtyard we lit up, and he told me his partner had been transferred. "John was on assignment here. It was never meant to be more than a couple weeks and now we're headed for New York. We've been in over a dozen cities this year."

And I knew he'd fucked someone else in each one, just like he'd done here, but all I managed was, "So this is it?"

"I'm afraid so, but if we ever get back this way...."

"I'll be here." I wanted to reach over for a farewell grope, but sucked my cigarette instead. On Monday I rejoined the little group of smokers in the courtyard. Nods and smiles were exchanged, but I let the others talk among themselves. I kept to my cigarette and thought of Adair and that incredible prick, and I realized I was going to keep on smoking and maybe, just maybe, one day a guy would join the group and he'd have this look and maybe, just maybe, inside those pants he'd have the cock of a lifetime. Until then I'd remain a dedicated pack-a-day man.

Scottie
R.J. March

We put Darren on top because he didn't mind sleeping so close to the ceiling. I wouldn't have been able to close my eyes, and rolling over would have been a problem because of the cast. I was knocking it into everything—furniture, doorjambs, people.

The table folded down and became a bed; covered with its cushions, it slept two. That's where Paulie and I were sleeping. Paulie found some blankets in a cupboard and put them down. I stepped out of the little camper, clipping my elbow on the way out. Darren was poking at the fire with a stick, listening to the radio. He looked at me, his face lit by the flames, framed darkly by his shoulder-length hair. His shirt was unbuttoned, and I could see the shadow between his pecs, the patch of hair that grew there, narrowing as it went down, making a thin brown line that rolled over the muscles of his stomach before making a sharp drop into his jeans, which were big and hung low, showing his hip bones and the dark fringe of his pubes. He'd been looking at me lately and not saying anything, as though he knew something about me, and I wondered what it was he thought he knew. Maybe he'd seen me go into the bathroom at the mall and not leave for an hour. Or maybe Joe Panotti let something slip about me—he didn't care anymore what people thought now that he lived in New York City and was practically married to a guy. I think he loved the looks he got from his old high school buds who'd named him "Pussy King." Everyone but me.

I wasn't gay like Joe. No, I was going to settle down and get married eventually. I thought the taste for dick I had would pass when I met the right girl. As far as I was concerned, I was still young enough for it to be a phase.

The way Darren looked at me got me all undone in a second, though, and I was going to say something—I just didn't know what—but then

Paulie stepped out of the camper. Paulie was like my little brother; he was most definitely my best friend. He walked across the sand to where Darren and I silently faced off, the fire going between us. I could hear the waves—we hadn't seen the lake yet, having come in so late. Darren had gotten us lost outside Watertown, and then we were heading south again and passing signs that said Syracuse was 50-some miles ahead. That's when things got a little tense, and Darren and I exchanged some shit, and Paulie, sitting between us in the little pickup cab, told us to cool it. Darren stopped, skidding into the gravel on the side of the road. The little Scotsman camper we were towing—Scottie, as we called it—nearly came up alongside us. "If you know the way, then you drive," he said to me. He got out and stood in the headlights, pulling out his dick to take a leak; I watched the arc glistening in the halogen spot. Paulie stayed where he'd gotten thrown—right up against me. He was always doing stuff like that—putting his arm around me, playing with my hair, leaning into me when we walked together. I guess some guys would have taken it to mean something, but coming from Paulie, it was like coming from your cousin or something—your brother.

I think, though, that his ease with me like that had something to do with some of the frustration I felt around other guys. I wanted to touch them the way Paulie touched me, casually, intimately, and that just didn't happen. It tied me in fucking knots sometimes, and I'd have to take a trip to the mall, sitting in a stall to sort things out, waiting until someone would try the door and find it unlocked and not mind that it was occupied. That's when the touching became easy, my hands doing their own thing, and I could relax for a while, my pants undone, my dick getting worked over, and I'd touch whoever's head, finger his hair the way Paulie sometimes touched mine. Those weren't the highest moments of my life, but the times I felt some sort of release—and I don't mean the obvious one—I would feel free for a while. But it was a short-lived feeling, and then I usually felt like shit, swearing that that was the last time, I was going to shape up and act like a man, and I'd call whatever girl I was seeing—because I was always seeing some girl—and ball her brains out. But the things I would think about while I was fucking had nothing to do with the woman underneath me. It was a phase, just a phase.

Paulie said we ought to check out the lake. Darren didn't move from the low folding chair he was sitting in. I picked at the frayed edge of my cast.

"Who's coming?" Paulie asked. He looked at me. I nodded. "Darren?"

Darren shook his head.

Paulie shrugged, but I was thinking, *What a fucking baby.* We were going to get punished because he fucked up and got us lost—he would be angry all week. I shook my head, tired of the asshole. It was going to be a long week.

We passed the dying fires of campers gone to bed. There was a moon in the sky, just a bit of it shining through some gliding clouds, and Paulie said something about it being late. We passed a trailer that was lit up, a couple inside playing cards, and I wondered if Paulie was still seeing that girl from Marcellus, the one with the braces and the mosquito-bite tits.

Paulie had been here before, so he knew the way. But the road was rocky and rutted, and the moon slid behind a heavy bank of clouds. Paulie led the way, and he kept swinging his hand back and hitting mine, screwing around or just making sure I was keeping up. I stubbed my toes a couple of times and cursed the fucking sandals I was wearing, and then the road went soft and sandy, and the waves sounded as though they would take us away. I saw the lake then, Lake Ontario, and it was black, and the breakers seemed almost to shimmer when the moon reappeared. Paulie's hand swung back and caught me hard in the nuts.

"Christ," I gasped.

"What'd I do?" he asked.

I fought the urge to crumble to my knees, but went down anyway. Paulie's hands went to my shoulders. "Are you all right, Chris?" he asked. I nodded, wondering how this simple movement could add to the most incredible pain I'd ever experienced. It seemed for a couple of minutes that the only way to be rid of the agony would be to have my balls removed. Then they dislodged from wherever they had gone, and some of the pain subsided, but I felt like a castrate anyway.

I stayed on my knees a while longer, and Paulie delivered a litany of remorse, but I could almost straighten up and walk again. "No big deal," I said, trying not to squeak. "I never liked kids enough to have any of my own anyway."

We walked over the sand, which still held the heat of the day's sun. The water was warm too, washing up over my feet. My groin ached dully, and I wondered if you could actually bruise your balls. Paulie put his hand on my shoulder.

"I'll tell you," he said as he leaned closer, "if Darren is going to be an asshole all week, he can leave now."

I agreed, but kept my mouth shut. Besides, Paulie's lips moving so close to my ear caused my dick to flutter. I was wearing shorts that were thin and baggy, and the wind went up my legs, blowing around my crotch like a horny old man. I went bony then, my dick twitching up and doing a little dance. I was glad for the dark and hoped my hard-on would go away before we got back to the campfire and Darren's moody eyes.

"Where's the toilet around here?" I asked. Suddenly I felt I needed a little time to myself.

"We'll walk back that way," Paulie said, facing the water.

"The waves are really a lot bigger than I expected," I said.

"How are your nuts?" he asked.

A tongue bath wouldn't hurt, I thought right away, giving myself reason for a stupid grin. "They're OK," I told him.

"We're going to have a great time," he said. He pinched the long muscle at the top of my shoulder, in a sort of Spock grip, and I pulled away.

I saw the lights of the bathroom up ahead on the left. "There you go," Paulie said, but he followed me in anyway.

The place stunk and buzzed with mosquitoes, reminding me again of Paulie's girlfriend. There were showers at one end, and Paulie stepped up to a long trough that passed as a urinal, and I got myself into a stall. I took the one by the wall; the one in the middle was occupied. I looked down—force of habit—listening to the steady stream of Paulie's piss ringing. I could see my neighbor's foot, bare and tanned, toes lifted off the concrete, the tendons along the top in sharp relief. The foot tapped soundlessly, making me wonder. In a mall the foot wouldn't be bare—I'd be looking down at a loafer or a Nike—but the tapping was usually some sort of sexual Morse code. Or not. I'd been wrong before.

"I'll meet you outside," I heard Paulie call out. I thought about Paulie getting undressed in that little trailer and sliding under the blankets with me, and I got a fatty all over again. The foot tapped some more, toes pulled up, tanned and sandy, a young foot. I moved mine, pivoting on the heel, bringing the toe of my sandal closer to the invisible line on the floor that separated our stalls. My cock was too hard to ignore. I started dry-jacking, listening to the papery noise of skin on skin, imagining what the man beside me looked like and if he could hear me. I wanted him to be young, my age, and I wanted him to have a chest covered with short dark hairs, and I wanted him to stick his fat cock down my throat.

I listened for bathroom noises from my neighbor—grunting or the use of toilet paper or even a trickle of piss—but there was nothing, although I did hear him sigh. And then I heard the sound that spit makes when it's used to jerk off.

There were no holes to peer through, no way to judge what this person looked like except for his foot, which I deemed beautiful. The toes were long, and there were sprigs of hair on each. I'd never thought much about feet, but seeing this one made me want to have it in my mouth, toes curling on my tongue.

His foot moved closer to that boundary. I squeezed my prick, and juice leaked out. I cleared my throat. I watched his toes flex and heard them crack. He sighed again, deeply, and my knees began to shake. I heard Paulie whistling outside—I was taking too long; he'd get suspicious. I moved my foot closer to his, wiggling my toes. And then he put his foot on mine.

I started dribbling, unable to control myself. Come bubbled up and out of my prick, running down my hand, falling on the toilet seat. I shuddered, holding my breath, trying to clean up with toilet paper, his foot still resting on mine. I felt the first drops before realizing he had come across our feet.

I practically ran out of there, barely able to compose myself. My cock tented the front of my shorts, and I was thinking there was no way Paulie wouldn't notice the big wet spot. My cock felt gigantic, the way it bobbed and swayed in my loose shorts, and I tried to push it down, but it wasn't going anywhere yet.

"Jeez, Chris," Paulie said, laughing.

I said, "What?" trying to sound innocent. Paulie laughed again. My wrist started aching the way it had been doing lately as we walked back to camp.

I dreamed about that toilet that night—that I went there to piss when everyone was asleep and all the lights were off. I felt around for a light switch and touched something that felt like a hard cock. *Well, it couldn't be anything else,* I thought, touching it carefully, fingering the loose sac of nuts that dangled beneath the firm rod. It was as hard as wood, jutting out at an angle from the wall, hanging like a trophy. *Not real,* I thought, although it certainly felt lifelike, and I decided, since I was alone, that it would be all right to suck the thing a little. *Need one of these at home,* I was thinking, touching my lips to the fat helmet. It was sticky with juices, and its end felt like the real thing, a cushion that gave way to a hard bluntness. I got it into my mouth—it felt bona fide to me, the real thing, thick and quivering with a life of its own—and started sucking it, getting my lips all the way down the base. I took hold of the balls and held them gently, letting them roll on my palm. With my other hand I gripped the shaft and must have tugged too hard, because there was a sudden flood of light. I blinked in the white glare, making out an audience of guys I did and didn't recognize, all of them laughing. And there was Darren in the back of the room, a huge grin on his lips.

"See what I mean?" he said, laughing. "I told you he was a cocksucker."

I awoke, and it was dawn. Paulie snored softly beside me, hugging the wall, keeping to his side of the bed. I listened for Darren in the back, pressed up against the ceiling. My wrist itched, and my balls still ached from Paulie's accidental blow the night before, and, of course, my cock was bone-hard again. Paulie said something, a mumbled nothing, caught in some dream. I put my casted wrist between my legs, giving myself something hard to hump against. It hurt less that way, and I held my breath. I closed my eyes and pictured someone—that hot Orioles baseball player— and rubbed my dick against my cast.

Darren moaned, and I stopped dead still. There was a thud. "Shit," he said, looking around the corner, rubbing his head. "Fucking bed," he said. "Paulie's sleeping here tonight."

He threw his legs over the side of the bunk, letting them dangle. They were long and covered with hair. He threw back the covers, and I saw the hard poke of his cock sticking up out of his boxers. It was tall and leaned to the left, its head shaped a little like the end of a baseball bat, blunt and flanged.

"Where's the toilet?" he asked.

"Up the road," I said. "Not far."

"What time is it?" Paulie said, rolling over, not opening his eyes. Darren looked at his watch, but didn't say anything. He noticed his bared dick and gave me a look as though it was somehow my doing. He eased himself down to the floor, covered himself up, and walked to the door. He stood there, not a foot away from me. His back was wide and brown, and he had dark hairs growing in a spade at the small of his back. Paulie pulled on the blankets. Darren held his hair back, twisting it into a ponytail. I always thought he'd look cool with a brush cut like Paulie's and mine.

"Where is it?" he asked me.

"The toilet?" I said. "It's, uh...Paulie, where's the toilet?"

"Might as well be in a fucking tent," Darren said.

Paulie lifted his head. "It's just up the road, asshole. There are signs all over the place. Even you should be able to make it there."

Darren smirked, looking down at us.

"You two look cute together. Ever think about coming out? Moving to Hawaii? Getting hitched?"

"He's an asshole," Paulie said to me when Darren was gone. I sat up, looking for my shorts, feeling the need for some cover. Paulie stretched across the mattress, stealing the extra room I'd given up. His arm lay across my pillow, tanned and copper-haired.

"He's got issues," I said, looking at his arm, wanting to put a finger on it where I could see a vein pulsing.

"You sound like that Danny guy," Paulie said.

Danny was someone I worked with, a really cool gay guy. He had said that about Darren the first time he met him—that he's got issues.

"What the fuck does that mean?" Paulie asked. "That's bullshit anyway. Darren fucks more chicks than the both of us."

Just like Joe Panotti, I thought. Fucking Joey and his sweet little prick— there was no end to that guy's libido that summer after we graduated, right before Joe went to college in New York. I remembered almost each time we dicked around because it was nearly every day: Joe dropping his pants in the car for a quick knob job during my "smoke" break at the restaurant; the times he took me to the mall and pimped me out in the men's room, joining in when he found someone he liked; the night he almost fucked me.

"Whatever," I said to Paulie, trying to shake the horny walk down memory lane I was taking.

"Danny would say that too," Paulie said. "You're hanging out with him too much. He's rubbing off."

"I work with him, for Christ's sake," I said. Danny was the gayest gay guy I knew. What I liked about him was that he didn't have the faintest idea of what I was all about. He'd flirt like crazy with me, then throw his hands up and shake his head. "I'm wasting my time with you, Chris, just wasting my time." He was always telling me all guys were bi, they just didn't know it. "Ask Freud, honey—he knew the score. Probably got his salad tossed all the time."

On the beach that day, I looked for my toilet buddy, and I thought I'd found him about 20 times. Every time I thought I'd nailed him, some other guy with hot-looking feet, long and hairy-knuckled toes, came walking by. I stayed on my stomach most of the time. "Your back's getting burned," Paulie said. "I know," I said, staying put.

"I'm hungry," Darren said, glowering, like it was our fault. I looked at his feet. His toes were stubbed, blunt-ended things. They didn't seem to have anything to do with the rest of him. They dug into the sand like pale and fat slugs.

There was a concession stand at the other end of the beach, close to the toilets, which were set back from the water. It was funny to see where everything was in the light of day, how close things were when they seemed so far apart the night before. I wasn't moving from my blanket at that point, so I threw my wallet at Darren and told him I wanted a couple of hot dogs and something to drink.

"I'll go with you," Paulie said.

I closed my eyes, the sun crisping my back. I could hear the waves and the music that Paulie brought along and could feel myself being pulled out and away. Paulie put his foot on my stomach. The wind blew across my shoulders. Darren whispered in Paulie's ear; I could see the white flash of his teeth. He asked if Paulie would shave his head. "It's lemonade," I heard someone say. I opened my eyes.

"Dinnertime, Sleeping Beauty," Darren said to me.

I went back to the toilet that night, hoping to relive the experience of the night before, but the place was empty. I sat in the stall for nearly an hour, waiting, getting hard, going soft, waiting. Someone came in and took a quick shit. I could see by his yellowed toenails that he was not the one from last night. And someone came in to brush his teeth. I squashed a mosquito that landed on my thigh and waited until I was too bored to wait any longer. I got up, flushed the unused toilet, and went to wash my hands—force of habit. I looked into the mirror, wondering when I would shave again, when this guy came walking in wearing soccer shorts and Adidas sandals, a towel over his shoulder. He nodded, glancing down at my feet, I thought, and I looked at his. My heart started pounding. It was him—I was sure of it. He walked over to the showers, throwing his towel over a bench. He slipped off his sandals and pushed himself out of his shorts. I stood at the sink, staring, hands drip-drying. He stretched his arms up over his head—his rib cage hollowed. He scratched the top of his head. He was ignoring me, acting as though he was by himself. He stepped behind the partition that provided some privacy, and I heard the water being turned on, the splash of it on the concrete floor.

I'm not sure exactly what I was thinking or if there was in fact any thought process at all. I went over to the bench and started undressing, standing in front of him, watching him, his wet skin, the water that ran over him, off him. I had no towel, no showering accoutrements. I turned on the shower directly across from him and stepped under the shock of cold water that took my breath away. I quickly stepped back.

"It takes a while for the water to warm up," the man said.

"Christ," I said, hugging myself. I stuck my foot into the falling ice-cold water. "How long is a while?"

"This one's hot," he said, his back to me. His ass was high and tight-looking, his crack a thin line. He reached back and soaped himself up. "I'm almost finished," he added.

"It's getting warmer," I said, going under the spray. I had to turn away from him because my cock was hoisting itself up, pulsing with blood.

"Pressure's good, at least," I heard him say, and I looked at him over my shoulder, ready to agree. His dick was lathered. He was facing me. He handled himself casually, sliding the tube of his palm up and down his shaft. He looked at me with green eyes, brown shoulders, flat stomach feathered with dark hair. Soap suds gathered in his pubes, dripped from his balls, ran down his long thighs. He leaned back in the water. I liked the way his toes curled against the concrete.

The door pushed open, and we both about-faced, a poor attempt to hide what was dangerously apparent. I listened to whoever taking a piss, and my cock deflated, and I was able to turn and look over at my shower partner. His ass cheeks shined. He looked over his shoulder at me, winking. It was a little too public for me, though, and I gathered my stuff together and wiped as much water off me as I could and left.

I went back to the little camper in an agitated state. My dick flopped around in my shorts like a salmon in spring. The guys were playing cards and passing a bottle of Jack Daniel's when they weren't chugging back beers.

"You're going to have to catch up," Darren said, shirtless, handing me the bottle.

"Did you swim?" Paulie asked.

"Yeah," I said. I took a swig and put the bottle on the table, looking at Paulie's shitty hand. I got a bottle of beer from the cooler and took it outside. I needed fresh air and something to look at besides Darren's bare torso.

It wasn't long before I was joined by him anyway. "Help me put Paulie up in the bunk," he said.

I looked up at him. "Are you sure that's a good idea?"

"I'm not sleeping up there again," he said, "and you sure as hell can't."

I looked back at the fire. "He'll be all right," Darren said. "Come on. Just help me get him up."

Paulie wasn't all that drunk. He probably could have gotten himself up there by himself. He acted helpless, though, and stupid, and let Darren and me push and pull him out of his clothes. Stripped to his briefs, he was smooth, compactly muscled, a little wrestler. I spied his soft prick, the way it lay cradled in his underwear.

"Get up there," Darren said.

"I'm trying," Paulie whined. Darren put his hand on the white cotton of Paulie's ass, pushing him upward. Paulie tumbled into the bunk, his arm and leg hanging over the edge.

I went to where Darren and I were going to sleep and started clearing the table. Darren stood behind me, taking off his shorts. He was naked underneath. I saw the bright white strip of untanned skin, the dark brown beard that surrounded his long prick. "You sleeping like that?" I asked.

"I never wear anything," he said.

Did last night, I thought but let it go. The thought of climbing into bed with him bare-assed like that wasn't exactly going to bother me much, or else it would bother me too much. I stripped down to the ratty old boxers I had on and got under the covers, hugging the wall.

"Fucking Paulie," Darren said, turning off the light. Paulie sucked up a snore and started coughing, mumbling something about an airplane, and Darren slid into the makeshift bed with me, his feet brushing against my legs electrically. He settled himself, nowhere near me, and I listened to his breathing. It stayed shallow and nasal, and I wondered what he was thinking. And then he spoke:

"You ever hear from Joe Panotti?"

I swallowed hard.

He accepted my silence. I thought I could hear him smiling, lying there beside me, flat on his back, his long legs bent at the knee to fit the short bed.

"He was a horny motherfucker," Darren went on. "I remember when we went up to Cross Lake for Senior Weekend, and he and I shared a tent. Fucker was all over me as soon as he thought I was asleep. His hand crawled into my boxers like a fucking spider. He started jerking me off once he got me hard. It was fucking insane. I mean, there we were with half the fucking ball team, and some of them were still up, drinking around the fire, you know? And besides, everyone fucking knew that Panotti had just gotten his dick sucked by Titties Janson."

I lay there in disbelief, my eyes crossing in the dark, my dick throbbing, trapped between my thighs. I didn't dare move, not wanting to betray myself or to give him any reason to quit his narrative. He shifted, bringing his arms up over his head. "And then he put his head under my sleeping bag and started blowing me." He kind of giggled. "It was my first one, man, I am not ashamed to admit it. I've had a few since—chicks only— but not like that one. Joey could suck the dimples off a golf ball, man."

Tell me about it, I was thinking, remembering a couple of blow jobs when he seemed intent on taking my dick off.

The next thing I knew, Darren rolled over me like a wave, and I felt his skin all over me, hot, a little sweaty. His mouth found mine surprised, and I tasted his tongue for the first time, never having imagined his flavor. He pumped his hips, digging his hard-on into my boxers. His hands found mine and held them to the foam rubber mattress.

"He told me all about you," Darren whispered.

"Yeah, me too," Paulie said, slipping under the covers, sliding up next to us.

"This is a hallucination," I said.

"Not exactly," Darren said.

"Move over," Paulie said, pushing Darren off me and coming closer himself so that I had them on either side of me. I tried to move myself to give them more room. "Ow," Darren said when I hit him on the head with my cast. Paulie's hand slipped into my shorts—at least I think it was Paulie's hand—and Darren kissed me some more until he leaned back and said, "OK, who's going to suck who?"

"It's *whom,* I think," Paulie said.

"I think he's right," I added. Paulie cupped my balls, his fingers edging the furry surroundings of my butt hole.

"Everybody could do everybody," Paulie said.

"I'm up for that," Darren said.

"How come you never let me suck your dick?" Paulie asked him.

"Wait a minute," I said, trying to sit up and shake this image out of my head. There was no way this was really happening—I was having some intensely realistic dream, I was sure, and then Paulie stood up, hitting his head on the cupboards overhead—"Fuck!"—and tried to stick his dick in my mouth.

"Open up," he said.

"I want to turn on the light," I heard Darren say, feeling him reach for it. The pointed tip of Paulie's cock brushed the stubble over my lips, and he complained. I put out my tongue to taste him, the moistened slit of him. He could have used a shower, but the smell of him was almost like perfume, and I opened my mouth wide just as Darren ducked under the covers and nosed around the opening of my boxer shorts. He pushed them down my thighs and licked my sudden boner, humping my calf with his sticky prick. Paulie's cock hit the back of my throat, nearly choking me, as Darren took me down to the pubes with all the ease of a sword swallower, and I made a noise that was supposed to sound appreciative.

"Did that hurt?" he asked.

I uncorked my mouth long enough to say "Huh-uh."

Paulie started pumping himself into me, trying sex talk. "C'mon, baby," he whispered, "take it all. That's a good boy; suck my big dick. Suck that dick, baby. Oh, fuck, yeah. Fuck—that's awesome. Fuck!"

"Paulie," Darren said, "just shut the fuck up."

"Sorry," Paulie muttered, and then he began to moan and groan.

"Paulie!" Darren barked. "Get down here." And Paulie dropped to his knees to chow down on the bone Darren offered. I watched Darren's lips come off my dick, a string of drool connecting us. He gripped my shaft in his fist tightly. "I want to see you sit on this," he said to Paulie. Paulie looked up from his suck, looking at the fat head of my prick and the five or so inches that stuck up out of Darren's fist, then he looked at Darren. Then he looked at me. I don't know why, but I winked at him. He looked cute down there with his mouth all full. And then he nodded, winking back.

The sight of his ass coming down on my pole was almost enough to make me lose it. He squatted over me and lowered himself slowly, and I saw his asshole glistening from the gob Darren had spat there, my head touching the wrinkled puss. He slid on like a tight glove, and I heard Darren whistle. He licked his palm and started jacking, watching the two of us for a while, and then he got himself behind Paulie and lowered his ass until it was right in front of my face. I tongued his tiny hole and fingered it too, and it was tighter than anything I'd ever touched. He gripped the tip of my finger and wouldn't allow any further access.

Paulie rode me, and I pulled Darren's thick pecker back through his legs and sucked on it, alternating between that and his little rosebud pinch. Paulie's ass lips made my hips buck, and I fucked into him, tonguing up Darren's hole, making him grab my head and jam my face into his ass crack. "Fuck," he breathed, and I felt him shudder as he unloaded across Paulie's back.

My nuts tightened, and my knob caressed a tender button inside Paulie's cunt, and I let him pull the come out of me with his sliding ass lips. He stood up quickly, his hole gaping and dripping with gobs of semen. "Ouch," he said, bumping his head again, and he jacked off over Darren and me, hosing us down with his hot spray of jizz.

"Hey," Paulie said, his shoulders heaving. "We need a shower now!"

We walked to the showers together in clothes we threw on. I think I was wearing something of Paulie's and of Darren's. There was much hooting and towel-snapping and soap-dropping. I was still convinced that I was in some walking dream state, that this would all make for a nice morning erection. I was ready to open my eyes for real and see the sun pouring in through the funky windup windows—what was it that they were called, *jalousie? Jealousy?* It didn't matter to me what the windows were called or how this dream was going to end up. I looked at Paulie as he stood under his showerhead and Darren standing under his and got hard all over again, and Darren said, "Looks like we've got a long night ahead of us, Paulie."

"Next time, you're getting fucked," Paulie said.

"What the fuck ever," Darren said.

"Christ," Paulie asked, "can't Darren get fucked next time?"

"Forget about it," Darren said, turning his back.

"Whose dream is this, anyway?" I said, and Paulie laughed.

I woke up the next day to the snuggle of Darren's back. He wriggled his behind. I turned, looking for Paulie, and found him up in the bunk, his foot hanging out of the covers. I was thinking, *Dream or real? Dream or real? Dream or real?* And then Darren rolled over and said, "Would you do me the kindest of favors and get your dick the fuck away from the general vicinity of my ass?"

"Sure," I said.

"I told you no last night, man—you ain't gettin' in," he said, sort of smiling.

"What?"

"You heard me," he said.

And then we heard *bump,* then, "Shit!"

"Hey, guys," Paulie said, rubbing his head.

Getting Even
Simon Sheppard

"Greetings! You have mail!" NstyLthrMan dragged his mouse and clicked. E-mail from one of his editors: that damn anthology was delayed yet again. He'd have to wait a month or two longer to see his story in print. And even longer than that to get his check.

He grimaced, found the "dirty gifs" folder on his desktop, and opened DutchguyWs's picture. The monitor screen glowed with the image of a perfect dick, long foreskin, a bright stream of piss. Seeing DutchguyWS always made him horny. He reached inside his boxers and tugged at his swelling dick.

Obviously, it was time to hit the chatrooms. He dragged the uncut dick to one side of the screen and brought up the list of online chat rooms. M4M Dungeon. Full. M4M Unusual. Full. Even M4M Feet was full. Daddies and Boys. Full. Hmm. Daddies and Boys. He pushed the Who's Here button. The list of screen names came up. Oldrtopman. CuteLngIslndStd. Long Island? Across the continent. Ah, NaughtyboySF. He clicked Find Info and brought up the boy's profile: 34; 6 feet; 170; bl/bl; muscular, gym 3-4 times a week; kinky; submissive; looking for Daddy. He opened the InstaMail window, addressed it to NaughtyboySF, typed in "Hey boy. What's up?" and clicked on Send.

NstyLthrMan waited, stroking his hard dick. The boy might be involved in three or four other chats. In any case, NaughtyboySF would want to read his profile before responding. He spit in his hand and stroked his dickhead, pressing into the swollen tip. He moaned with pleasure: he sure knew how to drive himself crazy.

With a little chime, a response appeared in the InstaMail window. "Hi, Gramps. What're u doing?" Gramps? Gramps?

"What a cheeky boy!" he typed back. "I'm more than man enough for you." Send. Second thoughts: it sounded too much like a challenge. Maybe NaughtyboySF didn't mean anything nasty by "Gramps." He typed in an additional line. "Just cruising around. You?" Send.

A second or two went by. Chime. "Cruise elsewhere."

How fucking rude. He took his hand from his dick. "Sorry to have disturbed your immaculate self." Send.

Chime. "Fuck you. It's trolls like you that made me stop going to gay gyms."

And, he thought, it's attitude queens like you that keep ME away from gay gyms. "First," he furiously typed back, "I am not a troll. Second, my regular boy is a lot younger than you. And nicer. Someday you'll get to be my age, if you're lucky, and then I sure hope someone treats you the way you're treating me." Send.

Chime. "Troll. Go pick on somebody your own age."

"You really are an asshole. What are you doing in the Daddies and Boys room, anyway?" Send.

A warning beep, and a window appeared. "NaughtyboySF is no longer online."

NstyLthrMan gritted his teeth in frustration. The rude little asshole had the last word and there was nothing he could do about it. He logged off and reached down for his now-limp dick. Fuck it! He was too upset to even jack off.

"Greetings! You have mail!"

NaughtyboySF clicked open his mailbox. Spam. A new fat-burning pill. An opportunity to make thousands of dollars while sitting at home. A website featuring all-nude girls. That was misaddressed. Delete. Delete. Delete.

Chime. An InstaMail window opened unexpectedly. A message from someone he'd never heard of. Gr8hardbod. "Hey, buddy. Liked your profile…" He pulled down the Members menu and clicked on "Open Member's Profile."

"Gr8hardbod: 25; 5'10"; 175; San Francisco; handsome, masculine, ripped; looking for kewl guys into good, dirty fun. Sounded good. Sounded great.

"Hey Hardbod," he typed back, "got a gif to swap?" Send.

Chime. "Sorry, no. So if you don't want to send yours, I'll understand."

NaughtyboySF felt disappointed; there'd be no exchange of pictures.

Another chime. "But I'm fucking horny and I'd like you to suck my hard-on. Wanna make a date? :-)"

NaughtyboySF felt his dick starting to stir. But he felt wary, too. There were a lot of liars and losers online. Men who'd send someone else's gif or promise to come over and never show. Predatory old guys and worthless trolls, guys like that grandpa who'd InstaMailed him the other day, a pathetic leather daddy he'd had to beat away with a stick.

Chime. "You still there?"

He decided to take a chance. After all, there wasn't much else to do on a slow Sunday afternoon. He started to unbutton his fly, thought better of it, and started tapping on the keyboard. "Sure am, stud. What're you into?" He clicked on Send. And reached for his fly again.

It was a second-floor apartment in a nondescript building. Gr8hardbod rang the bell, announced himself through the tinny speaker, and was buzzed in. The hallway smelled of frying hamburgers.

Apartment 207. Gr8hardbod knocked, and the door opened immediately.

OK, so NaughtyboySF wasn't a perfect match for his online self-description. Of course not. Still, he wasn't bad. 34? Yeah, probably. Six feet? Well, maybe a short six feet. 170 pounds? Kinda skinny for 170. Bl/bl? If his hair had been blond, it had grown out. Muscular? Trim was more like it. And looking more like an aging MTV boy than a hunky gym bunny. Short brownish hair, skinny sideburns. Cutish, but a little shifty-eyed. And, surprisingly, a piercing through his lower lip, one of those…it begins with an "L." Kinky? Submissive? That remained to be seen.

NaughtyboySF, on the other hand, was clearly impressed. His ad might have said "looking for Daddy," but he smiled broadly when he saw the breathtakingly handsome, well-built young redhead at his door. Gr8hardbod wasn't being immodest; when he glanced at himself in the mirror behind NaughtyboySF, that's what he saw—a breathtakingly handsome redheaded guy.

"Mmm, I love redheads. C'mon in." NaughtyboySF's tenor voice was just the faintest bit femmy. Gr8hardbod stepped inside and closed the door behind himself. In a split second, NaughtyboySF was all over him, grabbing at his butt, rubbing his hard crotch up against his leg. They kissed like a car crash. Gr8hardbod could feel the little silver piercing-ball pressing into his chin. He wondered where else the guy was pierced. He knew he'd soon find out.

"Want something to drink?"

"No, I'm fine, thanks."

"Come on with me, then."

NaughtyboySF waltzed him through the tasteful, slightly barren apartment, and into the bedroom with its huge bed, its big-screen TV, and little else. Now NaughtyboySF was tugging at him, pulling him down to the bed while trying to unbutton his shirt.

"Wait, let me get my backpack off."

"Oh, yeah, your...toy bag."

Gr8hardbod put the pack down on the floor beside the bed. And immediately NaughtyboySF was all over him again, undressing him, shoving his tongue down his throat. "I'm glad you're into older guys," NaughtyboySF whispered.

"Nine years isn't that much older. And anyway, age is no big deal."

But NaughtyboySF had already moved on to another topic, muttering about how pretty his nipples were. It was time to take control.

"All right, take your clothes off and get on your knees."

Yes, SIR!" said NaughtyboySF. He peeled off his tee-shirt and jeans. There was already a wet spot on the front of his Calvins. "Underwear, too?"

"Underwear, too."

"Yes, SIR!" He smiled, and the ball stapled to his lower lip winked with light.

"What're you grinning at, fuckboy?"

"Nothing, Sir!" He was pulling down his briefs. His hard dick bobbled as he pulled his underwear over his ankles. A hard, short, chubby dick, nowhere near the seven-and-a-half inches he'd promised, but fat enough, with a Prince Albert shining from his piss-slit.

"Now get on your fucking knees." Gr8hardbod kept his tone calm and level, knowing that a true Master didn't have to raise his voice.

"Yes, Sir." The guy dropped to the floor with a thud and knelt with his hands clasped behind his back, a purposefully blank expression on his face. His fat little hard-on jutted from his well-trimmed pubic hair.

Gr8hardbod spat in his face.

"Thank you, Sir!" NaughtyboySF said, spit rolling down one cheek.

This is going to be easy, Gr8hardbod thought. The guy didn't even notice I left his door unlocked.

Spit rolling down his cheek, NaughtyboySF looked up at the redhead's face. He couldn't believe his luck. He hadn't found it easy to hook up with younger guys who'd want to top him. Certainly not such a handsome, hunky, nasty guy. And a redhead to boot! God bless the Computer Age.

"You want to taste your Master's dick, fuckboy?"

"Oh yes, Sir!" said NaughtyboySF. And he meant it.

"Just a taste, then. If you want any more, you'll have to earn it."

NaughtyboySF stared straight ahead as his new Master unbuttoned his jeans and pulled down his jockstrap. A great dick, a beautiful dick, with a big mushroom head. And a bright red thatch of pubic hair. To stop himself from grinning, NaughtyboySF opened his mouth. Wide.

The redhead teased him with his dick, bringing it right up to his lips, then pulling it away. NaughtyboySF stuck his tongue all the way out and waggled it in a way he hoped looked seductive, not ridiculous. The big head slipped into his mouth. He nursed at it, swirling his tongue around the dickflesh. Gr8hardbod grabbed the back of his head and slid his shaft all the way in, filling his mouth and throat.

"Mmm," NaughtyboySF groaned.

He felt something around his throat. A collar, a leather collar. His Master was collaring him, claiming him. His chubby dick leapt. He'd do anything for this young man. Anything. Within reason.

With a tug at his collar, his new Master pulled out of his mouth.

"That's enough for now, fuckboy." Gr8hardbod's voice was soft and serious. "Now lie down on your bed. Spread-eagle on your back."

He did as his Master said, stretching his limbs wide, his throbbing dick pounding against his belly. He turned his head to watch Gr8hardbod, who bent down, reached into his backpack, and stood over him again. His hands were full of leather and rope. "Keep your head still and your eyes straight ahead," he commanded.

NaughtyboySF felt rather than saw the leather restraints being tightened down around his ankles and wrists, the ropes being fed through the restraints' metal D-rings.

"It's sure as hell time to tie you down, fuckboy," his Master said, looping the ropes around the legs of the bed, drawing them taut and knotting them till NaughtyboySF was stretched out, tied-down, and vulnerable. Vulnerable to this handsome young man he wanted so much to surrender to. He could feel more rope now, winding around his torso, then his legs, binding him down more securely. And he could feel the long cord being drawn through the ring of his Prince Albert, the ends being tied to the wrist restraints, his hard, sensitive dick being stretched out. The first slap on his dick made him jump.

"Stay fucking still." The same deadly calm tone.

"Yes sir."

Another slap. He tried not to move at all, to conquer his reactions, to give his captor whatever he wanted.

And another slap.

"Maybe it would be easier if I blindfolded you."

Without waiting for assent, Gr8hardbod reached into his toy bag again. NaughtyboySF looked up into the redhead's face, into something dangerous gleaming in his eyes. The blindfold appeared between them, and then the familiar contours of his bedroom vanished into the dark.

NstyLthrMan and his two friends had waited long enough. He opened the door of Apartment 207 and the three of them walked inside, locking the door with a little click. It wasn't hard to figure out where the bedroom was. NstyLthrMan smiled with satisfaction. A naked young man was tied spread-eagle to the bed, a web of ropes around his body. Lean. Big nipples. A line of dark hair leading down to his pierced dick. Blindfold. Ball-gag. Ear plugs.

Gr8hardbod looked up and smiled.

NstyLthrMan smiled back. His boy had done his job well.

NaughtyboySF felt the ropes being unwound from his torso. Unable to see or hear, he had no idea of what was happening. Was the scene over? His hands and feet were being untied from the corners of the bed. And someone—a second someone!—was pressing leather-gloved hands against his chest. Then he realized with a shock that there were more than two of them there, that a third person had entered the scene. He started to panic, jerked his body upward, only to be firmly held down. By more than one pair of strong hands! How many of them were there? He tried to yell, but the gag muffled the sound. He squirmed against the powerful grip. He yelled again. A hand came down hard on his cheek. He tried to arch his body upward, his still-hard dick throbbing against his belly. Struggling was useless. He was no longer spread-eagle, but his wrist restraints had been clipped together, pinned down above his head. His ankle restraints were clipped together, too. Ropes were being wound around his legs. How many of them were there?

His hands were forced down to his crotch and the wrist restraints were tied to the cord running through his Prince Albert. Struggling too hard could rip the steel ring through the flesh of his swollen dick. What the fuck was happening? What had he let himself in for? Reflexively, his hands closed around his dick, a feeble attempt at self-protection, but soon he was stroking his cock's veiny meat. He was sweating, rivulets running down from his pits. What had he let himself in for?

He felt strong hands lifting him off his bed, the air hitting cold against his sweaty back. Levitation. It was like flying, flying blind. There were at least three of them—no, four. His body was no longer his own. Whatever was happening, he had no say in it. He was powerless, along for the ride. He was being lowered down now, being stuffed into a box, a trunk, something. He was being manhandled, stuffed into a fetal position, his hand still firmly on his dick. And with a ka-chunk, the lid came down.

From the motion of the trunk, he could figure out that he was being carried, being hauled down the stairs, out to where? The street? A waiting car? It felt like the trunk was being slid across a surface. Then the clunk of a closing door. An engine revving. A van, then, he was being taken somewhere in a van. How did I get myself into this? the trussed-up boy wondered, on the thin edge of panic. His naked body was slick with nervous sweat. How the fuck did I get myself into this?

His weight shifted as they took the curves.

"He's a heavy fucker."

"Nah, it's the trunk that's heavy," said NstyLthrMan. "He's a real lightweight." He grinned. Everything was going as planned. Though, thinking of what his captive must be going through, he felt a little guilty. Oh well, if you didn't feel a little guilty, you weren't really having fun.

The four men wrestled the trunk into the abandoned warehouse. One of them shut the thick metal door behind them. And shot the bolt.

The lid of the trunk is flung back. They grab him, pull him out of the trunk. Take his blindfold off. There are four of them, the redhead and three others, leathermen who look as though they've stepped out of a Falcon video. Incredibly buff, handsome, masculine. They undo his restraints, his blindfold, take the gag out of his mouth. Fling him onto a table, get him on all fours. The redhead whips out his dick, that big, pink mushroom head again. He opens his mouth for it, sticks his tongue out expectantly. The redhead's meat plugs his throat. He feels hands spreading his cheeks apart, lubing up his hole. Fingers going up inside him, opening him out. The redhead pulls his dick out, leaving him hungry. The four strong guys are lifting him up, throwing him onto his back. "Who fucks him first?" a voice asks. "I do," says the redhead. Two of the leathermen grab his ankles. Lift his butt in the air. Spread his legs wide. The fourth man straddles his head. Pulls out an enormous dick. Shoves it into his mouth. He feels the redhead's big dickhead slide inside his ass with a pop. The two men let go of his ankles, move to either side of him. He reaches for their big, hard dicks, starts jerking them off. He has cock in each hand, cock in each end. "Who wants sloppy seconds?" the redhead asks. The guy in his mouth pulls out, goes around to his butt. The two guys he's been jacking off move up to his head. They both fuck his face, taking turns while the redhead's dick is replaced by an even bigger one. The redhead laughs and starts slapping his ass. No, he doesn't laugh, he...

"...You'd like that, wouldn't you?"

NaughtyboySF snapped out of his gangbang fantasy. It was almost as if whoever had spoken had been reading his mind. He'd been pulled from the trunk and was now standing up, naked, hands suspended above his head, cold concrete beneath his feet. The earplugs had been taken out. The gag and blindfold were still in place. But nobody had fucked him. Nobody had slapped him. They'd hardly even touched him. Not yet, anyway.

"Do you have any idea who I am, boy?" A firm, angry voice coming out of the darkness.

Who he is? Who he is? I have no fucking idea...

"I'm Gramps. The troll. Remember now?"

Oh God, which one? When?

"Remember?"

And then he did remember, more or less. And began to get deeply, truly scared.

"Remember, you little fuck?"

The blindfold came off. Before him were standing three men. Three men dressed in leather, their faces half-hidden by leather masks. Two white men, one black.

The first white guy had a neatly trimmed salt-and-pepper beard, a hairy beer gut peeking out from his leather vest. The second white guy was tall, lanky, sinewy, a leather harness over his smooth torso. And the black guy, wearing just boots, chaps, and a studded codpiece, was built like a brick shithouse, incredible shoulders and pecs. Nipple rings gleamed against his dark chest.

"That's my Daddy. My Daddy and his friends. Like them?" The redhead spoke softly, tauntingly, in his ear.

Which one was he, which of the three? He didn't remember any of the details of whatever-his-screen-name-was's profile.

"So you'd better watch who you insult online, asshole," the redhead continued. "'Cause you never know who you're talking to. Hell, it could even've been me, using my Daddy's account."

The redhead stood before him. The three older men moved closer.

"And now I bet you think you're in for a gangbang, huh? No such luck, asshole." The redhead smiled. "See, my Daddy wants me to do this...." And he held up a gleaming hunting knife. A long, long knife with a sharp, sharp blade.

NaughtyboySF felt a shiver of fear jolt through his body. He tried to kick the redhead, but his ankles had been shackled to the floor. Gr8hardbod slowly lowered the knife. Watching the descent of the blade, NaughtyboySF began to tremble.

"Hold still or things'll get really messy."

DON'T HURT ME, NaughtyboySF wanted to shout, but the gag made it into a muffled "Mmph." Tears were in his eyes.

The knife was against his thigh. The brutally sharp edge rested on his flesh. Slowly, slowly the blade ascended, up toward his balls, his dick, tracing a thin line in its wake. The knife was just an inch from his balls. The redhead smiled. The knife edge pressed into his soft ballsac. NaughtyboySF couldn't help himself; he lost control of his bursting-full bladder. He let loose a stream of hot piss.

"Some naughtyboy!" The redhead's voice oozed contempt. "Pussyboy is more like it, a pussyboy who wets his fucking bed."

Laughter. Derisive laughter. The leathermen all were laughing. Laughing at him. His face burned hot with mortification.

Then the redhead spat in his face, which didn't cool it down at all. One by one, the three older men came up to him, very close, and spat at him, too, big gobs which mixed with the tears running down his cheeks. This was very different from the games he'd played back in his apartment. This was, he feared, for real.

"You look like shit," said the redhead. "And your dick's nothing special when it's soft."

FLASH! One of the leathermen had a camera in his hands. A second flash. And the redhead stepped up close to him again, brought the knife back down to his crotch. He could feel its cold, sharp pressure against his cockflesh. The pressure increased. Oh my God, he thought. Oh my God. He closed his eyes and shivered, waiting. Waiting for a pain that never came.

"You learned your lesson, asshole? You had enough?" Gr8hardbod sneered. "My Daddy wanted to really work you over, but his friends talked him out of it. They figured you just weren't worth the fucking trouble. And they were right." The blade retreated from his cock. "So we're just going to get rid of you. No, not kill you, shithead. Too much of a hassle. We figure you won't make any trouble for us if we let you go. You won't, will you, pussyboy? Because it'll just be your word against mine, and I've saved our online flirtation on my hard disk. And then there's the pictures we just took. I don't think you'd like them to be posted all over the Internet. So you'd better behave. No more rudeness to your elders and betters. Got that?"

He slapped the boy's face.

"I SAID 'GOT THAT?'"

NaughtyboySF nodded, new tears burning his cheeks. He meekly allowed himself to be blindfolded again, to be bundled back into the trunk. The lid clunked shut.

Back in the van, NstyLthrMan looked at his friends, at his boy at the wheel. They were all laughing and joking. So why was he feeling so ambivalent? The boy in the trunk had been asking for it, needed to be taught a lesson. But had he let NaughtyboySF's insults get to him? Had he been ruled by his anger? Had he compromised his dignity? Maybe gone too far? Oh well, if you didn't feel a little guilty, you weren't really having fun.

The van drove on through the night. A light rain had begun to fall.

NaughtyboySF felt the van screech to a stop. The trunk was being lifted out, carried somewhere, then lowered with a thump. When the lid was opened he felt the chill of the night against his nakedness, the cold dampness of a light rain. He was lifted out, laid on cold, wet ground. The unseen men tied his wrists and ankles together. And then, minute after cold, wet minute, nothing. Nothing at all. At last, he tried the knots around his wrists. They came undone easily. He untied his ankles. rose unsteadily to his feet. Pulled out the gag, the earplugs. Took the blindfold off. He was standing, stark naked and all alone, in the middle of his own backyard.

NstyLthrMan sat staring at his computer. The gif on the screen showed a man in his 30s, his face contorted in fear, though it was hard to see that he'd actually been crying. His naked body was suspended by its wrists, and if you looked closely you could see a pool of piss darkening the concrete at his feet. There was a sign above his head, like the "King of the Jews" sign at the Crucifixion. It read "I am a rude, silly queen and a pushy bottom. NaughtyboySF."

In the few days that had passed since the scene, NstyLthrMan had gotten over his guilt. Now the humiliated boy in the trunk was mostly just a pleasant memory, a memory he'd even jacked off to once or twice.

And now the time had come to send the gif to NaughtyboySF. It was time to go online.

Suddenly, he felt particularly old.

"Greetings! You have mail!"

It was from NstyLthrMan, and it had a file attached. As he downloaded it, an image took form on his screen. An image of him, naked, kidnapped, tortured, humiliated. A taunt. A warning. A softly glowing souvenir of the worst, most unforgettable night of his life.

He felt his dick getting hard.

His left hand stroked the shaft while his right hand dragged the mouse.

There it was, the "Daddies and Boys" chat room. And there was room for one more. He entered the chat room, scrolled down the list of who was there. He found a likely screen name, checked out the profile, opened the InstaMail window. And he began to type:

"Hi there, Gramps. What's up?"

Spice Up Your Life
Nick Montgomery

"Now, young man," the doctor said. "Tell me what is bothering you."

He was a kindly looking Asian man, no more than five feet tall with patches of gray at his temples. He looked to me to be in his mid-60s, although he seemed unusually spry and alert for someone that age.

"I don't know what's bothering me," I answered, glancing nervously around his office. The room was a dark, cluttered enclave, with weird posters on the wall depicting human anatomy and charts of plants and herbs. There was no examining table, only two mahogany chairs with red silk cushions. Instead of being the usual glare of sterile white, his walls and ceiling were a heavy, dusty brown. Exotic music trickled faintly from a small adjoining room in the corner. *God only knows what's in there,* I thought.

"Then why did you come here?" the doctor asked. Noticing my nervousness, he smiled gently to reassure me.

But the smile didn't help much. I was already beginning to think it wasn't the best idea, coming to him for help. I had been under the weather for weeks. Not sick, mind you, just slow and sluggish and tired. Everything seemed to be blurry around the edges, as if I were observing life from under water.

"A friend recommended you," I replied. "She said you were an herb specialist, or something like that."

The doctor nodded. "I specialize in a number of things." He smiled again, then asked, "What are your symptoms?"

"I just feet bored and tired and sluggish sometimes," I said.

"Lonely?"

I had to think about that one. I had a fair number of friends and acquaintances, any one of which I'd go out for a drink with on a Friday night. But, when it came down to it, that's really all they were—minor friends and acquaintances. I guess my only real friend was my roommate, Eric. Only I wasn't quite sure what it was I felt for Eric.

"I guess I'm lonely," I said.

"Horny?"

I laughed out loud at that one. I couldn't help myself. What kind of doctor was this guy?

"Um," I managed to sputter, still giggling, "I don't know...."

"Do you masturbate?"

"Yeah," I said.

"How often?"

I stopped laughing. I didn't know what to tell, him. The truth was, I masturbated more than the average 21-year-old should, especially one in college, where sex was practically considered a major. Believe me, I'd had many opportunities, with both men and women. But I didn't feel like engaging in a few random nights of cheap sex with strangers. It was unhealthy, for one thing, but it also wasn't what I was looking for. So I usually ended up settling for my right hand and a bottle of lotion.

"How often?" the doctor asked again, his gentle smile never wavering.

"Very often," I quickly answered.

"What do you think about when you do it?"

"I'd rather not answer that," I said quietly. "If that's OK."

I felt bad, hiding things from the guy. But I didn't feel like revealing everything. I already assumed he knew I was gay. He seemed pretty astute. And I really didn't want to tell him that I usually thought of my roommate, and the time I caught him jerking off in his bedroom.

I had come home from class early, thinking the place was empty. I took off my shoes and padded down the hallway, past Eric's door, which was slightly ajar. Apparently, Eric thought the place was empty, too, because as I swept past his room, I heard a slight moan. I stopped. There was another moan. And another.

I turned. Carefully, quietly, I peered through the crack in the door.

Eric was naked, standing in front of a full-length mirror. His back was facing me and I had a prime view of his incredible ass, clenched and thrusting slightly. I also had the advantage of being able to see his reflection in the mirror. While I had admired Eric's body from afar many times, I had never seen him naked before. What I saw amazed me.

He was obviously a guy who had seen plenty of time both in a gym and on the playing field. I knew he had been an athlete in high school, and it still showed. His chest was hard and well defined, with rock-solid pecs punctuated by dark, dime-sized nipples. His stomach was a rippling wave of muscles, a tight washboard beneath his skin. His legs were hairless, tan columns, the muscles flexing slightly as he thrust himself in and out of his hand.

The biggest surprise, though, was Eric's cock. It was a good eight inches, and he could barely get his fist around it. Its shaft curved seductively upwards, the tip swollen and succulent.

At first, I was afraid Eric might notice me and suddenly stop, embarrassed. Or even worse, would see me and grill me about why I was watching him. I was about to leave when I noticed that his eyes were closed and his head tilted back. I decided to chance it and moved in closer to get a better view.

Eric moaned again. He ran a large hand across his massive chest, fingers fumbling with his nipples. His other hand was equally as busy, a clenched fist working his cock.

By this time my own cock was hard in my khakis, pushing against the fabric, threatening to break free. Keeping my eyes glued to Eric's body, I lifted my shirt, cautiously unzipped my pants, and pulled out my hard-on. Eric aside, I was no slouch in the cock department, packing eight solid inches and an ability to stay hard for hours. I lightly palmed the head, feeling a dab of precome stick to my hand. Then I started stroking, slowly at first, but gaining speed and force the more I watched Eric.

He was close to coming, I could tell. His face was flushed and a thin sheen of sweat covered his body. Also, his cock was pointing skyward, the head turning a light shade of purple.

I jerked myself harder, thrusting my cock in and out of my closed fist. I could feel a heat building in my scrotum, that pleasurable feeling that only meant more pleasure was on its way. The sensation moved through my balls and up my shaft and, before I knew it, my hand was dripping with nine full spurts of jizz.

I heard Eric grunt and looked up to see him douse the mirror with his own supply of come. Spurt after spurt hit the glass and splattered back onto his legs. He grunted and bucked until every last drop had been forced from his cock.

And then he looked up.

To this day, I don't know if he saw me or not. I thought I had been quick about it. I jumped from the door and shuffled into the bathroom, closing the door as hastily and quietly as I could. I stayed in there a good ten minutes, washing all traces of come from my hands. When I emerged, Eric was gone. But it fueled my fantasies thinking of that day. Not only of what I saw, but what fun it might have been if Eric had seen me and wanted to experiment more.

"It's all right if you don't want to tell me, young man," the doctor said.

"Thanks," I said, slightly embarrassed. Just thinking about that afternoon had given me a raging hard-on, one that I attempted to hide by crossing my legs.

"Besides," the doctor said, getting to his feet, "I know just what you need," he said. He shuffled off into the small adjoining room and returned a moment later with a small pouch tied shut with a blue ribbon. He plopped the pouch into my hand and smiled.

"This should do the trick," he said.

"What is it?"

"It will make you more attractive to people," he applied.

I was confused. I had no problem with my self-image. In fact, I thought of myself as a good-looking guy. Sexy, even. I liked my tousled brown hair and blue eyes. I liked the way my summer tan never seemed to fade. And I particularly liked what a year of going to the gym every day had produced—a solid body that could honestly be described as "ripped."

"I don't understand," I said.

"It's an aphrodisiac."

"Oh," I said, still confused, if not a bit startled. "Like Spanish Fly?"

"It's similar, yes." The doctor flashed me a mischievous grin. "Only more potent."

I studied the small pouch in my hand, kneading it with my fingers. It made a slightly crunchy sound as I felt the herbs being jostled around inside. Would this really do the trick? I doubted it, but I thanked the doctor and asked him how much it cost.

"No charge," he said, that ingratiating smile of his now at full beam. "I never charge for the first time. Try it and tell me if you enjoy it."

"Thank you very much," I said.

"You're welcome." The doctor shuffled into the little adjoining room and closed the door. I turned and headed out the front door, into the street and toward my apartment.

At home, I plopped onto the couch and examined the pouch in my hand. I sniffed it. It smelled pungent, spicy, exotic. I began to feel a little lightheaded and warm. What was this stuff made of? The doctor was right, it was definitely potent.

I thought about having a tiny bit and treating myself to an uncontrollable jerk-off session, but remembered my 4 o'clock history class. I had missed it too many times to skip it that afternoon so, reluctantly, I closed the pouch and left for class.

When I came home an hour later, I saw that Eric had invited three of his friends over. Austin, Pete, and Steve were your typical fraternity jocks—backward baseball caps, wardrobes from Abercrombie & Fitch, and bodies you couldn't help drooling over. Austin had jet-black hair and eyes to match. He always had a growth of stubble—which went well with his dark, Italian features. Steve was a red-head, all freckled face and farm-boy physique. And Pete was a brown-haired, green-eyed party boy. The most well-built member of the bunch, he had a habit of lifting up his shirt unconsciously and showing off his washboard abs. It looked like they had just sat down to dinner.

"Hey," Eric said. "I just made some spaghetti. Want some?"

"No, thanks," I said, making my way into the kitchen. I was about to get something to drink from the fridge when I noticed the pouch sitting on the counter. It had been opened, the blue ribbon curled next to it. I picked up the pouch. It was empty.

I practically sprinted back to the dining room. "Um, Eric," I said. "What did you do with the stuff in that pouch on the kitchen counter?"

"The oregano? I put it in the sauce. I hope you don't mind."

Before I could protest, I saw Austin shovel a forkful of pasta into his mouth. Then Steve did the same. Pete was chewing, a good third of his plate already empty.

"I don't mind," I said, wondering what the hell I should do next. "It just wasn't oregano."

"Whatever it is, it's damn good," Pete said. His face had reddened and I noticed beads of sweat forming on his forehead. "Is it hot in here?" he asked.

"I think so," Austin said. "Don't you have air conditioning in this place?"

"It's fucking unbearable," Steve added. He stood up and pulled off his T-shirt, revealing a freckle-specked chest taut with muscle. He ran a hand over his chest and down his stomach. "That's better," he said, before sitting back down at the table.

Austin and Pete stood up and did the same. Austin's chest was solid and dark, a thick mat of hair tapering down his stomach. Pete's was hairless and pale, with rosy-pink nipples that pointed straight ahead. Like Steve, their pecs and stomachs were nothing but muscle.

I stood speechless and motionless. Three incredible-looking guys were sitting shirtless at my dining room table, all under the influence of a mightily potent aphrodisiac. I could tell by their body language that something was going to give—and soon. I didn't know whether to run or fetch my video camera.

It turned out I didn't have time to do either. Pete and Austin began to eye each other, wicked grins forming on both their faces. Austin smoothed a hand through his chest hair then dipped it into the waist of his jeans. Pete pinched his nipples slightly, never taking his eyes off Austin's roaming hand.

"Shit, I'm horny," Austin said, his hand moving furiously inside his jeans. "I could sure do with a blow job right now."

"Me, too," Pete said, standing up. "I'm *real* fucking horny."

He slid off his pants and boxer shorts and stepped out of them. He had a great-looking cock, long and narrow, that stood straight out from his body. In no time, Austin was on his knees, twirling his tongue around the tip of Pete's dick. Pete tilted his head back and gave a long, guttural moan.

"What the fuck are you doing?" Steve asked, springing from his chair. But, instead of trying to break them up, he stood next to Pete and whipped out his dick. His was shorter than Pete's but thicker and more veined.

Without missing a beat, Austin moved from Pete's cock to Steve's. He alternated between the two, wrapping his luscious lips around one then the other. Steve put an arm around Pete's back and moved in close. The two began to kiss passionately, their tongues snaking in and out of each other's mouth. Low, animal-like grunts escaped their locked lips.

I started to speak but, due mostly to pure shock, couldn't produce any words. Obviously, it was an incredible sight, watching these three studs go at it. I didn't know whether to break them up or join in. So, I decided to watch a little more and see what happened.

Pete, meanwhile, moved behind Austin and slid him out of his jeans. Austin's cock outdid both of theirs in length and girth. It pointed skyward, rising out of a thick bush of pubic hair. Austin continued to deep-throat

Steve as Pete huddled behind him and began to tongue his ass.

"Yeah," Austin moaned before cramming his through with Steve's mighty cock again.

Pete had Austin's ass cheeks open wide and was plunging his tongue in and out of Austin's hairy hole.

I looked to see what Eric's reaction to all this was. He didn't say a word, only stared wide-eyed. It wasn't until I saw him pull out his own monster dick that I realized he was staring more out of pleasure than shock.

"Hey, Austin," he said sharply, cock in hand. "Suck this."

Austin crawled over to where Eric was sitting and immediately took all of his shaft down his throat. Eric tore off his T-shirt and grabbed Austin's head, guiding him up and down his saliva-slicked dick.

I glanced over at Pete and Steve, who were contentedly engaged in a frantic 69, each of them trying to take as much of the other into their mouths as possible.

"Take off your clothes," Eric told me. "Let me see your cock."

"I don't like this, Eric," I said, although my raging hard-on inside my pants was obvious to anyone with two eyes. "Make them stop."

Eric smiled at me and pushed Austin away. Then he stood up, cock still hanging out of his jeans, and came over to me. He grabbed my belt buckle and pried it open. Then he undid my jeans and yanked out my erection, bending down and running his tongue up and down the shaft.

"Stop," I muttered weakly. "We shouldn't...be...doing this."

I closed my eyes. Eric opened wide and I could feel my cock slide deep into his mouth. His tongue rolled around my head, my shaft, my balls. It was obvious he had done this before.

"Don't stop," I heard myself saying. "Don't fucking stop."

Eric didn't. He continued to gorge himself on my hard-on, seeming to take it in deeper and deeper every time. His tongue moved constantly, exploring every inch of my shaft. He cupped my balls in one hand, the other resting on my lower back, pushing me closer to him. All the while his masterful tongue didn't stop.

I suddenly felt my cock slide out of his mouth and slap against my stomach. I opened my eyes.

Pete was on his hands and knees, Steve standing in front of him, fucking his face. Austin had gotten a condom from somewhere and was behind Pete, stuffing his huge dick into Pete's tight hole. Pete grimaced and cried out at the initial penetration. Then he smiled and eased back onto Austin's cock.

"Yeah," Steve said. "Fuck him. Fuck his tight ass."

Austin, hands on either side of Pete's waist, began to plunge his thick rod into Pete's hungry hole. Pete, enjoying it now, once again went down on Steve.

Eric stepped in front of me. He was completely naked now, his body just as solid and beautiful as I had remembered it to be. He grabbed my head and pushed me toward his hard-on. His cock was so huge I could barely fit it into my mouth. But I soon managed, sliding my lips down it inch by inch until my face was pressed into his patch of pubic hair.

Eric moaned and moved his fingers through my hair. He bucked his hips, ramming his cock deeper down my throat. He tasted good—a mixture of salt, sweat and precome. I wrapped my tongue around the head, dipping into his piss slit. I worked his balls with my hand, kneading one, then the other. His thrusts grew more forceful. He had a grip on my hair now and was pushing me down, impaling me on his cock. I had to hold my breath, but I didn't want to stop, didn't want to do anything but feel his meat sliding in and out of my mouth.

And then, he came. He body began to shake and he shouted in ecstasy, the come shooting out of his cock and down my throat. I kept my lips tight around his shaft, making sure none of it got away from me, all the while swallowing, swallowing as spurt after spurt hit the roof of my mouth. When he was finished, I licked his cock clean.

Eric went to the table and shoved the plates to one side. He bent over, his ripe ass tilted upwards. "Fuck me," he said.

"Eric, I don't think you want me to."

"I need it," he said. "I need it."

He reached a hand behind him and inserted his index finger into his tight hole. I glanced over at Steve, Pete, and Austin.

Pete was still on all fours and Steve had just deposited a load of come onto his face. Pete licked at it hungrily. Austin, also still on his knees, pulled out of Pete, ripped off the condom and sprayed Pete's back with a massive amount of semen.

Eric, meanwhile, wasn't watching any of it. Instead, he was thrusting his hips back and forth, his finger going deeper and deeper inside him. "I have to have it," he moaned.

I grabbed his arm. "Come on," I said.

Quickly we made our way into Eric's bedroom. He closed the door and immediately grabbed me, his mouth pressing down on mine. His tongue parted my lips and slid into my mouth. His hands roamed freely across my body, pinching my nipples, cupping my balls.

My mind was reeling with pleasure when he produced a condom from his bedside table and slid it onto my hard, hungry shaft. He made a quick flip onto his back and before I knew it, I was fully inside him. We moved slowly at first, Eric savoring the way my cock slid in and out of him. Then we began to move quickly, frantically. With his legs flung over my shoulders, I gripped his thighs and rammed my meat into him again and again. Eric made a series of guttural moans, meeting each of my thrusts with one of his own.

And then, in a flurry of sweat and groans and tongue-filled kisses, Eric came again, sending a geyser of come onto my chest, neck and face. Tasting his sweet jizz on my lips, I felt the rumble of an orgasm deep inside me then filled the condom with an eruption of my own come. I landed on top of Eric, my cock still inside him. We exchanged one sweet, sensual kiss before drifting off to sleep.

Eric was still asleep when I awoke. I studied his handsome angel-face and began to dread what would happen when he woke up. I had quite a bit of explaining to do and wasn't looking forward to any of it.

I slipped on a pair of Eric's boxers and padded into the living room. It was dark outside. The clock on top of the TV said it was almost nine.

Steve, Austin, and Pete had left. I glanced over to the dining room table. It was still cluttered with half-full glasses and plates of spaghetti. There was also a note.

Eric, it said. *Thanks for dinner. We have to do it again. The Guys.*

"Are they gone?"

It was Eric. He stood silhouetted in the bright hallway. He had a towel wrapped around his waist.

"Yeah," I said.

An awkward moment passed between us.

"I'm sorry, Nick," he said. "I don't know what got into me."

I sighed heavily. "I have to be honest with you. It was the spaghetti sauce."

"What about it?"

"That pouch I had sitting on the counter. It wasn't oregano, like you thought."

Eric had a concerned look on his face now. It was beautiful, the way he squinted his eyes in confusion, the way his lips parted slightly. "What was it?"

"An aphrodisiac," I said. "An herb doctor gave it to me."

Eric laughed. "You mean, I put Spanish Fly in the pasta sauce?"

"Yeah. Only the doctor told me it was more potent."

"Geez," Eric said. "No wonder the guys were fucking their brains out. I've never seen them that horny."

Then he paused. The gorgeous concerned look filled his face again. Then he said, "But you didn't have any sauce."

I looked into his eyes; I knew what he was getting at. I had been caught red-handed. My secret was out. Eric knew.

"No," I said. "I didn't."

Eric began to walk toward me, slowly and with purpose. He smiled, then dropped his towel.

"Good," be said. He put his arms around me and pulled me to him. He was erect and I felt his steel-hard cock press against my stiffening one. "Because I didn't, either."

Invasion of Privacy
R.W. Clinger

"Hello! Is there anybody in here?" Of course there isn't. Point is at work, studying under the firm hands of a blond and handsome advisor, learning to build the tallest buildings, stack bricks, and mold cement. I am thrilled that the apartment is empty.

I have stolen the key from my roommate's boyfriend, who happens to be one of the maintenance men to the building. Simple and sweet. Robbie (me!) gets a key, peeks into Point's apartment from time to time, catches exotic glimpses of Point's life. To concentrate on him...be amused...understand him. Anything that makes something rock and roll inside my protruding, cotton Kleins.

"Hello, Point!" I yell again, touch the sofa where he sat naked in front of some man-on-man video, eating buttery popcorn with slick fingers. I caress the silver-plated edges of Point's photos on his dresser and other tablelike structures. Point standing in a skimpy bathing suit at the beach. Point drying off in the bathroom with one of those large cotton towels you can make love on. Point with his chiseled lines manipulating every inch of his well-designed, 23-year-old body. Blue, craving eyes. Rigid jaw. Lips that can divide a man into parts of rainbow lust, and could maybe whisper, "Robbie...you're the one," into my pulsating, needing-to-listen ears.

There's no one in the apartment. Empty. Just me. I make myself at home. I shower, shave with Point's razor, sniff his clean undies, drink his vodka, roll around naked on his bed. Of course I clean everything up before I leave, because Robbie doesn't want to ruin his Friday afternoons. And then, I lock the door to Point's rose-smelling apartment, tuck away the golden key to happy times, and end up back in my apartment across the street where I sit naked in front of a city window with my feet propped up against a chilled radiator, and wait until God Point gets home from his afternoon romp with his building buddy.

I observe for a living, get paid fair bucks for it. Robbie the sociologist studies the behavior of college students, observes how they perform in a classroom, how they concentrate on classroom objectives. That's how I met Point. He was a student, and I was observing him, but when he dropped out last semester, my professionalism ran astray, leaving me unable to stop observing, and then coincidence easily crept into my peering life, and I got a key to his apartment and, well, fix yourself and listen....

Of course we have seen each other naked, because our apartments are directly across from each other (coincidence again). I've seen his silken smooth sun-dark body in the summery light, and he's seen my ripened and massive one.

Just two days ago, after a 6 P.M. shower, having one of the cottony soft towels hang around his waist like a lover, Point caught me off guard. He made me stand paralyzed in front of my opened window as he stood in front of his window, man admiring naked man; strangers dancing with constant gazes. He ran a single, splayed palm from the V of his neck, down over each nipple, circling them, and then over each pulsating ab, even further down to the white rim on the cotton towel. The towel fell to the floor as our eyes blended and sealed. The hand strayed to the triangle of thick black hair between his legs, and then reached around his semi-hard, meaty friend, making himself harder than the buildings we stood in, harder than me...pumping and thrusting his hips forward, just Point and me in the world, like lovers. Eventually white ooze spurted from his fleshy cannon onto his cherry-colored wooden floor. His hips ground and melted me from so far away as some of the jism spit out the window, seven floors down...falling and falling.

As I run a long, thin finger down my outstretched, naked leg that's propped up onto the radiator, I think about catching his whiteness down on the street. Mouth opened, hands and arms outstretched, balancing myself for a good catch. White Point falling into my opened mouth, filling my needed craving. Swallowing.

I wait for him to arrive home. I wait to watch him walk from one end of his apartment to the other, pulsating and ripped, maybe showing off, all naked and horny and ready for golden-boy me. Usually, I watch for a long time. I gaze at him as he makes dinner with skimpy shorts on and nothing else; tight need-to-be-poked buttocks moving around. I gaze at his body as he pumps weights, sweaty and glazed, hard-on standing out of thick pubic hair. I admire the look he gives the 18-year-old Italian pizza boy upon delivery; one of those dazzling glances that says, "A cutie like you has time to stick around and collect his tip, doesn't he?"

Everyday things.

The Life and Times of Point Stevens.

But today is different, this Friday. I'm about to do one of the bravest things that Robbie has ever done. I'm about to show off like he did, give Point back what he gave me, my shaft in hand now, rolling it between fingers, feeling its plump, semen-filled head, sweat beginning to build all over my bent, needing-to-thrust body. I feel the trickling hairs on my lower stomach, stiff and yet soft. I touch my nipples, create hard brownish mounds. I lick my plump upper lip and get too excited, ready to expose a little of my white self to the real world. But right at the last second, before pumping everything I've got all over the floor, I whisper to the heated stillness of my top-floor apartment, "Stop...Point's not home yet," which leaves me to wait and dream of his poignant arrival.

Point arrives shortly after 7 P.M., as expected. He already has his shirt off, carries his hard-hat in his left hand. There are grease marks and dust all over his ripped jeans. I see mounds of Point-flesh through tears of denim as he plops the hat on an abandoned, manless couch. No boyfriend. No other man floats around him. Just me in my nakedness, across from him, ready and willing to surprise him with a big game of Robbie-Turn-On, invading his privacy.

He vanishes for a moment from the window view, comes back carrying a beer. Point pops it open, wipes a wet hand along his dark, dirty, muscle-popping chest. Wet perspiration and hair dangle over his intense eyes. He swings his head back, chugs the beer dry, and then...sees me in my persuasive window.

Next, Point drops the aluminum can, walks in a slow manner to his private window, keeps his eyes locked onto mine as if I'm some Herculean God, some *Playgirl* model. Part of his queer, dick-chewing mouth is open, leaving him in shock. He stands still, like a sturdy building, and begins to observe my masterful work. I have a chilly bucket of water sitting on the floor beside me with a bar of white soap floating inside it. I reach for the wet soap and roll it between my two palms, making lathering suds above my abs. The soap and hands find my neck first, work smoothly down my torso, touch everything I want Point to touch. Carved nipples. Popping pecs. Abs of metallic beauty. All turn-ons, willed to please only my single viewer from across Mount Street. A window (my window!) is transformed into some fascinating, high-feeling exhibit that possibly makes Point wish there was a tight clothesline between our apartments so he can dangle from it and mingle towards my man-infested abode with a gleeful smile written over his face that utters: need.

The bar of lathery soap reaches my navel. The chilled water cleans my burning meat-hard soul. I lather up triangular, burned-summer color pubic hair, dangling balls, growing shaft of delight that I want to open Point with. White suds drip off Zeus thighs and fall to the wooden floor. Like come drops that spurt out of the plump head of a Queen's dazzling, throbbing ass-poker. I lick lips with a constant observation as my hands drop the bar of soap to the floor. Feeling compelled to roll fingers over Robbie-sword, I see Point grow with exuberance. He's possibly charmed. Maybe tingling over there in his boyless apartment. And as infatuation sparks a harder erection between my spreading thighs, my accurate eyes watch the denim swell between his V-cut, pillarlike legs, and cause me to feel one quick jolt of silky pre-come erupt at the top of my slitted fag-beast.

I mouth, "Do you like what you see?" but Point doesn't respond…or rather, he responds (coincidentally, of course) by mingling one of his hands over hard denim, keeping his muddy brown eyes locked onto my evening performance of private invasion.

Pumping soapy cock is like having a lover shave you in the shower. It's totally remorseful. Intended work. Erotically cleansing. But when you pump a soapy cock for the construction worker across Mount Street, well, it's like having your wildest bedtime dreams sprinkled with golden stars or porn-model come droplets.

Willing my mushroomlike-capped meat with both slippery hands is not tedious work for me. I am willed to please, to satisfy. I see Point pick at a hard, popping nipple. He licks his own lips, moves a flat hand down into the rim of his denim and possible underwear. He touches everything he wants to press his fingertips into. And the look on his dashing, all-smiles and yet relaxed face, suggests that he wants to build something with me;

just between men, and just between us. Queer Builders Inc.

How long does he rock his hand down within his Levis-covered flesh? It seems forever as I manipulate my wet man-pole. But all good things cease—Don't they?—because that's what happens. Point unleashes his probing fingers and backs away from the window, leaves me to sigh heavily, but still with a thick, nine-inch rolling-pin structure in my massive hands. His window is empty for seconds, but he returns with what looks like a can of Pam or kitchen counter cleaning spray. Point closes his window and he accurately sprays onto the transparent pane of glass, which is directly in front of his crotch: NEED ME?

Intoxicated, I smile, feel another jolt of pre-come lift to the tippy-top slit of my desiring meat probe, and write on the soapy lather that has built-up on my chest: YES!

Moments later, I expect a single tap on my door, but nothing of the sort occurs. I keep my meat hard between my legs with two thrilled hands. I wait with utter patience for toy-boy builder to enter into the most necessary relationship. I wish the door were locked so he could break it down and…use building tools with me.

But builder doesn't knock. And the slender, tight entrance route to my seventh floor apartment is unlocked. Point invades, behaves as if it is his apartment. I hear the door click open, beige and dirty boots rap against the hard floor. He finds me, but I don't turn around and greet him. I simply utter with coldness and hard cock still in my rapping hands, "You're invading my privacy."

He laughs. Not in one of those sissy-ass boy ways; it's an intentional thick laugh, mixed with a solid cowboylike grunt that's filled with need and intimate care; one that's well practiced, and says he's ready to create a man out of the persuasive sociologist in the window.

Next, I hear a can opening and feel chilled beer rolling down and over my chest. Point utters with a sense of deliberated fineness, "I had to come over and rinse you off." He empties the beer can and tosses it to the floor. Clink! And then I feel his slab of bare, veined cock fall limp over my right shoulder as his fingers dance through my wavy, sun-bleached hair. I reach up as Point stands behind me and touch the tip of it, make it sticky with used soap suds and the drop of personalized cockjuice that sputtered free only moments before. I smell beer, man piss, and man sweat—and man need, too. Then, I simply whisper as I touch his massive, cut rod with a thick hand, rolling fingers over the hardening veins, "You don't have a boyfriend, do you, Point?"

His meat-beast grows with my immediate touch. "Yes, I do."

I drop my hand, unwilling to continue. I don't want to ruin things in his personalized life. I may be an exceptional viewer, but not a wrecker of lives. "Who?" I ask.

"I don't know his name. He's a hunk in some window across from my apartment." Slick Point reaches over my shoulder and finds one of my hands, directs it to his jism shooter again.

I smile, craving him. I endlessly need more of his time. Seconds speed by as I lean my head back on the wooden chair and whisper his name, blow a soothing, dainty kiss towards his dazzling, thin lips, intense cocoa-colored eyes, and well-carved cheekbones.

"How long has the sociologist been watching a guy like me?" Point asks. His fingers find both of my nipples, pinch hard. His lips kiss the top of my god-blond head.

"Since I spotted you at the college last semester." My one hand still rolls over my thrusting Robbie-rod. The meat stick stands proud and strong, showing off.

He laughs in that grunting, cowboylike way again that makes splinters of come want to fly from the top of my wet shaft, out the window, and onto Mount Street. I turn my head around and view his slab of building dick, and whisper, "I've found something here," and promptly lick the slit-hole on Point's intruding pointer.

He pinches my skin harder. His pounder-cock explodes in size. Out of the corner of my eye, I see ripped muscle on his dark chest that is built with lines of intense work. Pecs grow twice in size. Tips of nipples are the size of ten-penny nail heads. Abs look like ladders for me to climb so I can rest my lips on his narrow ones. To excite him more, I slip the tip of his Robbie-finder into my mouth, suck on it with impassive, mesmerizing care. Slurp. Roll of the tongue. Squeeze between my lips. Point arches his back, presses into my back, and whispers, "You're breaking some kind of law, aren't you?" in complete ecstasy.

I release his ass-plunger from my lips and chant, "Since the beginning of time with you."

But the conversation changes quickly, dramatically, and the next thing Point says is: "Do you want to seal this relationship up tight?"

And I turn to the side of the chair, cock standing straight up like a pink nightclub dancer named Rocketfinder, biceps tense and shaky, noticing denim around his ankles and dirty boots. I stand, slap my ass hard with desired excitement and whisper, "I've got a key around here somewhere," and feel my chest lay against his as our rock-hard nipples touch and he slips his probing tongue into my mouth.

Latex in square packages lay still on the wooden floor by the chair. I have my hands on the back of the chair, legs spread wide, cock pointing through wood bars of the chair, waving to other apartment observers across Mount Street. Point is somewhere behind me, definitely on his stiff, aching knees. He's separated my skin-tight ass with his kissable lips and then drives hard into my pink, queer shell with the tip of his long tongue. I feel an earthquake occurring beneath my bare feet. I feel Zeus fucking Hercules, muscle against muscle, as Point's tongue enters me, pulls out, enters me again. As Hercules bucks hard within my imaginary mind, Point finds my dangling soft balls and begins to roll fingers over them, plays with them, makes me feel as if I am between the Greek gods this time, all three trying to make me immortal and used.

I whisper, "Permission to intrude," as his tongue falls into me again, further this time, finding the heart and soul of the sociologist. I wobble as if I'm dancing. I almost fall and lose control. But Point holds me in place, presses his fingers hard around my balls, willing his other hand on one hip, keeping window-boy Robbie in place, determined to change, pull, push, throttle things.

Point comes up for air, spins me around, breaths real air like a skydiver or something, and says, "You've been a naughty observer."

I nod my head, gleefully smile. "Yes, I have." There is nothing but exquisite man before me. His own construction is model-best. Point's roving, hard shaft promotes direction to the ceiling of my heated window room. I reach out, wrap a hand around his thick, lined muscle of fag-heaven, bend for a square of protection and look up into his dazzling, dark eyes, uttering quaintly, "How naughty can you be, Point?"

"Enough to make you blind with passion." Not a very good poet, but he'll build just fine into one.

I rip protection open then, too excited, having my mind pop with Pointillism. I slip the condom down and over his reddened, erect pony, stand abruptly, ready and willing to take on what Point's got to give. After turning my offer back toward him, I hold a position with my fists clenched over the hard wood of the chair's back, spread my legs for natural queer-ness to take over, convinced with ease that Point from across Mount Street will manipulate me again and again, mischievously or in a dogmatic sense, whatever the moment allows. Looking behind me, turning my innocent but trusting eyes towards him, I whisper, "Prove that you're my new boyfriend."

Proving something of that nature is not a difficult task for the construction worker behind me. The head of his plastic-covered driver punches against my skin with utter ease, slips into me as if heaven were dripping over Earth, but, of course, it hurts like hell. His ten-or-so inches of testosterone-filled flesh feels like lumber in me, scrapes my insides, pushes and pokes at my entrails, feels as if Point has lodged it into the back of my throat, pokes at my society-accepting brain. It's one BIG thrust too! Not a pussy-ass push by some hand-wringing princess. It's one of those thrusts that has power behind it and is tainted with a sense of delirium and mischief.

Squinting my eyes, I shake all over and feel Point pull out as he takes a part of my insides with him. I am only left to moan the strangest, gurgling sounds that resemble: boyfriend, window, and separate.

With nails buried into the wood of the chair, Point squeezes my hips, pulls and pushes on them. His breathing grows wild, rough and animal-like. Pump. Thrust. Grunt. I sing some rock-n-roll baby-doll song in my head. I think of grease being smeared on a pane of glass as Point drives a little stare-boy like me wild. I feel like the tail-end of Italy is being shoved into my ass, heaving backwards onto him.

He leaves me to grunt, "More." But it sounds like whore instead. And I'm OK with that, because his pushing sends me to the bottom of the Atlantic Ocean and back. Pump. Thrust. Grunt. His hands latch onto my shoulders. They pull on me, force me to split more, to glow, and to hear him in a heated passion utter, "Robbie...I'm going to implode you."

Yes!...Dear queer God in Heaven...Yes! I think and dream as he pulls out and shoots onto my displayed back, over my head, too. I feel heated droplets of new Point-spew drip off my nose and watch it land onto the chair's seat. I feel some of his warm ooze on my forehead as he whispers, "Turn around, Woodboy, I want to finish you off."

I listen, because I'm in no position not to since my cock is ready to explode. My hands rest behind me on the chair's back, grasping hard wood. I feel woozy and almost unable to stand with hot builder juice dripping slowly down my back, over buttocks and man-crack, down Robbie legs.

Point's down on his knees, rolls his wet, jism-covered hands over my chest. His outstretched tongue meets my stiff cockhead once, teases me into disastrous, throbbing pain. And then he gropes the hard beauty of my world and begins to jerk on it, up and down, speedily, still licking the head of my cock.

I am left to think that I am a princess of windows as I feel his elaborate touch. I buck hips and moan and stare passionately down at his slender stomach, thick waist, bolt-upright cock between his thick legs. The last of his come drips off an eyebrow, falls to my lips. Salty pleasure. Thick man whiteness. Destiny sealed between us.

I still feel him inside me, coaching me with imaginable pressure, splitting me into two firm Robbies, but he really isn't there. Point wills me to come, pressures me, says things like: "Let that boy free." And that sends me over some ejaculating edge, which causes thick, white observing spew to fly out the tip of my rocky-ridged cock and splatter over Point's nipples, abs, shoulders, lips, and chin.

He cleans off his lips, because Point doesn't like to eat man-juice, just cock. His fingers delicately roll the spew away from them. I pump one last touch of ooze onto his working fingers and think of the golden key to his apartment, the photos, his underwear, shaver, shower, and his bed. I dream of laying against him this night, when it's completely dark outside, after midnight. I think of coupling with him, forming one figure. A mischievous grin of wildness controls my mouth. I know that I will trot across Mount Street and find myself slipping into Point's apartment again, having every intention to get him used to the taste of come, invasion of privacy, and me.

Hitchcock
Bob Vickery

Phil and I hang out all afternoon in the head of the Statue of Liberty, waiting for the crowd to thin. I spend most of the time staring out the windows, like James Stewart in *Rear Window,* only, unlike James, I don't witness Raymond Burr slicing up his wife, just the tugs and freighters steaming up and down the East River. Seagulls wheel around in the sky above, swooping and rising, like the crows dive-bombing Tippi Hedren and the schoolchildren in *The Birds.* Phil is pacing back and forth, growing more and more tense, his eyes shifting nervously like, like…John Hodiak in *Lifeboat?* Farley Granger in *Strangers on a Train?* Henry Fonda in *The Wrong Man?* No, I decide, definitely most like Robert Cummings in *Saboteur,* when he's hiding out with the sideshow freaks in the circus train as the feds search for him car by car. This is fitting since the fantasy we're about to act out comes from the same movie.

Phil glances at his watch and then at me. He really is a handsome man, his dark eyes snapping with intensity, his sexy mouth pulled down in a worried scowl. "This place is going to close in less than an hour," he says in a low voice. "If we're going to pull this off, we better act damn soon."

He's right, of course. I look around. There's been a steady stream of tourists since we first arrived, but a group of school kids has just left and now there's just us and three others. This might be as close to a chance as we're going to get. I sidle over to the exit door and look down. The stairs are narrow and steep, and I feel a wave of acrophobia, like James Stewart in *Vertigo,* when he's chasing Kim Novak up the bell tower. I don't see anyone. I catch Phil's eye and jerk my head. He nods, picks up his gym bag, and we race down to the first landing. The main stairs continue on down through the trunk of Liberty to the exit below. A wire mesh fence with a padlocked door separates us from a ladder that ascends up Liberty's arm to the lamp she's holding.

We both glance up and down the stairs. Phil quickly unzips his gym bag and pulls out a pair of bolt cutters. It takes just a couple of seconds to slice through the padlock. Phil and I slip through the door and close it behind us. I replace the padlock so that, unless someone looks at it closely, it still seems securely locked. Phil and I scramble up the ladder.

We push open a small door in the base of Liberty's lamp and find ourselves outside, on the tiny balcony that rings the flame. My heart is pounding with excitement. This is where Robert Cummings corners and accidentally kills Norman Lloyd, the Nazi assassin and bomber, in the final scene in *Saboteur*. A slight breeze blows in from Staten Island and ruffles through my hair. The sun is low in the sky, squatting over the Meadowlands and the apartment buildings in Bayonne. I glance over toward Phil. He's watching me, his eyes amused, his mouth curled in a sly grin. "We don't have much time," he says. "Let's get this show on the road."

"All right," I laugh. I pull Phil toward me and plant my mouth over his. Phil is a good three or four inches shorter than I am, a bantam cock of a man with a wiry, compact body, and I have to bend my neck down to kiss him. His tongue pushes through toward the back of my throat, and he starts grinding his crotch against mine. I reach behind him, cup his ass with my hands, and pull his body against me. I can feel his stiff dick push through the rough fabric of his jeans and rub against me. I slide my hands under his T-shirt and across the smooth muscles of his torso. I find the stiff nubs of his nipples and tweak them. Phil groans softly. He reaches down, unbuckles my belt, and pulls down the zipper of my fly. In a matter of seconds, my pants and shorts are down around my ankles. I step out of them, pull off my shirt, and stand naked by Liberty's torch. It takes only a couple of moments to strip Phil naked as well.

Phil reaches down and wraps his hand around both our dicks, squeezing them together. I look down at the solid mass of dick flesh encircled by his fingers: my cock, pink and fat, leaking precome, pressed tightly against Phil's blood-engorged prick. Phil may be short in stature, but he's prodigiously hung, his dick thick and long. It is so damn exciting to be bare-assed naked with my good fuck buddy out in the open on top of one of Alfred Hitchcock's most famous settings. A film buff's ultimate sexual fantasy. Phil starts jacking us off slowly, his hand moving up and down the twin columns of dick flesh.

I sink down to my knees, the pitted copper of the old balcony biting into my skin, and bury my face into Phil's fleshy ball sac, inhaling deeply, breathing in the ripe scent. I open my mouth and let his ball meat spill in, rolling it around with my tongue. Phil takes his stiff cock and rubs my face with it. "Yeah," he growls. "Suck on those balls. Juice them up good." I hold his cock at the base and squeeze it, watching it darken in color, its engorged head taking on the color and size of a small plum.

"Beautiful," I murmur. I slide my tongue up the fleshy shaft slowly, lovingly, and when I get to the head, I open my lips wide and take the whole cock in my mouth. Phil groans again and starts pumping his hips with quick, staccato thrusts. I reach behind and grab his ass, squeezing the muscular cheeks as his dick slides in and out of my mouth. My fingers burrow into his ass crack and massage his bung hole, teasing and playing with the pucker of flesh. Phil sighs.

I hear the low moan of a tugboat horn far off in the distance. It's followed shortly after by the higher-pitched call of the Staten Island ferry. As I feed on Phil's dick, I wonder what kind of show we're giving the traffic in the East River. *Can the ferry passengers make out any details, or are we too distant to be noticed?* I like to think that people are lining the decks, their binoculars trained on us, watching me give Phil head.

Phil's legs start to tremble. His balls are pulled up tight, and his dick throbs in my mouth. The fucker's just about ready to shoot. I take his dick out of my mouth and start jacking him off. Phil groans loudly, his body spasms, and suddenly his jizz spurts out, splattering against my face. Another spasm sweeps over him, and then another. By the time he's done, his thick load is sliding down my face in sluggish drops.

I wipe my hand over my face, sliming it up with his jizz, and start beating off. Phil pulls me to my feet, his hands playing up and down my body, pulling on my flesh, tugging my balls, stroking me all over. I close my eyes and arch my back as my jizz squirts out over the low copper railing into the empty air below. I wonder if any of it splattered against the windows in Liberty's head.

Phil wraps his arms around me and kisses me again. He breaks away, laughing. "Well, chalk up another Hitchcock landmark," he says. He glances at his watch. "Jesus! We gotta get out of here. It's closing time."

The next day we fly out to Rapid City, South Dakota. We rent a car at the airport, drop off our bags at a Motel 6, and head out toward the visitors' center at Mount Rushmore. The place is packed with tourists trying to milk the most out of their last remaining days of summer. Through the wide windows of the center, I can see Mount Rushmore loom over us, the four presidents gazing benignly off into the distance. It's just like the scene where Eva Marie Saint shoots Cary Grant in *North By Northwest*.

When it's my turn at the counter, I check out the ranger behind it. The guy could be a poster boy for the National Park Service: mild blue eyes, a strong jaw, neatly clipped blond hair, broad shoulders underneath his crisply starched uniform. He looks like a Midwestern Swede, one of those corn-fed farmers' sons that only the Bible Belt can produce. The name tag pinned over his right pec reads Johanson.

Ranger Johanson flashes me a polite smile. "Can I help you?" he asks.

I give him a cruisy smile in return, more of a knee-jerk reaction than a genuine effort to seduce. "You got any trail maps? My buddy and I are looking for some good trails to hike."

He pulls out a few maps from below the counter. I turn up the wattage of my smile. Ranger Johanson's eyes flick up and down my body, so quickly that if I weren't on the alert, I might have missed it. "Here you go, " he says, his voice pleasant and detached. I take them and join Phil over by the viewfinders.

"You're such a dick pig," he says.

"I just smiled at him," I reply. I pull out the maps. "It's going to be a real ball-buster hike tomorrow. We're going to have to get up extra early." Phil doesn't say anything.

That evening, armed with our *Spartacus Guide to Gay America,* Phil and I explore the gay side of Rapid City. Slim pickings, at best. We wind up in a place called the Rendezvous Club, something straight out of the '50s, right down to the crepe wallpaper, the wall sconces with crystal pendants, and the Patsy Cline records on the jukebox. I buy a pitcher of beer and join Phil at a table at the far end of the room, over by the cigarette machine. I feel uneasy. Try as I might, I can't conjure up a Hitchcock scene this bar might evoke.

"This place depresses me," I say. "Let's blow."

"Relax," Phil says. "We've got nowhere else to go. Would you rather hang out in that dump of a motel?"

I shrug and say nothing. I gloomily watch the pool game in progress a few feet away. After a few minutes of silence, Phil nudges me in the side. "Look who just walked in."

I glance toward the door and see Ranger Johanson standing at the doorway, scanning the room. He's wearing jeans and a T-shirt that hugs his torso, revealing a tight, lean body. Johanson's eyes turn toward us, and he nods his head in greeting. He walks over to the bar, orders a beer, and moves over to our table.

"You guys mind if I join you?" he asks.

I push a chair out with my foot. "Have a seat." I stick out my hand. "I'm Larry. My friend's name is Phil."

Johanson shakes our hands. "Mike," he says. His glance shifts from me to Phil and back to me again. "You find a good trail to hike?" he asks me.

"We know the general direction," I say. "We're going to the top of the monument. We've just got to figure out what trails will get us there."

Mike gives a slight smile. "You guys are ambitious. That's a killer hike."

We work through the pitcher of beer, making small talk. The conversation is polite, remote. I catch Phil sneaking a glance at his watch. Halfway through the next pitcher, Mike asks us how we know each other.

"We met at school," I say. "We're both studying film."

"Oh, yeah?" Mike says. "You guys want to make movies?"

"Yeah," Phil says. "That's the general game plan." He's having a hard time keeping the boredom out of his voice.

Mike takes a long sip from his glass. "You guys ever see that Hitchcock movie *North by Northwest?*"

I freeze, my glass raised halfway, and stare at Mike. "Yeah," I say cautiously, "what about it?"

"I fuckin' love that movie," Mike says. "I've seen it at least half a dozen times. You may find this dumb, but I think that scene where Cary Grant and Eva Marie Saint are chased down the presidents' heads on Mount Rushmore was one of the reasons I took this job here."

The blood is singing in my ears, and the background noise fades to a dull buzz. "You like Hitchcock?" I ask, trying to keep my voice calm.

"Like him?" Mike says. "I fuckin' love the dude! Especially his American movies. Except for *Marnie*, which sucks."

I glance over toward Phil. He returns my look, his eyes bright. I feel my dick growing stiff. I lean forward, pushing my beer glass aside. "Listen, Mike," I say, my voice rising in excitement, "as far as Phil and I are concerned, Hitchcock is God."

Mike leans back in his chair and looks at me. "Why are you guys hiking up to the monument?" Phil and I don't say anything. His eyes shift from Phil and back to me. "Come on," he says, "you can tell me. What are you two up to?"

Another silence. Phil clears his throat. "We just have a little ritual we perform."

"Oh, yeah?" Mike's eyes are curious as he smiles faintly. "Tell me about it."

Phil and I exchange glances. Phil nods slightly. "We're spending the summer having sex at as many sites from Hitchcock's movies as possible," I say.

Mike laughs. "No shit!"

"Yeah," I say, warming up. "We've fucked late at night on the steps of the Bodega Bay schoolhouse, where Suzanne Pleshette gets pecked to death in *The Birds*. And on top of the San Juan Batista Mission bell tower, where Kim Novak falls to her death in *Vertigo*. We've squirted our loads on the railway ties in the Santa Rosa train yard where Teresa Wright shoves Joseph Cotton in front of a locomotive in *Shadow of a Doubt*. Yesterday we sucked dick on the Statue of Liberty's torch, from *Saboteur*." I take a sip of beer. "And now we're going to do Mount Rushmore, in honor of *North By Northwest*."

Mike's gaze flicks back and forth to Phil's face and mine. "Let me tag along," he says. "Tomorrow's my day off. I can show you guys where the trails are."

Phil and I hem and haw, but after the fourth pitcher of beer we agree. We spend the rest of the evening quoting lines from scenes from various movies. The drunker we get, the funnier this seems. When we get to the part where I play Judith Anderson to Mike's Joan Fontaine in the scene from *Rebecca,* where Judith tries to persuade poor Joan to jump out of a window, I'm laughing so hard that beer is coming out of my nose.

The next day the three of us stand on top of the bluff, looking down at the view. Washington's nose is at quarter profile, but Lincoln's face is angled so that we can see it completely. We can just make out the tops of Jefferson's and Roosevelt's heads. My shirt is plastered to my back, and I'm caked with South Dakota grit. "Hell," I say, "Cary Grant had it easy. All he did was take a fuckin' taxi to the top."

We scramble down the steep slope between Jefferson and Roosevelt, rock debris slipping out from beneath our feet and pitching off into the distant drop below. I'm beginning to wonder just how good an idea this is. Lincoln looms on our left, like a Macy's Thanksgiving Day balloon float, while Roosevelt is right before us, in profile, staring off into the distance.

Phil points toward Roosevelt's eyes. "Check out his glasses."

Roosevelt's spectacles are connected by a broad band of rock, a couple of feet wide, running across the bridge of his nose. Without stopping to discuss it, Phil inches across the tiny crevices in Roosevelt's face, finding footholds and handholds in small cracks and ledges. In a couple of minutes he's standing on the band that connects the glasses. He waves at us. "Come on over," he shouts. "It's easy."

Mike seems to have no problem with this. He follows Phil's route, scrambling over the rock, and soon joins him. There's no way I'm going to chicken out now. I crawl across Teddy's face like a human fly, my heart beating like a piston. I look down briefly and see several hundred feet of cliff beneath me. I don't look down again. A couple of feet above my head, Teddy's giant eyeball stares down at me.

Mike reaches over and pulls me onto the band connecting the spectacles. I stand there for a minute, catching my breath. Lincoln's face on my left now looks like the face of God, filling the sky. Jefferson and Washington hang over empty air on my right. Roosevelt's giant nose sweeps out beneath me like a ski slope. Beyond it is nothing but empty air.

Phil is already pulling his shirt over his head. Mike's face is flushed, and his eyes dart between us. He reaches over and slides his hand under my shirt, tentatively at first. I can see his hard dick pushing against his shorts, and I give it a squeeze. I lean over and kiss Phil, sliding my hand over his sweat-slicked torso. As Phil and I tongue each other, Mike unzips my shorts and yanks them down. My half-hard dick flops against my thigh, and Mike wraps his hand around it. He turns and does the same to Phil. Phil and I keep on kissing as Mike squats down between us, playing with our dicks, stroking them, squeezing them, tugging on our balls. A moment later Mike takes my dick in his mouth and slides his lips down the shaft. I give a small groan of appreciation. Mike turns his head and starts tonguing Phil's balls, burrowing his face into them as he strokes Phil's dick. I reach over and tweak Phil's nipple, and his eyes flash.

Phil and I each grasp Mike by the arms and raise him. We carefully strip him, first pulling his shirt off, then tugging down his shorts and briefs. His dick springs straight up, hard and juiced, ready for action, already leaking jizz. I reach down and squeeze it, milking another clear drop of precome from it. I slick my palm with it and slide my hand up and down the thick shaft as Phil tugs and strokes the muscles of Mike's torso. Mike has a beautiful body: cut, lean, the chest furred with dark blond hair. His nipples are wide and dark pink, their nubs standing out like chewed erasers. I bend over and suck on them, first the left, then the right, gently nibbling on the rubbery tips. Mike groans. I reach down and cup his balls in my hand; they're covered with a light down and hang low, filling my palm in a meaty pile.

We stand on the ledge, jerking each other off. It is such a hot sight to have these two naked men on either side of me, stroking my dick, bringing me to the brink. Mike's dick is uncut, pink and fat, with a flaring head, not as big as Phil's monster schlong, but still a respectable handful. I press my back against the granite cliff of Roosevelt's forehead, a dick in each hand, and stroke them both lovingly.

I glance over toward Mike. He stares back at me, his forehead beaded with sweat, his mouth open, his eyebrows pulled down in concentration. "Mike," I say, "how'd you like to fuck my ass?"

Mike's blue eyes gleam. "What Hitchcock movie is that line from?" he asks.

"I don't think Hollywood released it," I grin. "He was ahead of his time."

I pull out a condom package and a small container of lube from my shorts pocket and hand them to Mike. He laughs. "You guys got this down to a science, don't you?"

"Let's just say we like to be prepared," Phil says.

Mike squeezes a dollop of lube into his hands and slides his fingers between the crack of my ass. I lick Phil's nipples as Mike slides a greased finger into my chute and starts working it in and out. Tingling sensations radiate from my asshole through the rest of my body. I bury my face into Phil's sweaty armpit and nuzzle it greedily as Mike removes his finger and replaces it with his sheathed dick. Mike grasps my hips and thrusts forward, his cock sliding in inch by slow inch. I groan loudly, and Phil pulls back my head, thrusting his tongue into my mouth. Mike grinds his pelvis against me, rotating his hips, and it feels as if I have two feet of cock inside of me. As he starts pumping his hips, I slide my tongue down Phil's smooth torso and take his cock in my mouth, sucking greedily on the thick shaft.

It doesn't take us long to settle into our rhythm, Mike skewering my ass as Phil pumps his dick in and out of my mouth. The sun has cleared the mountain behind us, and I feel its heat pour down on us. Sweat trickles down my torso and back, dripping onto the rock ledge below. The wind whips around the corner of Jefferson's face, pushing us against the granite wall of Roosevelt's forehead. I close my eyes and feel the two cocks of these hot men plunge into me from both ends. I fantasize that they meet deep inside me, spitting me on a skewer of cock. Mike is breathing hard now, each thrust of his hips punctuated by a low grunt. My hands wander up Phil's sweat-slicked body, feeling the muscles of his torso, sliding down his back, squeezing the fleshy mounds of his ass as it clenches and unclenches with each thrust of his dick down my throat. I wrap my hand around my own dick and start stroking, matching my rhythm to that of the two men thrusting in and out of me. One wrong twist of my body would send the three of us plunging onto the rocks below. I lean back harder against the granite cliff.

Mike's thrusts are coming harder and faster now, punctuated by grunts that are getting increasingly louder. He pulls his dick out just to the inner pucker of my asshole and slams it full in. I feel his legs tremble against me, and he cries out in a long trailing groan. He pulls his dick out and whips off the condom. Jizz squirts out, some of it raining down on Roosevelt's nose, the rest carried off by the wind. Phil's dick is as hard as the granite we're leaning against, and his balls are pulled up tight against his body; I can tell it won't take much to make him shoot as well. I replace my mouth with my hand and give his cock a series of deep strokes. Phil suddenly cries out, his body shudders, and his jizz splatters against my face in thick, ropy wads, one pulse after another.

I stand up and beat off faster now, Phil licking his spunk off my face as Mike tongues my balls. As my orgasm sweeps over me, I arch my back and let 'er rip. My jizz spurts out into the air and joins Mike's upon the massive bridge of Teddy Roosevelt's nose. My body spasms, and Mike and Phil have to press me against the granite cliff to keep me from falling off.

We stand together above Roosevelt's nose, our shorts around our ankles, our dicks slowly losing their hardness. The afternoon sun is beating full on us, and our bodies are drenched in sweat. We look at each other and start to laugh.

"Damn!" Phil says. "That's going to be a hard act to follow!"

We pull our clothes back on and carefully climb back to the top of the monument. Mike leads us down the trail toward the visitors' center. Night overtakes us before we're done, and we have to hike the last couple of miles by moonlight. By the time Mike drops us off at our motel, it's almost midnight. He looks up at us from his car, grinning.

"Thanks, guys," he says. "It's been an experience."

Despite the long day, I'm stilling feeling revved. And horny. Mike reaches over to start his engine, and I put my hand on his arm. "Don't go just yet," I say. "I just thought of one last scene. Why couldn't we pretend that this is the Bates motel in *Psycho*?"

Mike grins widely. "Sounds good to me." He climbs out of the car. "OK, guys. Let's hit the showers."

Bear With a Brick
Lance Rush

It's late. The gym is closed. He's alone in the shower. His machismo is lethal—if you like that criminal type. Boss hired him to keep an eye on things. The Boss is shady. Connected, I think. Must've owed someone a favor. Me? I'm just an Aerobics Instructor, minding my own business, keeping my jock clean. But I've seen this bushy man, this Bruin, stalking the gym. Hard-edged. Quiet. Thick with menace. Nobody fucks with him. One look and you see why. He's 6' 4" and 255 pounds of woolly danger. Yeah. I've seen him around, but never like this. I watch steaming hot water gushing over him, polishing his nakedness. His brooding face is unshaven, primitive. Looks even more dangerous wet. Got some rough miles on him. He's 40. Maybe 45. Damn well-preserved, though! Rock hard. No gut. Water runs off his taut, muscular endowments. Long tufts of black fur swirl across his chest and belly. I stand just feet away, fascinated by this view. Steam rises from his body. With his back turned, he resembles a big ole foreboding Grizzly in the wild, unaware of being watched. My eyes slide over wet pelted armor. Immense shoulders. Huge hulking traps. Great fanning wings. His dense muscularity slowly tapers down as streams of water run slick off the curves of his sloping buttocks. Shit! Fantastic! I want to worship this ass. Kiss it. Lick it. Sink my hard dick inside and fuck it raw!

I step into the shower, trying my hardest not to stare. Staring invites danger. But he turns and faces me. Strapping legs spread wide. A shock of black hair dangles in his face like a long, bushy Bear cock. Dangerous. Steam rises. He washes his massive chest. I see a crude tattoo roping along one bicep. A potent advertisement, the fucker reads: Thick as a Brick. Etched deep into the shaggy pontoons of his bulging pecs is another tat: 0779410. His inmate number. His ID. His hard-earned name from a former life. His body's a rippling testament to one man's frustrated energy. Energy carved and sculpted and made godlike behind bars. Do my glassy eyes dare dip to his genitalia? Could prove lethal, but... Oh MY! BIG, cut, brawny meat swings down from a wet patch of cock-hide. Hefty. Its wide pisshead is leaking. Even flaccid, his cock makes my mouth water! Seen longer dicks. But none this shaggy, this Hella-THICK! A real STOUT fucker! ENORMOUS HEAD! Under a knitted brow, his cool blue eyes turn mean. So piercing, so hot. I panic. He's seen me looking at that big leaking cock! What now? Do we fight? Do we fuck? Do I die? What? Have I offended him? Hell! What does he expect? I'd just stand there, soaping my ass, in his presence, and pretend his dick doesn't exist. I look away. But it's too late. Oh shit! I feel that heat rising in me. It's pulsing, jerking up, pushing blood through my stretching shaft. I quickly grab my towel and leave.

I can't let go of the moment. I've masturbated to this scene ever since. At the point where he aims those mean blue lasers at me, the soap slips from my hands. I bend to pick it up, and I feel him behind me. Burly arms enclose me in a killer's grip. All I see is "Thick as a Brick" as his furry biceps flex across my heaving chest. My wet body jitters. He pushes into me. I feel him thickening. He is full of damp heat. His breaths are hot. His unshaven cheek rakes my throbbing jugular. He doesn't speak. Doesn't have to. He kicks my legs apart, presses the small of my back and I bend. There's an urgent pulse thumping in his overgrown cockhead. It pounds at my cleft. With one push, it parts my burning asshole. OH! I feel a JOLT in me. OH! A vicious charge of heat. It burrows through my flesh. I grip his thighs. He slowly slides it all to me. Thick as a Brick. Thick as a Brick! He must pull my cheeks apart to fit his width. My anal walls enclose it. I want to scream when he drives it into me. I want to purr as he pulls it out. His fuck is hard. Sturdy. Rhythmic. His bearish balls smack beneath my thighs. He whips my dick fast in his soapy fist. His cock, his gruff touch, the machinery of his fuck, it's all electric! I close my eyes and settle in for the scratchy ride. Heat and lust war in my belly. My insides pound. He's thick as a brick. Thick as a fucking BRICK! I hear the sound of his wet flesh, clashing, thrashing, bashing into mine. I feel my balls churning beneath his flying fist.

His breaths, his wet, pricking fur sweep waves over me. I'm breathing his charged air. I'm a muttering fool. He pulls me in close and shudders, shudders like the earth beneath a roll of thunder. In that one hot moment,

I'm everything he wants. I'm his lover. His boy. His cock-slave, prison buddy.

He trembles, pulls away. My sore hole gapes! I feel so vacant. He sprays my back, my writhing back in wild charges. He whispers, "Yeah. Daddy's straight, boy. But your ass is my pussy. It's my cunt. My wife!" Seed from his unborn progeny rains over me. The water washes them away. He keeps beating me off. I spasm, detonate inside his sliding fist. My shooting jism flies high, directionless. But I awaken, alone. This hot cream from our fuck has splattered all over me. It's in my bush, my hair. It coats my nuts, my belly and panting chest.

It's foolish to fantasize about him. But I can't help it. What and who does he do with that dick? Is he straight? Gay? Bi? What did he do to survive in The Joint? Did he resort to fucking prison ass, for lack of pussy? I wonder about him. I don't know his name. Afraid to ask. I'll call him "Brick." He's an enigma. I've heard whispers at work, he'd done hard time for armed robbery. There are worse crimes. At least he didn't off anyone. I'm intrigued.

I see Brick almost nightly, sauntering through the gym, eyeballing patrons. He scares the shit out of them. He must've been hired for his intimidation factor. A big, gruff, roughneck menace, for pay. Beats digging ditches, I guess. Brick and I have a routine: I nod as I pass him in the corridors. He never acknowledges it. I want him. He ignores me. It's Destiny. I've avoided the showers for fear of one of those ill-timed hard-ons. Difficult to hide my eight-inch excitement for him. Man! I wonder how big his is when erect? Shit! I guess I'll never know.

Tonight, all this fantasizing has made me horny enough to hit the porno shops. There's one just down the street from the gym. A neon Adults Only Disney World awaits me. Straight, Gay, Bi, Tri, whatever the raunch du jour. It's a slow night. I buy my tokens. Walk down a dim hall. Step inside a booth labeled "Gay Daddies Ball." I close the door. It's dark. Dank. Sticky. Reeks of fresh come. It's got a glory hole. I'm home. A coin in the slot transforms the dark to a flickering fuckfest. I sit on a bench as the show begins. A tall, hairy Daddy stands naked in a mirror. Big low-hangers swing back and forth like pendulums. Shaggy fuckers. He's about to shave. He's lathering them up. Got a straight-edged razor at the ready. Hello! Another guy appears. Younger. More muscular. Naked. He falls to his knees. Oh! He's licking the cream off Daddy's balls. Man! That soft flexible dick is growing longer, harder. Mmm! BIG DADDY! Young dude takes its head into his mouth. I unzip. Let my eight inches breathe. The scene switches. Close-up: Big cock drilling tight asshole. It's a hard, rugged fuck. Who's doing who? I can't tell. But it's making my dick jump. Just as I begin to flog it, in mid-thrust, the fuck flick stops. Darkness envelopes me and my prick. Damn it!

A man's voice roars through this dark. It's so hard and coarse, it rattles my balls. It says, "Stick it through the hole!"

Right then, I could feel a dot of precome rise to the slit of my hard-on. It wants to be sucked. It wants be licked and sucked and slurped until my fucking brain caves in!

I turn, drop another token in the slot. The booth flickers. Mano a mano coupling. Two long fingers wag, beckoning me to this hole. In the shadows, I see a stranger's tongue wiggling, darting, anxious to suck my dick. I glide my cock to it, aim it through....

Oh! Yes! Shit yes! Moist lips enclose me, hungry for dick. His warm, slick throat engulfs me. My eight inches barely register a grunt. His tongue is hot, wild. Spinning. I feel a million nerve endings brushing over my hard dick. This tongue ravishes me! He laps. I push. He's deep-throating it. Oh! I shut my eyes and think of Brick. I imagine it's his long, wet tongue spinning on my cockhead. Brick's slick throat enclosing my throbbing shaft. I fuck this throat. No sounds but the rattling projector and the smacking of his lips. Oh! Yes. Suck it, Brick! He laps it so well; and this magnetic tongue spins, and coats, and feels so fucking good that, without warning, I'm shooting! I'm shooting my desperate charge all over his sucking lips! He pulls away. My dick still bounces and spits. Bounces and spits.

"Sorry," I say, panting. "I...I really needed that!"

I fall to the bench, exhausted, spent. It's quiet. Come drools down my balls. All is right with the world. But now I hear the clanging of a buckle. The purr of a zipper. I turn. This Big, Thick Daddy-Sized Dick flops through the hole beside me. Mmm! It's full. Succulent. Half-hard. Big Ballooning Head! Shit! You could show fuck movies on it. HUGE like Brick's. Just like Brick's!

"Grab my cock!" this hot voice demands. "Grab it, now!"

I grab it by its thick, furry root. Its powerful shaft pulses in my fist. Big Dick. Not fully erect. Still, Heavy Dick! I could play with it all night. Watch it transform into a man-sized boner. How big was it? I run my hand along its pulsing skin. I breathe its manly funk. It's ripe. I like that.

"Lick it," the voice says. "Lick my big dick!" I let my tongue tease its tip. The meat rises in jerks. I brush its thickening ridge. Salty. I lick down the fat shaft. Back and forth. He begins to moan. It grows and curves up, inches from my eyes. I take the swinging club inside my lips. It's heavy, salty. Mmm! Its skin is pounding, pulsing, throbbing! My lips fight to enclose it. He bucks forth. I gag. His joint's too BIG! His joint's too BIG! He could murder me if he tried. But his hips slide back slow, and I glide down the pipe. A singe of dick-juice wets my throat. OH! Big Dick! Big, delicious dick! I slurp where it curves and bends to my gullet. He trembles. It feels good. It's so weighty, yet I surrender to it. We move as one, sucking, bucking. My mouth is full of dick. I moan as cock veins pound on my tongue. His prick's rock hard now. I pry my lips away, see it jerk, glisten in my spittle. Wild hairs sprout from it. It's longer, much thicker than mine. His tool defies a ruler. Nine, ten inches maybe. Too curved to straighten out and measure. So FAT it would make a decent-sized wrist. Damn Big, that's for sure. All I see is BIG DICK! Big, thick, furry fuckin' dick!

"You want some of me?" he hisses. "You want this cock up that ass?"

I wonder, have I bitten off more than I can chew? The Big Dick disappears from the hole. In seconds, there's scratch at the door. The fuck film fizzles out. The booth darkens. It's pitch black. What now? Tension wracks my nerves. I hear nothing but his scratching and my heart pounding. I want to run. I want to fuck. I want to disappear through that fucking glory hole and into the night. But I can't. I won't. I'm horny for it, damn it! I want that dick up me. I pull up my pants and slide back the latch. The door swings open and bangs the wall. The stranger closes it in a blink, so quickly. All I see is a tall, wide silhouette. A big shadow with a big dick. It's breathing hard. Harder than both our cocks. He moves in, pushes his body into mine.

He towers over my 5' 10" frame. He dips down, plants moist lips along my pounding jugular. His face: I can't see it. But it feels like a sheet of sandpaper! I pull back and jam my hand down his jeans. His dick hair's wild, thorny. His cock's fat and warm. He runs his tongue down my neck. I fall to my knees. I hear him breathing. I rub my jawline along the swell of his cock. He says nothing. My darting tongue on denim speaks for me. I can't see it, but I feel it. My teeth prowl his zipper. He grabs my hair, pulls me away. He yanks down his zipper, hoists it from his jeans. Unleashed, his pants fall. I grab his ass. Oh! What an ass! A humping globe! Hard, furry spheres undulating. Mmmm! So round, so fuckable. But his prick looms, urgent. I slowly jack him off. Cockhead's wet and slimy. Feels bigger in the dark. Licking his throbbing shaft again, he grows hard, harder. Hard as a rubber bat. But the fucker doesn't stick straight out, doesn't project. Too thick, too fat and heavy, I guess. I stand, swerving my hot dick into his. He lifts his shirt, grabs my head, forces my face into his bushy chest. My tongue spins through pelt and muscle in search of nipple. He slams his naked dick into me. He grinds that fat club up my belly, then pushes it under my balls. My thighs grip tight to its full, warm pulsing. His breaths are loud. Mine are labored. I lick his pits. So shaggy and filled with the nectar of his funk. We dry-hump in the dark. He rips open my shirt, tongues my nipples. He bites and nibbles and tears at them. I pull away. I'll fuckin' explode if he keeps this shit up! We heave like animals. I take him in my hand. His width keeps expanding. I think it's gonna burst. But before it does, I want it. I need it. Shit! I need it. He spins me around, yanks down my jeans. I step out of them. He drops a token in the slot. We're bathed in the flicker of men fucking men.

Through thin shafts of light, I can finally peek at his profile.

Oh shit! It's…it's BRICK! I KNOW IT'S BRICK! It's HIM, and he's about to fuck my ass!

"Over on the bench! And spread them," he demands. The sweet talker.

I smile as I brace myself, hands to the wall. I spread my legs wide inside the semi-dark. I hear ripping. A condom packet. I turn to watch him peel it on. Big cocks in rubber turn me on.

"Don't turn around, damn it! Nobody said turn around! Head to the wall! Any cock shoots through that hole, you'd better sssssssuck it! You hear me, boy?!"

"Yes, sir. Whatever you say, sir! Just fuck me. Please fuck me, sir!" I pant.

"Now bend over! Stick it out! Poke it out!" he orders. I oblige him because it's BRICK!

Fingers first. Deep. Lunging. First one. Then two. Ah! Aw! Oooh! I gasp. Spread wider. I arch. Shove down, hard. OH! It impales me. I feel his knuckles! My man-smell fills the stall.

"You gonna give me this ass? Huh? Huh?" he asks, with a mean, sound slap to my cheeks!

"Yes! Yes, sir. It's yours. All yours, sir. Hurt me! Hurt me with your dick, sir!" Fingers leave. Replaced by something harder, far more Fierce. This hotness starts. I don't expect it to be this INTENSE! AW! That WIDE FUCKING COCKHEAD! AW! Stabbing at my velvet chute! Breaking it! Pushing through. OH! Yes! Fat. Snaking. Dick shaft. YEOW! His sliding is steady. Not brutal. But burning, pushing. Heat comes in a wave through my belly, down my thigh! Ooh! He kicks my legs further apart. Bears down. Oh SHIT! His joint, it's...so WIDE! Too fucking THICK! I can't breathe. He's in me. Deep in me. He's resting there. Fat, throbbing. Crammed and still, enclosed in my anus. Thick as a BRICK! My asshole's on fire! He wiggles it. A poker stokes my flame. "NO! STOP!" I cry. But he seems to get off on my pain. Fucking sadist! He embeds it there, then pulls back. Ah! I can breathe now. But then he lunges. FUCKKKK! Pulls back. Oh! Thrusts deep, and lets me have it. He's throwing it to me now. Fucking me with balls-out gusto! Fucking like a man who hasn't fucked ass in years. Hard, brazen thrusting. Blistering. Wild thrusting. He's ramming the shit out of me. This big bristled fucker. It's thick as a brick, tearing, driving, slicing at my hole. I wanna howl, bellow out: "Get this motherfucker out of my butt! This is fucking insane! It's too fucking much!" My heaving helps overcome the jolts. From the screen, a guy moans taking on a big Daddy's rod. But Brick's dick's not in him. It's in ME! He goes in nut-deep. Pulls out far. Goes in deep! My asshole clasps, releases, and clutches to every punch, every slap and slide of his prick.

Through the booth's flickering light, a long, hard cock appears at the hole. It's wavering!

"Suck it! Suck that dick! Suck it, I said!" Brick orders me.

He's thrusting deeper, faster. Rolls my nipples between his thick fingers. Fucking me with dick, slamming me with every muscle in that body. Pushing. Pounding. Urgent!

He's coaxing me, pushing my face right into that suspended cock. Its moist mushroom head wets my lips. I suck it. Shameless. The fucker in my mouth bucks. He's trying to choke me! The one in my ass is trying to kill me! Both fuckers find a rhythm in my butt, down my throat. Yet I take them on. My ass humps back and forth, riding dick. My mouth gulping, slipping forth, ingesting dick. Tonight I'm a just cockwhore. A slave to the prick. Buckwild and misbehaving for the prick. I feel my own, dripping a slow flood beneath me, and I haven't even touched it.

With another jolt, Brick pulls out of me and my asshole winces. The stranger's cock topples from my mouth. I stand in the shadows of two bloated dicks.

Brick nudges me from the bench. His ass flexes in semi-darkness. Those jutting mounds of muscle grab my fullest, hardest attention. My dick's so rigid it hurts! He bends over, shoots me a wicked look and says, "You want it? Go for it!" He tosses me a rubber. I slip it on, and I AM going for it. No easing it in slow. Soon as my cockhead touches his puckered seam, it opens, and like a snapping gyro, it captures me in a clutch. Oh! His moist asshole suctions in my dick crown. It flexes and vacuums me deep inside. Ah! Shit! It cushions my dick in tight anal walls. It's warm. Fits like a second skin. It gives way to each heated thrust. "Fuck it hard!" he yells. And I do. I pull back and SLAM it!

I'm shocked as I watch him gobble down that anonymous cock. His head jerks back and forth, slurping it with a mad hunger. Oh! I'm really lighting into him now. Pulling his legs apart, I ram his demanding chute with all the fury left in me! My pounding sets off tremors. Violent ripples flutter through bushy asscheeks. The harder I fuck, the harder his buffed arm flies as he fists his fat dick. I ride his bunghole with battering strokes. But oh! He's wiggling that pucker up and down the length of my prick. Oh! It brings me to my edge. I'm moments, nanoseconds away from shooting my wad. But Brick reaches his threshold first. A gush of white comets streak from his cock, smacking the walls as he shudders beneath me. Oh! Shit! These fucking guys must be synchronized! Now a vat of jism's rifling from that long suspended prick shooting from the hole. It's a fucking milk storm! It flies in a leap to Brick's sweaty face, over his back, and it smacks into my chest! Both men are sighing, grunting, cussing. Both dicks are shooting at once. Both of these copious explosions set me off.

I pull out of Brick's asshole. I rip off the safe and spray a vicious charge all over his hot, horny, rotating ass. An ass that humps and writhes in the flickering silence.

We dress in semi-darkness. He's quiet now. But it's BRICK. I KNOW it's him. He collects his stuff in haste and leaves me behind. I hear the door to the other booth open. The two men are whispering conspiratorially. There's something between them. I think they're lovers. I think this was planned. Maybe they're old prison buddies. Hell! Who the fuck knows.

But tomorrow, at the gym, will Brick and I resume our same stranger's routine? Will we fall back into that cool exchange where I nod and he broods and ignores me? Somehow, after fucking like this, I don't think so.

Out in the Woods
Brent Muller

Don't get me wrong; I love to go camping. But when my friend Rick asked me to go up to the mountains with him for the weekend, I had some reservations. Here he was, a straight guy, newly married, who wanted to go "roughing it" with a buddy because his wife hated the outdoors. And here I was, a horny dude who'd had his eye on Rick ever since we started working together on one of the firm's big accounts. I figured a weekend alone with him might just drive me crazy. Nevertheless, I agreed, and the next thing I knew, the two of us were pitching a tent in the cool air of the Shenandoah.

The ride up to the mountains had gone well enough. Rick had a great sense of humor, and we'd spent most of the drive joking about the hard-nosed bastards who made our lives miserable at the office. Only a few times did I have to check myself, keeping my eyes from gazing too long at Rick's handsome profile or at his snug-fitting thermal shirt, which seemed to show off every hard, lean curve in his athletic torso.

Once we were in the woods and started to set up camp, it was a different story altogether. The mountain air seemed to take away all of my resolve, and no matter how hard I tried, I couldn't stop thinking about sex. And not just sex, but sex with Rick in particular. As we put up the tent, I found myself watching Rick's every move. I couldn't help but stare at his arms as he drove the tent stakes into the ground, flexing his biceps with each strike of the hammer. And my eyes rested more than once on his round ass as he grabbed and hoisted up the sides of our canvas shelter.

By nightfall I had resigned myself to the fact that I had to harness my hormones or the weekend was going to be torture for me. After supper and a few games of blackjack by the open fire, we decided we both were tired and that it was time to hit the hay. I went to take a good-night leak on one of the big pine trees, and when I got back to the tent, Rick was lying on his sleeping bag with his hands propped behind his head.

"Ready to call it a night?" he asked with a playful look in his eyes.

"Sure," I said. "I'm really beat."

"It's been a long time since I slept with another guy," he said, and then started to unlace one of his hiking boots.

I didn't know what he meant by that remark, but I tried not to think too much about it. Straight guys are always saying things that sound ambiguous or slightly seductive. But, usually, they don't mean anything by it.

I tried to put the whole sex thing out of my mind, but as Rick started to undress, I couldn't help but glance over and sneak a few looks. As he took off his shirt, I noticed that the shadows from the lantern only accentuated his big arms and his nice-sized pecs. He had just the right amount of hair on his upper chest—not too much but enough to be sexy. And as he pulled off his jeans, exposing a pair of sturdy legs and that shapely round ass, I popped a big old boner right then and there.

Rick folded up his jeans and then lay back down on his sleeping bag; the only thing covering his body was a tight pair of white briefs. I wondered why he didn't get inside his sleeping bag, but at the same time, I was thankful for the scenery. I slowly undid the laces on my own hiking boots, taking my time in hopes that my dick would soften up a bit before I took off my clothes. I looked over at Rick's briefs and caught the outline of a pretty good-sized piece of meat. It wasn't really hard, but it didn't look exactly soft, either. He caught me staring and looked over at me.

"You sure take a long time to get undressed," he said with a little grin, and then he looked over my body.

Fuck it, I thought, *if he wants to see me with a rock-hard dick, then let him.* In no time I was down to my boxers, and I lay back on my sleeping bag, just like Rick was doing, looking up at the roof of the tent. I was sort of wondering what was going to happen next when my camping buddy answered that question for me.

"You know," he said, "if you like dick, you're welcome to munch on mine."

He looked over at me and rubbed his crotch, and the next thing I knew, I was pulling down his briefs and staring at an eight-inch, bullet-shaped dick. By now his rod was at attention, and I immediately got down and teased the tip of his shaft with my tongue, tasting just a hint of salty precome. I licked all around the head of his cock and then slid his whole big dick in my mouth, moving up and down on his shaft, while Rick let out a few soft moans. The musky taste and smell of his dick was driving me wild, and I had to stop stroking my cock so that I wouldn't shoot my load right off the bat.

I went up the line of his groin with my tongue, probed his tight belly button, then licked his rock-hard abdominal muscles. I sized up his nipples for a moment while he looked at me earnestly, as if he were worried that I might stop giving him attention. *No chance of that, buddy.* I started licking and flicking at his tender, brown nipples with my tongue as Rick tensed his body, and then relaxed and gave in to the sensation.

"Suck 'em," he said as he grabbed the back of my head and urged me closer to his chest. I willingly obliged, and he groaned with pleasure. I still wondered how far he'd let me go. After all, this was a guy who spent every night with his wife, a guy who wasn't used to being mauled by another dude. But I figured he'd stop me if there was anything he didn't like, and so I let my man-lust drive me onward.

He let me pry open his lips and stick my tongue down his throat. Then he matched me all the way, sucking hard on my tongue and then burying his own tongue deep inside my mouth. I pulled away for a second and then teased him by taking playful licks at his lips and his tongue. After a while, this was too much for him, and he forced my mouth down on his and almost sucked the life out of me.

When we came out of this lip lock, Rick pushed me off him, onto my own sleeping bag. Then he pulled off my boxers and grabbed my throbbing pole, which was wet and sticky at the tip with precome.

"Nice dick," he said as he held on to my thick, seven-and-a-half-inch rod.

"Then suck it," I said.

"Not right now," he answered, kneeling over me and then sticking his tongue in my mouth one more time.

He scooted down on my body and then started to suck on my balls, taking each swollen sphere fully into his mouth. For the second time I thought I was going to lose it and shoot my wad all over the place, but Rick seemed to sense this, and he let up on me at just the right moment.

"I want to fuck you," he announced, perched aggressively over my body.

I smiled, but didn't say anything. I don't usually like to get fucked, but this guy was turning me on so much that I was ready to give it a try.

"You better suck my dick first, to make it easier," I said as I pulled his head closer to my hot, pulsating rod. At first he was a little tentative, but then he started going up and down on my shaft like a seasoned pro. His warm, soft mouth felt so good that pretty soon I was aching to get fucked by him.

"Stuff your dick up my ass," I told him.

I watched him slather his eight-inch fuck stick with spit, and I wondered how he was going to get that thing inside me without any lube. *I should have come prepared,* I thought. But how the hell could I have known that all this was going to happen?

He lifted up my legs and teased my hole with the tip of his dick.

"Slowly," I warned him, but in reality I wanted it bad.

He got the head of his shaft in my chute and then gently pushed more and more of himself inside me. It was a little uneasy at first, but then I started jacking myself off, and it felt good. I took a deep breath and relaxed, and pretty soon he was pumping me, harder and harder, and I was loving it.

"You like this dick, don't you?" he asked, and I nodded my consent.

He slid his cock in and out of my chute in long, slow strokes, setting up a fuck rhythm that felt so good, I wanted it to go on all night. Then, all of a sudden, he began ramming my ass as hard as he could and giving my prostate the best workout it's ever had. The harder he fucked me, the more I wanted it, until I couldn't do anything but moan like a wounded animal. I knew I was about to explode, and just as my balls started to tighten up, he took out his dick, and we both shot our loads together, all over my stomach, my neck, and my face. Then I pulled him toward me, and he licked his own sweet come off my lips and my chin, and then let me taste his juice on his tongue.

By this time we were both sweating like pigs, and Rick fell on top of me in exhaustion. Within minutes I was nodding off, with Rick breathing softly into my ear. I don't know about Rick, but I slept like a baby and didn't wake up until daybreak.

The next day I woke up to find Rick starting an early morning campfire. I staggered out of the tent, still in a sleepy haze, and he looked up at me and smiled.

"It's about time for breakfast," he said, and then went over to light the Coleman stove.

"I usually just have coffee in the morning," I told him.

"Oh, no," he said. "Up here in the mountains, you're going to need your strength." Then he gave me a little wink.

Neither of us said anything about what had happened the night before, but that was all right with me. There was too much stuff to do. After breakfast we went for a long hike up to the peak of the mountain. It was beautiful up there, and we ended up seeing a couple of deer and even a wildcat running across our path on the hiking trail. Then we came back down to the stream near our campsite and fished for a couple of hours. We each caught a few perch, enough to make dinner, and then we set about washing and cleaning the fish, preparing them to cook over the open fire.

After all this we were both smelling kind of rank and fishy. I decided I wanted to take advantage of the showers at a nearby campground that was about half a mile down the road, and so I grabbed my towel and a bar of soap and told Rick I'd see him in a little bit.

When I got to the campground, it seemed pretty deserted, probably because it was the off-season. I went in, hung my clothes on a hook, and jumped in the shower. I love getting away from it all, but I've got to admit, this one remnant of civilization felt really good to me. The hot water running over my body was just what I needed after a day in the mountains.

No sooner did I start lathering up than I heard someone come into the shower room. I thought this was a little strange since I hadn't really seen anyone else in the campground. But what the hell, I thought, maybe it was somebody like me, who'd just come to mooch off the campground's facilities.

I could hear someone turn on one of the showers next to me, but I couldn't see him. For a few seconds I stood directly under the shower head, closed my eyes, and let the pulse of water massage my scalp. When I looked up again, there was Rick standing in front of me, dripping wet and buck naked.

"The water feels good, doesn't it?" he said, smiling and staring straight at my dick.

"Yeah, it's pretty nice," I answered, looking down at his cock, which was growing visibly larger every second.

"You mind if I join you?" he asked, and just like that, my dick went rock-hard. Before I knew it, he was kneeling down in front of me, taking every bit of my cock in his mouth. His lips on my dick felt really good, and I began fucking his month harder and harder. He took it like a man.

Then Rick stood up and backed me against the shower wall, jabbing his tongue in my mouth. We sucked and licked each other's tongues hungrily; we couldn't get enough of each other.

I picked up the bar of soap and began lathering up Rick's body, feeling the hard contours of his muscles underneath my hands. My soapy fingers went around his dick and balls, down his back, up his butt hole, then over the roundness of his perfect ass. I let the water rinse the soap off and then sucked on his dick for a few seconds, feeling it grow harder in my mouth. Then I turned him around so that he faced the shower wall, and I went down and tongued his crack, flicking in and out of his asshole. Rick started moaning a little, and I could tell he was loving this.

I spread his ass cheeks wider and went whole hog at his butt, licking and prying open his sweet hole with my tongue. I could have spent all afternoon down there with my face in his ass, but there was one more thing I was aching to do.

I stood up and sucked on my finger and then dug it up into his chute. It went in pretty easily, and I played with his hole for a while, relaxing the muscles. Then I took my dick and pressed it against his crack, teasing him a little, until I finally stuck the head of my dick in his hole.

"I don't know about this," he said, tensing up a bit.

"Just relax," I said, and I reached around and started jacking off his dick.

Within about a minute I'd pressed about half of my dick in his ass, and then I slowly eased the rest of my cock inside him.

"Fuck!" he yelled, flinching his muscles as I probed deeper inside.

I kept my dick stationed in his ass while I began to lick and bite the back of Rick's neck. The tight grip of his ass channel squeezing my swollen cock was like nothing I'd felt before.

I pulled his butt closer to me to better my position, and Rick put his hands up on the tile wall of the shower. I gripped his waist and started to move slowly in and out of him, feeling that he was beginning to relax a bit. As I looked down and watched my dick fucking his beautiful round ass, I wanted to shoot my wad right then. *No,* I thought, *I want this to go on a little longer.*

I started quickening my pace, fucking him harder and harder, and thrusting my cock deeper inside him. With every forward thrust, I pushed my dick in all the way to my balls. Soon Rick was bucking and groaning and meeting my every thrust. I could tell he didn't want me to stop.

Soon I was pulling my cock all the way out of his ass and then shoving it back in, impaling him with my rod. Each time I did this, Rick let out a little grunt.

"Fuck me, man," he shouted. "Ram me with your dick."

"You like a cock up your ass, don't you?"

"Fuck, yeah," he grunted.

I pried Rick's hands off the wall and turned him around so that he faced the shower room. Then I moved behind him and bent him over so that I could have better access to his fuck hole. I held on to his waist and rode him harder and harder, listening to the sound of his butt cheeks slapping against my legs. He had relaxed a bit since I started fucking him, but his chute was still tight, and every thrust brought me closer to spewing my load.

As I plowed his butt, giving him everything I had, Rick began stroking his cock, moaning that he was going to come. I could feel my own balls tightening up, and I knew that I was ready to blow. I took my dick out and turned Rick around, and almost simultaneously we spurted our jizz all over the shower and each other.

Rick leaned back against the tile wall, breathing heavily after our fuck session.

"Shoot," he said with a devilish smile. "I should have taken you camping with me a long time ago."

"Don't worry," I said as I pulled him under the spray of the shower with me to clean off. "We've still got tonight and all day tomorrow to make up for lost time."

The Wrong Guy
Michael Cavanaugh

"Hey, Cal, how about you and me...."

"Damn, would you look at that?" Cal cut me off in mid pick-up. "I'd pay money to shove my tongue up that ass." My spirits sank. Cal wasn't staring at my butt as he spoke. I followed his gaze over to Leo Costello's well-rounded backside. Leo worked in new accounts. He was a little nelly for me, but he did have a cute ass. He sure as hell had Cal's vote. "If you'll excuse me, Mark, I'm going to try and work my way into those well-tailored gray slacks."

"Sure, Cal. Good luck." I cursed office parties, downed my drink, then stalked across to the bar to get another. Looked like I'd be spending another holiday alone with my dick. My dick wasn't going to be any too happy about that.

"Hey, Mark!" Rudy Ferrin waved and made a bee-line towards me. Well, that sure as hell put a cap on the evening. All I wanted to do was look for someplace to hide, but it was too late. I really liked Rudy as a coworker, but I had no desire to hop into the sack with him. Unfortunately, he had a serious case of the hots for me—not that he'd ever tried anything. Rudy was too timid for that. Still, I recognized the symptoms.

"The party crowd too much for you, too?" he asked, coming to a halt beside me.

"They seem to be getting pretty lubricated," I agreed, looking over my shoulder at my coworkers. "When Davenport went face-down in the smoked salmon platter, I figured the time was ripe to slip away for a few minutes."

"Looks like Cal Logan managed to bag Lou Costello," he pointed out. I snorted grumpily. "I sort of thought you and Cal...."

"No, we're not," I snapped.

"Oh. Good." Rudy turned and caught a glimpse of my scowl. "I mean...uh, Mark, you deserve better than the likes of Cal Logan."

"Thanks for the evaluation, Rudy," I muttered, wishing to hell he'd just go away. "Got anybody special in mind?"

"I do, actually." I looked at him curiously. "Me."

"You?"

"Yeah." He smiled at me shyly. He had a nice smile. It made him look almost handsome. "I know I'm not the man of your dreams, Mark...but I dream about you." His cheeks flushed pink, but his gaze never wavered.

I stood there, looking at him. Rudy wasn't bad looking, by any means. It was just that he struck me as...hell, I don't know...he looked frail, like maybe he'd spent too much time reading books when he was a kid instead of playing baseball. He was tall, which was good, but I had a distinct feeling that under the suit, he was flabby. Flabby didn't do it for me. No way.

"At least come over for a nightcap. I've got a great view of the city from my place. What do you say?"

"What the hell," I said. Truth be told, it was the smile that got me. Something soft and sexy about his mouth. If only he hadn't been so flabby. "I have to say goodbye to the boss, Rudy. I'll meet you down in the lobby in about ten minutes."

He walked away, grinning like he already had his hand down my pants and was feeling me up. I downed my Scotch, rehearsing a million great escape lines to use when I got over to his place. A couple of frantic gropes and an awkward kiss or two, then I'd suddenly remember that I'd left the gas on in my apartment, or something equally unbelievable. If nothing else, we could give each other a quick handjob and go our separate ways. Hell, I'd spent worse nights in my life.

"So, what do you think?" Rudy and I were standing in the living room of his apartment, high above the city.

"You weren't kidding about the view," I said nervously. He was beside me at the window, standing close. Ever since we arrived, he had definitely been in control. I hadn't expected him to be quite so...forceful. His fingers touched mine, then intertwined with them till we were holding hands. I stiffened, but didn't pull away. It wasn't all that bad. Rudy's palm was cool and dry, and his grip was surprisingly firm. We must have stood that way, side by side in total silence, for ten minutes or more. Then he pulled me around till we were standing face to face.

"Kiss me," he whispered, his voice like velvet. His dark eyes glittered with the reflected lights of the city. I'd never noticed, but they were fringed with long, thick lashes, dark like his curly hair. It had been a long time since a man had kissed me—so long that I'd almost forgotten the sensation of someone else's lips touching mine. After the first moment, there was no doubt that Rudy knew how to kiss. He was no lunge-and-thruster, slobbering and panting as he tried to see how far he could wedge his tongue down my throat before I choked. His lips brushed mine gently, his upper lip caressing my lower, the contact sending a pleasurable shiver up my spine.

As the kiss became more intense, our lips parted and his tongue slipped between my teeth. It was a man's kiss, the lips firm, the stubble on his chin and upper lip prickling against my face, making me feel warm all over. As it continued, our tongues fought for dominance, parrying and thrusting back and forth, tentatively at first, then with increasing vigor. Rudy won out.

His intensity rocked me back on my heels, practically making me lose my balance. He sensed this and slipped his hand around my waist, pressing it against the center of my back. Then he did something to me that no one had ever done before—he began sucking the air out of my lungs, into his body. I fought him at first, but he persisted, blowing his breath back into me, swelling my chest.

We exchanged breath till I was dizzy. I grabbed him around the waist to steady myself as I filled my lungs with fresh air. I'd always expected him to be soft around the middle, but he was solid as a rock. Pressing my thumbs against his unyielding gut was a pleasant surprise. "That was wild," I grinned.

"You liked it?" His breath was hot against my cheek. "I want to see you naked." I started to loosen my tie, but he grasped my wrists and forced my hands to my sides. "I'll do it," he said. I stood there as he took off my tie and unbuttoned my shirt, pushing it off my shoulders.

"Beautiful," he whispered, eyeing my bare torso intently. He stroked my chest and belly, his hands molding every sculpted plane. His hands were strong, his fingers pressing hard into the muscle. When he leaned forward and flicked his tongue against my left nipple, I tensed my pecs. His teeth sank into the fleshy point, establishing a direct connection to my crotch. Rudy followed it up by insinuating his hand between my thighs, pressing up, cupping my cock and balls against his palm.

My cock strained against Rudy's hard, hot hand. He unbuckled my belt and my trousers dropped around my ankles. His thumbs hooked into the waistband of my jockeys, tugging them down over my hips. My cock swung out, the tender knob rubbing against the fabric of Rudy's slacks. His hand slipped back between my legs and he began massaging the thick ridge that ran from my balls to my asshole.

Rudy sank to his knees and buried his face between my legs. My prick throbbed against his cheek. He spit-shined my balls, then started tonguing my cockshaft, tracing the bulging veins from my pubes to my pisshole. He licked all around the swollen glans, kissed the tip, then went down on me fast, stopping only when his forehead smacked my belly. I grabbed his shoulders for support and groaned softly, reveling in the heat of his throat and the fancy dancing of his tongue along my prick.

He pulled off slow, with just a hint of teeth, sucked the head till it bulged, then swallowed me back down to the hilt, bouncing my balls off his chin. He sucked, his lips hot and wet against my belly and my balls. He rose up, slid down, first fast, then slow, his virtuoso tongue working variations on every thrust. If I really had left the gas on in my apartment, I didn't give a damn.

I pulled him to his feet when I couldn't bear the pressure of his lips and tongue a moment longer without spewing. Believe me, I was no longer in any hurry to spew. Rudy stood, smiled, and treated me to another of his toe-curling kisses. His mouth was sticky and faintly salty from sucking my cock. I got him stripped to his briefs and stood back to take a good look at him. He was built like a greyhound—pared down to the essentials, every muscle tight, direct, and to the point. His wasn't the body of a man who spent hours at a gym, but it wasn't the body of a guy who spent all of his time reading, either. I'd have to ask him what he did for exercise sometime. For now, however, I was content to explore the compact planes and angles of his sleek frame.

I started at his throat and worked my way down. Long, silky, dark fur feathered over his collar bones, forested the hollow between his pecs and ran in a thin line down over his washboard abs. I nuzzled the silken growth at his throat, letting it tickle my lips and cheeks. His nipples popped out stiff and tight from the rise of his pecs when I tongued them. As I sank my teeth into the rubbery flesh, his hand pressed against the back of my head and the muscles of his chest flexed against my lips. As I licked and chewed, Rudy was practically purring.

I reluctantly abandoned the tit and sank to my knees, my face pressed tight against his lean torso. The fabric of his briefs was soft against my chin. I pulled them down slowly and buried my nose in his curly bush. I had them almost halfway to his knees before his cock bounced free and smacked against my chest. The shaft was hot against my skin, thick drops of ooze leaking onto my hairless belly.

I sat back on my haunches and admired his cock. The knob on the end was big and shiny, puffed out like a mushroom cap. It was a fitting crown for the veiny shaft, which started thick and got progressively thicker as it approached the tangle of his pubes. I wrapped my fingers around the base of the shaft and started licking the head, savoring the spicy taste of his honey.

When my tongue found the nerve trigger tucked beneath the massive knob, his cock flexed, pushing deep into my mouth. I pressed forward, but couldn't even get as far as the point where my fingers wrapped around the shaft. I settled back on my haunches, content to polish the knob and lick his big joystick from crown to bush.

Rudy's grip on my shoulders tightened convulsively when I pushed his dick up against his gut and went for his balls. They hung low and heavy in their hairy bag, swinging back and forth temptingly as he spread his legs wider for me. One at a time they were a mouthful—together they were ecstasy, bulging my cheeks like a chipmunk's.

When I finally spit them out, Rudy knelt in front of me and pushed me flat on my back. He hooked my legs over his shoulders. His thumbs rubbed against my asslips, pushed slowly through the ring of muscle guarding my rear entry and began stretching it wide. The hairs on his chest tickled against the inside of my legs, taking my breath away.

"Fuck me," I whispered. Rudy's eyes locked with mine, willing me to open my body to him. He thrust his hips forward, his dick burning like fire inside of me as he plowed deep into my bowels. I looked into his brown eyes, watching his pleasure register in their glistening depths. He rubbed my belly as he wedged his cock deeper. His heavy balls rolled down over my tailbone and along my spine. Finally he was buried to the hilt, his huge cock skewering my vitals.

He started fucking me, pumping slow and easy at first, his thrusts increasing in speed and strength till he was pistoning in and out of my sluice like a pile-driver. His big balls slapped against my ass, making him grunt as he mercilessly battered the jism-bloated orbs against my sweat-streaked cheeks. I was getting close to spewing when he dismounted and flipped me over onto all fours. He climbed back on and started going at it doggy style. From this angle, every thrust brought his knob into contact with my aching prostate, unleashing bolts of pleasure that made me ache to come.

"Stand up," he murmured, nuzzling my ear. I struggled to my feet, careful to keep him in me. He turned me to face the wall of glass overlooking the city. I watched my pale reflection as he felt me up, stroking my arms from wrist to shoulder, squeezing the bulging curve of my biceps, tracing the definition of my triceps. His hands rose from my hips to my chest, his fingers pressing against the full curve of my pecs. He groaned in my ear, his prick flexing convulsively as he began pinching my sex-swollen nipples.

I gasped as he drove it in hard, lifting me up onto my toes. Without warning, the spunk started pumping out of me, arcing high in the air and splattering the polished glass in front of me. I felt his heat erupt in my gut as he began squirting his hot spunk up my asspipe. He kept right on fucking me till his cock went soft, churning his scum to a froth inside of me. After his big hot dick finally slipped out of my ass, he led me down the hall to his bedroom. I curled up against him on the bed and slept like a baby.

When I got to work on Monday morning, I hurried down the hall to Rudy's office. It seemed a little odd to be the one in pursuit, but my excitement at the prospect of seeing him didn't allow much room for embarrassment. "Got a minute?" I asked, slipping in and closing the door behind me.

Rudy laid his glasses on top of the memo he'd been reading and fixed me with his glittering eyes. I felt like a sweaty-palmed schoolboy. "You sure you got the right guy, Mark? Cal's office is across the hall."

"Oh, I've got the right guy," I retorted. He stepped around the corner of his desk and slipped his hands inside my suit jacket, pulling me close. "There is no doubt about that. None at...." I would've gone on, but he silenced me with a kiss. Oh yeah, he was the right guy, all right. No question about it.

Under Way
Dominic Santi

"Think about it, Henderson. You've been underway for six weeks. You're asleep in your rack, and you wake up to find somebody sucking your dick. Do you stop him?" Parker paused for dramatic effect. "Remember, you've been under way *six* weeks."

"I don't want to think about it," I groused, unhooking the chain on the guardrail surrounding the hole in the floor that led to the Pit. "I'm so fucking horny I'd probably let him!"

The hoots of laughter following me from the crew's mess echoed in the passageway as I stepped onto the upper rung of the ladder. I hooked the chain back into place and started climbing down into the 12-man berthing area below. Submarine sailors think they're such comedians. In quarters this close, Parker knew just which buttons to push with me. My almost constant hard-on lately was obvious. Still, I promised myself that one of these days I was going to deck the son of a bitch.

"One of these days," I muttered, descending into the darkness. At least in the berthing area the only human sounds were the gentle snores of the few people already crashed out in their racks. I was looking forward to the quiet. I was tired and grouchy, and my cock and I needed a reprieve from Parker's humor. Mercifully, by the time my feet touched the deck, the sounds from overhead were muffled by the soft white noise of the constantly moving machinery around us.

Sighing in relief, I turned and started down the short passageway, my eyes slowly adjusting to the dim red of the emergency lights. I liked the Pit. Only 12 of us were assigned there: six racks—two tiers of three each—on both sides of the room. And all of us had just enough rank that nobody had to share.

I was in the middle rack, in the back left tier. That was about as private as a person could get on a fast-attack sub. Right now my dick and I needed private. I stripped to my skivvies, then thought better of it and climbed in naked, shoving all my clothes except my underwear down by my feet. I was exhausted, but there was no way I was going to get to sleep without paying some serious attention to my cock. I pulled the curtain closed and hunkered down to get comfortable.

We had been under way for 43 days. To my way of thinking, that was way too long for a person to go without sex. Fortunately with my reading light off, it was dark and private enough inside my man-made cocoon for some serious self-abuse. At 5 foot 8, I was short enough to stretch out. I spread my legs wide, rubbing one hand fondly over my cock and balls, stroking them a couple times, letting them know they had my attention. With my other hand I reached under the edge of the mattress for my hand lotion. I flipped the cap open and squeezed. Then squeezed again.

"Shit!" I'd forgotten the tube was almost empty. I tossed it aside, too frustrated to work out the last few drops. I'd been going through so much of the stuff lately that, although my cock and balls were now luxuriously smooth, my supply of lube was running dangerously low. I was also too tired to get up and dig in the rack pan under my mattress for one of my last tubes.

I kept my voice quiet as I swore. While most of the guys from my area were on duty or still doing maintenance this time of night, I knew Jones from sonar would be asleep in the rack below me. I could hear snores from the first tier as well, so I knew a couple of the torpedomen who bunked there were sleeping too.

Resigning myself to dry stroking, I reached down between my legs and rearranged myself, running my fingers gently along the underside of the rim. I was half-hard already. No surprise there. After six weeks of nothing but solo sex, I was horny all the time. I started playing with myself, shivering with pleasure as my fingers stroked my hungry skin, tracing the outline of my rapidly lengthening shaft.

We had expected to pull into Sydney a week ago. My mind raced with the expectation of gorgeous blonde chicks—all of them ready to fuck me until my dick gave out, willing to suck my horny meat until I shot from my balls. My cock was ready!

Unfortunately, the U.S. Navy was not. I stroked again, trying to pretend it was some beautiful chick's soft fingertips holding me. I had no idea when we would actually pull into Sydney. With all the secret squirrel regulations associated with a WestPac, our knowledge of actual arrival dates was based more on rumor than fact. For all intents and purposes, I was trapped underwater with 122 other horny guys and no end in sight. And beating off was getting old. I needed a blow job like I'd never needed anything before in my life.

Just thinking about a warm, wet mouth closing around my throbbing tool made my dick snake up tight toward my belly. I was so hard I hurt—again. With my thumb beneath and my fingers on top, I played the exposed underside of my shaft, stroking the soft skin stretched taut over the rigid flesh beneath. After 16 solid hours of watch and maintenance, I wanted a quick spurt and then some sleep. I rubbed faster, wondering how long it would take me to come without lube. Maybe I could use some spit when I got closer. If only I weren't so fucking tired....

I dreamed I was getting a blow job. The best fucking blow job of my life. I was waking up, slowly, somewhere near the ocean, in a cave where I could hear constant rhythmic waves of sound in the background, drowning out the rest of the world. It was dark and hot, and someone warm and alive was making wonderful love to my dick. I couldn't see her face, but even in the darkness I knew she was beautiful. No doubt blonde and built. And she was talented. I shivered as she licked and sucked, poking the tip of her tongue in my piss slit. Taking me deep in her throat. Pressing her lips down tight against the base of my shaft....

"I can help you out with that," a voice whispered gruffly.

I sat up so fast I hit my head on the bottom of the rack over me. "What the fuck?"

A hand clamped firmly over my mouth. "Shut up, or we're both screwed."

I gasped as I heard the words growled in the darkness. The hands gripping me were definitely male, one holding my thigh firmly in place, the other pressing my torso back onto the mattress. Stunned, I lay back down. I was waking up quickly. There were no lights on in any of the individual racks, just the red light of the passageway. But even in the darkness, I was aware of the outline of a male head and shoulders jutting up through the bottom of the curtain. Whoever it was hadn't bothered to open the curtain, just slid his upper body through. At that height, he must have been kneeling on the floor.

"If you want me to stop, I will," the voice whispered. Definitely male. Not that there were any women on the boat, but I was still foggy with sleep. "I've seen your cock poking out the front of your coveralls, though. And I need the taste of man meat to get me off so bad I can hardly stand it. We can help each other out here," he said, his hand stroking up and down on my shaft, tugging the skin up ever so slightly, "if you're willing."

"I ain't no fag," I gasped, shuddering as he flicked his tongue over the head of my dick. "I like chicks," I moaned as he tugged lightly on my balls. My excuses sounded lame, even to my own ears. Despite my brain's ineffective protests, my dick was with him all the way.

"This ain't no gay-straight thing," he said. He licked again, this time a long, wet stroke that tickled under the edge of the rim. "It's a dick thing. Now shut up, or we'll both be talking to MS."

My dick jumped as his mouth teased me. At that moment I didn't care what Naval Investigative Services thought of homosexuals in the Navy. My cock needed attention!

And I'd placed the voice. It was Jones, from the rack below me. I'd never figured him for a flamer. He was slight, like me, but the guy spent every spare minute working out. Even I admired the way his nipples jutted out from his smooth, perfectly sculpted pecs. I'd pulled myself away from good horny daydreams a couple of times to watch him lift. I sighed heavily. At least he was blond. And apparently he purely loved to give head. I moaned as he licked me again. Damn, his tongue was talented.

I thrust toward him involuntarily—my cock knowing what I wanted even though my brain hadn't quite figured it out yet. Jones didn't take me back in his mouth, though. That's when I realized he was waiting for me to give him permission.

"You're really not making this easy," I groused, this time consciously lifting my hips up toward his pussy-hot, slippery mouth.

He laughed evilly, scraping his whiskers lightly along the shaft. "You want it or not?"

My dick had already decided. I arched against him, pressing my throbbing cock against his lips. "Do it, man," I said as his tongue wet my skin again. "You're fucking good at this."

"Yeah, I am." I felt his smile as he went back to work.

Fuck, it felt good. Jones sucked differently than any of my girlfriends ever had. His mouth was hungrier. Like he wanted the taste of my dick as much as I wanted the blow job.

"I like the way you grow." His voice was low, and it vibrated through my skin.

I grunted in response. Most of the time I'm a pretty average size. But when my dick gets interested, I can get pretty impressive. At the moment, though, I didn't want to think about Jones's opinions of my endowment. That was a little too much to take in. So I concentrated on how good his mouth felt.

This time he started at the base, bathing my shaft with spit as he licked his way up. Every so often he stopped and hit my cock against his cheek. It didn't hurt. It was more like pure sensation as our flesh connected. Nobody had ever done that to me before. I liked it—the way I liked everything he was doing. He kissed and licked, working the rim, stroking my shaft, caressing me with his lips until I could hardly breathe. I could feel how wet he was getting me. His hands played everywhere his tongue wasn't, slipping on his spit, gliding on my precome. I blushed as I realized he was tasting the pearls oozing from my piss slit. I leaked a lot. It had always embarrassed me.

"Mmm," Jones moaned, sounding like a kid with a lollipop. He squeezed the tip, smearing my juice around, mixing it with his saliva. "Make me some more."

I shivered at the vibration of his voice—and at what he was saying. I couldn't believe he liked licking my precome. But his tongue moved down again, licking just below the head, concentrating on the ultrasensitive skin under the V before his lips moved back up to suck lightly on the tip. I made him more—lots more. I couldn't have stopped if I'd tried. Then Jones's lips closed over me, and I forgot about thinking. His mouth was so hot and so wet and so fucking, fucking hungry. He knew every trick—all the places I'd thought only I knew were sensitive. He played the shaft, not too hard, not too fast, matching his movements to the way my dick jerked. If I could have sucked myself off, I would have done exactly what he was doing. He knew all the right places, all the right moves.

Suddenly he shoved something in my face—something soft and cotton. My underwear.

"Bite."

I did, without thinking. Damn was I glad. In his next movement Jones sucked me all the way into his throat. I wasn't expecting it. I almost screamed into the cotton. Fuck, it felt good. Fortunately, the fabric muffled my cry. But my whole body shook as he deep-throated me. I'd never felt anything like that before in my life. It was like fucking a mouth pussy, only better—tighter, more controlled—with all the attention focused on the center of my world, my cock.

It was way more than I could stand. I spit out the gag, gasping. "Gonna shoot!" I said. I hoped I was quiet enough. I was too far gone to tell.

"Go ahead," he whispered. His tongue dragged up my shaft. "I wanna watch."

Oh, fuck. Nobody had ever seen me come, ever looked at my dick close-up and personal while I shot. Just the thought was sending me over the edge. Jones lifted the bottom of the curtain. Dim red light highlighted the glistening shadows of my dick. He licked, mercilessly working the sweet spot below the head that made me twitch with every touch. His fingers played my shaft, sliding on his spit, tugging relentlessly on my balls.

"Bet it's gonna be one helluva load," he growled. "Gonna squirt right up out of your balls." He squeezed once more, his tongue digging in, his fingers stroking. "Gonna shoot like a fucking volcano out of this hot, hard fuck stick, just…like… this…."

"Oh!" My whole body shook as an orgasm of molten come exploded through my dick, just like Jones had said it would. Like my cock wanted to show off for him, to make him proud of the way it could spurt hot, thick man cream all over the both of us. He worked me just right, pumping me through the climax, his hand sliding on my sperm to make each stroke slicker, even more intense. I gasped as the sensation became almost too much, as Jones suddenly stopped, like he knew just when his touch was becoming more than my oversensitized head could stand. I felt like my heart had stopped, except I could hear it pounding in my ears from the most fantastic orgasm of my life.

It took me a minute to come down. I was totally blissed out. As my breathing slowed I felt Jones tensing next to me. His other arm was moving fast, pumping—jacking himself off, I realized. It felt so strange to be held by another man, to know that he was masturbating himself while be touched me, that he was turned on—that he was climaxing—because of me. That because of me his spunk was going to shoot through his cock, his bones were going to shake like mine had, he was going to fucking come because of me.

It was beyond erotic. It was the sexiest thing I'd ever done in my life. I felt close to him in my skin. I had to touch him. I leaned forward and tentatively kissed his shoulder, licking the salt from his skin.

"Oh, fuck, man…." His voice was soft in my ear, but I heard the wanting. The need. The fucking horniness that was every bit as intense as mine had been. "That feels so good."

I smiled, realizing with a jolt that I wanted to make him feel good. I tipped my head up, cautiously brushing my mouth over his whiskers, finding his lips by feel. I kissed him again, this time parting my lips and slipping my tongue inside his mouth, searching for hot flesh to taste. To suck and lick and bite.

"I want to kiss you," I whispered into his mouth, startled to hear myself say the words. I was awestruck at the thought that I was having sex with another man, that I was liking it. I was making another man's dick quiver—the way he had mine. And in the same breath I realized that I wanted to know what that quiver felt like—all the way through.

"Stand up," I ordered quietly.

"What?" Jones's hand stilled. His breathing was ragged, like he was too turned on to think straight.

"Come on and stand up. Smith is on watch. Grab onto his bunk."

Jones did. He moved slowly, like he didn't quite trust me.

"Poke your dick through the curtain."

I barely heard his whispered "Oh, shit."

But he did it. As the curtain lifted I leaned up on my elbow and took his dick in my hand. "My turn."

I felt, rather than heard, his grunt. All my attention was focused on the heavy flesh I held in my hands. It seemed to reach for me, the slippery head glistening with precome in the dim glow of the wall light. I'd never touched another man's dick before. Never seen one up-close and erect— and hungry for my touch. It seemed strange not to feel the pleasure twitch inside my own cock when my fingers stroked the velvety soft skin surrounding the steel-hard shaft underneath. Jones jumped when I rubbed my palm over the tip. I leaned forward and rubbed my cheek against his shaft. He jumped again. This time I sniffed. He smelled good. I nuzzled my face into his balls. He smelled really good. Musky and male. He groaned as I stuck out my tongue and started bathing the scent from one round orb.

"Quiet," I whispered. I felt my breath as it traveled over my fingers to his skin. Jones shivered. I tentatively lifted his sac and sucked one of his balls into my mouth, rolling it around gently on my tongue, the way he had done mine. He arched toward me, panting, as I tugged softly, first on one, then on the other.

I waited until my nose accepted the man smell trapped between his legs, until the taste of his wrinkled scrotum skin felt comfortable to me, until burying my face in his crotch felt good.

Then my hand still wrapped gently around his sac, I touched my tongue experimentally to Jones's shaft.

Man, did he jump. I don't know if he had thought I'd do it. I don't know that I'd believed I'd do it. But the relief that shivered through Jones's skin made my own dick twitch. I realized with a start that he probably needed a blow job as much as I had.

I also realized that one come wasn't going to be enough for me. I was rock-hard again. My face flushed hot at the idea of jerking off in front of another man. But the smell and taste of Jones's wet dick had me too turned on to care. I tipped onto my shoulder, slathered my hands with spit, then I slid one wet fist around Jones's shaft and wrapped the other around my own. I groaned with pleasure, feeling and watching him jump with me each time my hands tightened on his cock.

Then I started licking, exploring, doing the things to him that I would most like having done to me. Jones tasted good. Slippery and musky and slightly salty. I placed my tongue on his shaft, and I went to work.

Jones gasped, arching forward through the curtain as I wiggled and poked and licked.

Each time he twitched against my tongue, I stroked myself harder. When my taste buds were finally satisfied, when my own dick was drooling in response, I opened my mouth and, with just the insides of my lips, I kissed the head of his penis.

"Oh, fuck," he whispered. Jones's shiver vibrated through his whole body, echoed into mine.

"Shut up!" I said. I couldn't help grinning. I knew I'd finally gotten to him. The skin over his iron-hard cock was stretched silky soft. Curious, I pointed my tongue and poked it into the tiny hole in the tip. His chest lurched as he breathed in hard, his hips rocking forward to meet me as I licked inside his flesh-cushioned piss slit. I shuddered, felt my own dick leaking as for the first time I tasted the slippery sex juice of a cock that wasn't my own. I slid my mouth over him, slowly teasing him, making him want it even more, making him need it, just the way he had done to me. Making myself hungry for more of him. I waited until he felt comfortable on my tongue, until he was moving rhythmically against my lips. Then, with no warning, I sucked him all the way in.

Man, did he buck! I gagged when he hit the back of my throat. I couldn't take him deep enough for what he needed. I bobbed my head up and down over the tip, letting the saliva run out of my mouth as I wrapped my hand around him, trying to make a long-enough, tight-enough, wet-enough tunnel for his cock.

"So good," he gasped, his whole body tensing. "Fuck, man, I'm close."

I tightened my grip, sliding my fist up to meet my lips with each long stroke, jerking myself faster as Jones's dick arched out, hotter, thicker, twitching into my hand. I felt the tension even in my lips as he started fucking my face, thrusting toward his climax. I matched my rhythm to his as he stiffened, his abs clenching into a rock-hard wall.

"Gonna come," he whispered.

I pulled back, jacking our cocks mercilessly in my spit-lubed hands. I knew what I wanted now.

"Let me see you shoot," I said, fighting to keep my voice low. "I want to feel you come in my hand. Right..." my balls tightened as I jerked once more, hard and tight and slick "...now!"

"Fuck!" Jones started shaking. His body lurched five, six, eight times. I watched, fascinated, as his sperm shot out, pinkish-white in the dim red light. Spurts of thick, ropy cream pulsed out of his piss slit, ran hot and slippery down his glistening shaft and into my fingers. My gut clenched as the semen-rich smell of his orgasm filled my nostrils, and then I was gone. My come shot out, lubricating where my hand slid over my throbbing, spurting cock. I shuddered, trying not to cry out as I stroked us through our climaxes, relishing the feel of two come-covered cocks twitching in my hands until Jones reached out and pushed me away.

I collapsed on my mattress, resting my face against his sweaty, sticky thigh as he leaned against the upper bunk. I was exhausted, sated with the feel of our warm, live, and no-longer-horny bodies touching. Jones leaned over and kissed me gently on the cheek. I slipped my arm around his neck and pulled him down to my lips, kissing him back, long and soft and wet. The continuing snores around us told us we could take our time and enjoy ourselves.

Eventually we broke for air. "Thanks," I whispered, running my knuckles along his jawline, scratching my skin on the lengthening stubble.

"Any time," he grinned. His mouth moved against my cheek as he leaned closer and breathed into my ear. "It could be a while before we reach Sydney, you know."

"Could be a real long trip," I laughed back. "And we may need to get together in port." I smiled as I lifted my hand and stroked over the shadowy outline of his butt. "I'm still going to be checking out the chicks, but now I think my dick wants a taste of your ass too."

I jumped when he reached down and grabbed my butt, squeezing my ass cheek hard. "Sounds good," he said.

I gasped as his finger brushed lightly over my asshole. "Just remember that I can do things to you those chicks could only dream of."

"Now wait a minute…."

"You didn't think you would like the blow job either." Jones laughed, kissing me again as he pulled back toward the edge of the bed. "Think about it."

The curtain rattled ever so slightly as he dropped down into his rack. I felt my face get hot even in the dark. I was thinking about it already. An embarrassing itch let me know my asshole was thinking too. I was pretty sure what my answer was going to be.

I was going to love being Down Under.

The Harley
M. Christian

If they'd thought of BO, Mammoth would have kicked it over and tore out of there no problem. Hands down, the fucker had the most righteous stench—one like a rap sheet (fucking bad and sticks to your ass for life): body reek, oil, farts, old blood, dog shit—the works. But they didn't think of stink to settle the issue.

Now Monster, he would have won an ugly contest. Not that Mammoth was a dreamboat or anything—teeth like a shook-up graveyard, skin like a back road, nose like something grown from compost, hair a dry brush fire of greasy yellow just waiting for a match. Ugly as fucking hell, man, but fucking gorgeous standing next to Monster.

Bald dome scaly like an alligator with hives, mouth crooked with zigzagged old scars, beard a moth-eaten rug of steel brushes sloppily put together under a flat and wheezing nose. And those eyes, like two smoking sulfur matches floating in ripe piss or gasoline. Like most of them, Monster got yanked by the law a lot. Fuck, attitude alone (which stunk as much as Mammoth's pits) got him flashed and pulled over. He rarely got booked or nothin', though—most just yanked his chain till they saw those two match heads get struck by some interior spark, then they swallow their last meal that'd come up on them quick-like and just let him be.

But they didn't think of ugly to settle the contest over the Harley.

It was a fair draw for reps, as it ended up. But any ol' fucker knows that ain't a way to settle this that kinda shit: bullshit walks, right? Ain't no crazy motherfucker gonna say where and how much to anyone save his brothers—and then it's mostly bullshit anyway. Did anyone fuckin' see you cave that cop's dome by the Thrifty Mart? Fuck no. Did anyone see you blast through TJ with 10 keys of pure shit? No, but everyone's heard you fucking did so shut the fuck up about it, all right! Yeah, we've all heard it, fucker, about how you fucked that frat boy up the ass back behind Greenie's Poolhall with your ten-inch dick.

You can't count reps in this kinda thing. Especially with a couple of cast-iron pig fuckers like Mammoth and Monster. Two legends ain't gonna sit around no dried up waste of asphalt back by the Mosco's Speed Track throwing back and forth "I killed this dude, fucked this many, scored this, wasted that." Ain't that kind of scene with those kind of fuckers. Mammoth and Monster just stood and stared, scratched, flexed while Mammoth's Pup, perfect pale ass glowing in the track lights like a low, full moon, pissed like a racehorse into the mostly dead mesquite bushes as they tried to decide who'd get Bull's damned bike.

They didn't think of size, didn't toss it out like they'd tossed the other ideas out in two or three rumbling growls. Mammoth big. Pure big. Absolute big. Very, very, very fucking big—in three dimensions. No one called him, fat but that's what some thought seeing him sitting around his hog. Mammoth was big up and down and sideways—straining and stretching his colors and chaps, filling them with muscles laid on muscles. Mammoth wasn't a mountain as much as a boulder. Hands like outfielder's gloves, feet like phone books, head like a wrecking ball.

Monster was huge. They probably weighed the same: Mammoth big all around, Monster a skyscraper.

Birds had a tendency to fly around Monster. They came in all peaceful and calm and then screeched, banking when they saw that something tall and ugly had violated their airspace. When folks, civilians especially, saw Monster among his club they thought for maybe a beat, maybe a second, that he rode with fucking midgets. Maybe they'd smile, maybe they'd start to say something—but then they'd see, really see, that the rest of them were fucking big on their own, so that must mean that Monster was really, really…

…then they'd piss in their pants.

They didn't race for the bike, for Bull's prize Harley, cause they fucking already had. Two calls had been made when Bull had finally kicked after taking that bad spill on I-5. Everyone knew Bull had this cherry Harley sitting in his garage, knew that Bull rode with both Mammoth and Monster, knew those two fuckers hated lots of shit in this life but above all else each other, and fucking god and all his fucking angels knew that Bull just loved, fucking loved, to cause shit.

No surprise at all that Bull's old lady would make two calls right after

Bull got planted in his backyard. Something like "It's yours if you haul ass down here right now."

No fucking surprise at that. Big fucking surprise that both of those mean and ugly assholes got there together.

Pup finished his Olympic piss and hiked his jeans, bored as all shit that they still couldn't decide how to see who'd get the bike.

"Jesus fucking Christ," he said, drifting all light and wispy like over to Mammoth and running his soft hands down Mammoth's jungle of scratchy chest hairs and around the peaks of his leathery nipples. "Someone fucking die already, man. I wanna get out of this fucking shit-hole."

Lots of stuff said about the two of them, of Mammoth and Monster; lots even certified by law enforcement—usual and unusual—armed robbery, assault, battery, rape, possession, and possession to sell (usual); murder, assault on a police officer, transportation of illegal animal parts, bestiality, and suspected necrophilia (unusual). Cannibalism, as far as anyone really knew, was just a rumor. Both of them were like fucking storm fronts—tracked with precision by badges, rivals, and even their own clubs. There was even some bucks being shoved back and forth among riding "weathermen" to make sure the right kind of folks knew that the winds were just right or that one of the fucking hurricanes was bearing down on their vicinity.

Mammoth was an animal: He lived down deep with his wild urges, sharing space with all the old critters other folks might have fucking left behind. Folks may have been wild once, may have gone extinct in most, but Mammoth, though, he was, like, frozen in fucking ice when the rest of us were in school. He runs wild and free, feasting on the little folks who forgot that maybe we used to feel the same way. Mammoth likes it fresh and red and hot. He likes to sleep after and laugh and howl during. He didn't fight so much as explode. He just recently stopped biting as much as he used to.

Now Monster, he wasn't so much wild as thoughtful. The call of the wild didn't ring for him—rather, he was more of an intellectually ugly motherfucker. Rumor was—and rumors were all you could hear because no one, no one, was talking—Monster was always the real ugly sort, but was only on the outside till he was able to hear what folks were saying about his face, his size. Then he sort of took it to heart, started trying it on for size. Monster cultivated himself, they said. He measured, tested, and refined it till people never, ever said anything except for fucking "Sir!" to his face.

Lots about those two. Some about Bull's legendary prize Harley: the special one, the real good one. All original, cared for like only Bull could care for a machine. It cranked like a dream, growled like feeding time at the zoo, and could out race a rep across the country.

But, man, there was shit little about Pup.

Yeah, yeah, yeah—rumors. Always fucking rumors: the ex-cop, the ex-priest, the governor's son, the musician, and even the fucking astronaut. The best of them all, the ones not quite as big as Pup himself, said that sometime in the dim and distant (which wasn't that far back) Pup used to live in this placed called the Castro, used to work in this little place called Fashion Flowers (decorator orchids), used to wear a fucking lot of taupe sweaters and listen to a fucking lot of ABBA—till his little blond head got turned by a persuasive ass-fucking from a member of the Aces. From there he got passed around and around, not really a member of any club but more like a prize to be won. By 21 he was the Oscar for Most Vicious Motherfucker In Five States. Not only worth it, he was proud to be. Or so the rumors said.

He was Pup, and the one thing that was an absolute proven fact about the kid was that he could pull gas out of a bike without a hose.

"Look, bitch," Pup said to Mammoth (the only one, only one, who could say that to him), "it's getting fucking dark and my cock's gonna fall off. Will somebody please kill somebody so we can get the fuck out of here, OK?"

"Makes a lot of noise, don't he?" Monster said, leaning big and dark in shadows thrown from the track a hundred or so feet away. With a pop, the tall biker tipped a kitchen match off his thumbnail into brilliant flame and lit a fat cigar.

Mammoth snorted like he'd gotten stuck in tar or something and belched affirmative. "Does like to squeal a bit, he does."

"I'm fucking freezing my dick off here," Pup complained, hopping from one booted foot to the other, hugging himself while panting fading clouds of breath. "I want to get the fuck out of here."

"Shut the fuck up," Mammoth grumbled like rocks spilling from the top of a mountain. "I want the fucking bike, asshole."

"As do I," said Monster from the growing darkness, a toke of his cigar lighting his face like a red footlight.

"Well, I want to get the fuck out of here. I don't give a bleeding rat's ass about some motherfucking bike!"

"It's Bull's Harley," Mammoth said as if someone had questioned the color of the sun or the quality of Red Rose speed.

"It's prime," Monster said, agreeing with Mammoth for probably the first time ever.

"It's fucking cold, you cocksuckers. It's just a fucking bike, man. Can't it wait till fucking morning?"

"What does it take to shut him up?" Monster said, walking with earthquake steps from the dark into the brilliance cast by one of the racetrack lights.

"The usual," Mammoth said, smiling a flash of crooked yellow teeth as he levered himself off his bike and grabbed Pup by the shoulder.

"Aw, man, leave it willya? I want to fucking warm up already, OK?" Pup said, with a little less nellie in his voice, a tad more reason.

"Man don't know when to fucking quit," Monster said, close enough for Pup to get a face full of cigar smoke.

Between them, caught between the stogie and Mammoth's stink, Pup gagged and coughed a sudden cloud of breath. "Christ, give a fucking guy a break."

With a practiced move, Mammoth grabbed Pup's shoulder and jerked him around so he was facing the boulder-biker. "The trick, man, is to just keep him to fucking busy," he said, shoving Pup down to the asphalt with a creak and pop of his joints.

"You Motherfucker," Pup started, trying to get back up.

"Yeah, shithead," Mammoth said, popping his Harley belt buckle and unzipping his fly with one skilled tug. "Me motherfucker, you cocksucker."

They didn't think of cock size to settle the issue of Bull's bike. Maybe they didn't want to have it out, maybe didn't want their legends possibly…diminished in such a manly way. Maybe they just didn't have a reason to haul them out—yet.

As tall as he was around, Mammoth's cock wasn't: for such a bear he had a snake's cock. In the hard glare of the lights from the track his dick was like a fucking pool cue sticking out of his pants. Mammoth's dick looked like it had been cleaned, polished. White and long, uncut head making it even more like a fucking spear or something, it leapt from his jeans like it got thrown from Mammoth's crotch towards Pup's mouth, like it fucking naturally lived in the kid's throat and Mammoth just kept it on a leash in his pants. The fucking ten inches wanted—wanted, man—Pup's lips and throat. Wanted it hard and wanted it bad.

"Oh, geez," Pup said, putting a hand around Mammoth's mammoth and stroking it like you might polish a brass horn, "no one fucking rides for free."

Lips to cock, with a mighty roar of one the racers on the track nearby as fucking applause, Pup got right down to it.

Now you might expect that taking in something like Mammoth's cock would take some practice, right?—even for a righteous cocksucker like Pup. Fact is, man, Pup is what Pup fucking does—got it? He sucks cock. He polishes, licks, kisses, swallows, works men's tools. Some men, they say, just have a clear purpose in life. Mammoth, now, he stinks—in body and fucking attitude. Monster is the perfect bogey-man, the stuff of cop nightmares, homeowner terrors, and mothers' horrors.

Pup, like I said, sucks.

Like drinking a glass of water, Pup opened his mouth and swallowed Mammoth's cock straight down. Could swear, man, that his teeth didn't even touch his meat—just straight fucking down. Ever see, reader, a snake swallow a chicken's egg? Just like that, friend, just like that: jaws real, real far apart, Pup just tilted himself back and let it glide smooth and quick in his mouth and down his throat. Just as you'd think he'd start coughing or puking he just gave this little swallow, like, and took it all the way down.

"There," Mammoth said, "nice and quiet."

Soon, though, Mammoth wasn't. Even in the dim lights that spilled and splashed from the racetrack, Monster could see that were was some fancy throat work going on there between Pup's tonsils and Mammoth's cock: Like that snake swallowing that fucking egg, Pup started to work and pump and milk Mammoth's cock from down deep in his throat.

First Mammoth started to groan, then he started to whistle and mumble over and over, "motherfuckermotherfuckermotherfucker…" Soon he was grunting like a hog, howling like a wolf, and snorting like a bull.

Monster watched, at first with detached, but then with sly interest, at Pup sucking Mammoth's cock. He watched quite intently, and maybe a little hungrily, till this kind of light bulb went off over his head and he said, grinning from ear to hideous ear, "Pull out motherfucker. I got me a concept."

Mammoth pulled his dick out of Pup's magic mouth like a cork coming out of a bottle, the sharp "pop!" making Mammoth grin ear to ear.

"Speak your mind," he said, adjusting his now wet and dripping dick so his balls wouldn't scrape on his zipper.

Monster dropped down to one knee, grabbed Pup by his long blond tresses and tilted his head back, back. Pup squealed with more-than-likely delight and whimpered when Monster said into his dainty ears, "You like to make noise, right?"

At first, Pup started to nod, but found himself locked in the iron of Monster's grimy hand. So, instead, he swallowed, loud and liquid, and said, "Yeah, I do."

"Good," Monster said, suddenly letting go and leaving Pup to fall with a slap of denim onto the asphalt as Monster stood up. To Mammoth he said, "Man he makes the most noise for wins the bike."

Mammoth thought some time about this, working his great lantern jaw with a huge hands as he did so, as if the action somehow aided his reason. "Why the fuck not," he said with a broad smile that showed off his jumble of teeth to their worst in the hard lights of the track.

"Call it, motherfucker," Monster said, pulling a quarter out of his pocket and flipping it high and sparkling into the track lights. Just before it landed, Mammoth said, "Heads." It dropped down into Monster's great hand (looking like a dime laying there), who then slapped it on his greasy and tanned arm.

Monster lifted his arm. The tiny head of Washington blinked up at them from a jungle of tangled arm hairs. "Heads it is."

"Right, motherfucker. Eat my dust," Mammoth said with a typhoon laugh, pulling his pants down. Bobbing from his scrub of dark public hairs, his cock bobbed and swung as if it had been cored with reebar. Still wet and shining from a few minutes down Pup's throat, Mammoth's cock was a bright pink, almost a sunburned red, and it bent up at steep angle and slightly to the right. Down in the dark squiggles of his crotch, Mammoth's balls looked like hairy billiards in thick, wrinkled leather, and Monster, looking on with macho indifference, could almost imagine them banging together like the cue ball into the eight ball.

"On your feet, hole," Mammoth said, grabbing Pup and hauling him up by the front of his T-shirt till Pup was standing on the scuffed tips of his boots.

"I'm on them, I'm on them. Fuck!" Pup said, squeaking out from under the less-than-clean cotton fabric as Mammoth snapped his belt apart and jammed Pup's jeans down to his boots. No underwear. Not even a hard dick—yet.

"Assume the fucking position," Mammoth said with laughter in his thundering voice, as he spun Pup around and jerked him down again, hard, till the blond boy was on his knees again but facing away from the mountain in denim.

"What the fuck do you think you're…Jesus!" Pup said, startled into a shrill squeal by the iron of Mammoth's cock stabbing into his back. "Look, let me get fucking ready at least. Fuck!" This time it was the same brilliant, red, long, thin cock thrusting into his coccyx. "At least hit the fucking…Christ!"

In.

Not fast. Sure as shit not easy, and fucking, fucking, fucking not fun—for Pup. Watching from the other side, all Monster could see was Mammoth's straining, muscular bulk moving with very precise twitches as he stuck his cock around Pup's ass then—as he sighted down his shaft with the nerves in his cockhead—he jerked himself forward with perhaps (near as Monster could tell) half of his cock length.

Pup screamed, drowning out for a second the revving engines of the near-by race. The sound was sharp and high, the pain of Mammoth's iron jamming into his dry and pert asshole squealing out of him like toothpaste from a tube.

Mammoth pulled out and went in even harder.

Pup's cry cut like a sudden draft of freezing air around them, chilling Monster for a moment despite his size and sweating interest in Pup's getting fucked. After, though, after the scream was fading into the now dark night, Pup's sounds became more guttural, more visceral: with another pump from Mammoth his scream faded into a throbbing grunt and didn't match Mammoth's thrusts with his huge hips.

Pup's face also went from wide and contorted to a softening mask of forced, closed eyes, bitten lips, and puffed cheeks. As Monster watched, his own cock hardening in his tight jeans, Pup started to moan and cry in a tempo that slowly started to approach the bucking of Mammoth behind him. His arms started to shake, and he started to droop and drop with each slamming blow of Mammoth's hips from behind him.

Pup's lips started to blow and hiss, but alternatingly smiled and gasped in swells and surges of butt-fucked pleasure. Despite an image and rep far more immense and powerful than he was, Monster was enraptured by Pup's face as he got fucked by the stroking engine of Mammoth's cock. Before he could think the usual, automatic biker if I do this will I still be cool? Monster knelt down to stare into Pup's playing, rippling face: pain, pleasure, pain, pleasure.

Carefully, Monster put a cigar-sized finger in front of Pup's mouth and groaned himself, earthquake and passing train, as Pup's eyes snapped open and he gently wrapped lips as smooth as fine silk around his walnut-sized knuckles and began to carefully suck.

This obviously was something that Mammoth didn't care for, because once he figured out that his rival for Bull's Harley was getting his finger worked, he really started to buck: he wasn't just fucking Pup, he was slamming, colliding with his ass. Butt-fuck? No. Butt-fucking? Damned straight.

And damned straight that Pup screamed again—high and shrieking, like Mammoth's cock had grown ten times and barbed as well. He fucking screamed like his asshole was getting cored. His mouth opened so wide and full that Monster was surprised that he didn't chomp down on his thick and callused finger.

But Pup didn't bite him. Didn't once. In fact, after the pain seemed to fade into merely unbearable, Pup started to work Monster's finger again: gentle, gentle, gentle.

Behind them, a train with its brakes burned off, Mammoth chugged and pistoned faster and faster down that highway that led to "I'm fucking coming!"

Then he fucking did, jerking and snapping this way and that like his own dick had gotten wrapped in barbed wire somewhere inside Pup's velvety asshole. Watching Mammoth twist, grunt, and even cry out himself (in a macho kind of pig-grunt way), Monster felt sympathy for the recipient of his pool-cue dick: Hate to have that thing whipped and jerking on top of me, he thought.

Then, when Mammoth was done with his seizure, he said, "Fuck, Fuck, FUCK! Whew!" Panting like a bike on cheap gas that simply refused to die. "OK, asshole. Your turn."

Monster didn't say a word. He just kissed Pup on the forehead (feeling of wire bristles and lips surprisingly soft) and went over to his bike. When he walked back into the hard light spilling from the track he was carrying a pint of oil and sporting an unreadable expression.

"Fucker ain't yours yet, man," Mammoth said, hitching up his belt and laughing, low and mean, "and I don't think she needs any oil."

"Not for the fucking bike, asshole," Monster said, unbuckling his pants and dropping them to the asphalt.

If Mammoth's cock was a pool cue than Monster's was...what? Big? Damned sure it was fucking big. I mean, think about it, do you think a mean-ass motherfucker with the handle of Monster would have an ordinary cock? No fucking way—he would have a monster cock, right? A weird cock, a twisted, patched-up, piebald, bent, swollen thing—that's what would be hanging between Monster's legs, right?

Damned right: one ball bigger than the other (marble next to bowling ball), circumcised head swollen and lopsided like it had been patched by some unlucky loser in a crap game (so the rumors said), a cork-screwed shaft like maybe he'd been hard up and wasted and tried to fuck the transmission of a hog (rumor said), long puckered scar from halfway to base of his groin like Monster's cock had been stuck in some asshole or cunt and had to have been bled, maybe, to make it small enough to get it out (rumor again).

Of course Monster had a fucking scary cock. What else would you think?

And it was hard and throbbing.

Maybe something small and maybe even sweet took over Mammoth at that point, cause he took Pup's head in his hands and turned him so he couldn't look back and see that warped length of steel-hard pork that was about to take a trip up his ass. Maybe Mammoth had something like a burst of conscience and, maybe, he was worried about what Pup might do if he saw Monster's cock.

Just maybe—cause he knelt down and whispered in Pup's ear: "Whatever you thought it would be...it's worse."

Pup whimpered.

Pup whimpered even more after Monster popped the oil like a Bud and pooped it's thick gold onto his cock and positioned himself so that he was right up against Pup's throbbing and quaking asshole.

Then in.

Pup made a noise. No, not like you'd think. Nothing to war against the racetrack nearby and win, nothing hard and shrill and painful to hear. Pup made a noise, for sure—a simple, little kind of noise.

A good kind of noise: Part groan, part grunt, part moan, part sigh. It slipped out of his lips because the slow, pleasant, progression of Monster's twisted and fat cock into Pup's asshole was done gentle and smooth, lubed with 10-40 and a glacial patience.

Pup started to buck a bit as that good noise seeped out of him, trying to force the fuck that Monster didn't seem willing to do by forcing himself back against him and then pulling away. Between them, the sound of their fucking was a wet slurping, a sucking chest wound kind of noise.

Mammoth was laughing and rocking back and forth: "Come on you fucker, let's hear it!"

Monster smiled wide and sharp, gave Pup a hard slap against his pale, hard ass and started to return the buck—slapping his iron thighs against Pup with a steady and building rhythm. As he did, as he humped against Pup's asshole, he started to leak out a good series of grunts, too—a kind of cycling engine noise like a motor perfectly tuned and then slowly revved up to speed.

On the receiving end, Pup, too, started his own revving grunts as his bucked and slammed back and forth against Monster's escalating thrusts of his huge, misshapen cock. Slap, slap, SLAP!

Suddenly, Pup dropped down to the asphalt so his face was panting and heaving into the hard black surface and his ass was high in the air. Behind him, Monster could feel one of Pup's hands fumble with Monster's tight and aching balls and then vanish to, Monster guessed, stroke his own aching cock.

"I can't fucking hear you!" screamed Mammoth, rocking back and forth and laughing, laughing, laughing....

Pup screamed, then, low and growling like he'd reached down through his own cock and pulled a gritty, brilliant come out of himself. He jerked like Mammoth, but a Mammoth impaled on a hot rod of corkscrewed meat: He flailed and thumped the hard road with his free hand and drooled a warm pool of spit onto the black surface.

Behind him, Monster echoed and amplified: He bellowed like a great fucking beast with his cock caught in some kind of wild suction trap. He howled like a wolf getting one bitching fucking blow job, like a lion getting it from an elephant.

Then he pulled himself out with a slurping "pop," stood up with a sudden stagger and wiped his huge brow with a denim sleeve.

Mammoth was grinning and laughing and smiling and said, "Well, motherfucker, that was damned fucking quiet. Very fucking quiet. Hope you don't plan on riding it out of here."

"Nope, didn't plan on it at all," Monster said, after hitching his belt and helping a grinning and laughing and smiling Pup to his wobbling feet.

"Not at all," he added, putting a knurled hand on Pup's shoulder.

The bike, of course, went to Mammoth...and Pup? Pup went with Monster, of course.

The Beckoning
Jonathan Asche

It was as Cody and his girlfriend, Celia, were stepping out of his apartment Saturday evening that they encountered the new tenant as he was starting up the stairs.

"How's it goin'?" Cody said amiably, nodding and giving a slight smile, wanting to appear friendly, but not so friendly that the man would fear he was part of a religious cult.

The man seemed shocked to have been spoken to. "Um, fine, thank you," he replied, a trace of an English accent in his monotone voice.

Cody locked his door and stepped toward the staircase. "I'm Cody." He offered his hand, which the man regarded suspiciously for a moment before taking it.

"I'm Marcus, Marcus Fornier."

"And I'm Celia," Cody's girlfriend piped up, stepping forward to get an unenthusiastic handshake from the stranger on the stairs.

Marcus had deep-set, hooded eyes that, coupled with his severely arched eyebrows, gave him an almost dangerous appearance. His dark hair was cropped close to his head, and his mouth was framed with a neatly trimmed mustache and goatee. In each ear he wore a silver hoop. His form was hidden beneath a large, black overcoat, the hemline of which stopped just above his ankle.

"You just move in?" Cody asked.

"Yes. Last week. The third-floor loft," Marcus volunteered.

"Really? I didn't know."

"Excuse me," Marcus cut him off, "but I really must get to my apartment. I'm…I'm, um, expecting a call."

"Sure, yeah. Well, good to meet you," Cody said. "Talk to you later."

"Right," the man said before turning to continue up the stairs.

"Guess we shouldn't expect him to throw a housewarming anytime soon," Celia said with a sneer under her breath.

"Well, at least we were friendly," Cody said with a shrug, opening the front door to the building. "After you, my love."

It was after meeting Marcus Fornier that the dreams began. There wasn't much to remember at first: a blurred image of a man in a white bedroom. Cody couldn't remember what happened in the dream or if in fact anything had.

Cody did not put much stock in dreams. He often lost patience with Celia because she wanted to analyze every nuance of whatever image traipsed through her head while she was unconscious, hell-bent on determining the true meaning of her dreams. "Why does your path to mental health involve driving me insane?" Cody would say, only half joking. To him, the only real value of dreams was to give you a weird story to share with the person you woke up with.

For two weeks Cody awoke with the same memory of the man in the white bedroom. He found the dream less troubling than annoying. He was ready for his subconscious to switch channels.

In the two weeks since the dream began, Cody would awake feeling uncontrollably horny. The morning hard-ons were nothing out of the ordinary. Even the lust that built inside him during the night wasn't too unusual either. If he awoke in such a state and Celia was staying over, he'd lean over her sleeping body, sweep her blond hair away from her face, and begin kissing her neck until she awoke to reciprocate.

Now when he awoke, the desire he felt wasn't for Celia. Who it was for, he wasn't sure, but when his eyes opened and he looked over at Celia, his first impulse was not to touch her. Instead, he'd slide out of bed and lock himself away in the bathroom, stroking his dick until he spewed come all over himself and the bathroom floor.

His lack of interest was not lost on his girlfriend, however.

"Time to sleep," Cody announced, setting his book down on the bedside table.

Celia, reading in bed next to him, looked up from her romance novel and smiled. "Are you that tired?" she asked, her tone suggestive.

Cody gave her a perplexed look. "What do you mean?"

Celia placed her book down on her lap and leaned over to him. "You know what I mean," she said lasciviously, her smooth hand gliding over

Cody's broad, hairless chest, her lips close to his ear.

"Baby, not tonight."

Celia sighed, returning to her side of the bed. She wore an expression of disgust. "This is a switch," she muttered.

"What's that supposed to mean?"

"It means I could get more action in a monastery, the way you've been the past couple of weeks. What's wrong? Do you no longer find me attractive?"

"No, it's not that at all. It's just...I don't know. I haven't been in the mood."

"You looked like you were in the mood when you got up to go to the bathroom the other morning," Celia shot back.

Cody felt his face redden. "This is stupid. I've been understanding when you didn't want to have sex."

"You haven't had to be understanding for two weeks running," Celia said snidely. Immediately she apologized. "I'm sorry. You're right. I'm being selfish. It just makes me wonder if your feelings have changed."

"They haven't changed at all," Cody said, his tone soothing. "I'll bounce back. And when I do, you're going to get the best fuck of your life."

Celia giggled. "You promise?"

"Promise," Cody said, giving her a kiss before rolling over to go to sleep.

When Cody's eyes opened again, he was somewhere else. Someplace he had never been yet was entirely familiar with.

"Do you want to suck my cock?" a man asked. Cody looked in the direction of the voice. Across the room, sitting on an iron-framed canopy bed was Marcus Fornier.

Cody didn't respond. He could only stare silently at Marcus Fornier. He stood up from the bed, starting to walk slowly across the large, white room. He wore black silk pajamas, the top unbuttoned so his chest was exposed. The muscles of his chest and torso were firm, clearly defined beneath his taut, pale skin. Dark hair rose from beneath the waistband of his pajama bottoms in a single column before branching out across his hard pecs.

"You didn't answer my question," Marcus said. He was standing behind Cody now, his hands resting on Cody's shoulders. "Do you?"

Marcus's hand slid down Cody's arm, cuffing the wrist and pulling Cody's hand back toward him. Cody could feel his hardness beneath the silk. Instinctively he squeezed it.

"Yes," Cody finally replied, his voice a whisper.

"I know you do," Marcus said. His other hand glided down Cody's smooth chest, his rippled torso. It wasn't until this moment that Cody realized all he was wearing was a thin pair of boxer shorts, the front of which poked forward, the fabric pushed away from his body by his hard cock.

Marcus placed his hand over Cody's crotch, his fingers gently tracing the outline of Cody's erect prick. "You look like quite a mouthful yourself," Marcus whispered, his mouth inches away from Cody's ear.

Marcus Fornier planted his hands on Cody's waist, pulling Cody's body against his. Cody felt Marcus's rigid cock press against the crack of his ass. "Such a beautiful body," Marcus purred in his ear, rubbing himself against Cody's ass.

Cody closed his eyes. His breathing had become shallow. "Oh, yes," he sighed.

He could feel Marcus's hand sliding beneath his boxers, cupping a firm, round butt cheek. "So perfect," he said.

An index finger nuzzled his asshole, and Cody cried out. "Like that?" Marcus said teasingly. "Do you want more?"

Cody could only nod. "Then turn around," Marcus commanded.

Cody turned, slowly until he was facing Marcus Fornier. He was removing his pajama shirt, dropping it onto the hardwood floor. "What do you want to do first?" he asked.

His entire body consumed by lust, Cody sank to his knees. He buried his face into Marcus's crotch, prodding at his cock with his tongue while his hands desperately tugged at the waistband of Marcus's pajamas. "Let me help you," Marcus said, pulling the drawstring loose. The silk pants slipped off his hips, piling around his ankles.

Marcus's legs were solid muscle, covered with silky, black hairs. Just beneath his left hip was a small tattoo of an elaborately designed dragon. His cock was long and thick, the tip of the plum-size head trickling a thread of syrupy precome. His balls hung low in their loose, furry sac.

Cody grabbed the base of Marcus's dick and parted his lips. He leaned forward, guiding Marcus's cock over his tongue toward the back of his throat.

A grunt escaped Marcus's lips as his cock was engulfed in Cody's mouth. Cody swallowed his entire shaft, sucking on it hungrily. He reached around Marcus's legs, grasping his ass, which was amazingly smooth given the rest of him was so hairy. Cody kneaded Marcus's butt cheeks while his tongue swirled around the length of Marcus's dick.

Marcus was groaning, thrusting his hips forward. He curled his hand around Cody's head, grabbing a fistful of his ash-blond hair, pulling at it slightly as he fucked Cody's mouth.

One of Cody's hands strayed down to his own crotch. He fished his cock out, pulling it through the fly of his boxers. He rubbed his palm across the head, spreading his own natural lubrication around the shaft. Then he began to stroke his cock vigorously while his mouth slurped on Marcus's dick.

"Oh, yes, oh, yes," Marcus hissed. "I'm so close."

Cody felt himself nearing that same threshold. His body felt electrified, each stroke bringing him closer to the inevitable release.

Marcus pulled his cock from Cody's mouth, gripping it in his own hand. "Wait for it," he warned through clenched teeth, furiously pulling at his dick.

Cody raised his face, waiting to feel the shower of jism rain down upon his face when....

"What the fuck is your problem?" he heard a woman shout.

Suddenly Cody was awake. It took him a moment to orient himself. He wasn't in the white bedroom with Marcus Fornier, but in his own apartment. The sheets were tangled about his ankles. His torso and thighs were splattered with thick, white puddles of come, and his hand still gripped his now-softening cock. Standing beside the bed, her anger clearly visible in the thin light of dawn, was Celia. He could tell by her glare that no explanation he gave would meet her approval.

All he could manage to say was, "Damn, that was one wild dream."

After that morning, Celia became Cody's *ex*-girlfriend. She left saying she could understand if he favored another woman, but there was no way in hell she was going to figure out why he preferred his own hand.

"It doesn't bitch at me, for one," Cody said, unable to help himself. Celia slammed the door so hard three pictures leapt off their hangers and crashed to the floor.

Cody knew he should have felt more distraught than he did. He and Celia had been together for more than a year, and up until a few weeks ago he was sure he loved her. Now, his thoughts clouded by his mental rendezvous with Marcus Fornier, what Cody felt was a strange sense of relief. She would no longer be around to interfere with his growing obsession with the dreams and with Marcus Fornier.

In the nights following Celia's departure from his life, the dreams continued on much the same course. Cody would awaken in the same way, bathed in sweat and come. The dreams were so real that there were many times he had to stop himself from actually going to the third floor to confront Marcus Fornier, as if the new neighbor was actively invading his thoughts.

There was another reason Cody wanted to approach Marcus: The dreams were not enough. Cody found himself desiring the real experience. But he didn't know how to initiate such a thing. After all, up until a few days ago he believed himself to be exclusively heterosexual. Also, he had no idea what Marcus Fornier's sexuality was, either. For all he knew, the mysterious new neighbor desired women as strongly as Cody once had.

Such was not the case, however. Marcus Fornier apparently wanted to confront Cody as well and knew precisely how to initiate such an encounter.

Cody had just stepped into the building, returning from work. He was fumbling with the keys to his door when he heard a voice say his name.

Before he looked up he knew who it was. There was no mistaking that vague English accent for anyone else.

Cody looked toward the stairwell. Standing on the second-floor landing was Marcus Fornier. He wore a pair of black, silk pajama pants and nothing else. His chest and torso looked exactly as they had in Cody's dreams. Cody wondered if he was dreaming now, but was sure he wasn't. He hadn't gone to bed yet. The preceding moments of his day—getting ready for work, fighting the morning rush-hour traffic, the nine dreary hours at the office, then battling the afternoon rush—had all been mind-numbingly real.

For a brief moment, his and Marcus's eyes met. He was surprised to see a hint of a smile creep across Marcus's lips. Then his neighbor turned and started to climb the stairs.

Cody stood at the door of his apartment for a full minute before he made up his mind to start climbing the stairs. He'd hoped for such an opportunity, but now that it had presented itself he was hesitant. Dreams were one thing, but could he actually go through with this for real?

His cock had already made the decision for him. It had sprung into an intense erection within seconds of his sighting Marcus.

Cody began making slow, deliberate steps up the staircase.

The door to Marcus Fornier's apartment was partially open. Cody swung it open and entered, not bothering to knock (he'd been invited, hadn't he?). He closed the door behind him. The interior was familiar, though now he was aware of more of the details. At the front of the loft was a small kitchen and dining area. The walls were white. On the windows hung thin, gauze curtains that billowed in the breeze blowing through the open windows. The windows were also the only source of light, giving the loft the same hazy, gray cast as the outside sky.

At the far side of the room sat the loft's only significant piece of furniture: an iron-framed canopy bed, shrouded in the same white gauze fabric that draped the windows.

And sitting on the bed was Marcus Fornier, now nude and reclining on the plump, white comforter that covered the mattress.

Cody started to walk toward him. His dick ached beneath his pants; his heart thudded within his chest.

"Stop," Marcus commanded. "Don't you think you should be dressed for the occasion?"

Instinctively, Cody knew to strip. He pulled off his shapeless, navy coat. He clumsily removed his tie and began to unbutton his white shirt, aware of Marcus's gaze the entire time. Cody kicked off his shoes and started to unbuckle his belt.

"Wait," Marcus said. "Move closer."

Cody was about ten feet from the bed. He took about five steps closer. "Closer," Marcus encouraged. When Cody was less than two feet away, his neighbor told him to stop.

"Continue," Marcus nodded.

Cody finished unbuckling his belt, unzipped his pants, and pushed them down, kicking them off when they fell about his ankles. He now stood before Marcus wearing only his socks and, as fate would have it, a pair of boxer shorts. He made no move to take off his remaining clothing.

"So what are you, a porn star?" Marcus asked. "Take off the socks."

Cody shucked off the socks, but left the boxers on.

Marcus motioned for him to move closer. Cody stepped up to the edge of the bed, his thighs inches away from the mattress.

With Cody in place, Marcus got up on his knees and moved toward him. His cock was rigid and bobbed against his stomach as he moved. Cody noticed a dark patch near his left hip. "Is that a tattoo?" he asked.

"You can get a closer look later," Marcus said. His voice was low and calm, not at all the stiff monotone he had when Cody first met him.

He placed his hands on Cody's chest, caressing the smooth slabs of muscle that made up his pecs. "Just as I'd imagined," Marcus whispered. "Smooth and well-defined."

Cody closed his eyes as Marcus pinched one of his hard, tan nipples with one hand while the fingers of his other hand gently glided down his abs, producing a mild tickling sensation.

"Turn around," Marcus said, pushing him in the direction he needed to go.

Once he was facing away from the bed, Marcus leaned against Cody's back. Cody could feel Marcus's chest pressed against his shoulder blades, his dick resting against the curve of his ass.

"Tell me what you want to do to me," Marcus whispered into Cody's ear.

Cody stammered, finding the words difficult to say, though he'd heard them before. "I want to…I want…to suck your dick."

"That's a start. What else?" Marcus had reached an arm around Cody's body and was tracing the line of blond hairs that led from his navel to the waistband of his underwear.

"I want to lick your balls," Cody said, sighing.

"Better. Anything else?"

"And eat your ass." The sentence came out of Cody's mouth in a gasp.

Marcus pressed himself hard against Cody's back, his cock grinding between his butt cheeks. He placed his moist lips against the side of Cody's neck, taking tiny bites. Cody moaned and rubbed his ass against Marcus Fornier.

Cody felt Marcus's hands tug at the waistband of his boxers. His fingers slipped beneath the elastic, moving for Cody's stiff, throbbing cock. Cody closed his eyes while his neighbor delicately handled his prick, tracing the hard veins and caressing the swollen head.

The boxers were being pulled from Cody's body. So desperate was Marcus to have his conquest naked he nearly ripped the underwear from Cody's hips. Once Cody was nude, Marcus's hands began to feverishly trace the muscular landscape of his body. His hands glided over Cody's chest while he kissed the valley between his shoulder blades. His fingers dug into the ridges of his tight abdomen while he flicked the center of Cody's back with his pointed tongue. Marcus gripped Cody's sturdy thighs as he gnawed at the small of his back, his beard tickling the crack of Cody's ass.

Marcus's lips traveled down the dark crevice where Cody's butt cheeks met, prodding between the perfectly molded globes of flesh. He grabbed Cody's ass and pried his cheeks apart, exposing his tight hole. Cody took a quick, sharp breath as Marcus wiggled his tongue lightly over his asshole. Cody was unprepared for the pleasure this elicited. He cried out in both ecstasy and surprise. Bending forward, he pressed his ass into Marcus's face, wanting his mysterious neighbor to dive his tongue deeper.

Marcus Fornier didn't require much encouragement. He stabbed at Cody's ass with the ferocity a wild animal uses on its prey. He lapped at the tender hole, then poked it savagely with the tip of his tongue, forcing his way past the clenched muscle.

"Eat it!" Cody hissed. "Shove your tongue up my ass!"

The words sounded unreal coming from his lips. Cody almost felt as if someone else were speaking through him. But the pleasure was very real. His balls were churning, and his cock was quivering. A tiny thread of pre-come hung suspended from the head of his dick.

Marcus pulled his face away from the warm valley of Cody's ass cheeks. "Why don't you join me on the bed?" he whispered.

Cody turned around. Marcus was sitting on the bed, his butt resting on his ankles. Cody climbed onto the bed, straddling Marcus. He pressed his lips against Marcus's, his tongue sliding into Marcus's waiting mouth. Marcus's rigid cock was trapped beneath Cody's body, rubbing against his groin and ass. Cody's dick was pressed against Marcus's abdomen, creating a delicious friction.

"Suck my cock," Marcus said into Cody's ear. "I want to see you take it between those beautiful lips."

They disentangled their bodies, Marcus lying on his back and spreading his legs. Cody knelt between his legs, hunching over Marcus's body. He brought his lips to the hard, hairy surface of Marcus's abdomen, kissing and licking the soft curves created by the taut muscles that lay beneath his skin.

As his mouth moved lower down, traveling toward his dick, Cody encountered the dark patch at his left hip. Looking at it now at close range, he could see that it was in fact a tattoo. It was of an intricately designed dragon. The discovery took Cody aback.

"The tattoo," he said. "It's just like the one in my dream."

Marcus's only response was, "I know."

Although the discovery of the tattoo was bizarre, as was Marcus's reaction to Cody's mentioning that he had seen it before, Cody did not let it distract him for too long. His mouth kept moving toward Marcus's cock. He took the erect phallus in his hand, gently stroking it and admiring its size. Hesitantly, he brought his tongue to it. Marcus sighed as Cody licked his dick like a lollipop.

Cody then opened his mouth and guided Marcus's cock between his lips, just as he had in his dreams. The turgid flesh filled his mouth. He could taste Marcus's precome, savoring its salty flavor. He took as much of Marcus's dick as he was able, stopping when he thought it was about to catch in his throat. He started to suck it, mimicking the action he'd done only in his unconscious mind.

If Cody's lack of experience was hindering Marcus Fornier's enjoyment, he gave no indication. Marcus moaned and sighed; he put a hand on top of Cody's head and guided him toward his crotch. "Your mouth feels so good," he murmured, sounding as if he'd just been sedated. "Swallow that hard cock."

Cody took Marcus's dick in his hand, bringing his fist up and down the shaft as he licked and sucked the head. Marcus's body was quaking now, every muscle contracting as the pleasure intensified. Cody cupped his balls, delicately holding the two swollen orbs. His hand moved down farther, his fingers slipping into the sweaty crevice of his ass. Cody dragged an index finger over Marcus's hairy asshole, causing Marcus to tremble in barely controlled ecstasy.

Marcus pulled his legs up, bringing his ass into the air. "Taste it," he purred. "I want to feel your tongue in my ass."

Cody found his sexual trance momentarily broken as he considered Marcus's request. He regarded Marcus's ass, staring at the puckered hole surrounded by coarse, dark hairs, not sure if he could bring himself to actually put his mouth on it. As hot as it felt when Marcus was rimming him, Cody—whose homosexual experiences prior to this moment were only a couple of circle jerks in high school—wasn't quite prepared to return the favor.

But Marcus wasn't willing to be denied. He put his hand behind Cody's neck and forced his face forward. "Go on," he commanded. "It won't hurt you."

With trembling lips Cody kissed Marcus's asshole. He quickly poked it with his tongue, causing Marcus to shiver and groan. "That's it," he sighed. Encouraged by Marcus's response, Cody let his tongue linger, licking the tender opening of Marcus's ass. He found himself becoming more aroused by his partner's reaction. Each time Marcus moaned and sighed, Cody drove his tongue deeper. He had his face buried in Marcus's ass, licking his furry hole with long, sensual strokes of his tongue.

Cody continued eating Marcus's ass until his jaw ached. He reached a hand up and started to jack off Marcus as he titillated his asshole with his tongue, but his neighbor stopped him.

"Don't," he said, seizing Cody's wrist. "You do that and it's all over for me, and I'm not finished yet."

Cody looked up. "What did you have in mind?"

"Come up here, and I'll show you."

Rising up from the warm, wet recesses of Marcus's ass, Cody positioned himself over Marcus, straddling his chest. His cock rose above Marcus's face, demanding attention.

Marcus flicked the base of Cody's cock with his tongue. His tongue then swabbed his balls, sucking the skin of his nut sac between his lips.

Cody supported himself against the headboard with one hand, while the other hand gripped his dick and fed it into Marcus's waiting mouth. He swallowed it with ease, the muscles of his throat constricting around the shaft. Cody couldn't remember when he'd come this close to pure bliss. When he and Celia were together, their lovemaking never approached the excitement he was feeling now with this man he'd met scarcely a month ago.

Marcus took his mouth away long enough to stick two of his fingers between his lips. When he pulled them out of his mouth, they were dripping with his spit. As he resumed sucking Cody's dick, he reached around his waist and dipped the fingers into his ass, pressing against his clenched sphincter. His touch was delicate at first, but Cody got a jolt when Marcus managed to actually work one of his fingers inside him.

"Just relax," Marcus cooed, his lips less than an inch away from the slick head of Cody's cock. "Let yourself enjoy it."

Cody tried to do as he'd been advised, concentrating on relaxing his ass muscles, hoping that the pleasure wasn't far behind. It wasn't. He began to ride Marcus's finger, urging it deeper into his anus, while he fucked his hot, wet mouth.

The second finger was inserted, stretching Cody's asshole a little wider. It created a pleasurable tension that heightened Cody's excitement. As Marcus massaged his prostate and gulped his prick down his throat, Cody found himself aching for more.

"Fuck me," he breathed. "I want your cock up my ass!"

Marcus pulled his mouth away from Cody's dick. A little smile crept onto his lips. "I thought you'd never ask," he said playfully.

Cody got off Marcus and rolled onto his back. Marcus leaned over to a small, glass-topped table that stood next to the bed. Sitting on it were the accoutrements they would need: condoms and lubricant. Marcus took the bottle of lubricant and opened the bottle, squeezing a small pool of the gel into his palm. He rubbed it between his fingers before he rubbed the slick liquid over Cody's asshole, then slipped his middle finger inside him.

"Oh," Cody panted. "Hurry, I can't wait."

"Be patient," Marcus scolded, slowly inching his finger deeper. "I've got to loosen you up first."

Cody closed his eyes. Marcus added another finger, then a third. His body writhed as Marcus finger-fucked him, preparing his ass to accept for what was to follow.

Marcus withdrew his fingers abruptly. Cody opened his eyes to see Marcus lube his own cock. He tore open the foil wrapper of the condom, removed the rubber, and rolled it down his shaft. Marcus poured more lubricant into his palm and massaged his sheathed dick.

"Are you ready?" he asked.

Cody didn't answer right away. Marcus's cock was a bit larger than average—between eight and nine inches—and seemed almost two inches in diameter. Having never been fucked before, Cody wasn't sure he could handle it even if Marcus were below average size.

Yet Cody's desire was far greater than his apprehension. After a pause, he nodded. "Go for it," he said, hoisting his feet onto Marcus's shoulders.

Marcus took hold of his cock and brought himself to the slick opening of Cody's ass. He nudged the tight hole teasingly. Then he began to press against it harder, increasing the pressure until finally he forced Cody's asshole open.

Second thoughts immediately ran through Cody's mind as Marcus slowly entered him. His face knotted up into an expression of agony. He felt as if he were being impaled on a light post.

"Relax," Marcus coaxed. "It gets better. I promise."

Cody tried to do as he was advised, focusing past the pain. As Marcus began to thrust into him, his stiff prick massaging his prostate, the pain was quickly replaced with an intense pleasure.

Marcus smiled as he watched Cody's face melt into an expression of joy. "Like it?" he asked.

"Fuck me," Cody sighed, clutching Marcus's ass.

Marcus increased his pace, ramming his cock deep inside Cody's ass. Keeping his hands planted on his partner's ass, Cody pulled himself forward, wanting Marcus to plunge even deeper.

Marcus wrapped a hand around Cody's aching cock, jacking him off as he fucked him. Each stroke caused a minor explosion of euphoria throughout Cody's body. He began to tremble, his senses overloaded by pleasurable sensations. He tried to hold back and concentrate on other things to prolong this moment. His efforts were too little, too late, however. Marcus had aroused him to such a degree that his body, unable to take much more, succumbed. Every muscle tensed as Cody's cock fired its hot, thick load, splattering his chest and abdomen.

Seeing Cody get off increased Marcus's arousal. He started plowing Cody's ass with no restraint, his cock hammering in and out of him like a piston at full throttle.

"I'm almost there," he panted, his features contorted as the sensations became overwhelming.

He let out a harsh, guttural groan as he made his final thrust into Cody's ass, his load flooding into the rubber.

Gasping for breath, Marcus fell forward on top of Cody. They lay together, their bodies sweaty and sticky. The room was dark now, the sun having finally descended from the sky. Only the street lights outside illuminated the loft.

"Is this a dream?" Cody wondered aloud, running his fingers through Marcus's bristly dark hair.

"If it is, what a glorious dream it is," Marcus sighed.

Cody awoke in his own apartment. He was lying on his sofa, naked. It was still dark outside. In the dim light he could just make out the time on the clock on the far wall: 5:25 A.M.

He stood up. Memories of his night with Marcus began to flash through his mind. It could've been just another dream, but the soreness in his ass told him otherwise.

Cody went into his bedroom and hastily put on a sweatshirt and tattered jeans. He stepped out of his apartment and headed upstairs to the third floor.

When he reached Marcus's door, he stopped, not sure what to do next. After all, what would he say once Marcus answered? "Excuse me, but could you just confirm something for me: Did we fuck last night?"

But confusion and curiosity got the better of his judgment, and Cody knocked.

No answer.

He knocked louder. Still no answer. He began pounding on it until his fist ached.

A neighbor from across the hall came to her door—a frumpy, heavyset woman with tangled hair who was not too happy to have been awakened. "What the hell are you doing?" she snapped, tying a pink bathrobe around her thick body.

"I'm sorry. I was trying to wake my friend." Cody apologized.

"Well, you're not going to wake anyone up in that apartment," the woman groused. "No one lives there."

"No, someone moved in there earlier in the month. Dark-haired guy with a goatee. Has an accent. I was in here with him last night."

The woman glared at him. "Look, I've lived here for ten years. I may not talk to my neighbors, but I know who they are, and I'm telling you no one has lived in that apartment for two months. Now why don't you go back to your place until you come down from whatever it is you're on, or I'll call the police."

She slammed her door.

Cody stood in the hall for a full five minutes, trying to make sense of what had happened, what he thought had happened, and what the woman told him. Unfortunately, the only answer he could arrive at was he had apparently gone insane.

Then he heard a noise. He turned and saw that the door to what he once believed was Marcus's apartment had opened a crack.

Unable to turn away, Cody pushed the door open and stepped inside.

Base on Balls
T. Hitman

My ad read: *Red Socks I.S.O. Yankee pinstripes for between-the-sheets pennant chase rivalry. 29 y.o. bi-curious ballplayer seeks sports sex buddy. Me: 6' 3", dk blnd/blue eyes, mustache, mod. hairy. You: str8 acting, all-guy, into beer, baseball, in my bedroom. My hometown team loses to yours, I bottom. Your guys lose, you take the shame with me on top. Into jockstraps, sweat socks, sports, hanging out, no B.S. I'm real. Only same need reply. Write or call box #DSV-4600.*

Nervously, I dropped it into the mailbox and walked away, wondering if I was crazy. But the closer I got to the Big Three-O, the more I realized it was time to either give in to it or forget the whole crazy idea, settle down, try and get married the way it was expected of guys like me, and most likely be miserable for the rest of my life.

The replies started coming in about a week later, a few letters, two on the personal voice mail I'd gotten free for taking out the ad.

"I'm looking for a long-term relationship," one of them said. I wasn't, so I didn't jot down the number he left.

"You like baseball?" lisped my next prospective lay. "It's such a *slow* game. The men who play it whine too much, get paid too much…."

"What position do you play? Goalie?"

This went on for days. The same heat that had earlier filled my balls with an extra dose of load from thinking I'd meet the right kind of guy began to shrink them, along with my hope. You see, I'd gotten a taste of that kind of sex once before, and the itch to do it again never went away. We were both barely 18, playing on the same sandlot ball team the summer before he shipped out. It just sort of happened one night on a sleepover when I let it slip how much I was gonna miss our days together.

"Prove it," I remember him challenging me.

I did.

Funny thing is, I'd always liked women, too. But I'd never forgotten how another guy smells and tastes close up, and how, when I'd be playing with my cock over some centerfold, a few of the guys I watched on the hometown team would creep into my jack-off fantasies.

Shit—one day, I decided to take out that ad in the personals magazine, though it didn't look like I was gonna find what I wanted, needed, which was good old buddy sex. The kind that came with no strings, no apologies. The kind that's so good, you never forget it.

The kind it looked like I was never gonna know again.

I pretty much gave up on the personal ad thing by the end of the second week. Feeling dumb and depressed, I chucked the personals into the garbage on my way to the bathroom mirror. I'm no egomaniac. Never have been. But, shit, the face staring back from the mirror should have been getting it every night of the week. I keep my hair neat and short. I've got a 'stache and blue eyes, just like the ad read, and when I smile, those dimples sometimes make even me hard. I could probably get any woman I wanted, and have plenty of times. Problem was, I wanted to meet a guy like myself, a jock, a regular joe.

I was starting to believe he just wasn't out there when I caught a look in the mirror of the personals sticking out of the trash. An ad for a local gay bar capped the corner of visible newsprint. I didn't plan on going that route, but after an hour of hedging, I shaved, showered, tucked my wallet into the back pocket of my jeans, and headed out.

I'm not the kind of guy who should look nervous at any time. I parked my truck among a bunch of trendy small cars, a few convertibles, and started for the club's front door. But as I pulled a five out of my wallet and handed the bouncer my cover charge, I realized my hand was shaking more than I'd ever remembered. Pride's Landing on a Saturday night was full of people, most over-dressed compared to what I had on. One watered-down beer and a couple of stares from women dressed in tuxedos later, I came to the conclusion this wasn't a place for me and left.

What are you, fucked? a voice in my head kept saying as I drove away, doing the top of the speed limit, feeling wounded, stupid, lost. The erection I'd been trying to ignore for days, waking up to find it leaking in my hands, pumped out to its full eight inches, fell flat in my jeans. The solution would have been to go home, spend Saturday night alone, jacking off to whatever I could find—hopefully, baseball—on one of the four sports channels available on my cable system. Yeah, it would have helped, but only in the short term. There seemed only one sure fix for tomorrow, or the day after that. Forget this dream of meeting someone who just wanted to get hooked up for some buddy sex. A regular guy with regular needs. I knew I'd never be able to, but I had to try.

Halfway home, I saw the sign for Dan's Sportsbar. It was the kind of place where jock-types hung out, and lonely women came to find husbands.

"Why start tomorrow," I told myself. Braking, I pulled into the parking lot, this time resigned to the fact that I was stuck there—a man with a secret urge that would never be met.

It was a smoke-free bar. The pretzels were stale, but the beer was cold. I planted my can on one of the stools and ordered a draft. The place was fairly deserted. A game of adrenaline-juiced beach volleyball was on the tube. I tried not to think about the guys pounding the ball over the net, or their strong, hairy legs, hard asses, their bare, sexy feet, big hands, chiseled faces, so much like me and what I wanted. Shifting on the bar stool, I realized I'd gotten half hard again thinking about it. The more I tried not to, the worse it got. I knew my plan to forget it would be totally fucked when one of the customers told the bartender to flip on the Saturday night Game of the Week, and the TV turned to baseball. The lump in my jeans pressed painfully against my fly as the customer who'd made the beer man switch channels saddled over to the bar stool beside mine for a better view of tube. Giving me a casual tip of his head—a safe acknowledgment gesture for guys—he brought the bottle to his lips, took a deep chug, and stared at the screen. Me, as much as I love baseball, I couldn't help but look at my new bar buddy a moment longer. The fucker was totally beautiful!

Like me, he was pretty solid, a lean mass of muscles, no body fat. He made it easy for me to see how defined he was by the comfortable-looking khaki shorts and team T-shirt he had on. His legs were perfectly muscled and hairy, as were his arms. He wore white sweat socks, pushed down around his ankles, and an old pair of black name-brand sneakers. Except for a watch, the only other stitch of clothing on him was an old baseball cap.

But then I stole a look at his face, and knew I was ruined forever thinking that pussy could replace cock. He had warm, dark eyes, the making of a mustache, his square jaw scratchy from not having shaved for a day. With his dark hair buzzed on the sides, the trace of a scar on his chin, and the kind of mouth that just begged to be kissed, he was a total stud. I could imagine him in bed, that face going down on any number of women. He wasn't the kind of guy you'd think could be interested in anything else.

I'd only been staring for a second, but the guy tipped his head back at me, and we made eye contact.

"How's it going?" he growled.

I darted my eyes up to the game. "Good, guy. Yourself?"

"Just chilling," he replied. When I looked back, he had a casual, shit-eating grin on his sexy mug. "Daryl," he said, extending a big bear paw of a hand.

"Kent," I said, shaking back. Daryl's fingers had the cold dew of his beer bottle on them. I squeezed down on his grip, matching it in another typical guy ritual. We gave each other a pump hard enough to break the bones of lesser men, but his touch had another unexpected result—I felt my boner stretch fully stiff in my jeans. The handshake broke, and I glanced down. To my horror, I saw a small, wet stain expanding at the top of the bulge.

"Fuck," I grumbled under my breath, shifting again on the barstool.

"What?" he asked.

I shook it off and returned to the ball game, but I had the feeling of being watched from my left. When I looked at Daryl, I found him eyeballing my crotch, only briefly, but long enough to make things worse.

Not to mention *better*.

For the next two hours we talked casually about sports, mostly baseball, the fact Daryl had just broken up with his girl. He asked if I had anybody special. Taking that as a cue to avoid more disappointment, I paid my tab, only to receive a soft elbow jab from my left.

"The night's still young, dude," he said, his voice deep and thundery. "What do you have planned next?"

I wanted to tell him I needed to go home, pull out my dick, stroke it as I put him, my dream guy, through all the dream motions. I looked at the clock on the bar's cable box and settled on, "Go home, catch the ninth inning…."

Daryl reached into his back pocket and pulled out his wallet. He tossed a ten on the bar. "What about tomorrow? There's a day game, 1 o'clock."

My face suddenly warmed at the concept. "You want to come over to my place and watch it? I've got a big screen."

"I'll bet," Daryl said.

By this point, I wasn't thinking anything more would come of things. Sure, I liked him. I liked him a lot. But I already had a bunch of buddies I could hang with, play hoops, pucks, hardball with, shoot the shit with, or catch a game with. I wanted, needed, more. Still, I jotted down my number on a bar napkin and stood up, relieved that my dick had softened, and that the precome it had earlier leaked appeared to have evaporated.

"1 o'clock," I said, clapping Daryl's shoulder as I hurried out into the warm night. I was sure I'd get off quick in my own mitt once I got home, sure I'd jack off thinking of Daryl, his strong, hairy legs, his big jock feet. I'd come while imagining what he had inside those shorts, dressing him and undressing him in cleats, stirrups, athletic underwear, and a jockstrap. I'd imagine how he tasted, smelled, up close.

I only got halfway to my truck when I heard his voice behind me.

"You know!" Daryl said. "It's still real early, guy. I'd love to catch the end of that game."

I turned around in time to see Daryl perform a stretch. The action pulled his T-shirt out of his shorts and sent it over his stomach, exposing the ring of dark hair around his flat, solid belly button, the top of his white briefs, and even a tangle of curls along the edge of its elastic. He cracked a smile. I smiled, too.

"So, what do you say, Kent?"

All the moisture drained from my mouth. "S-sure," I stammered.

Ten minutes later, we both pulled into my driveway. I flipped on the tube, found what was left of the ballgame, and cracked two cold ones from the fridge. Sitting on the couch beside him, I felt Daryl's bare leg brush my jeans. Right after that, we watched the last batter get struck out in the bottom of the ninth.

"Fuckin' nice," Daryl howled, pumping his fist. As they flashed the box scores, I caught him studying my place. "So, you're flying solo?"

I nodded and muted the TV. "Right now. It's not really by choice."

Daryl leaned back on the couch, spread his legs, and casually scratched at the nut-bulge in his shorts. "Solo's good some of the time, but it mostly sucks. I know. Been going through my share of it recently, too."

There, so close to him, I couldn't help but follow his hand, which lingered between his legs a little too long. I could feel my heart beating faster at the sight of him, the way his stare held on a moment longer like his hand, how he seemed so relaxed, yet so eager. This was new to me, the sense that maybe something was taking place. Was it my imagination, wanting him so badly it had blinded me to what was really happening? The most I could manage was to squeeze the beer bottle in my hand, my grip becoming a vice. "Big stud like you," I joked nervously. "I bet you got a whole stable full of ladies."

"I done OK," Daryl coolly answered. He fondled his bulge. When I looked down, the meaty pouch of one of his balls, still snagged in his clean white underwear, was hanging in the open. All the moisture drained from my mouth as I looked up to see his eyes narrowed, his hairy throat knotted with a heavy swallow. "Sometimes," he continued, his voice a deep growl, "a woman can't do everything. Not the way another man can." That said, Daryl reached over and gave the stiffness in my jeans a good, firm squeeze. I nearly dropped my beer bottle I was so stunned.

"Whoa, guy!" I gasped, almost passing out from the feel of his hand on my manhood.

"Don't act surprised," Daryl thundered. "I figured you were interested by the way that pecker of yours was spitting up ball-snot back at the bar."

"It was that obvious? Oh, fuck," I moaned as Daryl felt me up. For a minute, I let him play with my dick, loving the strong, comforting feel of his hands on me.

"You like that?" he growled under his breath.

"Aw, man," I answered. Then I eased one of my hands toward him, setting it on his hair covered knee.

"That's it, buddy," Daryl urged. He put his free hand over mine and pushed my fingers up, into the hot, packed fullness between his legs. I rubbed the ball he'd let slip into open view. I could barely believe the incredible feeling at the tips of my fingers. Before, there'd always been guilt in wanting something like this. But now, there wasn't. It all seemed very right. "I fuckin' want you, dude," he said, cementing things. "I wanted you from the moment I saw your hot ass on that barstool."

"Fuck, Daryl," I sighed, sliding my hand up into the hairy skin beneath his underwear.

We sort of moved together. Daryl's breath, smelling hot and male, filled my next shallow gasp for air before our lips met. Kissing another guy was so much different than the soft, smooth mouth of a woman. Daryl and I kissed hungrily, deeply, running our rough faces across one another. As we kissed, we abandoned baseball caps, kicked off sneakers. I broke the kiss long enough to haul my T-shirt over my head. Next thing I knew, Daryl's shirt was off. I put a hand on his pecs and rubbed him from the damp hair of his armpits down to the pelt around his stomach. Daryl let out a deep growl and started to undo his shorts, but got no further than the top button when I pulled his hand off.

"No," I huffed. "Let me do that."

Daryl spread his legs and leaned back, allowing me easier access. Tucking my hands into the top of his shorts, I pulled down his zipper, watched as he raised his ass up off the couch to accommodate me, then yanked them down his legs, off his big feet. This left him only in his sweat socks and a pair of white briefs, and I quickly took care of the socks.

Peeling off the sweaty cotton, I raised Daryl's right foot and studied his long, flat toes.

"You like my feet?" he growled, his voice an invitation.

I answered him by running my nose—then my tongue—along the underside of his toes, inhaling the sexy, clean smell and taste of his foot sweat. Both of us groaned, him from the sensation, me from having given myself the pleasure. From there, I moved to his other foot, then higher, into the hair of his legs. By the time I reached Daryl's knees, he took my head between his hands and guided my face to the tent in his underwear.

"That's it, buddy," he thundered. "Show me how much you crave my dick."

I groped Daryl's bulge, pumped him a few more times in his underwear before pulling them down and off. The handsome fucker's cock—rugged and solid like the rest of him—pointed straight up over two full, fat balls covered in black hair.

"Fuckin' nice," I sighed, taking Daryl's cock by the root. I played with his dick while licking and sniffing the perspiration off his hairy low-hangers, drunk more on the taste and smell of Daryl than the beer in my system. I had just moved up for that first taste of his cock when Daryl leaned forward. He took hold of my belt buckle and hauled me back to my feet.

"Not yet, slugger," he said, yanking down my fly. I pushed down my jeans, kicked them off my feet, and stood wearing only the jockstrap underneath that had kept my cock rock-hard most of the night. "You hot fucker!" Daryl howled. He took hold of my pouch, pulled it aside, then sat there with my bat in his mouth as I pumped his.

I don't remember how we made it onto my bed, just that I found myself in a rough-and-tumble 69, rolling on the sheets, sucking hungrily on his hairy cock like I might never get a taste of one again. From time to time,

I would feel Daryl's hands as they rubbed the sides of my ass, my stomach, stroking my balls before he spit out my cock to suck on them.

The taste of dick wasn't anything new to me; I'd had it, all those summers before. But as I licked my way through the tangle of fur toward the base of Daryl's balls, my tongue darted into the gamey pelt surrounding his asshole. Unlike the sweetness of cunt, Daryl's manhole was tangy, sour. Three licks into it, however, I knew I was hooked.

Daryl spit out my cock. "Yeah," he groaned, "that's it, buddy!" Taking my point, I felt the warm, wet press of his tongue between my butt. With his hand on my bat and his mouth on my hole, the pressure in my balls started to erupt.

I was still coming when Daryl howled for me to grab hold of his cock. Two firm strokes later, a fountain of thick, musky ball juice sprayed up into my face.

I woke rubbing my tired eyes, feeling drained and disoriented in my own bed, but happy in ways I'd never dreamed possible. The clock on the bedside table burned the hour into my pounding temples.

"Holy fuck," I groaned, more because I saw the stack of used, full condoms lying discarded beside the alarm. It hadn't been one big jack-off fantasy!

Stretched out on the bed, one hairy leg spread against mine, was Daryl. His face looked a little hairier, but handsomer than any I'd ever seen in my nearly 30 years. My shifting on the bed must have startled him awake. His eyes slowly opened. He grinned and yawned, smelling of sex and morning breath as he put a hand on my chest to toy with my pecs.

"Mornin'," he growled.

"Morning yourself," I smiled. The words tasted of Daryl and the previous night, hot and thick on my tongue.

"What time is it?" he asked.

"Noon," I yawned.

"Noon!" he said disbelievingly, working his hand down to my cock. "The game's on in an hour."

"I know," I said, reaching over to give him a kiss. "We got time."

"Time for another game," Daryl groaned, moving into position. Time for another chance at happiness.

Sharing Jeff
Barry Alexander

By the time we finished planting Karen's new flower bed, Scott and I were drenched in sweat. Every muscle in my body ached. But I had to admit, it was worth it. Thanks to my wife's eye for color and Scott's green thumb, the yard was becoming a real showplace.

Karen came over and gave me a kiss, then pushed me away in mock disgust. "Someone needs a shower," she said with a smile. She jerked her thumb at Scott. "And you better take him with you. I'm not serving any sweaty men in my dining room."

He grinned wickedly and clutched his chest. "Alas, yon fair lady has wounded me to the heart." He staggered across the lawn, then fell, doing a cartoon imitation of a death scene. Acting is not one of Scott's talents.

I walked over and looked down at him sprawled in the grass. Scott's dark hair was windblown. Sweat gleamed on his tanned shoulders and the V of skin exposed by the cut-out wedge in the front of his old sleeveless T-shirt. A drop of sweat trickled through the stubble on his chin and into the soft hollow at the base of his throat. I swallowed hard, forcing back a surge of desire, and held out my hand. "Come on, you idiot. Corpses don't giggle."

Scott caught my hand in his and before I could brace myself yanked me down on top of him. We rolled around in the grass for a minute, then he pinned me. He looked down at me, and the laughter went out of his eyes. I could feel the heat of his groin on my stomach. I was grateful for the bagginess of the sweats I usually wore when Scott was around. I shook my head slightly, and Scott let me up. "Sorry," he said softly.

"You two are worse than the boys," Karen scolded. "Dad will be dropping them off soon. Good thing he kept them entertained today. The four of you would have goofed off all day, and I wouldn't have my new flower bed."

Karen walked over and stood on her toes and kissed Scott's cheek. "Thanks, Scott. Stay for supper?"

"Thanks, but I do have to live up to my wild bachelor reputation some nights."

Karen sniffed. "Then you better hit those showers too if you expect to get anywhere with the ladies."

We went into the house to shower. Karen stayed outside to admire her flowers and wait for the boys. As I stood under the warm spray and lathered myself, I tried to force my thoughts away from the fact that Scott was doing the same thing in the basement shower. He was so damn close, but I didn't dare start anything, not with Karen just outside and likely to come in at any minute.

It didn't work. I couldn't help picturing Scott's naked body under the shower, water sluicing over his broad shoulders, cascading over his chest and the rippled planes of his stomach. Water beading in the dark pubic hair flattened against his dripping skin. Water running like rain along his erect cock and dripping off his balls. I thought of how that water would taste as I licked it off.

I turned my back to the spray and covered my hard cock with a handful of foaming body wash. It was Scott's hands stroking my cock, teasing my balls. It was my fist wrapped around his cock, pumping up and down as we brought each other off. It didn't take long. Come bubbled over my hand and shot over my stomach, mingling with the foam that covered my skin. I turned into the spray and let the water wash me clean. The release had felt wonderful, but it wasn't enough. I still ached for Scott.

I was a bit relieved that Scott wasn't staying tonight. I couldn't get the imagine of that single drop of sweat out of my mind. I loved spending time with Scott no matter what we were doing, but sometimes it was really hard. He was so close, and I didn't dare touch him. That had to wait until my weekly "night out with the boys" or an occasional quickie in the garage. I loved Karen and my sons; I did not want them hurt.

Family night. Touch football with the boys, then pizza in the living room as we watched videos. Just me and Karen and the boys—and Scott. The boys sprawled on the floor to watch *Terminator* and *Homeward Bound.* Scott claimed the recliner.

Karen sat in the wing chair with her feet tucked under her, sketching. I wondered what she was drawing this time, but I knew better than to try to look. She never wanted anyone to see her drawings until they were done.

I couldn't resist looking over at Scott. Long legs stretched out in front of him, he appeared engrossed in the story of the lost pets, but I knew he had to be as eager as I was for the movie to be over. He caught my look and shifted restlessly in his chair.

Karen saw the look too. "Oh, go on. I know you're dying to show him your new circular saw. You and your tools," she said with mock despair. Karen pretended to complain about all the gadgets I bought for my wood shop, but she was really proud of the things I made and always pointed them out to guests.

"Are you sure you don't mind?" Scott asked, always the gentleman. "I don't want to drag Jeff away from family night."

"Go ahead. The boys are half asleep anyway."

The smell of fresh-cut wood greeted me as I opened the side garage door. Scott followed me inside. In seconds I had him pressed against the door, devouring his mouth.

"God, it's been a long week," he said when I let him come up for air. I didn't give him long. Before locking my mouth back to his, I pulled his T-shirt over his head and ran my hands over the dark hair that stippled his chest. His breath caught as my fingers brushed over his nipples. I bent down and sucked one in, pressing my tongue against the pebbly ring and feeling it stiffen into a hard nubbin. One of his hands cupped the back of my head and held me in place while the other kneaded my cock though my trousers. I licked along the line of his ribs and up his side. Scott raised one arm over his head, giving me the access I wanted. The musky smell of his fresh sweat made me even harder. I pushed my groin into his hand and buried my face in the hollow of his pit, licking the dark hairs and sucking the sensitive skin.

Not content with groping me through two layers of fabric, Scott hurried to unbuckle my belt. In seconds, my slacks were open and down around my ankles, along with my underwear, hobbling me in place. Scott dropped to his knees in an instant. He licked up the inside of my thigh, along the crease, and over to my scrotum. His wet tongue tasted my ball sweat, and he began to lap. I spread my legs as wide as I could as I leaned against the door.

"Oh, God, that feels so good!"

I slowly fisted my cock as he continued to lick and suck my balls. Only when they were soaked with spit and riding my shaft did he turn his attention to my aching dick. He took the head into his mouth and swirled his tongue over the dark red crown. My legs trembled as his tongue found my slit and tried to wedge its way inside. His hands roamed over my buttocks, pulling me closer.

He looked up at me, holding the head of my cock in the wet cavern of his mouth, but not licking. His eyes were wicked and innocent at the same time. I didn't think I'd ever seen anyone more beautiful. He waited, his lips encircling the tip of my cock.

"Please," I said. "Suck me. I need it so bad."

He opened his mouth and inhaled my cock. His lips pressed against my pubes for a second, then he began to suck. I sighed and buried my fingers in his hair as his mouth moved up and down. Scott had such a talented mouth.

It was two weeks before I could arrange an evening alone with Scott. We tried to have at least one night a week just for us. Karen said a night out with the guys was good for me; I was always less tense the next day. But things kept coming up. I had to cancel the previous week at the last minute. Mark hadn't told me until the last minute about the extra soccer practice the coach had arranged. Scott pretended it didn't matter, but I knew he was hurt. He understood that I couldn't let my sons down, but I hated to let him down too. It seemed like lately things just kept keeping us apart. This week it was overtime. But I was determined not to let it stop me. Scott couldn't always be last.

I rushed through all the things I needed to get done—I was not going to be late this time. I was exhausted by the time I got to Scott's place.

"Long day, love?"

I didn't answer, just pulled him into my arms and kissed him hungrily. He was hard for me. There was something so right about feeling a hard male body pressed against mine, to feel the easy strength in his arms as he held me. I ground against him, trying to melt into his body. I'd have fucked him right there, but Scott pulled back to catch his breath.

"We don't need to rush; we have all night. And I made dinner."

I stretched out on the couch in front of the fireplace, my head in Scott's lap. We didn't say anything, just watched the flames, our fingers locked together as he idly stroked his fingers through my hair. God, it felt so wonderful to be close to him again. The scent of him, warm and male, the hardness of his muscled thighs under my head, the gentleness of his fingers. My cock was half hard with desire. And in a minute I was going to get up and show him just how much I'd missed him. My fingers brushed against the hard mound inside his slacks. I smiled. *Going to have to do something about that in a minute,* I thought with a contented sigh.

"Time to go, Jeff."

Warm lips brushed against mine. I woke up slowly and opened my eyes. I'd fallen asleep on the couch, my head in Scott's lap. He was smiling down at me.

"Oh, my God, I fell asleep on you. I'm so sorry. Why didn't you wake me?"

I snuggled against the lean strength of his body, reluctant to move. Scott's arms tightened around me for a moment. I pulled him down into another kiss. Our tongues tangled for a moment, then he pushed me away.

"Don't. There isn't time, and Karen will be waiting."

I groaned. "I don't want to leave, but you're right, damn it. I'm really sorry, Scott."

He forced a smile. "It's OK. I know you've been working too hard. It's just sometimes I wish I could have you for the whole night, you know?"

"Karen and I don't have sex every night."

"No, but she gets to curl up next to you and wake up beside you in the morning. I really envy that sometimes. Hey, don't worry about it," he said when he saw the look on my face. "You're married. You have obligations. I'll take what you can give me."

"I love you. Don't you know how important you are to me?"

"I know. I just wish sometimes there was a place for me in your life—a *real* place."

I slipped under the covers. Karen swung around and snuggled close, soft breasts pressed against my chest and her legs tangling with mine. I put my arms around her and held her. She curled against me, her slow breathing ruffling the hairs on my chest.

I thought about Scott. I'd known things were hard for him, but I'd never really thought about it from his point of view. Seeing me with Karen, knowing that he had to share me, having to pretend we were only friends, had to be awful. Maybe he saw himself as just the guy who sucked my cock—someone I turned to for a little sexual variety. God, I hoped not.

I loved my wife. Karen is a warm, beautiful woman. She is fantastic in bed and a good friend. But there were times I just needed to be held by a man. To feel a rough cheek against mine, to feel a hard cock pressed against my own. To feel the strength in male arms, to smell male scents. And the only one I wanted was Scott. I couldn't imagine my life without him. I had to make that clear to him. Scott was such a sweet guy. He didn't deserve to always be consigned to the backseat.

Friday, Karen decided to drive up to her sister's for the weekend so they could have a shopping orgy sans husbands in the Mall of America. She had her parents pick up the boys after school for their monthly weekend. She said that would give me a chance to take care of some of the things I'd had to neglect lately with all the overtime.

Family night. I had the house to myself for the first time I could remember. I didn't intend to waste a moment of it. A whole weekend of Scott. I could have him anywhere and anytime I wanted him. No frenzied groping, no frantic kisses, just long, sensuous lovemaking. I could sleep with him in my arms and wake up with him in my arms.

I was checking the dining room one last time when I heard the door open. I wanted this evening to be perfect.

"Hey, where is everyone?" Scott called.

"In here." I stood facing the door so I could see his face when he came in.

Scott came through the doorway and stopped when he saw the table: Karen's best china, her grandmother's silver, the pair of champagne flutes he'd given us for our anniversary. I thought I saw something flicker in his eyes, but he broke into a big smile.

"Hey, you should have told me you two had a romantic dinner planned. Give Karen my best. Enjoy."

He turned to walk away but not before I saw the trace of hurt in his eyes. God, I'd done it all wrong. I'd wanted to surprise him. I came around the table and swung him around to face me. I could see the glint of unshed tears in his eyes.

"Scott! Wait. Karen's not here. It's just us."

"Us?"

"Just us. The whole weekend. You're as much a part of my life as Karen and the boys. I couldn't do without you."

We stared into each other's eyes as we sat down to dinner. The candles brought out the green flecks in Scott's eyes. I watched the corners of his eyes crinkle when he smiled at me. I wanted to kiss the tiny lines, but I knew I wouldn't be able to stop with one kiss. My dick was already half hard. As Scott took a bite of linguini, a splash of marinara sauce painted his lower lip. His tongue swept over the spill.

"I wanted to do that!" I protested.

"You'll get your chance later. We don't want to let all this go to waste."

I tried to keep part of my mind on the meal, but it wasn't easy. Scott was no help. Something rubbed against my calf, and I was about to push the cat away when I saw the wicked gleam in Scott's eyes. He leaned back in his chair, and his foot slowly moved upward. By the time his toes reached their goal, my cock was hard and straining against my slacks. He traced the contours of my genitals, then kneaded the shaft with his toes. I gasped and almost dropped my glass of wine, but I managed to set it down carefully.

"Dinner is over." I stood up and moved around the table.

"But I haven't finished yet. I'm really, really hungry."

"Too late. You should have thought of that before you stirred certain things up."

"What things?" he asked in his low register, trying to sound innocent.

"Why don't you come over here and I'll show you." I undid my pants and revealed my hard cock.

Scott stood up. To my slight surprise, something very hard tented the front of his slacks. He'd either not worn his usual briefs or some time during the meal he'd reached down and freed himself. I wasn't sure which idea I found more exciting. There was already a dark stain on the front of the light gray fabric, and I didn't think it was marinara sauce.

I reached for him, and he sprang back. "Uh-uh," he said in a deep, sexy growl. "You want it, come and get it." His eyes gleamed with mischief.

Scott ripped off most of his clothes as I stalked him around the dining-room table. His shirt buttons pinged as a couple of them ricocheted off the china. He pulled the shirt off his broad shoulders, baring his chest. His nipples popped up like those little timers that tell you when the turkey is done. He unbuckled his belt and unsnapped his slacks. The mass of flesh straining for release forced the zipper partially down. Crisp curls of dark hair coiled around the thick base of his cock. I was so intent on the view, I tripped over his discarded shirt. Scott took the opportunity to shuck the rest of his clothes. He wasn't wearing briefs. The empty pouch of a white jock dangled beside his furry balls. His hard cock pointed straight at me. The head of his beautifully cut dick glistened with the profuse amount of fluid he was leaking.

When I finally caught him, he kissed me so hard I thought he was going to suck the tongue out of my mouth. I could have flung him across the table and taken him right there, and maybe I would tomorrow, but tonight I wanted him in my bed. As if reading my mind, he tugged on my cock and turned to race up the stairs. The golden moons of his ass beckoned, framed by the white straps of his jock. I took off in pursuit.

Scott stopped just outside the door and stood looking at the bed. "Maybe we should do this somewhere else?" he asked, suddenly serious.

I took his hand and led him over to the bed. I sat him down and waggled my cock at him. "Oh, no you don't. I'm not going to keep this guy waiting while you play Goldilocks and test all the beds."

"But—"

"Shhh," I said as I pushed him back against the pillows. I was not going to let this get awkward. "There's only the two of us here. This is my bed, and this is where I want you."

His golden skin looked wonderful spread across the sky-blue comforter. I wanted him so much I had trouble with the buttons on my shirt. Scott scooted over to the edge of the bed to help. He ended up doing it all. I was too involved with the sensations he was creating in my body.

After the first couple of buttons were undone, he slid his hands inside my shirt, tracing the line of my chest. He dipped his head inside the opening. His warm lips nuzzled against my pec. I gasped at the first flick of his hot tongue. His mouth closed over my nipple, sucking it to hardness and rubbing his tongue over the sensitive peak. He slid my shirt off, then went to work on my slacks. He gave a lingering kiss to my nipple before moving lower. I shuddered and pulled his head to me as he rimmed my navel.

He tugged my slacks down to my ankles. I kicked off my shoes and stepped out of my slacks. He combed his fingers through my bush and looked up at me. My cock quivered, dripping another filament of pre-come. He caught it on his fingertip and drizzled it like icing around my cock head. I could barely hold still while he smoothed it in, making the deep-red helmet glisten.

"Under the pillow," I said.

"I thought the maid was supposed to leave the mints on the pillow," he said as he found the green foil packet.

As soon as he had the condom in place, he took me into his mouth. I knew I wouldn't be able to take much; I was too eager for him, and Scott was just too damn good with his mouth. He knew exactly the right pressure, the right pace, the right places. He must have sensed my urgency. After a couple of minutes, when my shaft was slick with his saliva, he pulled away and scooted to the center of the bed.

Scott rolled back, knees locked in the crook of his arm, exposing the most intimate part of himself for me. I looked at the brown bud nestled between the smooth curves of his cheeks. I leaned down and kissed him there and felt him tremble. He dilated, exposing a hint of the deep pink interior for a second. I knew he wanted me inside him as badly as I wanted to be there. But I forced myself to slow down. I didn't want to rush this.

I loved that first moment of sliding inside him. The way his sphincter resisted for a minute, then suddenly seemed to recognize me and welcome me into the warm, dark secret place of him. I slathered some lube over my cock and worked some of it inside him with my fingers. He was so hot and silky. His cock jumped every time my fingers bumped his prostate. I leaned down and took his balls into my mouth for a moment, rolling them around on my tongue, tasting him.

I knelt up, moving closer until my cock brushed the bottom of his ball sac. I tilted it down until I felt the heat of his pucker. I leaned into him, sighing with pleasure as he opened for me. I felt like I was sliding into liquid fire; he was so hot and silky around me. My hands slid up his thighs as I pressed deeper. Scott wiggled his butt to take more of me. I gave a last push, and my balls smacked against his buttocks. I held still for a moment, looking into his eyes as he smiled up at me.

I began a slow rhythm—slow deep thrusts that made me aware of every inch of my dick. I loved the look on his face every time I bumped his prostate. I changed the angle and the tempo, massaging it with the rapid thrusts of my cock. God, he felt so good, so hot and tight around me. I wanted to get deeper and deeper inside of him. To get so close, nothing could separate us. I took his legs on my shoulders, leaning over him so I could kiss him. His hard dick was trapped between us. My abs were soon sticky from all the precome his cock was leaking. Our mouths locked together, forming one more connection as we rode toward the peak. I slipped a hand between us and found his cock. His balls hugged the rigid shaft. I wrapped my hand around it, and Scott started fucking my fist.

My hips drummed against him. Scott thrust upward, locking his heels against my buttocks. His body arched, and his head lolled back, his face in a grimace of tortured ecstasy. Hot semen gushed against my chest and stomach. His guts spasmed around my cock. Powerful ripples surged up and down my shaft. The rich male scent of him was a potent aphrodisiac.

I couldn't hold back. I slammed against him, trying to drive every inch of my body into his. I gasped against his neck, and my hips locked against him as my orgasm tore through me. Crescendos of pleasure rose and broke over me, shattering me with their force. I sprawled across Scott, my heart hammering against this chest. "I love you," I said as soon as I got some breath back.

Scott wasn't in much better shape. "Love you," he gasped and pulled me down into a kiss neither of us had the breath for.

I woke early. Scott and I were twined together so closely, I wasn't sure where he began and I ended. His head lay on my chest. I could feel the slow, steady beat of his heart against me. It felt so right to have him finally in my bed. I stretched and took a deep breath. Mmm. Fresh coffee. Bacon. Mmm.

Suddenly, I sat straight up. Who in the hell was cooking bacon? Scott stirred sleepily. "What's the matter?"

"You didn't get up and fix breakfast, did you?"

"This early? Don't be silly. Come on, let's go back to sleep, unless you..." His hand wandered down to my cock. I pushed it back.

"You'd better get dressed," I said quietly. "Someone's down in the kitchen fixing breakfast. And I have a good idea who. Stay here."

I tried to run through all the other possible scenarios in my head as I headed downstairs. Mom and Dad had brought the boys home early. We hadn't locked the door, and the neighbors had walked in. A burglar was making himself at home. None of them were convincing.

For some reason Karen had come back early. She'd started breakfast. Had she come upstairs and seen us? Would I find a short, bitter note on the table? "I'm taking the boys; go to hell, pervert." No, that wouldn't be like Karen. She'd tell me to my face. So that meant she hadn't been upstairs yet. That was good. Maybe there was a way out of this. Then with a sick feeling I remembered Scott's clothes all over the dining room. How in the hell was I going to explain that?

I had visions of my life without the boys and Karen. I couldn't lose them. They were my family. And then I thought of my life without Scott. Without the man who had held me so tenderly last night, who had met the intensity of my passion with equal desire. I couldn't stand the thought of life without Scott. He was family too.

My brain was still running down blind passages looking for a way out when I pushed open the kitchen door. Karen turned from the pan of eggs she was scrambling and smiled at me. "You'd better call Scott down for breakfast. It's almost ready." I looked with astonishment at the table. It was set for three. "We've got some things to talk over."

Scott and I lay in bed exchanging kisses and slow caresses. We were still in a bit of shock. Karen had gone back to her sister's for the rest of the weekend. There never had been a shopping spree. Apparently she'd suspected for some time. It didn't bother her.

"I'm not blind, darling," she'd said. "You're a wonderful husband and father. Scott is a good friend. If I have to share you, I'm glad it's with him. We just need to lay down some ground rules and make sure the boys don't find out."

Then she'd taken out the drawing she'd done a couple weeks before of the two of us. I guess that's when she knew. Karen had drawn the two of us looking at each other. The drawing captured all the passion and longing I felt for Scott. No one looking at the drawing could doubt that the two men were in love with each other.

Scott smiled and snuggled closer. After our little talk, he no longer doubted that there was a place for him in my life—in all of our lives. He was family. And I definitely had more than enough love to share.

Unraveling Hayden
Lance Rush

A 3 A.M. stream of traffic cruises the Metro. I should be asleep, but I'm alone and frustrated on my fire escape, smoking a Newport. Fucking neighbors are fighting—again! Their voices come booming through the walls, and this one sounds serious. I turn and see Hayden, stark naked by his door, watching me, watching him. A shaft of moonglow settles on his dick beneath his dusky crown, lighting that smooth area just above his circumcision scar. For six sexless months we've shared this apartment, and I'm hooked. I've fallen in lust with the sight of Hayden's big limp dick.

"Somebody oughta call the cops! This shit is ridiculous!" Hayden's roused cock seems to say. He folds big looping biceps across his chest. He's restless. He and his dick are pissed off. All thoughts lead to Hayden's dick. I've even written poems to it. Poems he will never read.

"Maybe I should go over there and knock that motherfucker around some. See how he likes the abuse! Listen to that!" he yells, midnight eyes flashing as he starts banging on the wall.

"This is New York, man! Mind your business! Fuckin' lunatic could be packin'!" I say.

Hayden's dick swings as he grabs the phone to dial 911. Watching him, I realize how unfair I've been to objectify the Brother. I mean, there's so much more to Hayden than that long cocoa organ swaying between his well-carved legs. Sure, he's got a Big One, but he's got an even Bigger Heart. This city hasn't left him jaded, yet. He really cares about people. Even strangers. "Hello. Could you send a patrol car to 810 West 101st Street? Apt 5G. Got a real violent cat over here trying to kill someone! My name? Doesn't matter. Just please hurry up, man!"

The look on his face is merciful. But his looks are deceiving. You'd never know it from gazing his smooth tan face, but he's a former Golden Gloves

Boxer. At 29, he remains one fine and sexy looking individual. All his fineness tops a big, muscular, don't-fuck-with-me frame endowed with an almost dangerous athleticism. Plus, my man's got a sharp mind. Reads Russian literature. Teaches sign language. Yes. Brother's got mad education, and fisticuffs skills to boot. But I look at his dick, and all my horny mind wonders is, When the fuck is he gonna let me suck that thing?!

"Even in New York, your mind is your act!" he says cryptically, slamming his bedroom door. He's always saying weird metaphysical shit like that. Zen stuff that I'm supposed to ponder. Your mind is your act?! What you talkin' bout, Hayden? Hell! If my mind was my act, I would've been sucking Hayden's big, beefy, benevolent bozack all night long!

But Hayden's troubled mind has indeed become his act. Cops come. Cops go. It's quiet at last. We can sleep. Well, at least Hayden can. Standing on my fire escape above this city's streets, I stare out at the tolerable freak show. Restless, I haul out my raging dick and masturbate. I stroke and I smoke until my come falls in a shower of nasty thoughts inside the night's debris. Sleep still eludes me. I lie in bed and compose another poem. A poem to Hayden's dick:

"In my blue banana solitude, it haunts me, and every cinnamon nippled sin of my mind.

I dream some indigo evening, I'll be a Nubian Tarzan who swings from your jungle vine!"

"My mind is my act. My mind is my act." It becomes a mantra as I drift off to sleep. I'm having another Hayden dream: We meet in the backroom of a leather bar. A bunch of surlies are gathered around a sling where a young, Leonardo-blond lays ass-up. Hayden's clad in latex shorts. He's slowly, skillfully fisting his squirming prey! My dick and I stand amazed, as his slave cries, "More! Please, Sir. More!" Maybe it's the sheer power of those jutting muscles swelling his 5' 11" frame into a danger to be reckoned with. He's all sneering copper and midnight eyes blazing. One glimpse at his mysteriously thick chunk shooting through black latex and it's cock-lust at first sight. Blond boy vanishes as a bold Hayden latches onto my leather-bound cock.

In this dream, I'm in my hard-to-get mode, so I push him away. But he lunches forth, unfazed. Smoke emanates from his body. The others disappear. The Lance in my dreams wants no part of him. But he is adamantly

slamming a big restless bozack into me. His dick's a 10-inch slab of kryp-
tonite, weakening my puny Superman act. Uh-oh! What's he doing now?
That wicked tongue is coursing in a slow, slow trail down my pounding
neck. Oh shit! He's lifting my T-shirt, and heading for my spot! No! Not
the nipples! Ah! Daaaamn!

Hot tongue spinning around, white teeth seizing the tip of each slow-
sizzling orb. My iron resistance is melting, melting against his shank of
tempered steel. He's throbbing, pushing, mounting into a fucking 10-inch
rod against my weakening thigh! This hot motherfucker's tripping all my
tripwires. The man's some kind of sexual terrorist, pushing my libido's red
button. I'm about to go down in flames! His sultry-dark eyes pierce black
laser beams through mine. I'd swear those eyes are fucking me.

"Are you in love with me?" he asks in a knowing whisper, tongue fluttering below my waist. "Hell, no! You're a pain in my ass. So fuckin' righteous! No one's good enough for you!"

"But, you love my big dick, don't you?" he insists, his teeth grazing my
clothed cock.

He rises, pushes all that hard, unruly prickage into mine and jams his
tongue down my throat. I catch a firm grip to his nipple ring and yank the
fucker—hard! Our kiss turns violent. He smacks my ass! I punch his chest.
He thrusts. I lunge. Two long, wet, deep kissing minutes later, we break for
air. Fixing me in those coal-black eyes, he says, in a demanding growl,
"Unzip me and take out my dick!"

Just as I'm about to go for the ultimate gusto, the ALARM RINGS! It's
7:30. My sheets are soaked. 31-fuckin'-years old and still plagued by wet
dreams! I need help. Maybe Hayden's dick would cure me. All thoughts
lead to Hayden's dick. Over the breakfast table he buries his face in a cere-
al bowl. All I see is short wavy curls and an intense scowl. Mmm. Never
noticed how bushy Hayden's brow was. Hmmm. I wonder. Sometimes a
man's eyebrows can directly correspond to a dense lurking jungle below.
Man! I do like a nice hairy thatch. A nice bushy mat framing a big black
cock. You see? It's like a disease. All thoughts lead back to Hayden's dick!

I go to work. I'm a robot, doing a competent job. Still, visions of big
dick stab randomly through my brain. I come home. Ah! Hayden's there.
But, damn it! He's not alone. These hot sounds are emanating from his
bedroom. Every anguished grunt hurts me, slowly.

"Oh! Yes! Yes! Hayden! Baby! Fuck me! FUCK ME! Don't stop! Aw! Yes!
Fuck!"

I bang my head against the wall, but all I see are stars and lights, and lime-green chromatic streaks play in my eyelashes. They all morph into, guess what? Hayden's cock. The fuck noises continue. What is Hayden's dick doing to that crying boy? It should be in ME, not that punk! And who is it tonight? The Spanish Cop or the Irish Fireman? That burly Italian brute of a power lifter? Or maybe it's that bodaciously butch Physical Therapist with Arnold's build. Goddamn serial fucker! He's always sticking it into macho trade. It's what he attracts. I hate them all. Every moaning, groaning hunk that passes through our door—I resent them, whoever they are. Hell! If he's going to be a whore, maybe I should just ask him to leave. But where would that leave me? Beating my dick to a memory?

His door opens. He's nude. He wants me. I want him. Finally, it's going to happen. He hauls it to my lips, and I'm sucking it. We're outside on the fire escape, and I'm slurping it like a piece of raw fruit. Oh! It's pounding, pounding between my eager lips. Feels too good, too hard to be true. "Ah! Yes! You suck it so well. You blow cock like you can't get enough! You're my fucking dick junkie! Oh yes! Easy, now! Don't want you to O.D.," he croons. "OK. That's it. You're done. Good night, Lance," he says. Good night? I don't understand. I'm ass-out and shivering over Manhattan wondering, "What?"

I awaken to drenched sheets—again! There are over eight million freaky stories in this Naked city. But I wonder, has a Black man ever drowned in his own come?

Tonight, I find myself alone again on the fire escape, smoking my last cigarette. Maybe I'll quit smoking. Just give up all my vices. Hell! It seems I've already given up sex with anyone but myself. But Hayden's hunky company has left, and he quietly joins me outside. "When are you gonna quit those things" his voice asks.

"What's the profit in it? Getting fat? Don't think so." I exhale.

"The profit? Well, clean lungs. A healthier life. Fresher breath. Better smelling clothes. And a man could kiss you without the stink of ghetto mouth! Straight up, Lance. We both know you're fine. You've got lots of potential. But, personally, well, smokers never did turn me on."

What? Just hearing this, I flick my butt with a quickness to the street below, and as I turn…Hello! Hayden's sitting on the ladder, naked legs spread, red boxer shorts housing a monument. "See that! You look better already without that fucking cancer stick between those hot lips. Yep. You're looking pretty tasty right now," he grins, taking flirting to a whole new level. He's squinting inquisitively, as if to see how far I'd go, or maybe he's trying to measure my kink factor. But if this is another dream, I don't want to wake up, ever! Wanna pinch myself 'cause, he's stroking that big red silk-clad cock and staring at me with a look he reserves for a lover.

"Where's your friend? Gone back to the home gym early?" I ask.

"Gone home hurt is more like it!" he says with a smirk.

"So, you really threw it on him, huh?"

"More like threw him out! That's over. Not the right type."

"So what exactly *is* your type, Hayden?"

As I stand before him, he wraps his legs around me, pulling me closer into him. But this is no embrace. Hayden's thick, strong legs are endowed with the vicious strength of a Pro Wrestler. And then, it happens. He flips the waist of those boxers and Mt. Olympus rises over the Harlem skyline! His King Cobra stands, hard and naked as new birth. As far as dicks go, this is truly one of The Choice Ones. A long, ripe, viciously big mahogany prick, more fantastic than any dream! A vein, a smooth J-shaped vein courses along its shaft. It stops just an inch from his great puckered glans. The nuts. Ah! The nuts are two potent eggs in a large brown bag. This dick of my fantasy is surrounded by enough pubic hair to make a decent Hi-top Fade! A virtual bird's nest of coarse black fur frames a cinnamon shrouded rod! Oh yes! Sheeeit! Hello, Beautiful! Man! I would've have quit that nasty nicotine habit long ago if I'd known Hayden would be mine for the asking!

He slides on a condom with a nasty grin, stands up and nestles against me, his body full of heat. Yes! Don't let me be dreaming! I'm feeling Hayden's dick! Gigantic and thick, long and hard and Black as Harlem streets! Yes. Finally I'm alone with Hayden's dick! He gazes at me with shaded eyes, a look I've never seen before. His lips are so moist, those hot eyes shining, and so determined to fuck.

The torrid shaft spasms heavily as it pushes down my throat. Its broad roping veins pound hot rhythms on my tongue. The very feel of it, throbbing in my mouth, instantly hardens my dick.

I surge down, gulping, spitting saliva along the great rutting tube. I'm amazed at how quickly his inches unfurl from seven, to a hard eight, to nine, to a mighty, thick 10-inch rod. I slowly bob my head as he swerves his taut brown hips, coasting, lunging that fucker deeper down my throat. He gropes my spinning skull, leading me up and down the wide, slick shaft. "Ah! Yes! Sssssuck it! God! I love those lips, man! Suck my fuckin' dick!"

I nibble and tease his head as every muscle of his body pitches. "Oh! Shit!" he sighs. He's losing balance. Leaning against a fifth floor ladder, he must hold onto something as he's weakening to my suction. My savage throat encloses him. Ah! Yes! Hayden! But his endowment scrapes my tonsils. I pull away, gasping for air, and head back for more. Mmm! The fuck club wavers as my tongue flutters his swollen knobby crown. Outside, in the dark of night, it looks even bigger, thicker, harder! Streetlights blink and flicker shadows across the long, wet shaft. I aim the meaty slab back to my lips and commence to lapping it strongly, loudly, wildly! Deep brown nuts clap and slap my slurping chin, and he's thrusting as I suck him.

"Easy! Slow it down, baby. Here, let me do you," he insists.

I grudgingly leave his well-polished dick and switch places against the fire escape's ladder. Hayden clutches his donkey's dong and slowly goes down on me. His teeth rake my angling shaft as his hot tongue sails down, down to my prick's root! Ah! A cool wind stirs up my asshole. I pull my cock from the depths of his gobbling throat, and plunge deeper! But he takes it all down in one long, greedy swerve. Oh! Every fucking corpuscle of my pleasured cock is percolating!

He's beating that fierce prick between the rungs of the ladder with hard, frantic strokes. I'm so erect, so fucking excited, I wanna scream over Harlemworld. But Hayden swirls down and laps my hanging nuts. That nasty tongue's rattling at my sac as a gusty wind hums along the skin of my balls. This duel intensity is putting a heat and a chill in me! I shudder, wanting more, more!

Squeezing biceps tighten around my ass, and Hayden jabs two wet fingers up my fuckhole! Aw! It startles me! Shit! He's circling, pushing, twisting those thick boxer's digits deeper, harder, knuckle-deep! Oh! Yes! My hot writhing ass is a pitching furnace about to explode! A wicked stream of come bursts out my fiery cock, anointing his surprised chest in gashes of white!

"I want to fuck you, right here! Right now! Damn it!. No one's watching, baby, " he assures me, kissing my neck. "We both know you've been wanting this!"

I turn and toss my leg up two rungs, so goddamn horny my hole's as open as a 24-hour porn shop! He leads the dickhead in, real slow. I emit a gruesome moan as his cock knob burrows through my wincing crack. Shit! Hayden's dick's so wide, so fucking engorged, my fucking rectum trembles.

I want to growl, howl deep from my balls. But it's mad-late. I'd only star-
tle our neighbors into calling the cops. He pulls back. My panting breaths
sustain me. But OH! He punches through my asshole with a boxer's force!
AW! He's trying to pound me soundly into unconsciousness! Shit! He
draws back, tears deeper. My body thrusts forward. Oh! That dick's stretching my fuckhole. My anal lips grip tight to it. With no lube, Hayden's
fierce fuck tube's slowly killing me! He goes in deeper, pumping, strong
legs smacking my boiling cheeks. He jams, shimmies, jams and shimmies,
bringing power, pressure, and pain with each stroke. God! My man can
fuck! His cockhead pounds, his shaft rams, jolting intensely at the pit of
my asshole!

He pulls me closer, taut bronzed hips whipping, rocking into mine. Oh!
He latches onto my swinging, windblown prick, working it hotter,
stronger in his fist. I thrust my wild hips into this sparkling city night,
fucking the driving air around me!

Discarding my smoker's breath, Hayden goes in for a kiss. Moist, full
lips bang at my lips until his tongue pries them open. With burning
tongues, surging, lunging, we battle for the depths of each other's throat.
Suddenly I know why I've been a fool for him. It's in the heat of his dick.
Somehow, I knew it would be like this. This rhythm, this sheer Black
manly rhythm of his fuck. I imagined his kisses would be like this, so hard,
wet, and desperate with passion.

Oh! He's rolling his ass, jamming that fat dick up my wiggling asshole.
I'm pulsing, flaring in his hot hand. He's tugging my seething meat with a
swift and volatile speed. His hand pistons my drooling cock, pummeling
my load out of me! Oh! I'm pitching, lunging, crying into the night.

We're both about to spray the mean streets of Manhattan! But before we
do, I want him. "Let me fuck you, now! Come on, Hayden! Let me get a
piece of that ass," I pant.

His plowing ceases. His thinking cock pulses within me. Is he man
enough to take me up his ass? A silent argument wages between his cock
and his asshole. When he pulls out of me, I know his ass has won. I miss
the heated pressure of his dick already. But another pleasure awaits me.

I turn and I see Nirvana is a warm, buttery vision of muscle spreading.
He parts his globes, and shows me the world! Pinched brown spiral winces
for my dick. I jab two fingers in it. His whole body jumps. He lays his head
against the ladder, spreads his hefty legs wider. He's ready. My fingers leave
the warm tension of his chute as he demands, "If you're gonna fuck it, bet-

ter fuck it good!"

I aim my stiff eight-inch, condom-bound cock up his beckoning fuck-hole. Shit! The rubbery knot breaks. His bushy guts clamp hold of me, pulling me further, deeper through a moist, flexing tunnel. Yes! It swallows up my plunging cock in one primal suck. Shit! It's a fucking vortex! "Fuck it! Fuck that ass! Give it to me, Lance! Yes! That's it! More! More! Plow me, damn it!"

I pull back and ram him! His body arcs, donkey dick slams the railing. "Fuck me!" Inner man-muscles grip tight to every fucking inch of my burning prick!

"Oh! Damn! Hayden! You've got such a sweet ass, baby!" I manage to sigh. I pump him hard, steady, increasing speed with each thrust. My nuts tap, then slap his cheeks.

"Fuck me!" We set a hot boning rhythm. In deep, out far. In deeper, out farther. With each stroke I feel myself building, building to a monumental come! "Fuck me!" He pushes back, bucking that anxious truck of an ass into me. I grip his waist with one hand, his monstrously hard cock in the other, jacking it swiftly, roughly, bullying it to come! "Fuck me!" he cries as his pipe surges like something wild in my fist. I bear down harder, faster, hips banging his pumping hips.

Suddenly, he clutches my fucking rod intensely against those anal walls, and spasms. "Oh! Shit! Damn you, Hayden! I'm gonna shoot!" I warn. My body heaves forth, and I must pull out. Soon as the rubber's off, a stream of jism hurls swiftly from my dick, followed by strings of frenetic blasts, vaulting like mad into night's wind! Hayden quickly spins around. Shit! I see his pisshole widen, and there he goes! Oh damn! Porno stars get paid extra to shoot the way Hayden sprays. He comes hard, thick, and so copious it resembles rice pudding. It shoots in long arcs of white-hot slush, like there's just no stopping it! Then, he leans back and falls to the ladder, a giant, sputtering a trail of come down his thigh. His fine brown body's coated in a sheen of sweat. He shudders silently against me. We haul our bodies along the rail of the fire escape, breathing ferociously.

On the street below, I see the spinning red moonbeams of a patrol car. A lone cop gets out and runs into our building. "You don't think he's heading up here, do you? " I ask. "Naw! No way! I mean, we didn't make that much noise. Did we?" From the jar of our buzzer sounding, I guess we had. But that's the Big Price a man has to pay once he unravels the long, dark mystery of my roomie's big, hard, make-ya-wanna-holler dick!

Line Cabin Fever
J.D. Ryan

The foreman fixes me with a steely glare. "Jesse, you and the Kid take the valley. See if you can bring in that brindle cow this year."

I stifle a groan. I'd hoped to pull duty with my old pal Earl. This early in the year, that hanging valley could well get snowed in. And the idea of spending a week or so trapped in a line cabin with the new hand just didn't get my juices flowing.

Jed's no kid, of course. He'd just let it slip once how he was the youngest on the spread, and Cookie had branded him then and there. He didn't seem to mind the joshing—didn't seem to mind much of anything. No, he was a right peaceable man, easy to get along with.

So why am I so all-fired disappointed? Well, me and Earl, we've been working together since I hired on nearly a year ago. We know how to keep busy on a long night. And when that cold wind starts whipping snow underneath the door there's only one way for this cowboy to keep his ass warm. That's with a steaming rod of manflesh pumping me full of hot cream, and Earl's balls slapping my asscheeks.

Of course, you don't just come right out and tell everyone you ride for that brand. And it ain't like me and Earl spend all our free time balling each other, either. I mean, personally, I'll hump anybody that'll let me. I ain't awful particular about what they've got between their legs. So long as somebody gets fucked, I'm happy.

But the Kid's a wild card. I'll have to tread easy, see which side of the fence he sits on. I glance his way, trying to read his sign. He's a big brute, that's for sure, way over six feet of muscle. Sandy hair over a baby face he's trying to age by growing a scraggly mustache. Blue eyes—a couple of times I've seen a wicked little twinkle in there that makes me wonder what's under that easy-going surface.

I reckon he's seen 20, but I'll bet my paycheck he's not over 25. And I'll walk naked through a patch of prickly pears before I let on I won't see 25 myself for another six months. Jesse ain't no Kid.

I catch Jed looking back, and head for the barn. I know what he's seeing: little, wiry fellow with dark hair and eyes. Lots of hombres make the mistake of thinking, because I have to stand on tip-toes to get to get the halter over my horse's ears, I'm a pushover. Lots of hombres wake up next morning nursing a black eye and minus a good chunk of pride, too. Mostly it works out, what I don't hump, I wallop.

I grab my gear and hightail it for the corral. The ponies have already got it into their heads that they'll be going to work this morning, and none of them likes it too much. I drop a loop over a frisky little chestnut I've rode before and liked. While we're arguing about who's the boss, the Kid comes alongside the gate toting his own gear. We nod to one another, and he singles out a broomtail for himself, a big gray that moves a touch too slow for me.

Once we've convinced our four-legged partners that they're going to cooperate, we stop by the cookhouse for supplies. All too soon for me, we're on our way to the valley.

"Hey, Kid," Cookie calls from the doorway. We rein up a bit. Jed glances back.

"You watch out for ol' Jesse, you hear," the cook yells. "Ain't none of us ever seed him without a hard-on, and them nights is gonna get mighty lonely up there."

I wheel the chestnut, raise up in the stirrups, and make a big show of grabbing my crotch.

"You're just wishing you had some of this, Cookie," I call back. "You get too horny, you hoof it up to the line cabin, you hear? You beg for it enough, I might just give in and let you have a little taste."

The boys all hoot, and Cookie retreats into his kitchen. Don't nobody out-smartass this cowpoke.

Jed looks at me as we ride off, like he's wondering what he's got himself into, but he keeps his mouth shut. In fact, he keeps it shut for the next few days while we ride the brush looking for strays. Not that this bothers me to any great extent—I generally talk enough for two or three men.

Things come to a head the third night. It's been particularly rough day, and I'm sweating like a pig. So, once we finish our victuals, I set a pot of water on the fire and start filling up the washtub.

"What in tarnation are you up to, there?" Jed asks from his side of the cabin.

I pour the first pot of scalding water into the tub, and set another on to boil. "What's it look like?"

He stands up to watch, I glance over and see his mouth is open in shock. "You're gonna take a bath? In the middle of the week?"

I put my hands on my hips and give him my best schoolmaster glare. "For your information, Kid, this is the 1890s. Civilized folks take baths when they're sweaty."

It ain't long before the fireplace and the boiling water have that tub steaming. I start unbuttoning my shirt.

"You can turn your back if you want," I tell the Kid, dropping my grubby shirt to the floor. I can wash the clothes once I'm clean.

He grunts, which I take to mean he don't mind if I strip buck naked, so I do. Earl once told me I have all the morals of an alley cat, and I guess he's right. I slosh a bucket of warm water over my head to rinse a little of the dust off, then sink into the tub.

I can hear Jed's feet shuffling, and glance up to see he's putting the coffee pot on the fire. He looks down at me, and colors up right fast. I chuckle and wriggle down into the water, running a hand between my legs to ease the ache in my lonely cock. My nine inches are standing straight up, like always, and Jed's eyes are about to pop out of his head looking at that hard rod sticking out of the bath.

"Damn, Jesse, what's a little fellow like you doing with all that meat?" he mutters. His ears are glowing so hot I'm afraid they'll catch his hair on fire.

I grin. "Partner, I'm doing anybody who'll stand still long enough to take it."

His eyes got real wide and he swallows. "But what if there ain't no girls around to take it?"

I put on my best innocent look. I know I look like about as innocent as a coyote in a sheep pen, but I just can't seem to help trying—I widen my eyes, paste a big smile onto my face, and look him straight on. "Then I guess I'll just have to see if there's an hombre in sight that might be feeling as lonely as I am," I say. "I ain't picky."

He shuts his month, turns back to his coffee. After a while he pours himself a cup and sits on the edge of his bunk. I'm about through washing myself now, so I stand up and let the water drip off. When I towel myself dry, I make sure to bend over so the Kid gets a good look at my throbbing asshole, too. Then I start to toss my clothes into the tub.

"Hold on there," Jed says, standing up again.

I glance up, my eyebrow cocked. He's blushing so hard it's lighting up his end of the room, but he keeps coming.

"If civilized folks are doing it," he mutters, "I reckon I can take a bath, too."

"The water's still warm," I say. "And we may as well wash all the clothes at once, anyway."

I pour myself a cup of joe and watch the show. Once he gets out of those sweaty clothes, I see Jed's got the kind of lanky body I like. Just right for wrapping around a little fellow and keeping him warm. He's hairy enough to be right comfortable, too. Looks almost like a ginger-colored grizzly standing there in the firelight, his face the color of a ripe chili pepper.

I expect he'll turn his back on me, but he hunches down in the water like I'm not there. I watch his hand lather that fur, and lick my lips. When he slips the bar of soap between his legs, I clear my throat. "I might could do your back for you, if you want," I say softly. He looks at me, then at the hard pole I've got in my left hand. I give it a couple of good pumps, and he swallows hard.

"I'll be honest with you, Jesse," he replies. I just ain't never thought of such a thing. I don't think I'm the kind of hombre that can spread my legs like a woman."

"Did I ask you to?" I snap back. I grin to show I'm not mad, then step up behind him. I grab the soap out of his hand, set down my coffee, and start lathering what feels like an acre of hard muscle. He quivers, but Jesse knows how to break a wild stallion. "You got nothing to worry about. Kid," I murmur, my hand easing the knots out of his back. I ain't the kind of man to take what ain't offered." I keep rubbing and he loosens up in spite of himself. I grin—he might not know it yet, but he's already hooked.

"How does…" Jed mutters, then stops to clear his throat. I wait. "How do two men do what a man and a woman are supposed to do, anyhow?"

Gotcha. I slide my hand around his waist. He tenses when my fingers close over his family jewels, then relaxes when he finds out how good it feels. I move my hand up to grasp his cock. "Getting any ideas yet?" I ask.

His reply is a gasp.

I chuckle.

"You…you want me to…?" he chokes out.

"I don't want you to do anything you don't want," I say, sliding my hand up and down his meat. He's not as long as I am, but way thicker. Feels like a fence post in my hand. I imagine how it's going to feel stretching my ass wide open, and my heart starts pounding against my chest. My mouth and my cock are already drooling.

"Then what...?" He's panting now, his hips starting to shove against my fist. Suddenly, he pushes me away and stands up.

I look up, trying to grin and hoping I'm not about to get my face pounded in.

"I got to get some things straight in my head before you do anything else," he announces. "What, exactly, is it you're proposing?"

I grab my coffee and sit down on my bunk. He watches me from the tub, his hands on his hips.

"All I'm proposing is that we take care of each other," I say. "You're as ready as I am. I could take care of it for you, is all."

He dries off, pours himself another cup, and goes to his bunk. We stare across the room at each other, naked as two jaybirds. A couple of times he opens his mouth to say something, but then he closes it again. I stretch out on the blanket, sipping my coffee.

"Alright, then," he finally says. I lean forward to listen. "Alright, I admit the idea has got my attention. And I admit it's been a while since I had anything but my own hand for company." He fixes me with a steely glare. "But this don't mean I'm about to start licking my lips every time you walk by!"

I paste on the innocent expression again, and shake my head. "Only an emergency measure, I assure you, Partner."

He stands up, and I meet him in the middle of the room. I'm on my knees before he can ask me what I'm doing. My mouth fits around that pole like it was made to. He gasps as my lips wrap around his swollen head. I slide my tongue under his foreskin and tease at his slit, and his knees buckle.

We move back onto his bunk, and I kneel between his hairy legs. I'm starting to get warm, but my ass is still chilly. If my plan works, though, I'll have that monster cock heating it up pretty soon.

I suck his cock back into my mouth. It's a tight fit, but I swallow hard and it slides past my tonsils. Jed lets out a moan, and his hands come up to clench in my hair.

"Good God, what are you doing?" he whimpers. Of course my mother taught me not to talk with my mouth full, so I can't answer him. I just start pumping his rod in and out of my throat. Pretty soon, he's shoving against me again.

I watch his stomach muscles tighten up, and slide his cock out. He stares down at me.

"Wha...why we you stopping?"

I grin. "Lie back," I tell him. Meanwhile, my hand's feeling around in my saddlebag. My grin gets wider as I feel the tin of grease I packed inside for just such an occasion.

Jed's mouth drops open as I climb up onto the bunk with him and start greasing him down. I straddle his pole, a grin already on my face.

"Wait a minute, there," he says, flailing about with his arms. I lean onto his chest.

"What's the matter, Jed? I thought you wanted some relief."

His eyes are as big as saucers. He looks at his cock, then my ass, then back to his cock.

"There ain't no way," he mutters. "You're gonna bust something."

"Wanna make a little bet on that?" I say. He shuts his mouth and watches.

I've got his cock greased, now I get myself centered with that big head right under my hole. I brace myself, and shove hard. Thunderation, but it feels like a fence post!

Jed's face is screwed up with worry, and he once or twice puts a hand out to try and stop me. I just shake my head no, and keep pushing down. There's a sharp flash of pain, then it's inside. I take a deep breath, and impale myself on his shaft, sinking until my ass grinds against his legs. "How's that feel?" I ask, only it comes out more of a gasp on account of that lodgepole pine I got shoved up my nether regions.

"God Almighty, that's good!" He sets his big hands on either side of my waist and gives a little shove. I swear the head of that thing's tickling the back of my tonsils.

I slip my hand back, take hold of his balls, and slide them around my fingers. Jed throws his head back and bucks up. I let out a grunt, but don't try to get loose. This is one stallion I'm gonna ride to the finish.

I spread my legs out a little more, brace with my hands, and pump up and down. I'm spearing myself with that pole, and it feels like it's splitting me right in two, but I'm loving it. I never had anything so big up my ass since I started taking cocks. I lean back a bit and groan, it's so good. The pain's wore off now, and Jed's hitting my joy-spot dead on. I buck up and down like I'm going for a rodeo prize. We're both grunting every time I shove down, and his hands tighten around my waist like he's trying to shove his balls up there alongside his rod.

"Hellfire!" Jed screams. I feel that pole thicken up, deep inside me, and I know he's gonna shoot any second. I slip my hand back down between his legs and shove a finger into his tight hole.

His eyes pop open wide, and he lets out a little gasp. I know it's the best feeling he's ever had, and I just grin down at him and keep grinding on his cock. Now I'm shoving my finger in deeper, and he's pushing down to take it. His balls jerk away from my hand, toward his rod, and I feel hot juice shoot into my innards.

I shove backwards, taking him as deep as I can. He bucks up to meet me. I push another finger inside his ass, fucking him.

He shoots three loads into my ass, then lies back and stares at me wide-eyed. I slide my fingers out of his hole, and he gives a little quiver. Instead of jumping off my mount, I just lean forward onto his chest. He jerks when my tongue connects with his tit, then he sucks in a deep breath.

I nuzzle under his thick mat of chest hair, sucking his hard nubs. He wriggles under me, and I pull harder.

"If you don't quit that, I'm gonna get hard again." he gasps.

I grin around a mouthful of fur. "What do you think I'm trying to do?" I ask. "If you get on top this time, you'll likely get me to cream without having to touch my rod."

He glances at my eight inches, bouncing against his hard belly. Then he looks me in the eye. I feel a huge palm slide around my meat, and something inside me melts.

I've been wanting to touch it, though," he mutters. "I have to tell you I never bedded a woman who made me feel like you just did."

His pole starts hardening again, deep inside my canal, I moan a little, squirming on top of it. I want him to take me hard this time. I want that big body pinning me to the bed and taking everything I got to give.

His hands tug at my rod, He's never done it before but he learns fast when I put my hands on top of his and show him how I like it. Pretty soon I'm grunting and wriggling to his rhythm, His cock is throbbing again, filling me up.

"God, Kid, I need to get fucked!" I gasp. "Get on top and ride me hard!"

It takes some doing, what with him so new at it, but we maneuver around so I'm underneath. I hoist my legs up to his shoulders and lie back. He gives a few soft, gentle shoves, I reach behind him and slap his ass, hard.

"Fuck me, dammit!"

His mouth flies open, He's not sure if it hurt or not, so I give him another wallop. All of a sudden, it's like he gets the idea. He gives a growl, grabs my wrists and pins them down with one hand. Then he leans onto me and starts huffing like a locomotive.

I can't catch my breath for a minute, then I'm panting and gasping. He's got me so tight I can't even squirm, and I roll my head back and let out a yell. His hot cock stabs past my throbbing hole again and again. He spreads my legs wider, splitting me apart.

I feel my balls churn. My belly quivers and my hips try to slam up to meet Jed halfway. Fire shoots out of my cock, spewing over my chest. My second volley hits Jed on the chin. He looks down, startled, then pounds me even harder.

I can feel his rod getting ready to unload in my ass while mine's shooting all over my chest and belly. Jed lets go of my wrists and grabs my ass. He hauls me down, holds me tight against him. I can't move an inch—not that I want to—as he thrusts harder and faster. My cock bounces on my belly. I hear myself whimpering. I try to say something but I can't control my body,

I'm still shooting my load, my belly shivering. Jed's filling my ass with so much cream I can feel it leaking out every time he shoves inside. I can only let out little grunts when his balls slap my ass. I feel like I'm about to pass out, it's that overwhelming.

I'm lying there, trembling, probably with a dumb grin on my face, when something touches my lips. I open my eyes, and Jed's kissing me. I'm so surprised I can't do anything but look up at him.

He leans back down and kisses me again. This time, he wraps his hand around my jaw pulling my mouth open so he can slip his tongue inside. I close my eyes and melt into it, shoving my own tongue against his. My arms go around his waist without me telling them to.

When he surfaces for air, he grins down at me.

"Now I know why all the hands are so hell-bent on teaming with you, Jesse."

I open my mouth, but nothing comes out. This could be a real tragedy if I don't get back in control—I got a reputation as a smartass to uphold.

Jed moves his hand up to tousle my hair. "I might not be getting too much sleep up here," he says.

I finally find my tongue. It's licking the raw places on my lips where his whiskers took the skin off. I put both hands on his chest and shove.

"If that's the case," I snap back, "you're gonna get rid of that mustache or I'm not gonna have any hide left."

He chuckles, the deep rumble shaking the bunk, "You always gotta have the last word, don't you?"

I scowl up at him. "You're damn right I…."

He shoves his tongue into my open mouth, stifling my retort. I stiffen, then lean into his kiss. Plenty of time for smartass comments after he gets me good and warm again.

Virtual Virgin
R.J. March

Malcolm filtered, getting himself through the crowd in Letitia Blaze's living room. What she'd wanted more than anything was a loft, but couldn't find one within her budget, so she rented a place with a big living room and moved all of her furniture into it. She called the bedrooms closets. People stood in between her bed and her kitchen table. "Where's the toilet," Malcolm heard some inquire. "I'm afraid to ask," was the reply.

There was some beer somewhere and Malcolm was looking for it. He didn't look at anything but elbows and shoulders. The lighting was bad anyway. He heard Letitia's laughter and the marching band music which seemed appropriate. "Where did you get that?" he asked someone tall, pointing to the beer bottle the man was holding.

The beer was in the bathroom, the tub a makeshift ice bucket. Someone stood by the door, just out of the light. "Are you going to be long?" he asked Malcolm. "I'm expecting a call."

Malcolm got himself a beer. "That long," he said, lingering to open the bottle. "So who's calling?"

The man smiled, looking away. "My mother actually," he answered. "Her dog died today."

"I'm sorry," Malcolm said, feeling as though he'd put his foot in it. The man was tall, in tight black clothes, looking a little like a mime, Malcolm was thinking. He had a mime's face, expressive, animated. It made him seem loud, even though he spoke very quietly. An attractive mime.

"What's with the music?" he asked.

"Letitia used to be a drum major."

"You can major in drum?"

Malcolm made room for Simon Devray who wanted to get into the bathroom. They'd dated once, he and Malcolm, and now weren't speaking to one another, each pretending not to remember the other.

"What's your major?" the tall man asked. Malcolm shrugged, grinning. The tall one smiled back. He was very handsome, Malcolm decided, liking his hair and that it moved, unarrested by gel and catching the stray light from the bathroom when Simon stepped out, air-drying his hands. He winced at Malcolm, who winced back.

"I'm a poet," Malcolm lied.

"Really?" the tall man said, holding his beer up to his temple and regarding Malcolm as though in a new light. They both heard Simon snort his way down the hall. "So you've probably read Jewel's new book—just kidding."

"So was she, I hope," Malcolm said.

"My name's Tom Curry," the tall man said, extending his hand.

Malcolm took it. "Letitia's new personal trainer?"

"Uh, no," Tom said, "But thank you. I'll take that as a compliment."

"It was," Malcolm replied.

"I'm thinking this is risky," Tom said. He was getting himself out of his black turtleneck.

"I've got condoms," Malcolm said, his feelings a little hurt.

"Not what I meant at all," Tom said, setting his hands on Malcolm's shoulders. "I meant doing this here in Letitia's bedroom."

"I told you—this is her closet."

"Someone's going to come in," Tom whispered, running his tongue along Malcolm's jaw. He undid the fastenings of Malcolm's trousers and they fell fast to the ground. Malcolm lifted Tom's T-shirt and put his mouth on a dark rubbery nipple. He felt Tom's hand wander the breadth of his back, dipping low, sliding under the waistband of Malcolm's briefs, grabbing his ass cheeks. Malcolm fingered the tab of Tom's zipper. He could already feel the thick bulge of Tom's prick. He thought about his not wanting to come to Letitia's party tonight, dreading the ride up in her pissy little elevator and the "eclectic" mix of people she'd promised, not to mention the curious lack of finger food.

Until now.

Not that Tom Curry's dick could have been considered finger food.

"I'm sorry," Malcolm said, turning on the lights. "I have to see this."

Tom Curry's ass, bared, was hairy enough to comb. The bottom half of him was, in fact, goat-like, furry; he appeared to be half-dressed for

Halloween, waiting for the rest of his gorilla suit, which suited Malcolm, who had grown weary of stubble-covered boys trying to cheat their hirsute fates with razors and waxes and depilatories. He tugged off Curry's white briefs, avoiding the heavy swing of his oversized prick.

The rest of him, his chest and arms and back, was remarkably devoid of hair. Malcolm pushed him toward the bed upon which he fell easily, onto the dark cushion of coats. Malcolm could smell Simon's Drakkar-soaked cashmere car coat, which he aimed to mark up with some egg-white streaks of come, purely out of spite. He knelt shakily, ankles bound, and kissed Curry's red mouth, lips like pillows, eyes sparkling despite the dull, low-watted light on the bureau.

"You're tall," Malcolm said.

"Thank you."

"I usually don't like tall men."

"I see."

They kissed again, and Malcolm stretched out over the tall, half-furry Tom Curry, feeling the bulk of him coming between them. It's like a misplaced arm, Malcolm thought, dragging his belly across it. He moved down the smooth torso, tonguing into the belly button, aside which lay Curry's log. He licked the whole thing from top to bottom, getting it very wet, very slippery. He replaced himself atop Curry and humped his own dick against Curry's huge piece, sharing spit and mixing it with pre-come, a very pleasant combination, he was thinking. Maybe too pleasant. He watched Curry tip his head back, chin to the ceiling, mouth open, his whole demeanor resembling ecstasy. Houston, we have a problem, he thought as Curry gurgled sexily, tensing his long thighs, stretching cruciform across the coat-covered mattress. He felt the first shot like a wet bullet—all the rest gushed out like what's left in a fire hose when the water's turned off, and there was lots.

They both held their breaths.

"I don't—" Tom began.

Malcolm felt the warm wetness spread between their bellies.

"I can't even—" Tom began again.

"No problem," Malcolm said easily. "It's fine. It's fine." He eased himself up, glancing at the thick white puddle on Curry's belly. There was enough of it on Malcolm's cock to make him at least look as though he was satisfied.

"It's not fine," Tom said. He got up on his elbows and his come slid down a sudden ravine, dripping glutinously onto someone's—Simon Devray's?—dark coat. Malcolm, on his haunches, was not as disappointed as he was surprised. He waited for the excuse, the logical explanation— haven't had sex in three months or been jacking off all day without coming or I'm taking theses vitamins that...

"We could always..." Tom said. "I mean, I could—"

Malcolm pressed his palms between his thighs. He had huge thighs. He was a squat powerhouse, a little powder keg, a fire plug, compact and muscled, one of those guys who usually had a chip on his shoulder. He would have wrestled in school, but he'd hated the look of cauliflowered ears and mistrusted his ability to separate sex from sport, especially a sport that seemed more like thinly disguised sex. He contented himself and his lost opportunity with taped collegiate wrestling events on public television, whacking off to them like any of his favorite fuck films.

And then the excuse: "I'm kind of a virgin," Tom Curry said quietly. "Ostensibly."

"An ostensible virgin," Malcolm said a little too loudly. He was actually thinking of his wrestling tapes now. He liked the short guys the best, the little ones who weighed in at 170, 185, the little bruisers. It was a form of self-love, he realized, straddling the elongated thighs of Tom Curry. He looked at his own thighs, doubled in size because of the way he was sitting, little swirls of dark hairs covering them. It was like loving your own thighs, he was thinking.

The bedroom door opened, and Simon stood in the doorway, mouth agape, misinterpreting, thankfully, the situation, mistaking it for post-coitus. "I'm so—" he said.

"Sorry," Malcolm finished. The door closed. Malcolm looked at Tom who looked, not stricken, but maybe struck.

"I'm not happy right now," he said. He sat up. "Clothes," he said. "I feel particularly naked.

"You know," he continued, pulling up his trousers. They were nice, not shiny, black slacks made of moleskin or something like it. "I didn't want to come tonight—to this party, I mean."

"I see," Malcolm said, finding his shirt and shaking it out, putting it on. There was a knock on the door.

"My coat," they heard Simon bleat.

"Come in," Malcolm said, zipping his pants. The door opened slowly. The marching band music had stopped— how long ago? Was the party over? he wondered. Simon stepped between the two half-dressed men, glancing quickly at both of them with the agility of someone with a photographic memory.

Once Simon left them, the men finished buttoning and tucking in silence. Malcolm picked a speck of white from Tom's shoulder, unable to help himself. He turned around and found his coat on the bed with the pile of others. He checked to make sure it wasn't his that got marked up.

"Are you leaving now?" Tom asked him.

Malcolm made a sad smile. "I am."

"I'll wait then," Tom said.

"Why?"

Tom paused, his mouth open enough to show the tip of his tongue. Malcolm felt his own eyes narrow and focus. "People will think we're leaving together," he heard Tom say.

"We're not," Malcolm said. "But what would be wrong with that anyway?"

"Well, nothing, really—it would just be inaccurate, that's all."

Malcolm sat on the edge of the bed.

"You're really a virgin?"

Tom turned to look at himself in the mirror, adjusting his turtleneck. Malcolm couldn't wear turtlenecks, unable to find any that would accommodate the girth of his neck. "In a manner of speaking," he sighed.

"Ostensibly," Malcolm said, noticing for the first time the gold band around Tom's finger. He reached for another speck of white on Tom's shoulder.

"Do I have dandruff?" Tom asked.

"Lint," Malcolm replied. He watched Tom look at his own reflection as he would at something not unpretty.

"What's worse?"

"Depends," Malcolm answered. "Dandruff, I guess."

"No, I mean being a real virgin or a virtual virgin."

"Are you saying you're not really a virgin?"

"Well," Tom drawled. "You know what I mean, don't you?"

"But you're really married."

"Well, yes," Tom said, glancing down.

There was a knock at the door. Simon poked his head in, so much like a turtle that Malcolm had to laugh. He stuck his arm in through the crack, holding a coat. "Not mine—do you mind if—"

Malcolm got himself away from the enigmatic Tom Curry and his wedding ring problems and thought better of himself. "I can't be a home-wrecker," he told Letitia, who had called inquiring just what he and Curry were conspiring in her closet the night of her party.

"Was it some teenaged kissing game? Five minutes in the closet?" she asked. "How did it go otherwise?" and Malcolm caught an image of her, phone pinned between her head and shoulder, chucking her bare foot under the furry chin of her Lhasa-poo, Baron Von Richter, better known as Bear.

"Otherwise?" he said, exhaling. "Otherwise, he was incredible. Absolutely incredible." He began imagining Curry's prick uncovered.

"Not him," she said, annoyed. "My party, darling, the soiree."

Malcolm straightened his back. "I have three words for you, or maybe it's four, Miss Blaze: hors d' oeuvres."

The next phone call was from someone he'd met at another party a month ago, the wrestler who had trained on the DuPont compound until it had become too freaky. He was a young one, fresh from an Iowa high school, graduating class of '89, and his name was Cal, and he was wondering if Malcolm was doing anything tonight.

"It just so happens," Malcolm said, rifling through the pages of wallpaper as though it were his engagement calendar, "that I have a few hours free."

What he liked best about Cal was his spontaneity, these impromptu hook-ups, and that Cal was just shy of five-six and had a killer leg-lock. Malcolm quickly changed the sheets, but left them mussed, took a shower and towel-dried his hair and did a few calisthenics, shooting for that lightly-man-scented thing that seemed so popular these days.

There was no pretense with Cal. He came for two things: beer and ass. He drove through the door with a hard-on, the fly of his jeans half-open, and he pushed Malcolm with his broad chest into the kitchen, pinning him against the counter by the refrigerator, getting a bottle of Red Star for himself. "I have wine in the bedroom," Malcolm said.

Cal eyed him suspiciously. "No candles, right?"

"None," Malcolm said. "I swear."

"This has got to be quick," Cal said. "I have an awards banquet to go to tonight."

"Dressed like that?"

"Is that all you think about? Clothes?"

Malcolm undid the fastenings of Cal's jeans.

"I hope you realize you just opened up a fresh can of whup-ass," Cal said, his grin all toothy like a perfect row of pearly white corn.

Cal believed that foreplay was for girls. He let Malcolm suck on his hard joint just enough to wet it good, then he spat a gob on Malcolm's pucker. Malcolm, on his knees, chest to the mattress, his butt up and almost ready, closed his eyes. The initial stab was always the worst, but Cal had a cock that was perfectly suited for fucking—narrow-headed, flaring out at the base, giving him some formidable girth, and a set of rocks that swung furiously once they got going, banging Malcolm's balls hard, making them ache.

"You are going to take your shirt off, right?" Malcolm asked. He wanted, eventually, to be able to see Cal's chest, his huge areoles, the wispy corn silk that grew in the dip between his pecs, and the little tattoo of Casper the Friendly Ghost on his right hip.

Cal sighed, taking a deep dip into Malcolm's slick hole, and Malcolm gasped, not wanting to, but unable to help himself, and thinking, for some strange reason, of Tom Curry, maybe because of the tickling fuzz on Cal's thighs, reminding Malcolm of the hairy man at Letitia's party.

"I fucking missed this ride," Cal said, plunging, going up on his toes to get in deeper, wrapping his big arms around Malcolm's waist, his wrists trapping Malcolm's sweaty cock.

"Tell me you love Cal's dick," Cal whispered.

"I love it."

"Say it."

"I did."

"No, like I did."

"I love Cal's dick?"

Cal stopped fucking, though firmly planted. "You're asking?"

"No," Malcolm panted, wanting to feel the rough ride of Cal's prick against his prostate where it had been the last five or so minutes. Its absence was driving him crazy. "I love Cal's dick," he shouted. "I fucking love Cal's fucking cock!"

"Oh yeah, baby, that's it, that's it." He made his thrusts short and quick, and Malcolm quickly realized that the ride was coming to an end. It was like being on a rollercoaster—for all its brevity, it was a hell of a ride.

"Oh, shit," Cal bellowed, and Malcolm lifted his torso, his back pressed against Cal's front, Cal's sliding cock buttering up Malcolm's insides,

Malcolm loving the buttons of Cal's tits against his shoulder blades, as Malcolm shot out a terrific amount of come that would require another change of the sheets.

Cal grabbed his beer and drank it down, pulling himself out of Malcolm's manhole. "Dude," he said, "I'll be in town next week. See you then?"

"What do you think?" Malcolm said, his thighs fluttering girl-like, sensing the imminent drip of his asshole.

He ran into Tom in the lobby of the Strand theater. Wife's in the bathroom, Malcolm figured, and wanted to make a quick exit, but no, he'd left her home.

"She's not much for visual stimulation," Curry explained, and Malcolm nodded. "Which movie are you seeing?"

Malcolm bit his lip, a little embarrassed. "The *Mail* one," he said, adding, "I'm a sucker for Meg Ryan. You?"

"She's the blonde, right? She's all right, I guess."

"No, I mean which movie."

He looked up at the listings. "I hadn't really thought about it. *Armageddon* I guess." He shrugged his shoulders. He was wearing a fuzzy sweater that gave him footballer proportions. "I just wanted to get out of the apartment."

Malcolm looked over the listings himself, coming across a foreign film and getting an idea.

"You know," he said, "I heard this *Dead Dog Day* is awesome. Want to see that one?"

"Who's in it?" Tom asked.

"It's Asian—probably Jackie Chan."

"Who's she?"

He's an angel, Malcolm thought, stepping up to the counter. "Two for *Dog*," he said.

As he'd expected, the theater was empty save for an elderly couple sitting in the third row, sharing popcorn and talking loudly.

The two men sat in the back. Malcolm was eager for the lights to dim, having decided there was no dishonor in wrecking a marriage that was already earmarked for the divorce courts. He was beginning to consider himself as a divorce counselor and prepared himself to go down with the lights.

Tom Curry sat quietly, his big hands flat on the wide wales of his corduroys. He stared at the blank screen.

"You know," he started, turning to Malcolm, his gaze not eyeward, but downward. "I spent a lot of time this week thinking about that party."

"You have?"

"A lot," Curry said, dragging his stare up the front of Malcolm's torso.

The film started. Up on the screen a mangy yellow dog licked himself in the middle of a dusty unpaved street until a battalion of small boys—"Are they Vietnamese?" Curry whispered, and Malcolm shrugged— pelted the rough-looking thing with rocks. Subtitles announced the film's title and the names of its actors. Malcolm settled in, growing in his seat, spreading like germs, until his massive thigh pushed roughly against Curry's.

"They look Vietnamese," Curry said, his leg moving ever-so-slightly in a nervous-feeling up and down motion. "Jackie Chan's not Vietnamese, is she?"

The film, as far as Malcolm could tell, was about the preparations this small village was making to celebrate a holiday—Dead Dog Day.

"What's the big pot for?" Malcolm asked. A huge cast iron kettle, the likes of which one usually saw in cartoons about cannibals, simmered in the center of the village, the fire under it ministered to by the old women, squatting and cackling and poking the fire with sticks day and night.

"I'm not sure," Curry said.

Malcolm increased his leg pressure, and Tom responded in kind so that they seemed both to be jockeying for more room with neither making any headway. Suddenly, Malcolm reached over and into Tom's crotch, taking a handful of his package and squeezing.

"I'm sorry," he said lightly. "I thought we had popcorn."

"I thought you might have forgotten where you were and wanted the remote control."

"It is bad, isn't it?"

Curry nodded.

"Well," Malcolm confessed, "I was thinking that the film would become something like background to something else."

"Like what?"

Malcolm smiled. "Like if those two up front turned around they'd only see one of us."

Tom puzzled a moment. Malcolm saw it on the man's face, and then it cleared, amused. Curry began to fiddle with Malcolm's fly, the sudden ministering causing Malcolm to harden, his dick doubled up and about to bust in its cramped quarters. One after another, the buttons of his fly were undone, slowly and with much finagling as the holes were smallish and the fit rather tight. It might have taken 20 minutes, but Tom managed to open Malcolm's jeans single-handedly, all the while trying to make the other hand look casual on the back of the seat beside him.

"I just want you to know," he said, glancing up at the screen, "that my experience at this point is perhaps not as extensive as what you might be accustomed to. I almost blew an acolyte when I was eighteen." He drew back the waistband of Malcolm's briefs, baring the high-tension buzz of Malcolm's cock.

Malcolm watched the dark head tip forward and felt the hot breath, Curry's tongue darting then slowing to a long fat swab, Malcolm's prick handled delicately, like a cracker-full of caviar. Tom kissed the wet head, making it wetter, smearing his lips with Malcolm's salty balm. His lips parted, toothy gates lifting, and Malcolm entered the hot foyer of Tom Curry, his tongue flat as a welcome mat, the hole dripping with an inordinate amount of saliva. Would the back door be so soft and wet, Malcolm wondered; would he even be allowed to make a delivery like that?

Tom's fingers walked up abdomen steps, hard rubber plates of muscle, up to fat, flat nipples hanging off the undersides of Malcolm's pecs. A fine spray of hair covered his belly, tapering at his sternum. His shirt, tight black rayon, rolled up his torso like a pair of nylons.

Tom's oral fixation made up for his lack of experience. He explored Malcolm's cock from tip to base, every millimeter of skin, sucking on the piece like it was candy. He favored the head, tonguing and teething the rim of it and hitting that funny gut-sucking spot near the split that triggered a steadier stream of pre-come. Tom slurped loudly and froze. Up on the screen, a little boy was feeding a puppy in a bamboo cage. "You're safe now, little one," the subtitles read. The couple up front were engrossed and oblivious, and Tom's slip of the tongue went unnoticed.

Curry jiggled his nutty handful and unsucked a moment for some feedback. "Super job," Malcolm intoned, feeling slippery and kind and close. "Back to work," he said quickly, replacing Tom's mouthful. Tom worried his way between Malcolm's formidable thighs again, rubbing them briskly as though to warm them, as if they weren't hot enough. Malcolm tensed them, and they turned to stone. Tom moaned, coming off of Malcolm's hair-trigger piece to tell him about a dream he'd had: "And you had your legs locked around my waist and you were squeezing the hell out of me. I couldn't breathe and it hurt like hell, but I had a hard-on like you wouldn't believe, and I woke up just as I was popping."

"Nice, nice, yeah, but—could you—" Malcolm whined.

Tom gripped the steely prick, Malcolm's juices running like candle wax. They both regarded the swollen head, flat capped, blunt. Tom licked his lips and bowed his head. This was the end.

His orgasm seemed to originate mid-thigh—the hairs there stood and waved. His balls tightened, shrinking up into him, and the bands of muscle above his groin spasmed. He whispered, "Look out."

Curry's uvula received the first shot. It caught him unaware, despite the warning. He coughed, falling backward, hitting his head on the seat-back behind him. "Sweet Jesus!" he said, watching in amazement the fountain of come that leapt from the split end of Malcolm's cock—eight ropy wads of semen.

"Switch," Malcolm said, once he'd recovered, unsure of what to do with the big mess he'd made of himself, but otherwise determined to show Curry a good time. He scraped himself off and flicked the excess—and what excess—off his hands. Curry looked up from his haunches, shrugging.

"What?" Malcolm said, trying to get down on his own knees for a little reciprocation.

"No need," Curry said, plucking the front of his pants.

"Seriously?"

Tom shrugged again. "It doesn't happen like this at home, I'll tell you that much."

Malcolm lifted his eyebrows.

"I'm not kidding—I usually have to fake and hope the little precome I have suffices."

"Any kids?" Malcolm asked.

"What do you think?" Curry asked. "Are you dissatisfied?"

"Not really," Malcolm answered. "A little incomplete."

"I hear you," Curry said.

Malcolm grabbed Tom, who had stood, getting ready to return to his seat and watch the rest of the film, albeit uncomfortably. Malcolm turned him around and undid the man's belt and threw down his trousers. "You might experience a little more delay this time around," Malcolm said, spinning Curry around and getting his come-sodden dick between his lips. It was soft, but big, a hefty droop, sweet and musty smelling. It buckled, filling his mouth, and he felt the brush of pubes under his nose, and the soft skin of Curry's balls against his chin. The cock pulsed to monumental proportion.

He tickled his fingers into the fuzzy split of Tom's ass, feeling the end of his spine and, lower, the wrinkled kiss of Tom's butt hole. He stopped trying to swallow the man's dick down whole and asked, "Ever?" pressing a finger into the little volcano.

"I don't think so," Curry whispered.

"Think?"

"Well," Tom said. "I'm not sure I'm following you."

Malcolm pushed his finger a little deeper. "Ever get it up here?" he asked.

Tom dropped his ass a little, sucking up a little more of Malcolm's digit. "Not that I know of," he said. "Although, I was almost fucked by my first roommate in college."

"Hmm."

"Does that count?"

"Did he stick it in?"

Curry shrugged. "He was this big hockey player, nose like a cliff, fists all scabbed. He actually scared the shit out of me. But his dick was so—not that I cared or anything, but—small."

"But did he penetrate you with this little thing?"

Tom made a thinking face, slowly shaking his head. "We were doing shots of tequila." He pressed his fingertips to his eyelids. "Does it really matter?"

"That I'm the first?" Malcolm asked. "Not really. Not at all, really."

"Do you want to—" Tom asked.

"Fuck you? Yeah."

Tom looked up at the screen. He looked like someone waiting for a bus. He leaned against the back of the seat in front of him. "I imagine it hurts the first time."

"But this might be the second—you can't remember."

"It does make a difference to you."

Malcolm shook his head. "No, no, no—I'm trying to convince you to go for it, for Christ's sake. Just go for it."

Tom looked down at Malcolm's flag pole, thought a moment, then turned around and sat down.

"Jesus," Malcolm muttered.

"My sentiments exactly," Curry gasped. "I guess I wasn't ready." Pulling out hurt him even more, but they were able then to slick up Malcolm's cock with spit, and Curry, a firm believer of getting back on the horse that threw him, sat down again, and Malcolm's wet prick slid into him with very little resistance. Malcolm put his hands on top of Tom's thighs, and Tom kept his hands on the back of the seat in front of him, and they worked together silently, some sort of human engine, fuel-injected, piston-popping. Sweat ran down Tom's back, into the furry ravine of his ass, over Malcolm's honey-dipped cock. "Is it hot in here?" he asked.

"It's just you," Tom breathed, reaching behind him, under Tom's shirt and finding two pearls to twist and turn. He grabbed handfuls of pecs, gripped them mercilessly. "Oh God," Tom whispered.

The movie, unfortunately, had come to an end. "Jesus, that was fast," Tom muttered, pushing his fanny onto Malcolm's prong with a little more urgency. "If they aren't credit watchers, we're screwed."

"You most certainly are," Malcolm said, standing up, his cock slamming Tom's insides. He bent his dick-recipient over the seat-back and fucked him with tight, rabbit-like humps that caused Curry to hold his breath and fist himself in a strangling manner, hosing out a spray of freshly manufactured come. Malcolm felt his eyes cross, and he fell over Curry's broad back, his cock pulsing, emitting a nut-clenching load up Curry's ass.

"Jesus," Malcolm sputtered, sitting down shakily while Tom flicked his own spew from his fist. "Yeah," Tom agreed.

"Are you hungry?"

"For what?" Tom asked, turning around. The couple up front were getting up, satisfied with what they'd seen. "Remarkable," Malcolm heard one of them say, and he agreed.

"Yes, quite."

Of Monsters and Men
Wendy C. Fries

"No tongue implied," he whispered, smiling.

It had been an accident, pure and simple.

"It's Kin's birthday," Pam had said as they broke for lunch. Like a dozen others, Michael Delphin had hugged Kin and given his cheek a quick peck, but Kin turned to speak as the peck descended. "This—" he'd begun, and Michael had managed to kiss part of the boy's tongue.

Kin had looked mortified. "No tongue was implied there!" he'd said. "That was an accident!"

Eight hours later, alone on the beach, Michael laughed. "No tongue implied," he murmured again, assuming the stars were as charmed by its sound as he.

But, you know, I think I want there to be an implication there. Yeah, I think I do.

Michael had been alone quite awhile.

He'd created *Alien Justice*, scripted half the weekly episodes, directed some. Too much to do for one man, and it had left him even less time for lovers. But that time was ending; he could feel it by the flitting in his chest, by the movement of his body while it whispered to itself of lovemaking.

Kin Quon. Eurasian, with enough white blood in his line to soften his cheekbones, not enough to destroy the angle of his eyes or the color of his skin. Their relationship had been short and sweet, when in film school together more than 12 years ago. Michael didn't know if Kin remembered, having never mentioned it since he started working on *Alien Justice*. One thing Michael did know, though, Kin made one hell of a monster.

Kin licked the pustule.

He stepped back, grabbed a desk light from Cynthia's messy desk, and shined it on the purple skin of the beastmask he was creating.

The spit made the swollen skin of the pustule look about ready to burst; it seemed a mere moment away from spewing yellow alien goo onto the nearest good guy.

"Lovely."

Well, almost. Kin had to find something to replace his spit. He couldn't very well follow the actor who'd be wearing this monster suit, licking at two dozen pustules before each shot.

Ten minutes later: "Perfect match." The mineral oil worked just as good as saliva.

Kin grinned, kissed the deformed face of the alien on what would pass for its lips and said, "Have I ever told you you have beautiful sores?" He winked at it, stretched, looked at his watch. He swore. It would be pointless to go home only to be back in four hours. For such emergencies three cots lived permanently against the wall in the hallway by the bathrooms.

Five minutes later Kin stretched out on his back, quickly passing into another restful, dreamless sleep amongst the terrors and terminal cases of the special effects house they called the Beast Bungalow.

And if you wanted to talk dedication, Michael could explain the concept by pointing at Kin and the rest of the team. They put in more hours for the show than Michael himself. He had probably called the Beast Bungalow at every hour in the 24-hour cycle and he couldn't recall a time when the phone had gone unanswered. Someone was always there—molding, designing, articulating, painting. They made possible what Michael dreamed. He dreamed mutants, freaks, and ghouls; he had nightmares and the team crawled inside his head and brought them out, big as life and six times as ugly. If Kin or Cynthia ever quit, Michael figured he'd have to hang up his haunts and go back to the beach and forget about it all.

Which was a good reason to step back and forget about accidental kisses or a man's smile. What if they got involved and then messily uninvolved?

Assume it won't work, Michael told himself, *and forget about it. Besides, there's just too much else to do right now.*

But Michael didn't take into account the act of falling in love—with a monster.

Nineteen hours later that's just what happened.

The beach was dark, moonlit, and beautiful.

It was also littered with cables, lights, cameras, and a crew as they filmed the last scene for the week: a lone alien, crawling wounded along a dark shore.

The susurrations of the creature as it made its bleeding way across the sand were hideous. It sounded as if it were drowning on its own spit and bile. And the way it moved: it was a nightmare of crippled muscle in laid-open flesh. It should not have been able to breathe much less locomote, but it dragged its painfully ruined body across the dark shore, moaning each time the salty water splashed up and into its wounds. Its anguish was palpable; hanging in the air like the fumes of something burning. It was weak, barely able to raise its scabbed hand to claw at the sand or push out another wavering mewling sound. Then the creature paused and...

—In the cable-strewn shadows Michael lifted his chin and counted to five in his head—

...bit its own arm. A huge blob of translucent ooze pearled fat and thick on the creature's skin. The creature bent its head and sucked.

"And...Cut!" Michael shuddered, a discrete little motion there in the dark. "Oh yes," he sighed, a man having a religious experience bordering on ecstasy, "Oh good heavens, yes."

He felt like crossing himself and so he did, but got it all wrong and didn't know and didn't care. He blinked and looked away from the sight of the "creature" before the actor inside started to speak or move like the human she was.

The moment was too holy to ruin with reality.

He mumbled a response to his assistant's question and then stumbled off, over cables and cords, and went up the beach, forgetting where his car was, and when he found it, he fumbled with his keys to unlock it. He felt drunk.

He had something he had to do.

It was an hour before midnight when Kin opened the front door, wearing a backward baseball cap and a pair of shorts. He smiled. "Hey, I—"

Michael tripped over the door sill, but it didn't matter because Kin was there. Michael caught himself against the other man's body, his hands flying up to Kin's face, holding it for several seconds. Then he kissed him hard on the mouth.

Kin didn't move.

Michael finally stepped back after four weeks that were really four seconds and said in a rush, "I can't have your first-born, but I can adopt any mutant fetuses that creature produces." Michael rolled his eyes and moaned like the creature. "My God, it was beautiful, Kin. It looked so wretchedly real I almost threw up. It was that great. Oh, you are beautiful, you are just beautiful."

Amazing the stories eyes can tell. Because Kin's spoke for him despite the fact that his larynx was on a deep and meaningful vacation. What his eyes said were: I am utterly and totally surprised that you kissed me.

Michael stepped back, tripping on the door sill again. "Oh! I'm sorry!" He was mortified. "I thought you...I thought...I didn't know...I...shit!" He clamped his eyes closed and fumbled for the handle of the door. "I am so, so sorry, and forget I ever came and...and I never meant to." He was halfway out when he remembered to say, "But the creature was disgusting, Kin. Thank you."

Kin murmured to himself while he worked, "Why did you do that, you twit?" He shaved off a half inch of clay. "Why?" He used his fingertips to smooth the wound left behind by the shaving. "Well..." He wet the spot with water, patted it. "...because I had no idea he felt that way again."

Kin shrugged, "Yet the signs were there. But you just work too damn hard. So...we just need to smooth this little misunderstanding out. Yeah, that's all."

Kin smiled, putting the final touches on his apology.

The crew broke for lunch, and Michael went to his trailer, tired as hell again.

He slammed the trailer's door and was about to tumble to his tiny couch and collapse for half an hour but....

On the table, the gargoyle perched, fangs level with Michael's throat, eyes burning and staring straight into his.

Michael froze.

The creature's vampiric wings—exquisitely formed so that veins stood out between the bones—rose up behind its back in a great arch over its head. Muscles cut through in strained bands at its shoulders and along the crouch of its haunches. Its muzzle was long, griffin-like, and its eyes slanted up—thin and sharp.

The gargoyle was three foot tall, white-gray fired clay, and terrible in its beauty.

Michael's mouth hung open, and when he felt the couch at the back of his knees he collapsed on it with a soft grunt. He didn't blink or look away, and every breath he took was short and shallow.

The wings—scalloped at the ends, each point corresponding to a finger bone and claw of the gargoyle's 'hand.'

The eyes—faceted, pupiled, completely dimensional so that their gaze met yours no matter where you moved.

The clay—a dull sheen, making it seem as if the beast had lightly perspiring flesh.

The face—though the teeth were bared and the eyes sharp and hard, the look in its eyes was more of exultation, of glorying in being alive.

"Michael Delphin" propped between the beast's clawed toes, a white envelope. Michael thought about getting up to get it, but he couldn't right now. He just had to sit there a little and let his heart stop kicking at his chest.

It took a while.

Finally he stood up. But he didn't touch the envelope, he touched the gargoyle. She was cool and smooth as skin.

He ran his hands along her sharp cheekbones, over her fangs, along the ridge of tongue. He cupped his hand beneath her jaw, ran it along her neck, down to the cords of muscles swelling along her side. And then he touched the perfect, perfect wings and for just a moment felt a rush of wind from their imagined beating.

He sat down again, but this time his open mouth smiled and he murmured, very inadequately, "Wow."

Five minutes later he at last plucked up the envelope, opened it, and took the single sheet from it.

I've named her Glori though she isn't mine to name.
My gift to you,
Kin

"We can't. We shouldn't…"

Other than those few words, mumbled over and over, Michael did not know what to say.

Nor did Michael know what to do.

So, naturally enough, Michael went to find Kin, so that he could say and do…well…nothing.

"If you won't say anything, I will. And what I'll say is this, Michael: Forget already that I work for you. Don't worry about it, because it really doesn't matter. You're not a child. I'm not a child. We're madmen without straight-jackets, remember?"

Kin smiled. Michael didn't. Instead, he wondered why in God's name he'd come to the Beast Bungalow at 2 A.M., trying to find words to explain why they ought not to pursue this when all the while Kin was grinning, insisting that they really should.

The smaller man advanced on the larger.

Michael backed up, hit a table, heard something slide and crash to the floor. He turned, blinked, then squatted and picked up a skeleton arm and put it back on Cynthia's workbench. "I know you're not a child, it's just that…" Michael slid along the edge of Cyn's bench and backed up, toward the wall. "…it's not really fair. You work for me, for crying out loud, how can this be fair?" Michael's shoulder jammed up against a shelf, he turned, glanced into the eyes of one of last year's wart-ridden plant people, or, more precisely, the latex headmask used for same.

Kin leaned against Cynthia's table, followed Michael with his eyes as the man slid along the shelf—14 feet long and crammed with the heads of almost that many freaks and furies.

When the shelf ran out against his back, Michael stumbled, almost fell. He tripped into a metal folding chair, sat down hard. A closed bucket of gelatinous glue pressed against his ankle. The outside of the bucket was still sticky from use earlier that day; in about three seconds the side of Michael's shoe and his pant cuff were held fast. He didn't notice. Yet. "I mean, I want you to understand that I would never do anything to jeopardize the beautiful working relationship we have. You're…" Michael's expression went solemn and reverent "…truly sick, and I'd hate to lose that. This show really needs you."

Kin stepped around Cyn's desk and leaned his head against the shelf. "I know you wouldn't jeopardize our working relationship. I've always known that. We didn't nickname you Boy Scout for nothing."

Michael's brow wrinkled, "Boy Scout?"

Kin slid along the shelf to the next head: a gray-faced alien with immense eyes. "For your honorable reputation. When the show first started we used to call you Boy Scout because you were so damn fair and so damn nice to everyone." Another step brought Kin even with a heavy-browed head with huge glistening lips that covered half its face. "And you still are.

We don't call you Boy Scout anymore though. Usually."

The next creature didn't have eyes, mouth, or nose; it had a cranium filled with cratered pits. During shooting those pits had dripped white pus.

Kin took another step and another and finally Michael realized what was happening. He stood up and—felt something.

He looked down and finally noticed the glue bucket. "Oh, mother of all things!"

Kin was in front of him already, and how quietly he had moved, how quick. He grinned and said, "The Beast Bungalow claims another victim." He leaned forward. "Let's fix that."

Fingers reached for a belt buckle.

"Hey! Don't you understand? I don't think...."

While Michael talked, Kin leaned over and reached behind him. He dragged the metal chair around and stood on it. He was now a touch over a head taller than his boss. "Shut up," he said very softly, looking down into wide brown eyes. He leaned over until Michael's head tilted back. Their mouths met and were carefully introduced. Then their tongues greeted one another like old friends. Except for this one place, they touched each other nowhere else.

The kiss went on a good long while. Long enough to allow the discrete acceleration of two hearts, the all-over perspiration of two skins, the pleasant hardening of two cocks.

Kin stood straight finally, his breathing fast. "I'm a little older than you; I don't think you know that. You think I'm young." He smiled. "It's because I'm short, I know." Kin stepped down off the chair, pushed it away with his leg. "But we're both the same size lying down." When Kin touched Michael's belt buckle again, Michael said absolutely and wisely nothing. And when Kin hooked his fingers around the waist of jeans and underwear, pulled them down, and went, and stayed down with them, the only thing Michael said was "Oh."

Then his knees tried to give out.

He shot his hand up beside him, grabbed the shelf hard enough to make it shake. The heads rolled.

Plop.

Plop.

And half a dozen plops more.

Kin took his mouth away from Michael's erection, but it wasn't to notice the alien heads and mutant craniums bouncing briefly on the linoleum or to watch them as they stilled, their swollen eyes or eyeless faces staring off in all directions. It was to take Michael's hand and to put the fingers of it in his mouth, to suck on each, to slide his tongue in the crevices between and then, finally, to tug that hand down in invitation.

Withdrawing his feet from his jeans, Michael sunk to the floor without hesitation. Pulling Kin on top of him, he held the smaller man's head with his hands and tugged on Kin's lip with his teeth before sucking first it and then the tongue that wiggled out.

Kin reached between them and undid his own belt buckle and the top of his pants. Without breaking the kiss, he shoved the pants down and then felt Michael helping him.

The heat of Michael's cock against him made Kin squirm. He wanted to go down again, part Michael's legs and take that cock into his mouth, run fingers through short dark curls and hold Michael's firm but yielding sac.

Michael tilted his hips up and all thought of want fled from Kin's mind. Need came now: need to fuck, need to get inside, need to feel the tight hot....

Michael arched his neck, pulling his lips away. His eyes were closed tight. "Condoms," he said hoarsely. "I don't have—"

"I do."

Kin pushed his fingers into Michael's hair, pulled his head up toward a kiss and said against his mouth, "Don't let the monsters get you," and started to get up.

Michael grabbed Kin's wrist and sucked on his middle finger a moment or ten thousand and said, "The best one already has."

Kin attempted speech, but merely grunted. He rose unsteadily and went to his locker in the corridor to get his backpack.

Which wasn't there.

Which wasn't there?

Wallet, keys, backpack, all on the table this morning. All on the table....

Kin smacked his head against the locker's metal door. Wallet and keys on the table, backpack on the chair. On the fucking chair!

He hit the door with his forehead again.

He specifically put condoms in there because he hoped Michael would come here, and he knew what he wanted when that happened.

Oh, mother of all things!

He started to hit his head on the door again when he heard: "What's happening?"

Kin slammed the locker shut. "I'm ritually impaling myself on a dull walrus tusk." He came back to his naked lover, romantically surrounded by the bodiless heads of their children. Kneeling beside Michael's prone form he said, "I forgot them."

Michael smiled and shrugged. "So?" He touched Kin's chest, his fingertip abrading the nub of the nearest nipple, then ran his nails lightly down Kin's belly and into the black nest of hair between his legs. Then, licking his own hand, he closed it around Kin's waning erection and began to stroke.

As before, words escaped him and Kin grunted. The sound was unmistakably one of pleasure.

Kin rose up a little, thrusting his hips toward the wet, warm hand. He hung his head back until the faraway lights on the trestle ceiling shone in his eyes. It was never the same when you touched yourself, never. Another's hand on your body, doing exactly what you may have done a hundred times before, always felt a thousand times better.

Then Michael's mouth, wetter and much hotter than Michael's hand, covered Kin, and the sensation went happily right off the scale.

Kin's hips lifted faster, harder. Glazed eyes stared right up into those lights, but didn't see them at all. Leaning back on his palms, he could feel his elbows melting. They were ready to disengage and send him sprawling. He was seconds from it when Michael's arm wrapped around his waist and pulled him down, on top of him.

Kin's legs clamped against Michael's hips. Their cocks ground together, and he thrust, hard and frantic, his hands clamped to Michael's shoulders, Michael's hands at his hips as he thrust in return, his face turned to the side, his eyes shut hard and tight.

Michael's expression of delicious pain, his open-mouthed breathing, his writhing beneath him...the sensations gathered like a hot river rushing from all points in Kin's body, down to his groin. Hearing himself begin to keen, he felt Michael's nails dig into his skin as his body went rigid.

Kin began to come moments before his lover, their limbs locked around each other, Michael's moan going on forever.

A thousand earth years later, they lay side by side, facing one another, their bellies mutually sticky with each other's come—though, Kin reflected, it almost looked like something a very strange mutant or alien might ha—and then Michael had pried his tongue into Kin's mouth and Kin's sub-conscious shut up for awhile.

They awoke to banging, and it wasn't theirs.

Kin opened his eyes and knew instantly what the sound was. "The doors are locked," he told his lover, "I changed the combination in case someone tried to come by last night. I didn't think we'd be here until morning though. It must be Cyn. We better get dressed."

Kin tried to sit up. It was difficult. Michael tried to join him. This was also difficult.

They looked down at themselves.

The glue-bucket had come undone in the night and had glued their discarded clothing to their bodies in new and creative ways. It had also glued several severed alien heads to them.

The banging on the door grew louder and Cynthia Yakovleva could be heard to swear.

"Mother—" Kin said.

"of—" Michael added.

"all—" Kin opined.

"—things!" Michael collapsed and stared at the ceiling. He knew, he just knew knew knew that getting involved with people who worked for him was going to get sticky.

The Opportunist
Derek Adams

She was the first thing I saw when I entered the café. No, make that the first thing I *heard*. She was in a booth across from the jukebox, waving her arms, her voice shrill. I couldn't hear her exact words, but I could tell from the tone of them that she was ripping some poor bastard a new asshole. Once I got about even with the table I glanced over and, sure enough, there was a guy with a totally hang-dog look on his face, shoulders drawn up, eyes cast down, peeling the label off a bottle of Bud.

I stuck a quarter in the jukebox, picked out a couple of tunes I hoped would be loud enough to drown out the ranting blonde, then took a seat at the counter and ordered me an ice-cold beer.

"Here you go, handsome."

"Thanks, Reba." Reba and I had been in high school together and had always been good pals. We had us a little thing going a few years back, but decided that we made better friends than lovers. Reba assured me that there was absolutely nothing wrong with my performance in the sack—it was just that she knew my heart wasn't really in it. That had led to one of them all-night confessionals with me spilling my guts to Reba. Turned out she'd known all along. And here I'd thought I was being so clever about slipping away to the city on the weekends so I could enjoy a little man-to-man action.

"Things ain't sounding any too good over there, are they?" I hazarded.

"Maybe not," Reba allowed, "but they're not looking so bad, are they, Clay?" I shrugged my shoulders noncommittally. She rested her elbows on the counter and lowered her voice. "I've seen more than my share of men, but rarely have I seen one engineered quite so well from the ground up. God must've been in a fine mood the day that boy was born. Oh yes."

I had to agree with Reba—there was no faulting the broad shoulders, the biceps straining against the sleeves of his shirt or the full curve of his denim-encased thighs. The fellow also had a nice profile—jutting chin, prominent nose, and smallish pink ears that I wouldn't have minded nibbling on for a starter course.

"Well, you can just shove it up your ass sideways, Lenny!" The blonde gal jumped up from the booth, sending Lenny's beer flying. She spun on her heel and stalked towards the front door. "What the hell are you two looking at?" she snarled as she stormed past me and Reba.

"Y'all come on back now," Reba crooned. "And kiss my butt," she added under her breath. She grabbed a towel and went over to mop up the mess the blonde had left behind. I slipped behind the counter and pulled a beer out of the cooler—one of the ones Reba kept tucked back by the refrigeration coils just for me. I practiced a smile in the mirror above the cash register, then made a beeline for Lenny.

"Here you go, buddy," I said, setting the beer down in front of him.

"Huh?" He looked up at me, obviously still dazed.

"I'd like to buy you a beer. Mind if I sit down?" I eased into the booth without waiting for his reply.

"Got no moss growing on your back, Clay Phillips," Reba muttered. "Not by a long shot." I flashed her a big grin and she shook her head. Before she walked off, she mouthed something at me and flicked her eyes towards Lenny.

'Opportunist.' That's what the word had been. Reba had first pulled it on me the other day. She'd been reading a magazine article and told me it fitted me to a T. What it meant, near as I could figure, was a guy who recognized a situation and took advantage of it. Now, I don't know about you, but I don't think there's anything wrong with that. I mean, it's not like I was going around holding a gun to anybody's head or anything like that. I just recognized in Lenny a guy who was in need of some comfort. I thought of about 13 different kinds of comfort I could offer, and a cold beer was as good a place to start as any.

"Thanks for the beer, mister," Lenny said, eyeing me woefully.

"Clay," I replied, introducing myself. "Clay Phillips."

"Hey, Clay." Lenny shook my hand. He had a nice grip. "I'm afraid I ain't going to be much company. Me and my gal just broke up."

"Don't need to talk to be company, Lenny," I assured him. "I know what you're going through, buddy." I heard a muffled snort from Reba, but I didn't look over at her.

"I don't know what it is, but that Sue Ann...." Lenny was off and running. All I needed to do was supply a sympathetic ear and keep the beer flowing. About an hour into it, I signaled Reba and ordered us a couple of steaks. I sure didn't want Lenny to pass out on me. By the time we got to the end of Lenny's relationship, we had finished the steaks and pretty much put an end to Reba's supply of ice-cold beer.

"Why don't you come back to my place?" I asked while we were paying the bill. He had confided that he was gonna be spending the night in the cab of his truck. I hated to think of a big strong guy like Lenny folded up in the cab of a truck like a pretzel. It just didn't seem right somehow.

"You sure it ain't a bother, Clay?"

"Hell, no," I assured him, clapping a hand on his shoulder. The man was a rock—a warm, flexible rock.

"You're a pal, Clay," he said, his fingers closing around my upper arm like a vise. I flexed and he gripped harder. I took that as a good sign.

When we got to my place, I left Clay in the living room while I made a trip to the can. Before returning, I detoured through my bedroom and stripped down to my boxers. What the hell—it was hot and I was hoping for it to get a lot hotter before the night was over.

"Just make yourself comfortable, Lenny," I suggested when I sauntered through the living room on my way to the kitchen. "I don't stand on no ceremony around here. Want a beer?"

"Sure, Clay." I popped the tops of a couple of longnecks and returned in time to watch Lenny peel his shirt off one of the prettiest torsos it had been my pleasure to see in many a day. Long, dark hairs feathered up over his collar bones and swirled around his fat brown nipples. A narrow trail of the same silk trickled down the middle of his flat belly.

"You mind if I take off my jeans?"

"Suit yourself, Lenny," I replied nonchalantly, watching as buttons slowly popped, revealing a crotch bulge upholstered in scarlet.

"Sue Ann got me these," Lenny announced, eyeing his shorts uncertainly. "Ain't much to 'em." He wriggled out of his jeans, pushing them down over his thighs, then his calves. When he bent down to take off his boots, I got me a dynamite view of the twin mounds of pale flesh that had been left high and dry by the tiny triangle of fabric that made up the back of his briefs. When he stood up again, I saw that the designers hadn't wasted a lot of material up front either.

"Hey, man, on you they look good." I handed Lenny his beer. He took it, then his eyes zeroed in on my chest.

"Whoa, Clay! That is wild, man!" I'd had my left nipple pierced on one of my recent trips to the city. "Does it hurt?"

"Hell, Lenny, it was like paving a four-lane highway from my tit to my crotch."

"Can I...can I touch it?" This was almost too good to be true. I nodded, watching his fingers as he slowly reached out to me. When he touched the thick steel ring, every muscle in my body flexed. He slipped his forefinger through the hoop, rubbing his nail against the rubbery point of my tit. He tugged gently and my pec twitched. "I've got no feeling in my tits," he remarked, twisting the hoop from side to side.

"I don't believe that," I countered, wondering whether he'd give me a chance to prove my point. "You know how good it feels when you play with your nuts?" His eyes got wide and he blushed scarlet. "Well, your tits feel every bit as good." He shook his head stubbornly. "I can prove it to you."

He didn't speak, so I took the initiative. I reached up and grazed the thick points of his nipples with my callused thumbs. From the way he jumped, you'd have thought somebody'd crammed a cattle prod up his ass. I half expected him to put the couch between us, but he didn't. Once he'd stopped weaving around, he was right back where he'd started. I touched him again, only this time I pinched his thick tits and held on so I wouldn't lose him.

Lenny's eyelids drooped, and he let out a low moan when I began gently tugging on the sensitive tabs of flesh. I kept waiting for him to grip my wrists and pull my hands away, but he didn't. All he did was lean forward slightly when I tugged, then rock back when I pushed him away from me.

After a couple of minutes of this, Lenny grunted, and I felt something hot and wet pressed against my belly, right above the waistband of my boxers. I looked down. Lenny's cock had escaped from his skimpy shorts and was now spanning the distance from his body to mine. It was a nice cock, thick and stubby, jutting out of a bush of gleaming brown curls.

"Uh...sorry," he stammered, grinning at me goofily. If he was embarrassed, it wasn't slowing him down any. "I...uh...I must be a little drunk."

"Yeah, Lenny," I replied. "Me, too." Just so I wouldn't look like a piker, I reached into my shorts and fished my cock out through the fly. It was growing, but hadn't quite risen to attention.

"Oh." Lenny was looking down. "Yours is bigger than mine."

"Not so much," I replied modestly. "Yours is prettier."

"Huh?"

"What I mean is, its more in proportion. I think it's a real nice dick."

"I…uh…I like yours, too." Lenny all of a sudden got this real serious look on his face. "I…uh…I don't think I should be doing this, Clay."

"You ain't doing anything, Lenny," I countered, more or less truthfully. "You're horny, right?" He nodded. "This feels good, right?" I twisted his nipples. He nodded again. "I just want you to feel better, man. You've had a hell of a day." He blinked his big brown eyes at me. "Tell you what, you give me about ten minutes of your time, and we'll see whether or not I can put a big old smile on that mug of yours. OK?"

Lenny nodded one last, fateful time, and I sank to my knees, stripping his red shorts off in one smooth move. I gripped him firmly by the waist, letting my fingers curl against his delectable, rock-hard buns. I took a deep breath, bobbed forward, and started working on the fat purple knob that capped his spike. When I made contact, he sucked air so hard it damn near made my hair stand on end, but he made no effort to extract himself from my hot mouth. I tightened my lips around the rim of the crown and began to poke at his pisshole with the tip of my tongue.

One pretty consistent thing about straight guys—they don't get much first-rate head. That, once you get 'em in the right setting, makes 'em easy pickings for a dude who knows how to suck cock. Well, the setting was right, and Lenny's hot little rod had come to the attention of a real pro. I lunged forward and butted his belly with my forehead. He grunted, and his balls clipped my chin on their way up to his armpits.

While I was doing my best to suck Lenny's brains out through his dick, I was also letting my fingers take a walk over the silky terrain of his backside. I had no doubt that the flawless globes of flesh were uncharted territory. As my wandering digits got closer and closer to his crack, the atmosphere got warmer and more humid. When I touched the tightly puckered ring of muscle that kept him from taking on water when he sat in the tub, his dick damn near poked a hole in the roof of my mouth. He wiggled around a little, but made no effort to stop me.

Encouraged, I sucked his bone a few minutes longer, then left it standing tall while I burrowed between his furry thighs. I polished his knotted balls for a bit, then pushed along the swollen ridge that ran back to ground zero. I coaxed his feet apart and wriggled my way between his legs, spreading them like a wishbone. When I flipped myself around and looked up, there it was, all tight and pink, encircled by a mossy ring of brown fuzz, throbbing with his pulse. Paradise, dead ahead!

I tore into his ass like a pig rooting for truffles. Poor bastard didn't have a clue what was happening till I had my tongued jammed in deep. Just to make sure I didn't lose him, I reached between his legs and grabbed his cock, pulling it down and back. He leaned forward and braced his hands on the coffee table, head down, eyes closed, mouth gaping. I punched my tongue up his chute, then took a long slow lick down the length of his cock. It flexed and drooled a big glob of thick, clear lube. I lapped it up and licked my way back up to his twitching asshole.

After several similar round trips, Lenny's hole was loose enough for me to slip a finger into him beside my plunging tongue. I glanced at his upside-down face. The fucker was in total bliss, shaking his head from side to side, moaning incoherently. I blew a little air up him and sneaked in a second digit, then a third. I twisted the plug of fingers deep and wiggled them. I made contact with his prostate and Lenny quivered.

"Lenny," I cooed, still pumping my hand in and out of his ass. His eyes fluttered open. "Reach in that box on the table and grab me one of those packets." He fumbled for the box, pulled out a foil-wrapped rubber and eyed it dubiously. "Wanna open it for me?" He gripped a corner of the packet between his teeth and ripped it open, cupping the glistening rubber in his palm. "Wanna put it on me?"

"Huh?"

"You know how to put a rubber on, don't you?" Another nod. "Just like doing one on yourself, only you grab my dick." He hesitated briefly, but once he touched me his grip was firm. He plopped the lubed circle on the tip of my prick and rolled it till he ran out of rubber.

"Looks like a big old sausage, man," he said, chuckling softly. "What you gonna...aahhh!" I cut off his question when I jammed my fingers in him up to the webbing. I finger-fucked him briefly, then stopped moving. Lenny's hips took over, and he continued to bounce up and down on my hand.

I don't think he could've sworn to the exact moment I substituted cock for fingers. I simply switched tools and slid up into his hungry hole, pushing ahead slow and easy. He was hot and tight inside, his assring gripping me firmly so I wouldn't accidentally slide out. Lenny continued to wiggle, and I started wiggling myself, watching my latex-sheathed prick disappear between those milky globes of flesh.

Lenny started tipping forward, and I grabbed him by the hips. He put his hands on top of mine and took a quick inventory. "What...?" he muttered.

"Just massaging that old hot spot, buddy." I crammed my knob hard against his prostate and the muscles in his back danced. He looked back at me uncertainly. I pumped him again.

"Oh, man." His head drooped and his subsequent conversation was confined to a series of increasingly noisy groans as I kept on savaging his lush ass.

I stopped one pump shy of shooting, focusing on the tickle in my gut that mounted in intensity till it became unbearable. I pulled out slow, felt the pressure build, then shoved it back in up to the hilt as I started to spew. I reached under Lenny, grabbed his stiffer in both hands and pumped him off, savoring the sensations as his whole body quivered and convulsed. I stayed behind him, smearing jism over his belly till he spasmed and spit my cock out of his hole.

The following Saturday I was sitting at the counter talking to Reba when Lenny and Sue Ann moseyed in and slid into the booth across from the jukebox. Lenny waved at me and smiled. Sue Ann glanced my way but did neither.

"Looks like those two are speaking again," Reba observed, propping her elbows on the counter. Sue Ann's voice rose in volume. "For now." She pulled her order pad out of her apron. "Better go over there and take their order while I've got the opportunity."

"Good idea, Reba," I agreed. "It's very important not to let opportunity pass you by. Never can tell when you'll get another chance."

"Maybe not, Clay," Reba replied, "but I'm sure you'll be ready and waiting." She shook her head, grabbed a coffee pot and set sail across the cafe. While I sat there listening to Sue Ann's voice rise and watching Lenny's shoulders droop, a big old shit-eating grin struggled to take over the bottom half of my face.

Santee's Equation
Dale Chase

"I write and I fuck," said Paul Santee, "not necessarily in that order."

"That's it?" I blurted, expecting a larger life from such a figure.

His laugh was short, dismissive. "What else would you have me do?"

"Nothing, I guess. It's just hard to imagine you that contained."

"Actually it's quite the opposite. Imagination, like the cock, knows no limit."

He was legendary on both fronts and his presence alone was getting me hard. He knew this, of course, and played me like he had so many others. I saw myself entering the ranks, rows of naked young men bent forward at the waist. A phalanx of asses, mine now included. "I never thought about it like that," I offered, reeling myself in.

"You're not creative, then?"

"No. I like to read. I've read all your books, some more than once. But I don't have a gift for imagination or at least not for putting it into words or on canvas or anything. I guess that makes me a realist."

"As am I. That's where imagination comes into play, a vehicle of escape where reality has no hold and things can be reordered at will. Imagination is actually a place, a sort of parallel world or, no, not parallel because it's far superior."

"Would you rather be there than here?" I asked.

He slid a hand down onto my ass. "Not at the moment. Don't forget the other half of the equation."

The party was in his honor so he couldn't make too early an exit, never mind his personal agenda. When admirers swept toward him, he gave me a hard look and said, "Don't leave," before allowing the throng access.

I got another drink and watched him from across the room, six feet tall and starting to thicken with age, but still impressive and, of course, exuding sensuality on a grand scale. His dark hair was graying, enriching already stunning good looks, and his lips were full—God, mouths do it for me. I could feel him on my dick. Maybe I had an imagination after all.

A good half an hour passed and I never took my eyes off him, so caught up was I in my good fortune. He periodically looked past his adoring fans to drill me with promise. I figured his cock was as swollen as mine.

For someone who disdained all but writing and fucking, he worked the room with skill, and each person who basked in his presence came away happy. I could see it in their faces and their animated gestures as they hugged into tight little groups buzzing with excitement. But it wasn't charisma that captured them, it was a power so absolute it reduced everyone to willing pawn. And there was none of that inflated ego bullshit that infected most of the high-and-mighty, this guy was real, far more man than I'd ever encountered. Ever. Writing and fucking. I let it run through my mind like a masturbation mantra.

He finally unstuck himself from the crowd and worked his way toward me. I was near a terrace door, and he guided me out into the night. We leaned on an iron railing, San Francisco spread out below. "I want to do you right here," he said without prelude. "I haven't heard half of what's been said and fear I've done nothing more than parrot myself because you are…." He paused, drew a long breath. "I have a thing for blondes," he continued. "Fair skin, sweet pink pricks, little rosebud puckers." We moved to a remote corner far from the party's eye, and he groped my crotch. I did nothing to him in return, too intimidated by who he was to even think about anything reciprocal. As he prodded, I offered a squeal, which got a grin out of him. "Ripe," he said.

"Yes," I managed, riding his palm. I wanted so badly to let go, but he pulled back. "Let's get out of here."

He had a car and driver, but nothing flashy, and this bit of understatement became yet another attribute piled on an already sizable heap. Inside the car he raised the tinted barrier, and as we drove toward his house across the bay, he unzipped my pants and pulled out my cock.

"Magnificent," he said, running his fingertip through a gob of precome. "So ready." He played around with my knob until I began to squirm, then said, "Go ahead. I like to watch."

He held my shaft while I pumped and after several thrusts I let go of what felt like a pint of jism, erupting with exquisite agony up onto my shirt front. As my dick squirted I noted the sizable bulge at his crotch.

When I was done he held on, playing with me like I do after a good solo session. His hand was large and long-fingered, an artist's hand. I knew his prick would be massive and wondered if all artists were well hung. I must have chuckled at the idea because he asked, "What?"

"Your hand. Big, long-fingered. I'm thinking major cock."

"Patience," he counseled, going under to fondle my bag. As he rolled my balls in his hand he said, "I never got your name."

"Nick," I managed.

"Nick what?"

"Tresser." I spread my legs to give him further access, and he worked a finger back toward my pucker. "Nick Tresser," he repeated as he skated my rim. "It's good to meet you, Nick. I'm sure we'll be fast friends."

I couldn't respond because his fingertip was prodding my hole, pushing in just enough to make me squirm. "Eager," he said. "We're going to have a fine time."

He kept me like that until we arrived at his house. As the car stopped he withdrew his hand, and we sat for a moment while I regained my equilibrium and stuffed my erection back into my pants. Santee seemed oblivious to his own, which made mine all the more unmanageable.

The house was completely dark. Santee dismissed the car, and we walked up a long path to what appeared a rustic cabin-sized home, nothing of what you'd expect for the famed man of letters. He unlocked the door and once inside said, "Undress."

I was nearly down to my underwear before he turned a switch and I found myself bathed in the kind of eerie backlight that gives the impression you're headed toward another dimension. Santee disappeared, and I kept stripping, tossing clothes over an easy chair near the fireplace. It was only when I was naked that I took a good look around and found the room surprisingly plain: overstuffed furniture, dark trim, drab carpet, everything worn and looking quite old. Writing and fucking. I was beginning to see what he meant.

When he returned he was clad in just a white terry cloth robe, untied. As he moved about the room, pouring us drinks, making a fire, I was driven to the edge trying to get a good look at his equipment, and he knew it. Had he entered the room naked it wouldn't have had half the effect. My dick, which had softened in his absence, was again on the rise.

He offered me a drink as if we were still at the party, handing me the glass and moving past to poke the fire, toss a couple pillows onto the floor.

Then he turned and leaned against the mantelpiece, which pulled open the robe and gave me what I wanted. I set my drink aside and moved toward him. His cock was long and thick with a great flared purple head. It jutted out at me from a dark forest that splayed up onto his stomach and chest. When I reached him I dropped to my knees.

I'd never had such a mouthful. It was more like trying to accommodate an arm, the knob alone a substantial meal. I sucked on it for some time before he began to thrust, and I opened and took as much as I could, driven to near frenzy not only by his prick in my mouth, but by the thought of it going up my ass.

Periodically, I withdrew to play and lick and glance up at the man I adored far too much. He had his hands on his hips and watched the action, dark eyes wide yet still so restrained, as if he could maintain for hours, as if control was a given. I made a show for him, drawing back to caress his knob, to settle it onto my tongue for a long moment before closing my mouth and sucking in all I could. This got a moan from him, and I thrilled to his first note of approval.

My own prick went unattended. Never mind hard, it was insignificant in the presence of the master, and when Santee resumed an easy thrust I stopped working him, held still, and simply received. He slid his hands down onto my ears and fucked me gently, great crown in my throat, mighty shaft filling my mouth. He kept this up for some time, never with any urgency, then withdrew and took off his robe.

When he had me on a thick rug before the fire he surprised me because he did not go where I expected. Instead of the much anticipated fuck, he settled his body atop mine, his cock atop mine, and began a slow sensual humping as he kissed me. I couldn't have gone higher had I been drugged.

His tongue moved with a kind of restrained voraciousness, prodding mine while those lips I coveted worked my own. This, coupled with that log of cock rubbing against me and his great body pressed to mine, was too much. I started squirting jism, bucking beneath him as I unloaded. His mouth never left mine, his humping never changed, he just kept on, cream now saturating the crevice between us. Finally he eased off of me and sat up. He ran a hand down my chest and into my bush, played a bit with my spent cock, then gently turned me over. Totally satiated, I felt almost fluid in his hands.

He raised my hips, pulled my legs up underneath me, and I heard the condom packet and the lube jar open. My asshole clenched in anticipation, and Santee quietly murmured his approval. He took his time greasing my channel, fingering me at length, squeezing my butt cheeks, playing up and down my crack. Here was a man who truly appreciated asses, who didn't just drive in for a quick squirt, but savored the rosy pucker and everything in vicinity. I felt his breath against my skin and a brief nibbling, then a long pause and, finally, deliciously, the great cock pushing in.

Slowly, by millimeters it seemed, because he knew no rectum was built for him; deftly, if such a word can apply to a fuck, and I found out it can because later on I looked it up, and it means neat and skillful in action, adroit. That says it all: adroit. And, of course, it just kept on going, blazing new territory, because even though I'd taken a lot of cock I'd never had one up in my gut headed for parts unknown. When he was finally all the way in he ran a hand up my back and along my neck. "Exquisite," was all he said, and then he began his fuck.

If feeling him going in had been a unique experience, pulling out was even more, and I issued a sort of frenzied gasp as I anticipated his next stroke, realizing I had a human ballistic missile up there toting the ultimate warhead. I pictured Santee pointed toward other countries, other worlds, fully capable of wiping them out.

He took his fuck slowly at first and, as his hands squeezed my ass, I knew he was watching his own show, because not only did he thrust, he squirmed and wriggled, grinding himself into me until I could not refrain from crying out. "You like it up there," he said, and I squealed at another long thrust and managed only, "I can't believe it."

"Believe it," he replied, riding me a bit now as if he was preparing—no, considering—a climax. I wondered how many asses it took to gain such control, how many fucks, but such thoughts were fleeting as that prick slid up into me and I felt yet another rush of pleasure.

When he withdrew to add more lube I moaned, the gape of my asshole unbearable. Momentarily abandoned and so incredibly open, I whimpered until the great knob tickled my rim. I couldn't wait to get him back inside and pushed at him, which got a chuckle out of him. "Hungry little mouth," he said poking at me until I began to beg. He let me go on a bit, then took hold of my hips and plunged in again in a single long stroke, which got a cry out of me as I realized where we were headed.

Once he began fucking in earnest, he never let up and I never stopped squealing, moaning, calling, begging, yes begging, because even though he was plowing me thoroughly I still wanted more, as if I could get the man himself up inside me. "Oh, God, fuck me," I said over and over, and he finally replied, sounding so calm, "With pleasure."

His staying power was fitting. Nothing premature for a man of his stature, he could come when he goddammed well felt like it, and so he rocked up into my rectum for what seemed an hour while I swam in a kind of sexual frenzy I'd never known before. If an asshole could come, mine was.

By the time he did unload, I was completely gone. He owned me, ass first, everything else a distant second. Santee announced his climax with a growl, and I felt the great animal slam into my backside as the great prick delivered what surely was a massive load. It took him some time to empty, and I pictured huge balls high against his root, pumping cream from what had to be an inexhaustible supply. When he finally eased up, he collapsed forward onto me, kissed my neck, then withdrew and hurried away. I dissolved into the rug. I could not move.

I felt him return, but didn't stir, and he settled beside me and ran a hand over my butt. "Do you have any plans for the weekend?" he asked as if I could be conscious of anything beyond him. My life was no more than vague recollection, and I answered no when I really hadn't a clue. Life? Who cared. I had been fucked by the great Paul Santee, and he was telling me he was going to do it again.

"Good," he said. "I'd like you to stay."

It was Friday night, no, Saturday morning most likely. Or had time stopped? That seemed entirely possible, everything in abeyance for Paul Santee. "Fine," I said.

He rolled me over, and I looked up at an expression I hadn't seen before, a bit more relaxed, possibly even accessible. He smiled. "You're beautiful," he said, fingering my nipple until it hardened. "And you have an ass I intend to inhabit completely." He slid his hand down onto my stomach and into my bush, played around my limp cock, then went further. I raised my legs to accommodate, and he drew both my balls into his hand. "Sweet innocent little pair," he said. "There is so much I want to do with you. You'll remain naked, as I am quite the voyeur."

"How about you?" I asked.

"Me?"

"Works two ways. Your body is incredible, and if I'm going to be around it for two days I want to see all I can."

"Fair enough. Now let's call it a night and see what tomorrow brings."

I awoke before him and spent some time savoring the idea of where I was and with whom. It wasn't enough to stare at this man the world adored, it wasn't enough to draw back the covers and steal a look at his morning erection, I still had to say it. Paul Santee. I was in bed with Paul Santee. I looked about a room darkly masculine, cluttered with books and papers. His world was as inviting as the man himself.

I wouldn't have nosed around if I hadn't had to pee. From the bathroom I glanced at his still sleeping form, then slipped out into the living room, realizing only then how small the place was. His writing desk was in an alcove beneath a large window, and I allowed myself a brief stint in his chair and a look at his wooded view, imagining him there creating his masterpieces.

As I started back to bed I noticed a stack of what appeared to be manuscript on a corner table. New novel? It had been two years since his last, and I could not resist a peek, but what I found wasn't what I expected. Santee discovered me some time later there on the floor amidst his scattered papers.

"What in hell are you doing?" he demanded. I froze as he strode toward me, steeling myself for the worst, while having no idea exactly what that would be from such a man, only that I would deserve it. When he reached me, however, he stopped as if he'd suddenly changed course. "Surprised?" he asked, and I nodded, too scared to say anything. "It's all right," he assured me. "Come on, get up."

He made coffee, and as it brewed I ventured a comment. "It's wonderful," I said.

He laughed. "What porn isn't?"

"No, it's so much more, it's so you, your style, everything that's in your novels channeled into—"

"Fresh young asses like yours."

I basked in the compliment, then went on. "What name do you publish under?" I asked, trying to appear worldly. I was a porn devotee and knew none of the authors wrote under their own names.

"It's not for publication."

"You mean nobody knows?"

"I know."

He poured coffee and I sat on the sofa while he gathered up his stories. "Writing and fucking," he said as he carefully sorted his work. "Combining the two is the ultimate pleasure."

"I'll bet."

"There's only one thing missing in the equation."

He never told me what that was, but when we'd finished our coffee he went to his desk, took up pad and pen, and began to write. I was left entirely on my own. To watch. I had no idea what his story was but soon got the gist. As he filled page after page his prick began to rise, and I became enthralled with the sight, pen never hesitating, hurrying through line after line as his arousal seemed to increase proportionately. Half an hour passed, pages were completed and stacked to one side, while the great cock oozed in readiness. Finally Santee put down his pen.

"Come here," he said, eyes fixed on his work. When I reached him he opened a drawer, took out condom and lube, prepared himself, and said, "Get on."

As I climbed aboard he turned me toward the desk, and I straddled carefully until the great knob was at my rim, then eased myself down onto it. Santee never moved. As that pole of his worked up into me, I wriggled and squirmed, enjoying once again that singular ripple of pleasure. Once I had him all the way in, my ass resting against his bush, he said, "And now, if you're as gifted as I think you are, I want you to read aloud. It's not fucking and writing at the same time," he added, "but it's pretty damned close." And with that I began to read a story about a fair young man with a rosebud pucker lured to a writer's hideaway, and as the great cock slowly pumped up into me I stumbled over the newly minted words, much to Paul Santee's amusement.

The Daddy Thing
Bob Vickery

He's leaning against the strip of brick wall dividing a porn-video arcade and a Korean mom-and-pop, his pose not pathetic—if it were pathetic, I'd just drive on—but awkward, self-conscious. He's young, but not young enough to be a runaway, somewhere in his early 20s maybe. Unlike so many of the others hustling the street, he doesn't look wasted or strung out. Or schizophrenic and dangerous. In fact, I'm not even sure he is hustling. *Is he a police decoy?* I wonder. *Or maybe just waiting for a bus?* But he seems too ill at ease to be a decoy, and the nearest bus stop is two blocks down the street. I'm interested, but I'm also feeling very wary.

I circle the block and then slowly cruise by him again. Our eyes lock, and he doesn't turn away. I keep on driving. The third time around the block, I pull over alongside the curb. I've got Vivaldi's "The Four Seasons" playing on the tape deck, and as "Winter" pours out of the speakers, I let him have it with my heaviest eye fuck. After a couple of minutes of glancing at me, then away, then back to me again, he ambles over to the car. I turn down the music and lower the passenger window.

"Howdy," he says.

"Hi," I answer. I like his face. He's got an expressive mouth and dark eyes that are large and set wide apart, giving an impression, however spurious, of innocence. He's wearing a loose flannel shirt and those stupid baggy shorts slung down low on his hips, so it's hard to get a clear impression of his body. The hang of the shirt suggests leanness. I'm grateful to see that he's got nothing pierced—at least nothing I can see. The last time I did this, the guy I picked up had a Prince Albert. I had to call the whole thing off, paying him $50 for his trouble. Kids.

I scrutinize him closely, looking for anything, a glance, a tone, that might hint at possible violence. I detect nothing, and I unlock the passenger door. "Get in," I say. I'm feeling very conspicuous, a middle-aged man in a late-model BMW in this neighborhood. He slides in, and I pull away.

"What's your name?" he asks, as I swing onto Van Ness Avenue.

"Sam," I say. I glance over toward him. "What's yours?"

"Coyote," he says.

Jesus. I'm sure there's some colorful story behind the name, but I'm not interested in pursuing it. "Look," I say, "I'm not good with nicknames. Do you have a real name I can call you?"

He gives me a sharp glance. "Chris," he finally says. We ride on in silence. I keep waiting for him to ask me what I'm "into" and to start naming prices, but he just sits there quietly, looking out the window. He's got his elbow bent and his arm draped over the back of the seat. His hand is surprisingly large and strong. I notice that he bites his nails.

"How long have you been doing this?" I ask. It's a square thing to ask, but I'm curious.

He shoots me another sharp look. "Doing what?" he asks, all innocence.

"Hustling."

He doesn't say anything for a long moment. "Two months," he finally replies. "How long've you been paying for sex?"

I've pissed him off. I decide not to rise to the bait. "Longer than two months," I answer pleasantly.

I wonder if he's telling the truth about the two months. Still, it might be true. He certainly seems raw. "I just moved to San Francisco four months ago," he says, as if reading my mind. "Nobody told me how fucking expensive this city is. And how hard it is to find a job."

"Look," I say. "Just so there are no misunderstandings, I'll pay you $100, which I believe is the going rate."

"Yeah, fine," Chris says. We don't talk for the rest of the ride back to my place.

He takes off his clothes in my bedroom like he's alone in the room, going to bed. I'm already naked, lying on top of the bedspread, watching him. He's lean all right, the muscles in his torso as cleanly defined as the girders of an unfinished building. His arms are powerful, the biceps rounding nicely, the forearms popped with veins. His nipples poke through a light dusting of chest hair that fans out across his pecs and descends down his flat belly. I take in the tone of his muscles, the clear smoothness of his skin. Sweet Jesus, but I love the bodies of young men!

When he pulls down his briefs (which are ratty and torn), his dick springs up, half-hard, and sways heavily between his thighs. *I got lucky tonight,* I think.

He looks at me from the foot of the bed, slowly stroking his dick, his face blank. "So what do you want me to do?" he asks.

"Sit on my chest," I say.

Chris climbs onto the bed and straddles me, his knees pressing against my sides. His strokes have gotten him fully hard now, and his dick points at the ceiling, gently twitching. My eyes trace the veins that snake up the shaft. I lightly run my hands over his torso, my fingers barely touching him. Chris puts his hands behind his head and poses for me. My caresses are more urgent now; I tug at his skin, squeezing his muscles, feeling their hard smoothness beneath the silkiness. I reach up with both hands and squeeze his nipples, not gently. Chris closes his eyes.

"Scoot up," I say. "Drop your balls in my mouth."

Chris's balls hang loose in their fleshy sac, filling my mouth. I roll my tongue over them, sucking on them gently, as I continue squeezing Chris's nipples. Chris slaps my face with his dick. My eyes travel up the muscled expanse of his body to his face. His dark eyes return my stare, giving nothing away. I inhale deeply, breathing in the sharp, musky scent of his dick and balls.

Chris rubs his dick across my mouth, smearing my lips with his pre-come. I open my mouth, and he slides his dick in full, until his balls press against my chin. He stays there motionless for a moment, his cock head pushing against the back of my throat. "Yeah," he croons. "You got a hot man's dick in your mouth, uh-huh, fucker. That's what you wanted, right? To suck on a hot stud's thick cock?"

Yeah, I think, *that's right. Talk dirty to me.*

He begins pumping his hips, sliding his cock in and out of my mouth. His large hands grasp my head on either side, not forcefully, just to keep my mouth a steady target as he fucks my face. One of my hands moves over his body, squeezing the hard muscles of his torso, twisting his nipples, as my other hand furiously strokes my dick. Our eyes lock together, and his lips curl up into a slight smile. "You like having the dick of a hot stud in your mouth, fucker?" he growls. "You like feeling the stud's balls slap against your chin while he fucks your face?"

It's a little hard to answer with my mouth full of dick, so I just grunt my agreement.

He pulls out of my mouth and scoots back a few inches, posing for me again. His cock bobs in front of my face. I raise my head to suck it, but he pulls away. "Just worship it for a while, fucker," he says.

It's a dick that deserves worship. My eyes feed on it hungrily as he strokes it slowly, teasingly. He makes me beg for it before I finally get to suck it again.

When he finally shoots, his load pulses out and splatters onto my face, one squirt after another. I shoot when he does—in fact, I've been holding back, waiting for him, and I cry out as my body spasms with my orgasm. After the last of my load oozes out between my fingers, I collapse back onto the bed, panting.

I look up at Chris. "Damn!" I say. Chris laughs. I let him use my shower, and 15 minutes later he's out the door, my $100 in his back pocket. I make sure to get his phone number before he leaves.

Alex, a friend of mine, looks at me quizzically across the table at the Cafe Flore. "So how many times have you seen this guy?" he asks.

I take a sip from my wine cooler. "I don't know," I say. "Four or five times, maybe." Actually, I've seen Chris nine times, but I feel embarrassed admitting this. "Lately we've been talking a little after sex." I shake my head. "You wouldn't believe this guy's life. He's got no job skills. He doesn't even have a high school diploma. He lives in some slum residential hotel with a bunch of crackheads and speed freaks. The only way he can support himself is through hustling."

"So?" Alex asks. "You're happy with the arrangement, aren't you?"

I don't say anything for a while. "I keep wondering where he's going to end up ten years from now," I say. "It won't be pretty."

Alex shoots me a hard glance. "Christ, you're not falling for this guy, are you?"

I take a long sip from my drink. "No," I finally say. "I'm not." I look away. Across the room two men sit at a table by the window: one is middle-aged, the other much younger, early 20s maybe. They're smiling, and the older man has his hand resting on top of the younger one's.

I shake my head and look back at Alex. "You know, I never did get 'the daddy thing' before, why an older man would want to hang out with someone much younger. I could see the sex part, but afterward? What the hell interests do they have in common, with all those years between them? What do they talk about after they've finished fucking?"

Alex shrugs. "Maybe they don't talk."

I give a small laugh. "Yeah, right." We sit in silence for a while. I watch a fly buzzing against the window, beating its head against the glass. "I've been thinking about how cushy my life is," I finally say.

"Are we on a new subject now?" Alex asks.

"No," I say. "Not really." I look at him. "I make good money; I've got a nice place; things are all right." I lean forward. "But you know, Alex, there are all these things I know, things I've learned. And I have no one to pass this knowledge on to. This kid is making so many goddamn stupid mistakes, and there are so many things I could teach him."

Alex groans and rubs his hand across his face. He looks at me. "Just what do you have in mind, Sam?" he asks. "Reforming him?"

I take a sip of wine. "A straight man has sons and can pass what he learns on to them. A gay man's only option is to go out and find his sons."

Alex laughs. "You're showing your paternal instincts in some mighty strange ways." I don't say anything. Alex leans back in his chair, his eyes trained on me. He shakes his head. "Holy shit, are you ever setting yourself up for a major fall."

I glance back at the couple across the room. "You think so?" I ask absently.

I dream I'm at the opera, watching *La Traviata,* and someone's cellular phone is ringing. I keep waiting for the moron to switch it off, but it just rings and rings. After a while I realize the phone really is ringing. I groggily pull myself out of my sleep and glance at the clock. It's almost 2:30 in the morning.

I fumble for the receiver. "Hello?" I mumble.

"Sam?"

I recognize Chris's voice right away. I pull myself up, rubbing my eyes. "Do you know what fucking time it is?"

"Sam, I'm at the police station."

That wakes me up quickly enough. "What happened?" I say. I can hear voices in the background. Some woman is shouting, loud and drunkenly. Chris says something, but I can't make out his words. "Will you speak louder?" I ask impatiently.

"I got busted for robbery," Chris shouts in the phone.

I let a beat go by. "Jesus Christ," I say.

"They're going to throw me in jail, Sam." There's a brief pause. "They gave me one phone call, and you're the only person I could think of to call." I can hear the desperation in his voice now. There's another pause, not so brief. "I was hoping you'd post bail for me."

"Oh, yeah? And just how much is bail?"

I hear Chris talking to someone in the background. "Five hundred dollars," he finally says.

I run my fingers through my hair. *This is just fucking perfect,* I think. I don't say anything.

"Sam, you'll get it back after I appear in court." Chris's voice is tense. I still don't say anything. "Please, Sam," he pleads. "If you don't do this, I'll go to jail!"

"What station are you at?"

"The Mission Station. Over by 19th Street."

I sigh. "OK, just give me time to get dressed. I'll be there in an hour."

A long pause. "I really fuckin' appreciate this, man." Chris's voice trembles with relief.

"Yeah, right," I say. I hang up.

We don't leave the station until after 5. Chris is slumped in the front seat, wedged against the door. His face is strained, and there are circles under his eyes. He stares sullenly ahead.

"You want to tell me what happened?" I ask.

Chris shrugs but says nothing.

"Look," I say. "You dragged me out of bed at 2:30 in the morning. I've just shelled out $500 to bail your sorry ass out of jail. The duty officer told me you mugged some guy and stole $100 from him. The least you can do is tell me your version of the story." I notice I'm using the same tone my father used on me during my more serious juvenile fuckups. This is not a happy revelation.

Chris pulls a cigarette out of his jacket pocket. I'm about to tell him he can't smoke in my car, but I decide to let it ride. Chris lights up, inhales deeply, and exhales a long cloud of smoke. "I didn't rob anybody," he says. "The old fuck owed me the money."

"Christ," I mutter.

"He did!" Chris snapped. "He picked me up on Polk Street, drove to an alley, and said he'd pay me $100 if I went down on him." Chris glares at me, as if I were the guy. "I don't usually do that, but I needed the money, rent's due, and so I sucked his stubby little dick. After the old shit came, he told me to get the fuck out of the car, that he wasn't going to pay me anything. So I hit him a few times and took $100 out of his wallet." Chris's voice is getting louder. "He had more. I could have taken it all, but I just took what the motherfucker owed me. I got out of the car, and a couple of blocks later, the cops pulled me over. That bastard had waved them down and told them I'd mugged him."

I don't say anything for a long time. The streets are turning gray from the early morning light, and cars are beginning to switch off their headlights. I glance toward Chris. "Do you have any idea how fucked up your life is?" I say. "You need to take a long, hard look at yourself. You are one sorry bastard."

"Yeah, well, fuck you!" Chris says.

I slam on my brakes. The car behind me honks loudly. "Get out!" I snap. Chris doesn't move. I shove his shoulder. "I said get the fuck out!" I shout.

Chris turns to me. There are tears in his eyes. "OK, I'm sorry," he says.

I look ahead, gripping and releasing the steering wheel. More cars are honking. "I don't fucking believe this," I finally say. I start driving again.

"Can we go to your place?" Chris asks meekly.

I glance at him. He looks like he's on the verge of losing it big time. I don't say anything for a while. Finally I sigh. "All right." I turn the steering wheel and head toward home.

The first thing I do when I get back is call in and tell my secretary I'm taking the morning off. Chris stands in the middle of the living room, watching me as I talk to her. After I hang up I look at him. "I'm going back to bed," I say, "and try to get a little of the sleep I lost last night." I start taking off my clothes. Chris stands there, still watching me cautiously. "You look like you could use some sleep yourself," I say, less harshly.

We strip and climb under the covers. I close my eyes, feeling Chris's body press against mine briefly, before he rolls over and faces the wall. We've never actually slept together, and it feels strange having him in bed with me for reasons other than sex. After a couple of minutes, I drift off to sleep.

When I wake up, the clock says it's almost 11:30. I stir and glance over toward Chris. His eyes are trained on me, and I get the disquieting feeling he's been watching me all the time I was sleeping. "Did you get any sleep?" I ask him.

He shrugs. "A little." He still looks subdued.

I'm feeling more charitable now. I reach over and squeeze the back of his neck. "That guy's not going to press any charges," I say. "He's not going to risk the embarrassment."

We lie in bed together without speaking. I keep on massaging the back of his neck, my fingers gently kneading his flesh. Chris closes his eyes. I pull him to me and kiss him gently, my lips just barely pressing against his. I'm still not fully awake, and my kisses are sleepy and distracted. We kiss again, harder this time. Chris shifts his body and wraps his arm around me, pulling me against him. I reach down and squeeze my hand around both our dicks, feeling his cock swell and harden against my own. I start stroking them both, dick flesh against dick flesh, balls pressed against balls.

Chris rolls over on top of me. He takes hold of my wrists and pins my arms above my head, his mouth still fused to mine. He begins dry-humping my belly, his now-stiff dick pushing against me. He bends down and buries his face in my armpit, licking it, bathing it with his tongue. "Yeah," I murmur. "That's right, lick it good." His face burrows deeper into my pit and then travels down across my torso. I close my eyes, feeling his mouth on my left nipple, flicking it with his tongue, nipping it. His mouth continues its trip down my body, across my belly. He runs his tongue up the length of my dick and then swallows it whole, sliding his mouth up and down my shaft. Chris has never sucked me off before; until now it has been an unwritten rule that cocksucking falls outside the services he's willing to offer me.

"Turn around," I say. He pivots his body, and soon we're both eating dick, both having our dicks slobbered over. Chris worms a finger up my asshole, working it in knuckle by knuckle as he sucks me off. I groan, my voice muffled by my own mouthful of dick. Chris's lean body writhes on top of mine, flesh pressing against flesh. He's got another finger up my ass, and he jabs both of them in and out in quick, short strokes. All these things he's doing are new; he's pulling sensations out of me that I've never had in bed with him before. I start sucking on his balls as my hand slides up and down his spit-slicked shaft.

"Why don't you fuck my ass?" I ask him.

"OK," Chris says. All his confidence is back now; it's like the scene in the car never happened. He breaks free and fishes the condom and lube out of the drawer in the nightstand next to the bed. I lie back, hands behind my head, watching as he rolls the condom down his dick, admiring once again the muscularity of his body, the smoothness of his skin. My lust is quickly melting away all my previous aggravation. I arch my back as he slowly impales my ass.

Chris lies on top of me, his cock full up my ass, and grinds his hips. I groan, and he smiles slyly. He may be hopeless outside of bed, but he's in his element now, and we both know it. He starts pumping my ass, his strokes deep and sure, and I wrap my legs around him, pushing up every time he slams into me. He bends down and kisses me again, thrusting his tongue into my mouth. I slide my hands down his smooth back, squeezing the hard flesh of his ass, feeling the bunched muscles of his thighs. Chris's torso presses against mine, I can feel his muscles flex against my body.

We roll over, and now I'm on top. I sit erect so I can look down at Chris. I run my hands over his torso, flicking his nipples, pinching them. I squeeze my ass muscles tightly just as Chris thrusts his dick hard up my ass. Chris gasps. I do it again at his next thrust, and Chris gives a full groan this time. *Yeah, sucker,* I think. *The old guy is good for a few tricks himself.*

I reach behind and massage Chris's balls with my hand, squeezing them gently, imagining the creamy load inside them. They've pulled up tight against his body, and I know it won't be long now before he shoots. Chris's lube-slicked hand is wrapped around my dick, stroking it in synch with each thrust of his hips. He pulls his dick almost completely out, holds the position for a second, and then plunges in hard. I feel his body shudder, and he cries out sharply. The orgasm sweeps over him one spasm after another, and I ride it out on top of his thrashing body, feeling his load pump into the condom up my ass.

Chris continues stroking my dick, and I feel myself getting close. "Slide down," he says, "and let me suck on your balls."

I move down his chest and drop my balls into Chris's mouth. He tongues them as he strokes my dick. I lean back, eyes closed, feeling Chris draw me to the brink. When I do come, I groan loudly, my load squirting out, splattering against Chris's face. I collapse onto the bed beside Chris and then kiss him, tasting my come on his lips. I roll over, and we lie there silently, our bodies pressed together.

I glance at the clock. It's a little after 12. "I've got to go," I say. "There's stuff I have to do in the office."

"All right," Chris says. As I climb out of bed and head toward the bathroom, I glance back. Chris is lying on the bed on display, his hands behind his head, his legs spread open, his half-hard dick pressed against his thigh. He's wearing a small, self-satisfied smile, and I know he's convinced he's running the show again, that our having sex has swung the balance of power back to his side. Along with the inevitable arousal, I feel a flash of irritation.

I think about this as I shower. When I come out of the bathroom, Chris is sitting on the edge of the bed, slipping on his boots. I dress in silence. I glance at Chris in the mirror as I knot my tie. He's propped up on his arms, watching me, his eyes shrewd. I pull my wallet out of my pocket, fish out a handful of bills. "Here," I say.

He looks at the money, startled. "You don't have to pay me, man," he says. "Not this time." But he keeps his eyes trained on the money.

"Yeah, I do," I say. "I want to keep things between us on these terms." I hold the money out to him. "I included an extra $50 for the oral sex."

Chris looks at me, and some of the cockiness drains out of his face. Neither one of us moves for a couple of beats. Finally Chris reaches over and takes the money. "Thanks," he says quietly. I feel the power shift back to me again, but I get precious little enjoyment from it. "I'll give you a call," he says, "when I find out when my court date is."

"All right," I say. He leaves a couple of minutes later.

I look out the living room window as Chris walks out the front door of the building and onto the street. His hands are jammed into his pants pockets, and his shoulders are slumped. I just stand there watching him, my eyes following his back until he turns a corner and is out of sight. The son of a bitch is such a lost soul. "Christ," I mutter.

Even as I negotiate the city traffic a few minutes later, I can't get that last image of him out of my mind. I turn on the radio and listen to Otis Redding sing "Sittin' on the Dock of the Bay." Downtown there are ragged men on nearly every street corner, holding out signs begging for money, styrofoam cups clutched in their hands. *Chris in 20 years,* I think. Otis sings about how his loneliness won't leave him alone, and I can feel the tears well up in my eyes. *Maybe I will go along with him when he goes to court,* I think. A car behind me honks, and I see that the light has turned green. I put the car in gear and head toward work.

Jacked In
Alan Mills

The door opened automatically as soon as I walked in range of its sensors. I stepped inside quickly, anxious to try out my newest purchase. The metal iris closed behind me and the lights came on. I gave my 16 x 18 compartment a quick glance and felt safe. I'd been jumped once this year—I wasn't about to let it happen again.

My space was quiet. The steel walls creaked from the transference of pressure. I walked up to my porthole and looked out. The external lights came on, and I watched white bits of detritus flow past in the murky waters outside.

"External light override, off light," I said, and the image outside turned black. In the distance, I could see the faint glow of the next city over: I.O.-249. I imagined it to be a different place with different ways, but I knew better. It was just like where I lived. Every city is the same.

"External light resume function." The light went on, and I turned my back on it, seeing turquoise ripples play across my walls before the light turned itself off. I went to my terminal, and the wall screen came on. My alarm was still set, and my security functions had no intrusions to report.

"Internal camera closed circuit." My image appeared on the screen before me. I unzipped my black plastic shirt and let it fall back over my shoulders and down my arms. I had a torso that was powerful, healthy, having, as I did, the strong, unengineered genes that pirates hunt for. I peeled off my boots and pushed my plastic pants to the woven fiber floor.

I looked at my toned, muscular, and well-endowed body, and felt grateful. Sure, I was natural, a mistake, and I could never live more than 90 years, but I was entirely intact and I had only one implant—the one I had to have.

I lifted my pants off the floor and reached into my pocket, pulling out a small aluminum vial. I started getting erect just thinking about what was inside.

I screwed off the cap and the contents poured into my palm. It was a clear, hexagonal crystal with a red label on one end: Dorothy's Dirty Garden.

I held the crystal to a wall light. It was clean and see-through and not a bit opaque. There weren't any flaws or fractures that might indicate secondary programs or functions. No, this was pure data, a primo Red, labeled as a caution indicator, and I had it in my hands.

My dick was fully hard now, and I walked up to my terminal and slid the crystal into my drive. I watched the screen as the security codes and protocols downloaded into my system. In seconds, the escort program linked up. The words "Dorothy's Dirty Garden" appeared on my screen. They were followed by a list of conditions, warnings, and copyright information—nothing out of the ordinary.

I went over to my bed and laid down on my stomach, squirming to adjust my erection on the mattress. I hugged a pillow to my chest and stretched to get my interface cable. Inspecting the golden tip, I pulled some lint from it, then reached back, touching the plug to the small of my back. I didn't find the right spot with the first try, so I looked back toward my ass and saw the small circular port at the base of my spine. I touched it with the golden tip, and my whole body tingled and felt warm. Precome soaked into my covers, and I let out a soft, "Oh God," just before I fully jacked in.

The upload was quick, and I instantly found myself standing in a semi-hydroponic garden, like the ones found in most city plazas. I thought I'd end up someplace exotic. "Boring," I said out loud. My voice sounded like a cannon exploding among silence. I was alone.

I noticed my clothes: they were expensive and formal, made from cotton and leather. I touched the jacket. It was the sleek kind worn by the wealthy at cocktail parties. I smelled it. This was real cowhide, softened and dyed to a perfect matte black. The white shirt underneath was soft, comfortable…silky…and tailored tightly to my body. The pants were nice, too, and flattered me almost provocatively.

That's when I discovered the privacy breach. This was my body, not my virtform. I touched my face and hair. This wasn't right. I had checked the crystal for secondary functions, including memory scanners. I reached back for my plug. I had to find out how deep the crystal was digging.

"Um, hi."

The sound scared the shit out of me. I turned and covered my rapid beating heart. "Fuck!" I shouted. "Don't do that."

"Oh, sorry. It's weird being alone, huh? Um, I've just been wandering around."

I stared at him.

"Sometimes," he continued, "with new programs, there's an empty time early on, before most people get turned on to it. And this place doesn't even seem to have any internal system virtforms, which is kind of strange, don't you think?"

I kept staring at him. Something about him wasn't right.

"I mean, this is a pretty weird set-up. I think the audience is kind of exclusive, and then, there's the fact that we...."

"Look like ourselves."

He looked down, ashamed. "Yeah."

I figured out what was wrong. He was beautiful, without being perfect. It was boyishness. Who would want their continuant to grow up looking so boyish?

"Um, since we're here, do you mind if I ask your name?"

I glared at him. "This is a Red. That means it's sexual. You're not supposed to ask somebody's real name in any program, let alone a Red. It's a security risk."

"Oh, uh, I meant a fake one."

I went to jack out.

"Wait! You're really handsome."

I stopped, not knowing what to say or do. It wasn't exactly a normal statement for a man to make. I paused, curious about what would happen next.

"I didn't mean to piss you off. It's just that, I don't really know what to do under these circumstances."

"Yeah," I said, "I guess I can understand that."

"Sorry," he stammered, "but are you, well, you look nat."

"What the fuck!" I yelled, pushing him away from me.

"I'm not a gene pirate or anything, it's just that...."

"Get the fuck away from me!"

"It's just that you'd have to be...to be here and look so...."

I jacked out, feeling virtlash rip down my spine as I pulled the interface cable out of my port.

Still a bit dizzy, I jumped up and scanned through the warnings and conditions on the screen. There wasn't anything about privacy breaching. This couldn't be legal. I ejected the crystal and looked at it again, and then I saw it. Right underneath the red label was a thin, horizontal secondary function disguised as a refraction of the red imprint. Whoever aligned this crystal was extremely clever and had something to hide. "Scan for security breaches." There weren't any. My system hadn't been violated. No data had transferred in or out, and my system hadn't been backtracked. Only my upload and…then I found it: a brief and specific neuron scan. That's how the program bypassed my virtform settings and found out what I really looked like.

But, that wasn't like hacks. Surely they'd want to know more about me than my appearance. That data would only help them if they were local. The Red I'd purchased was distributed globally. I sat down, took a deep breath, set down the crystal and calmed myself. Whoever aligned the crystal probably just never thought a nat might use it. I was probably safe.

I knew my Reds—I jacked with them a lot. Whenever a Red got too personal, it was usually because the aligner never gave the consequences too much thought.

But I preferred Reds to other, tamer escorts. I liked seeing a man's tight ass going up and down, even if his oversized virt-cock was plugging a woman. On rare occasion, I'd get together with a guy myself. If you stand around long enough, you attract the daring or the curious. And no one really cares anymore if two guys get together. It's too rare to be an issue. No one pries, either, for fear of looking criminal. It's a perfect world. Society has reached a point of total tolerance, but science had already made everyone practically the same.

To be truly homosexual you have to be natural first, and almost no one is natural. Natural birth is now an inefficient way to seek continuance. It only happens by accident, when two people do in real life what they should only be doing in virt.

I was the rarest kind of nat. My parents had been natural too. My genes were pure and unengineered, and everyday, I had to fear for my life.

Despite the excitement, or maybe because of it, my cock was still hard. I decided to take care of it the primal way. I was too freaked to do another upload. Lying back on my bed, I stroked my dick and pictured the strange young man I saw in virt, his auburn hair, his barrage of questions.

In moments, my cock erupted, and I looked down to watch real semen pour from my slit. I couldn't help but wonder what would have happened had I not jacked out.

I worked as a cyborgist, doing repairs to replacement limbs and organs. The day after the Dorothy incident wasn't easy. I went through 22 patients before my last one of the day, and I still had two hospitalizations to process and five overnight leg repairs to work on. Reception systems had no compassion no matter how you tried to program them. "Reception," I sighed, "summon Patient 23."

A few moments later, yet another perfect man walked into my lab. He was tall, with brown hair, a bit lighter than mine. His eyes were brown, too, and engineered for resilience. His muscles were awesome, and he flaunted tan, radiation-resistant skin.

Right from the start, he did what everyone does; he stared at me for a moment. Despite my looks, people always get the sense that something's wrong, that I'm just a bit too short, or that I have some subtle lack of symmetry, or that my skin is a little too light. They're right, but they never quite figure it out. It startles them, however, almost every time.

"Doctor?"

"Yes. How can I help you Patient 23? Please, sit down." I gestured toward my examination chair. Both he and I were cold and defensive, knowing what talking too much to strangers can lead to.

"I'm having a sensitivity problem."

"Numbness?" I asked.

"No, the opposite. Do you think it might be neural interface damage? I hate the hospital."

"That's rare. Most cases only require recalibration or a new energy pack."

"I hope so. I'd hate to have to leave it here for repairs."

I glanced over his body, looking for the man-made part, but I couldn't see it. "So, Patient 23," I said, "you clearly had some great skin work done. I can't even tell which limb it is."

He shut his eyes and pulled down his shorts. "It's right here."

I stared at it. He had a full penis and testicle unit with absolutely no work done to disguise its nature. It was huge, its soft and pliable surface shining like well-polished chrome. And, it was throbbing—vertical, engorged, shaking up and down.

"Um…I'll have to do a diagnostic. What systems do you have in this?"

"It's got vibration, collapsing thrust, multi-climax, auto expansion, anti-climax, power ejaculation, and rapid nanobotic sperm regeneration."

Handling it gently, I examined it. He shuddered with every touch. It was definitely an impressive unit—the kind that prostitutes get. Focusing on my job, I lifted the testicles and plugged my diagnostic system into the small port in his perineum. "What exactly is the problem?"

"It's way too sensitive. I had to keep switching to anti-climax just to get over here."

"Why didn't you just detach it?"

"Oh come on, Doctor. That just feels too weird."

I started running the diagnostic. "Was it elective?"

"That's personal data, but no, it wasn't. There was a shuttle accident when I was in development."

"Well, your commissioners bought you quite a package."

"You ask a lot of questions for a doctor," he growled. "My commissioners didn't get this for me. They had me reconstructed to look normal. I got this later. I mean, why not? A guy can make a lot of money with one of these on him. People can't get all their kicks in virt, you know."

I got the results. "You've cranked your multi-climax function too high. All I need to do is recalibrate it. It will reduce your rate of orgasm a bit, but you're going to have to live with that unless you want to get a newer unit."

"Yeah, OK. Just do it." Suddenly, he threw back his head and his machinery shot a massive load without being touched. Nanocome rained down on the floor several feet away.

"Sorry. I had to turn your functions off. I didn't realize that you'd been building up an ejaculation."

Intensely post-coital, Patient 23 panted and dug his fingers into the armrests. "That's OK, Doctor," he panted. "Just fix the problem."

"Alright, I've got it recalibrated. Tell me if the sensation is normal."

He gripped his mechanism and stroked it. "Yeah, it feels normal."

"OK, I'm sorry about this, but I've got to check your multi-climax."

He looked down at the diagnostic terminal in my hands. "You know, there are other ways to test this. Have you ever felt one of these up your...."

I hit "ENTER" and nanocome rapid blasted from his cybercock. His body shook violently as orgasm after orgasm wracked his nervous system and erupted into the world. As the climaxes continued, he gripped my shoulder and braced himself against my chest. As the program ended, he rested his head on my shoulder and slowed his breathing, his burning lips almost touching my neck.

"Are you OK?" I asked.

"Yeah. Just give me a minute."

He slowly recovered. "How much?"

"You can take care of that with the reception system outside, thank you." With that, Patient 23 stumbled out of my repair room, leaving his artificial semen scattered across my floor.

I was horny, to say the least, as I shoved my way through a crowded corridor in the Plaza on my way to a tube. Near the entrance, I got stopped by congestion. It was the end of the day, and people were heading back to their quarters in droves. I thought of just staying in the Plaza and eating out, but I had to go easy on my credit. If Dorothy's Dirty Garden wasn't safe, I had to buy another new Red. My old ones were boring me.

As I waited for the next transport to arrive, I noticed someone staring at me from a few feet to my left. He was cute, but I didn't know him. He smiled, and despite my better judgment, I smiled back. He made his way toward me, and I was so horny, I didn't think about the consequences.

He grinned. "Hi."

"Hi."

"Don't worry," he said, touching my neck. "It will be over quickly."

My eyes widened. I could feel two spikes piercing my skin. He had a gene extractor in his hand.

"Officer!" I screamed as I fought to escape. I felt like I was going to black-out. In a second, the spikes would burrow their way inside me, where they'd hunt for healthy chromosomes and rip them from my cells. Depending on how many, the result would be paralysis or death. If I survived, I'd be a full cyborg, assuming I could afford the reconstruction.

Out of the frightened crowd, a woman lunged forward and pulled the guy off me. She did her best to get between us, scratching at his face to keep him and his extractor at bay.

"Take it easy, bitch!" he yelled. "I just want the nat!"

"No!" she screamed, even as officers poured in around us, tagging the pirate with restraining rods.

As he fell to the ground, his extractor escaped his grip and rolled away. One of the officers picked it up. "Pirate!" he said from behind his reflective face plate, and the rest of the officers scanned the crowd.

Their mirrored and emotionless faces settled on me. One stepped closer. I couldn't see his eyes, but I knew he was staring. "You OK, sir?"

Shaking, I said, "Yes," and gently touched the small cuts on my neck.

He turned back to his unit. "Two and Three, escort this man back to his home sector." He turned back to me. "Don't worry, sir. They'll be discreet."

"Um, thanks." Everyone was staring as the two officers lead me toward a transport. The woman walked with me. She was beautiful and young, like all the engineered. "I'm glad he didn't get you. That whole industry makes me sick." She smiled compassionately.

She was right. It was a sick industry, but as I looked upon her kind face, I wondered if she'd feel the same way when her manufactured DNA started breaking down, when the only thing that could save her would be the natural bonds inside my genes.

I stepped into the transport with the officers, and the crowd just looked frozen as the portal closed. Many of them had never seen a nat before, and most of them were weighing a familiar dilemma: which was more valuable, their lives or mine.

I asked to be dropped off one sector away from my quarters, just before the outer rim. I walked the rest of the way cautiously and made it home without another incident.

I fell onto my bed, shaking all over. That one had been too close. And, it took place in the Plaza, in the same place I'd have to be tomorrow and every day after that.

I'd have to move again, but every place was the same, and for someone like me, every city was lonely.

And then there was the issue of credit. I was low, and I wouldn't have enough to get out anytime soon. I wanted to get out of the Indian Ocean. I needed to escape to someplace far away, maybe the Pacific. But, I'd have to save for months. If I was lucky, I'd be able to make it to the next city over: I.O.-249—the village that promised to be different, but wouldn't be. Still, I'd have to leave a lot behind.

I kept obsessing on escape, but no way out was apparent. Reaching back, I caressed my port. The metal was warm. I had a deep need to jack in. I felt like I was falling apart. I needed to touch someone. To talk. To not talk. Like I said, I had a need.

Only one face came to mind.

After jacking in, I found myself in the same plaza, wearing a slightly different suit than I had been placed in before. I still looked like me, however, and that made me nervous. I looked around. The gardens were much more crowded. Everywhere I looked, men were talking or just holding hands. A few kissed, but still, all of them looked engineered. Clearly, they were just deviant adventurers from all over the world, looking for the something exotic that their normal lives could never afford.

As I walked slowly through the gardens, men were jacking in and out all around me. I looked from one face to another until finally I saw him, the nat, the anomaly, the one like me. He was leaning on a railing, looking at the mezzanine below. Holding my breath, I walked up to the railing and stood next to him.

"You came back!" he said, grinning sincerely. "Just got off work, right?"

I looked into his eyes. They were green, a natural trait one would normally hide. "I'm sorry I was so rude," I said. Green, it was weak, I knew, but it amazed me. "You must have the rarest eyes in the world."

"What?! They're not covered?!"

I kissed him quickly, full on the mouth, opening his jaw with my tongue. He kissed me back with equal passion. I felt overcome. Our arms encased each other, our overheating bodies aching to merge.

I pulled him down to the grassy floor and fed desperately from his lips. I fought to get his jacket off, and he ripped open my shirt, exposing my chest and stomach. I rolled onto my back and he straddled me, staring at my body. His hands traced the ridges of my stomach and stopped at a tiny birthmark. He seemed entranced. "I've never been with a nat before."

I tore his shirt open, exposing his beautiful torso and a small mole near his navel and another next to one of his nipples. "Me either," I breathed.

We undressed each other violently, desperately trying to get closer to each other's skin. We kissed and licked. It was all a blur, like we'd been on narcs. But, that was the nature of Reds. Every sensation was bigger than life.

A crowd gathered to watch us explore with hands and mouths. I ran my tongue along his shaft. He pushed his cock down my throat, and I closed my eyes, tasting skin, thinking only of the flesh opening my jaw.

He kissed his way down my torso and wrapped his lips around my cock. As his mouth went down my shaft, I looked up at the men around us. They were dumb with amazement. I defiantly stared into their strong brown eyes until one of them finally spoke: "I think they're both nats."

"Yeah," said another, "gay nats."

"That's really strange. Do you think they're internal or real?"

My lover recaptured me with his eyes. "Ignore them," he said and kissed me, pushing his tongue through my lips. As he sucked on my mouth, his wet hand caressed my asshole before one of his fingers pushed slowly in. "Yes?" he asked.

"Yes," I said, and he lifted my legs over his shoulders and pressed his spit- and precome-wet cock to my ass.

It was an incredible moment. We were lost in each other, poised on the brink of self-destruction. "We're meant for each other," he whispered before shoving his cock all the way in.

His cock sliced through me, and every virtual nerve in my body was set on fire. He pulled out and filled me again, his gaze locked on mine.

His cock moved a little faster, and I felt like I couldn't breathe. His cock was big and fat, but normal, as close to real as virt could get. He closed his eyes, lost in the feeling of us together. I was lost too. I wanted it to never end.

"Oh yeah," someone shouted, "fuck that nat ass!"

"You love cock, don't you, nat?!"

I glared up at the crowd. Many of them had their dicks out. I wanted to yell at them, tell them that their perfect world sucked, that they weren't even really human anymore.

Suddenly, the cock sank deep into me. My lover's nuts pressed firmly against my rim. "This is about us!" he grunted, pounding me again.

He fucked me harder, much harder, and I barely heard the Holy Shits and the Motherfucks. He gripped my cock and all put threw himself inside me. I could feel warm come dripping out my ass. I came violently, my virtual semen exploding, hitting his face, my face and beyond, my natural semen flooding between my legs in a world that, at the time, seemed unimportant.

He pulled out quickly and straddled me, sitting on my come-covered and still-hard cock. I filled him completely, and more come escaped from his cock, flying free and landing on my chest. I kept coming too, my semen filling him and dripping back down my shaft and balls. As the onslaught subsided, his sweaty body collapsed onto mine. My cock slid from his ass, and he held me, kissing my neck and then my lips…the way a real lover would. The men left us then, too turned on and too into each other's perfection to care about us anymore.

"So," he said, "are you going to tell me your personal name?"

"I shouldn't. You know that."

"I already know everything else."

"What?" I asked, still a bit dazed.

"You're DW-0926. You live in I.O.-250, sector 29, compartment A37. You're in cyborg repairs, collect Red virt, and have a credit list at 206,570."

I pushed him off me. "You fuck!"

"No," he said laughing, "don't worry. I'm not gonna...."

I jacked out in a hurry. I didn't have much time. I pulled on my clothes, ignoring the come sticking to my legs, and fled my compartment.

I stepped into the corridor and saw them, three gene pirates—extractors in hand. "There he is!" yelled one. I ran as fast as I could to the local tube.

"Give up, nat!" one of them yelled behind me. "This won't hurt much if you don't resist."

With a good head start, I saw the tube in front of me. A transport had just arrived. It's portal was opening. I threw myself inside and hit the "Plaza" button. The portal closed slowly, but one of the pirates got his hand inside, triggering a safety sensor.

I sank to the floor. The pirate laughed. "You knew we'd find you." He was on the older side, probably closing in on breakdown himself. Already going cyborg, it wouldn't be long before old age ate the rest of him. "Make this easy on yourself," he grinned sardonically, "and we'll get a good harvest." I curled up in the corner. "OK, let's hook him up."

Another pirate entered and smashed the controls. As the third one stepped in, I heard him yell and collapse.

I looked up. Standing in the door was an officer gripping his restraining rod. Bursts of light reflected off his mirrored face guard as he tagged the other pirates before they could resist. In seconds, the transport was quiet, smelling slightly of burning skin.

"Are you OK?" he asked. "Did they get anything from you?"

"No, um, yes... No they didn't."

"I'm honestly sorry," he said. "I didn't imagine they'd be tracking you. They must have tagged you earlier."

"No, it was..."

"Relax. Luckily, I was on my way here to apologize."

"For what?"

He took off his helmet, letting his auburn hair and green eyes show.

"For upsetting you." I touched his face. "I followed you after Two and Three left. I shouldn't have done that, I know. Please trust me now. More pirates will come soon, but I'll get us out of here."

I was still dazed. "How?"

"I'm with The Department of Order. I can do whatever I want."

He kissed me, and it felt strange. I'd never been kissed out of virt, and it felt like a Red. No, it felt better than that, better than the hottest virt. Fuck, it was even better than Real Thing.

AD-0728 slept next to me on the shuttle, his head resting on my shoulder. Outside the window, clouds rushed past as the ion engines propelled us silently across the sky. It had been a long time since I'd seen real clouds. Virt ones were clearly poor substitutes.

AD had set up a transfer to a different outpost, and our government was footing the bill. From now on, we'd actually be living on land.

I looked at AD closely, still amazed at how far he'd come. He'd been born in a fetus farm and allowed to grow as a stud. When the operation was seized, he was incorporated into government service. Sure, ours wasn't a perfect world, but it still had its good moments.

Across the aisle, a little girl smiled at us. I smiled back. She would live some 300 years and still be young when we were old and near to death. I held my lover's hand. He and I were unique. What we had took a lot to keep alive, but the feeling I had inside when I looked at him was vibrant like the real life clouds and the sun dropping over the horizon. No matter how we stood out, he and I were real, and I wasn't willing to trade that for all the miracles that science had to offer.

The All-Nighter
T. Hitman

R-i-i-ing! Paul's eyes shot open. At first he thought it was the alarm clock that shattered the forbidden dream. His right hand still gripped his cock, which was half-hard, just a few strokes shy of getting him off into the sheets that had felt, in his dream, like the warm folds of a familiar mouth.

R-i-i-ing!

Paul's left hand reached for the snooze button. But when the ringing continued, his right-handed choke on his cock relaxed, dropping the moist, precome-soaked sock of foreskin from finishing off the unconscious jack job he'd been giving himself as he reached, now conscious, for the phone.

"Hello," he growled, his deep voice cracked and sleepy.

A gruff man's baritone answered, "Pablo!" Paul knew right away who it belonged to. "It's me, dude. I'm at the police station. I need your help!" It was Buster, and he sounded like he was verging on panic. "I need you to bail me out! If my dad finds out, he'll tan my ass." Buster's voice rose even faster and higher, causing the ache in Paul's dick to pound.

"I'm fucked if you don't come help me out, dude!"

"Slow down, bro," Paul said. He pinched the tired corners of his eyes before looking at the clock. It read a quarter to 3, and one quick glance out the dorm window at the early-morning darkness confirmed it. "Did you say you're at the police station?"

"The campus cops busted me. I wasn't doing nothin'!"

Paul knew better. He knew Buster better. Stretching out on his back, Paul reached down and teased the slick, itchy flesh of his cock, causing the moist pink head to push its way out of his darker-colored foreskin. "So big man on campus got cuffed. Buster's been busted!"

"This ain't funny, Pablo," Buster huffed into the phone. "I'm in big time trouble, dude!"

Paul sighed and let go of his recently awakened dick. He gave his balls an absent scratch and said, "What can I do, buddy?"

Fifteen minutes later, Paul Aguillara stood outside the bullet-proof glass of the teller's window at the campus police station, checkbook in hand, $200 poorer, with two exams staring him in the face on Monday morning. He looked at his reflection in the glass. Usually he was neatly kept, but tonight he appeared to have been hit by a freight train—or rather 200 pounds of full-steam running back that was Buster Varitek.

"He'll be out in a minute," the woman behind the glass informed him. Paul hesitated a second longer, staring again at his tired brown eyes, the day-old stubble of his square-jawed face, his jet-black hair, usually so perfect and gelled, now barely combed. Even his clothes—a T-shirt under his old leather jacket, his seersucker shorts—everything looked wrinkled. At least his black sandals, pulled on in haste, showed off his legs, so solidly athletic with their sheen of black hair, and his perfect size 11 feet.

Soon the electronically sealed door buzzed open and Buster was led out into the reception area in front of the uniformed storm trooper who had arrested him. A wounded scowl covered the big guy's handsome face. At that moment Paul had a rush of anxiety at the sight of his best buddy— Buster with the buzz-cut hair and baseball cap turned backward. Big muscle dude Buster, the pussy magnet, who sometimes drank too much and puffed his chest too much and who was always getting into trouble when he didn't score—on the field or off. Paul felt anxiety, because at that moment he remembered his dream.

"I'm releasing him to you," the officer growled. Paul only half heard the statement. "You can pick up your car Monday morning. You're gonna have to pay to store it Sunday. That's 40 more bucks each day it stays here."

"Yeah, whatever," Buster said, clutching his yellow copies of the arrest papers that matched the color of Paul's bond receipt. He didn't say much more until they reached Paul's Jeep and the doors were shut, the ignition started. As Paul drove back toward the dorm, he could smell the stale stink of beer on Buster. The punch Buster had taken to the side of his face was easier to glean in the warm glow of street lights than it had been beneath the cold white fluorescents in the police station.

"So you were fighting again," Paul said. He was still pissed off. With everything on his plate, the last thing he needed was this. But he was also shocked by how much relief he had felt at seeing Buster safe, at helping him out, something fatherly, protective, maybe more, dare he even think it?

"It wasn't like that," Buster said, folding the papers and raising his ass high enough off the seat to tuck them into the back pocket of his shorts. It took him several tries to finally accomplish the task, during which Paul's gaze couldn't help but be drawn to the fullness tenting the front of Buster's shorts, his crotch now thrust up, the outlines of his manhood, pure iron that hadn't accomplished its goal to hunt and conquer, to plug the choicest pussy at some pub in the campus town. Even before Buster settled his ass back down on the passenger seat, Paul had to look quickly back to the road. With a rising sense of embarrassment, he felt his cock begin to stir, constricted by the boxer briefs under his shorts. He had gotten half-hard before he could stop himself, the pressure working down to his balls, making it feel like someone was giving them a painful twist while alternately jerking the foreskin over his cock.

"So was she sweet?" he asked, hoping to divert his thoughts away from what it was that kept teasing his memory, that fucking dream, and what he had felt when he first caught sight of Buster at the police station.

"Real fuckin' hot, dude. Nice set of cans. Real small ass in a miniskirt so tiny, I swear you could see her fuckin' pussy lips crack a smile," Buster answered. "Only problem was that when I offered to buy her a drink, her townie boyfriend got a little offended."

"Did you think he wouldn't?" Paul asked, eyeing Buster.

"Not at me, dude," the big guy said. "He took it out on her! Pulled her off the bar stool and dragged her to the door, calling her all sorts of names you and me only say to each other after we've fucked some hot piece of tail—and not to their faces. It ain't gentlemanly." Buster cracked a sexy smile that showed off his perfect white teeth. "See, like I told you, it's not how you think it was."

"You went to jail because some other dude was rude to a woman? Took a punch?"

"Yeah," Buster shrugged. "But you should see how many he took."

"You can sleep it off here tonight," Paul said, peeling off his jacket, then his shirt, tossing them onto the desk chair after closing the door behind Buster. "But, man, I've gotta study when I get up. You're out on your ass before breakfast."

Buster answered with a deep, sour burp. Over the next few minutes Paul watched Buster fumble as he tried to take off his shorts, his beat-up old sneakers, finally his socks. Then, with Buster dressed in just a well-packed pair of white briefs, any trace of exhaustion vanished. The temperature inside the small dorm room seemed to double as Paul tried not to stare at Buster's hairy chest and solid athlete's physique. Paul kicked off his sandals and tucked both thumbs into the top of his shorts, ready to shuck them like the rest of his clothes. But when he realized that he'd thrown wood again in his boxer briefs, he left them on, sure he would push them down once the lights were out and the weird thoughts he kept trying to blame on lack of sleep could be forgotten.

Paul grabbed the folded-up quilt at the foot of the bed and one of his pillows and then tossed them onto the floor.

"Your bed," he yawned.

"Fuck that," Buster chuckled. "I'm the guest. You get the floor."

"No fuckin' way," Paul said.

"Wrestle you for the bunk," Buster said. Before Paul could argue, the big football player had him flat on his back on the bed. Pinned by the hair-covered tree trunks of Buster's solid legs, Paul watched in horror—momentarily paralyzed—as the big guy clamped down on his hands and ground his almost-naked body, putting them face-to-face, cock-to-cock, on the dormitory bed. Buster leaned down and grinned. At such close range, Paul couldn't deny it, couldn't say his tough-assed buddy wasn't the most beautiful fucker he'd ever laid eyes on.

"Get the fuck off me!" he half-laughed, pushing back against the pressure. For the moment, Buster's hands—and cock—had him pinned, and the longer Paul struggled, the harder Buster seemed to get. Soon the decent lump in Buster's briefs had tented obviously, its crown straining to the point that Paul noticed a tiny circle of wetness form on the crisp white cotton. Buster too appeared to sense something more than the usual routine had taken place, and at one point he looked down at himself. This was Paul's opportunity. He pushed up, and in a flash flipped the football player onto his back. The scratch of their bare legs, bare chests, near-bare cocks rubbing together filled Paul's eyes for a blinding moment with a shock of white light. Once the stars had cleared, there was Buster, looking just as dazed, twice as incredible and handsome.

"So, you gonna share your bed?" the big guy asked with a sheepish grin on his face.

Paul drew in a deep breath. The air smelled strangely electric, of male sweat, beer breath, and the unrivaled jock scent of Buster's skin.

"It's almost 4 in the morning, fucker," Paul said, shaking his head and taking a deep breath.

"I know." The shit-eating grin on Buster's face flattened, becoming serious. "I really wanted to get some pussy tonight, Pablo," Buster sighed. Paul felt him push upward, just as he ground down. The action mashed both their dicks together, and even through his shorts Paul felt the warmth and wetness of Buster's excitement. Paul's dark brown eyes fell into the big guy's baby blues. The room became silent, deathly so.

With his chest and dick pushing into Buster's, Paul grew aware of his racing heart and the way it was beating faster, faster. The moment could have erupted into something more. But just when it appeared it would, when Buster opened his mouth, ready to say something, Paul rolled off. The change in pressure on his dick was like a sucker punch.

"You get the floor," he said, now avoiding Buster's eyes. Standing, he flipped off the light, bathing the room in total darkness except for the poor glow of the alarm clock, the fucking alarm clock that kept telling him how fast the minutes were speeding by at some points, dragging slowly at others.

Saying nothing, Buster slumped to the floor on his back. Paul heard the big guy groan as he assumed the position, long legs stretching out on the floor. In the dark, however, he knew he couldn't conceal the truth that their wrestling match had caused him to get hard too. Paul dropped his shorts, even his boxer briefs, at long last freeing his uncut six-incher and the meaty sack of low-hanging balls that, a minute earlier, had been pressed into his best buddy's. He tried not to think about Buster and the fact he'd felt his cock, as hard as his own, pushing into his own, staining it with precome, inviting him to make a move.

Sleep would solve everything, Paul told himself. The big running back would wake up hungover and not remember what had almost happened. Paul would be too busy cramming for his tests to think about the incident. Yes, he thought, sleep will solve everything.

But it didn't.

Paul was half out of it when he heard the steady whap-whapping from the side of his bed. The longer he thought about it, the louder, wetter the sound grew, and the further he was pulled from sleep.

"Fuckin' wanted some pussy," a deep, whispered voice growled. This was accompanied by the sound growing louder.

Paul had nearly fallen asleep on his back, one hand at the side of the bed, the other draped over his forehead. He slowly lowered his hand, tipped his head to the left. There in the wan red glow of light from the alarm clock's digital numbers an image took form. Buster too lay on his back, but he'd arched one of his big, strong legs up and had pulled his underwear to one side. Poking up, above the egg-shaped balls that were hanging to one side, was the running back's stone-stiff cock. Each upward stroke by Buster's hand intensified the wet sound, and the rounded head glistened visibly in the red light. The big guy was getting himself off, right there at the side of the bed, within hand's reach.

Between his own spread legs, Paul felt his cock rising up at the sight of Buster's display. He took a heavy swallow, only to find that his mouth had gone completely dry. Part of him wanted to join Buster; the other was paralyzed by what such an action would mean. But the heavy swallow and the curious shift of Paul's weight on the bed again gave Buster the upper hand. The big guy tipped his head toward the bed and continued to jack his dick. Paul thought about closing his eyes, pretending to be asleep, but he didn't. He watched for a few more seconds, seconds that felt more like hours, until Buster aimed his dick toward the side of the dorm room bed—and Paul's open hand.

The warm, spongy skin brushed his fingers. Paul flexed his thumb, running it along the sensitive underside of Buster's cock head.

"That's it, Pablo," the big guy growled. It was all the urging Paul needed. Wrapping his fingers around Buster's shaft, he began to jerk the eight-inch cock the same way he'd done it to himself, teasing the knob with the skin of its shaft. Buster's cut cock reacted by releasing a trickle of fresh precome into Paul's palm. Before he could stop himself, Paul pulled back and licked the salty-sweet nut juice off his hand before taking hold of Buster's cock again. The big guy lurched up with each stroke, moaning deeply, but saying little else than "F-u-u-uck!"

The more Paul jacked on Buster's cock, the clearer it became to him that what he really wanted, needed was a better taste of his best pal's boner.

Paul slid off the bed. Buster must have known what was to happen. He maneuvered Paul's 180-pound mass of solid muscles into position, spinning him around into a reverse sixty-nine on top of him. This time Paul did not question it or worry about the outcome. He didn't care about the exams or losing a whole night's sleep or being awakened by a call from the police station. There was only Buster, Buster's cock, and the feel of it as he took it into his mouth, sucking the running back closer to getting off. The taste was salty and comforting, something that Paul had only imagined in his dreams before this night.

At one point Paul felt the rough fumbling of a hand down his bare ass, from his crack to his hole, from his hole to the sensitive skin between his can and his ball sac. Buster reached lower, freed Paul's uncut six-incher from where it was trapped between his own stomach and the big guy's pecs. Buster didn't say anything as he explored the moist folds of foreskin, then their hard center, gently stroking it, even once extending his tongue for a lick of it. This excited Paul almost as much as having Buster's cock in his mouth, the fact that the horniest and handsomest dude on campus wanted him so badly, he'd taken a dick between his lips. Still, nothing got to Paul more than what came next.

Through the low moans and staggered deep breaths, Paul heard Buster grunt, "Fuck, Pablo, I really want to tea-bag some pussy...."

The strong hands holding onto his sides pulled Paul back, forcing his ass flush against Buster's face. Something warm and wet inched its way between Paul's cheeks. Buster moaned again, as did Paul, but this time it got muffled up inside Paul's asshole. The big running back started to eat him out, tonguing him the same way Paul knew he licked pussy.

Paul thought about protesting; sucking cock was one thing, but getting his ass worked over was another. The incredible feel of Buster's mouth on his hole silenced any arguments. Paul resumed sucking harder and faster as the licks across his asshole went deeper, hungrier. With his mouth clamped onto Buster's dick, a hand teasing his foreskin, and the big guy's face shoved halfway up his crack, Paul knew it wouldn't be long for either of them. Buster confirmed it when he grunted an impassioned "Pablo!" up into Paul's butt. Right then Paul pulled back, catching the first squirt out of the big guy's cock between his lips. On the next blast Paul's body tensed, and the hand teasing his foreskin pushed him over the edge. He was still gulping Buster's powerful-tasting load when he blasted five scalding volleys of his own jizz across the running back's hairy chest.

"Here you go," Paul said. He put the Jeep in park and clapped the knee of his best buddy. Both of them seemed tense from the contact.

Buster forced a weak smile. "Thanks for everything, Pablo. I'll pay you back." That was all that Buster said as he reached for the door handle.

Most of the morning had gone the same way—few words, none about what had happened the night before in Paul's dorm. Still, when Buster closed the door behind him and leaned in, with his shiner, day-old stubble, and nervous, caged expression, his was—Paul conceded—the handsomest face he'd ever seen. "It's OK," he said, smiling back.

Buster lingered at the open window. "So, dude, you got anything lined up for the weekend?"

"A date, I think," Paul answered. "Nothing major."

"Why don't we go out together?" the big guy asked.

A sudden rush of warmth lit Paul's insides. He felt his cock begin to stir in his shorts.

"I mean," Buster continued, his smile widening, "I need you there to keep me out of trouble."

Paul chuckled and sighed.

"That all I'm good for?" he asked. "Saving your ass each time you get into some shit you don't want the old man to find out about?"

Buster shook his head.

"No, dude. You're a really great friend, and you're good for a hell of a lot more."

The Deceivers
Jordan Baker

Heat baked Rory's skin, burning into his naked flesh with the intensity of a death ray. In his mind's eye, he pictured the South African veldt stretching endlessly before him. Automatic gunfire and shotgun blasts dotted the darkness with sounds he'd longed to forget since the afternoon shrapnel had taken his sight.

Squeezing his eyes tight against the memory, Rory pressed the back of his head tighter against the rough blanket and concentrated on another kind of heat.

Wet flames engulfed his cock, sliding up and down its length in steady, measured strokes. Sean's tongue deftly buffed the underside of Rory's eight-inch shaft as the stubble of his beard grazed Rory's inner thighs.

The rhythm took on a life of its own, Sean's mouth tightening as he tugged at Rory's cock, trapping the head between his tongue and the roof of his mouth while pulling away. Just as the blind man thought he must slip free, Sean loosened his grip, swallowing him quickly, taking his length deep into his mouth with a hunger more fierce than the sun.

It was at the peak of this movement, when Rory was thrusting his hips upward with all his might, that the warning would come. Just as he felt the head of his cock testing the opening of his lover's throat, Rory felt the razor stubble rake the tender flesh of his inner thighs, agony and ecstasy mingling in the darkness.

That was the point, after all. This was all about testing limits, coupling on the veldt surrounded by death and gunfire and unwanted memories, hammered by an invisible sun. If you could forget the war outside the shack, you could take pleasure in the comfort of a blowjob.

Rory's mind was ripped from thoughts of war to the sensation of Sean deep-throating him with bullheaded Irish determination. At least three inches of Rory's cock was down Sean's throat now. Rory felt his friend's face pressing hard against his pelvis as Sean refused to withdraw. Instead, the younger man was whipping his head from one side to the other like a hound shaking its prey.

"Fuck!" Rory swore, balling the blanket in his fists as the muscles in his belly convulsed. "Fuck, fuck, fuck!"

Out of control, he stabbed his hips at Sean as he came, mainlining his jism into the condom's reservoir. The muscles in Sean's throat began working as he swallowed, their rippling grip struggling to arouse Rory even more as the younger man continued milking Rory's cock.

After an eternity, Rory's orgasm ended, leaving him panting on the cot. In the darkness, Sean coughed and gasped for breath.

"How the fuck do you do that?" Rory asked.

Ignoring the question, Sean grasped the older man's legs, ducking his head between them and forcing them over his shoulders. Rory felt himself being doubled on the bed as Sean's hands found his asshole and began coating it with lube.

"Give me a chance to catch my breath, you crazy Mick," Rory growled, but Sean's only answer was a satisfied chuckle as he pressed the head of his cock against the opening of Rory's ass.

For a moment, the older man allowed himself the luxury of attempting to detect the feel of the ever-present condom, but the cool kiss of lubed latex against his opening was soon replaced by the savage pressure of Sean's cock bullying its way inside him. The tight ring of muscle surrounding his asshole burned with the effort as it clenched around Sean's member. Then, Sean was inside him, moving in and out of his ass with the same practiced rhythm he'd shown while giving head.

Responding to the cues twitching through his partner's cock, Rory thrashed his hips from side to side, upping the friction until he heard Sean give way with a soft moan. Tightening his legs, Rory squeezed his knees against the younger man's head as he felt Sean go limp.

His own orgasm subsiding, Sean wriggled his torso between Rory's thighs and slumped forward for a kiss. The men rested in each other's arms for a few moments until Sean worked his way free, gingerly removing the condom.

Slipping off the cot, Sean padded across the room and the shelling stopped in mid-screech as he shut off the tape player with a decisive click.

"You felt like you were back in the action for a minute, didn't you?"

Sean asked.

"For a moment," the blind man grinned ruefully, rubbing his eyes. "Can you turn on the air conditioning? It feels like a furnace in here."

"Heat lamps," Sean said, flicking half a dozen plugs from their sockets. "They give the illusion of the South African sun. The cot's real army surplus, as are the blankets. It should have been the perfect illusion."

"Almost perfect," Rory agreed. "You're a master of deception, but I knew it was just a game. I had to cooperate to get into the mood."

"Maybe next time we can do an alien abduction fantasy," Sean laughed. "I'll get you good and drunk and you'll think it's really little green men giving you an anal probe."

Rory sighed and shook his head.

"Now that you've mentioned it, if I were to be abducted by aliens, I'd assume it was something you'd rigged."

"You're becoming jaded," Sean commented. "Games aren't doing it for you anymore. You want the real thing."

"Not likely to happen without sight," the blind man sighed. "My adventuring days are over."

The next night, it was Rory's turn to host the game. That was the rule. However, where Sean sought to give pleasure through deception, Rory used illusion to heighten his friend's senses.

"Let me know when you're ready," Rory advised his lover.

"I'm naked," Sean laughed, "does that count?"

"Almost. Put this on," Rory replied, tossing a blindfold in the direction of his friend's voice, "and assume the position on the bed."

Dutifully, Sean hopped onto the bed, carefully arranging himself on his hands and knees.

"Ready," he said.

Feeling his way toward the bed, Rory ran his hands over Sean's face, caressing the younger man's skin with his fingertips.

"You've shaved," he noted.

"No need to appear as a scruffy mercenary today," Sean joked.

"Tell me when you recognize something," Rory chuckled as his fingers played over Sean's lips.

Circling them with his tongue, the younger man drew two fingers into his mouth, sucking at them lightly.

"Odd place for those, don't you think?" he quipped as they were removed.

Strawberries were next, followed by a series of items, sweet and dill pickles, a banana, a bit of a leather belt, an object he couldn't identify, and finally Rory's cock.

Dutifully, Sean took each in the spirit it was intended, savoring the taste and feel as he sucked them in turn. It wasn't until Rory fed him a raw carrot that the Irish man rebelled. "God, I hate carrots," he said. "Give me back the dick...or at least the strawberries."

"You can tell the difference by taste," Rory observed, moving behind him and running his hands over Sean's ass. "What if you couldn't taste them?"

"If you've got a pepper in that shopping bag, I'll rip your head off," Sean growled.

"That's the point," Rory sighed, moving back to Sean's head and tracing the line of Sean's lips with a pickle. "I don't know what this is. Could be a dill, could be a sweet pickle. I can't tell because I can't read the bottle."

There was a loud crunch as Sean bit the pickle in half.

"It's a dill," he said. "Good thing, too. I hate sweet pickles. Too cloying."

Abandoning the pickle, Rory slipped his hands to Sean's shoulders and guided him onto his back on the bed. Trickling a line of juice from the younger man's chest to his groin, Rory smiled to himself at Sean's gasp. Leaning forward, he warmed the trail with his mouth, kissing his way over his partner's nearly hairless chest and belly until reaching his crotch.

Sean began humping softly against him as Rory warmed his thighs and cock with his breath. Warm, callused hands fondled Sean's cock, bringing it to life with short, sure motions as Rory unrolled a condom along its length. Cupping Sean's balls, Rory tickled the tight flesh with the tips of his nails until the younger man was ready to explode.

Moments later, Rory swooped down on him, taking the length of his cock into his mouth in a swift gulp. The icy shock of the act was incredible, causing Sean to cry out as his cock momentarily froze before warming beneath his lover's kiss. Pumping him with his mouth, Rory continued giving the younger man head until he sensed the muscles in Sean's stomach relaxing into comfort.

Releasing his friend's cock, Rory took another swig of chilled gin and attacked him once more, bringing the chill of evaporating alcohol to bear on the sensitive flesh of Sean's dick.

"Christ," Sean gasped, humping his cock into the warmth of Rory's mouth.

By the fourth repetition, Sean anticipated the cold and his gasps were less intense as he learned to expect the warmth that followed. After half an hour, Rory stopped bothering with the gin, simply devouring his partner's cock with a feverish devotion until Sean's orgasm peaked.

Rory held him tight in his mouth until he felt Sean's cock deflate as sleep overtook them.

The next weekend, Rory awoke to waves of searing heat washing over his sweat-soaked body. Flames popped and sizzled in the darkness and the cold fingers of fear gripped the pit of his stomach. The moment soon passed, and Rory laughed at the sound of sirens and wood splintering as a fireman beat his bedroom door in with an ax.

"You've outdone yourself, Sean," he laughed. "But I'm not buying it. You should've gotten me drunk and tried for the alien abduction."

"Sir," an unfamiliar voice piped up, "I don't know what you're talking about, but we have to get you to safety. This whole building could go any moment."

"Yeah, so could I," Rory laughed. "You better give me mouth-to-mouth…or better yet mouth-to-cock…I might be suffering from smoke inhalation."

As if on cue, the acrid scent of burning plaster reached Rory's nostrils, prompting another burst of laughter which soon turned to a coughing fit as the smoke choked him.

"Bloody hell," he heard the fireman curse, "this damned queer really is going to need mouth-to-mouth."

Exploding in mingled laughter and coughing, Rory doubled over in the bed, helplessly lost in the humor of the situation.

Strong hands appeared out of the darkness, firmly pressing him flat against the bed as someone pinched his nose and tilted his head back. Warm, hard lips were pressed to his as Rory's rescuer prepared to blow. Before the fireman got the chance, Rory flicked his tongue into the other man's mouth and wrapped his fingers into the fireman's close-cropped hair.

In shock, he realized Sean would never crop his shoulder-length hair for a practical joke. Running his hands over the fireman's slicker, he realized the man was much larger than Sean, much more muscular.

Damn, damn, damn, Rory thought as the fireman pulled away from him.

In the darkness, even above the crackle of flames, he could hear the rasp of metal catches popping open. He cried out more in fear than in pain when an ember landed on his leg, momentarily scorching it. Scrambling to his feet, Rory tried apologizing over the flames.

"I didn't realize this was a real fire," he babbled. "I thought it was a joke."

Rough hands grasped his shoulders, twisting him and bending Rory over the bed.

"What the hell?" he cried out as he heard someone spit behind him. Moments later, Rory felt someone using their fingers to rub saliva around the rim of his asshole.

"OK, buddy," a voice snarled behind him, "if this is the way you want it."

With a shock, he felt the fireman penetrate him, brutally thrusting a cock deep into his ass with a single stroke. As Rory cried out in surprise, a second cock forced its way into his mouth. He suddenly realized the fireman was wearing a grape-flavored condom. The thought was still forming as a third man began covering Rory's own hard-on with another rubber before taking it in his mouth.

Moment's later, Rory found himself buffeted back and forth among three firemen who fucked him with abandon while bantering back and forth about the developing fire.

"You better come pretty quick, Jake, or these walls are going to collapse," the man fucking Rory's ass croaked as more embers sizzled onto the blind man's back.

Unable to cry out, the blind man continued sucking the cock in front of him, desperately trying to get the men off before the flames engulfed them all.

The man fucking Rory's ass was the first to come, disappearing altogether after his orgasm, leaving Rory free to concentrate on the other two. As Rory's own orgasm found release, the man sucking his dick grasped Rory's hands and pulled them to his hard-on. Moments later, he came as well while Rory jerked him off with frantic strokes.

Someone was screaming about the walls caving in and there was a huge crashing noise filling Rory's ears as the final firefighter came, his cock leaping inside Rory's mouth as the man sank his fingers into Rory's hair and pulled his face tight against his groin.

Unable to breathe, Rory screamed, the vibrations driving the man he was sucking even further over the edge of his passion.

Whether from fear or passion or lack of oxygen, Rory slipped into a darkness even deeper than his blindness, his senses overwhelmed by heat, sex, flames, and jism.

Rory awakened on the starched sheets of a hospital bed. Gingerly, Rory brushed aside the flimsy gown and felt his skin for burns, bandages, or IV needles as he took inventory of his condition.

"Let me help with that," a familiar voice said, and Sean began gently massaging his chest and shoulders. "Good to see you back among the living. Your house is a mess."

"How bad is it?" Rory asked.

"You're fine," Sean answered. "Some smoke inhalation and a few minor burns, but nothing more than you'd get from a little hot wax or cigarette ash. Your place is totaled, though."

"Fuck," Rory sighed, collapsing back on the bed. "I thought it was all just a joke. I didn't even believe the place was on fire."

"You're becoming jaded," Sean pointed out. "That's what the lesson with the blindfold and the groceries was about, wasn't it? Our games aren't doing it for you anymore because you know they're games. That's what you were trying to show me with the hot and cold blowjob treatment. Once you know what to expect, it's not as intense."

"We're not kids anymore," Rory sighed. "We need to grow up and quit playing games."

"Uh-huh," Sean said, carefully unrolling a condom over Rory's dick. "Nice to see this hasn't had an adverse effect on your friend here. He still seems to work nicely."

"I was almost killed, I've lost everything I own, and that's all you've got to say?" Rory asked incredulously.

"Well," Sean smiled, flicking his tongue out to tease the tip of Rory's cock. "There is one more thing I'd like to know."

"What?" Rory asked.

Chuckling softly, Sean flipped the switch to start the fire recording and asked, "Could you tell which fireman I was?"

CBGB 1977! (Hunting the Wild Mapplethorpe Model)
by Jack Fritscher

The media call it "Punk Rock" and to me punking always meant fucking. I got my curiosity through the *New York Times* and from hanging out with sickboy Mapplethorpe who was all over his punk diva, that poetic Patti Smith girl who was actually happening. So I figured to check it out. The clubs are a gonzo dream for a New Journalist in search of kink and ink. Editors pay by the column inch for reportage any man would do for free in the underground world of black leather, rock 'n roll, and sex. Mixed with art and cameras, social devolution is only interesting served raw before it becomes pure style on the runways and in the malls. CBS News got a boner showing a clip of "punk dancing," which to me looked like a lot of fighting, punching, and kick-boxing with a beat. So I split out of Mapplethorpe's loft where I was staying on Bond Street, fucking with him among his cameras and curios, and exited by Bleecker Street and headed to the bottom of the Bowery, stepping over for crissakes winos cadging tourists for bottles of Tawny Port.

Somewhere in the middle of all this lower New York garbage, *Time* tells tourists, and Mapplethorpe tells me, lies CBGB, the hole-in-the-wall capital of Punk Rock. CBGB stands for "Country/Blue Grass/Blues." Shit. Those initials long ago lost their meaning. CBGB is closer now to heeby-jeeby with a gothic-mod crowd that downshifts the concept of fabu to a new low cool. So no wonder Mapplethorpe, Hasselblad in hand, mentioned to keep an eye open for models if I met anyone with a "Look."

Outside CBGB, a Bowery drunk and his three pals were tossing up cookies in the doorway. (Hey, man, New Journalism reportage is what it is about! And punk is about the Stuff of the Night. Fluids. Sex. Blood. Art. And other outrageous dark voodoo that scares Mom and Pop like the inside of CBGB). I stumbled in through the gloom over loose floorboards, tripping on gigantic roaches, and plopped my ass into a wobbly chair made in a correctional facility for terminal assholes, trying to see the goddamn stage. Outside, the Bowery Bum Ballet had sounded like all four faces on Mount Retchmore doing an upchuck quartet. Inside, CBGB was stirring like a morgue of necrophiliacs anticipating a hot autopsy.

Tonight. On stage. Live. Sort of. Was appearing the punk rock group, SMEGMA 4SKINZ.

Looking around, I saw weirdos. I mean young, young, young weirdos. Before hippies, people didn't get weird till maybe 25 or 30. These babies were born weird. All of them, not old enough to grow a moustache, looked cloned out of what was left of James Dean. They had deadwhite faces made up over black leather jackets.

Fuck. Gimme an empty table. Quick.

To my right sat Fan Tan Fanny. One fan came out of her crotch and spread out over her tiny chest. The second fan came out of her ass and reached up and across her pale shoulders where the two fans joined, baring her mortuary sides. Her small dead breasts dangled forward as she leaned to light her Camel from the table candle.

She was no apprentice nymphomaniac.

The guy behind me was no guy to have behind me. He was a burnt-out 22, 6'2", and 300 of the ugliest pounds this side of a fat man's amputated left leg. His tit-length beard, parted in the middle, spread out to two sticky points. His shaved head was covered with Day-Glo green bristle. His tits, his nose, and his left ear were pierced. The lobe stretched, like something out of National Geographic, halfway down his neck. Through the hole in his lobe he had stuck a big, corked test tube. Inside the test tube crawled two live cockroaches.

Suddenly the stage was lit. The houselights dimmed to black. A deafening hum buzzed feedback from the speakers on either side of the floor. A disembodied voice announced, "Ladies and Gentlemen! SMEGMA 4SKINZ!"

As the stage lights blazed bright, then down, something dark pulled up a chair to my table. In the candlelight, I saw he was young and leathered. Our eyes met. Some fucking enchanted evening. His face had the tough hollow look Jim Morrison had perfected in that bathtub in Paris. He took out a Gauloises Blondes. I struck a match. He moved his face to the flame. The cigarette dangled. He inhaled and sort of grunted thanks. I dropped the lit match into his leather crotch. Our thighs touched side-by-side under the table. He smiled and licked his lips. He sucked on a cut across his knuckles. "I punched a guy," he said. He held out his bloody fingers. "Want a taste?"

"SMEGMA sucks," I said.

"Mr. Gauloises" smiled and snorted his agreement. I checked him out again. He looked at me as if he were asking for something I knew I had.

The music was too loud to make normal conversation.

On stage, Pontius and Pilate, the leaders of SMEGMA 4SKINZ , were laying out their opening number. Pontius Smegma wore a blue ski jacket and stretch pants. He stood stage-rear moving his hands without any particular effect up and down on a synthesizer. He made elevator Muzak sound like the Pachelbel "Canon in D." Pilate Smegma's leather jacket was torn to shreds. How the fuck can anyone tear up a leather jacket? His black Korvette's $1.98 wig slipped to his stencilled eyebrows as he struggled to look EVIL.

"Sixty-nine Comeshots!" Pilate Smegma shouted, then hit himself in the side of the face with the microphone torn from its stand. POW! "Sixty-nine Comeshots! SIXTY-NINE COMESHOTS!" He screamed. Then POW! POW! POW! Slamming himself in the side of the face.

"WHAT'S YOUR NAME?" I yelled into Mr. Gauloises's ear.

"You can call me 'Bryl.'"

Behind his nose ring, he looked like his parents called him "Buddy."

I pretended not to hear him and leaned over for another listen using his right thigh to support my weight. I pressed hard. Very hard. "Did you say 'Bryl'?" I asked.

"Yeah," he said "A little dab'll do ya. Brylcreme. But nobody ever calls me 'Mr. Creme.'"

Crissakes. This kid was straight out of the Toob.

The music was maxing. The crowd was rushing the stage for a taste of SMEGMA. The bleeding performer was alternating his mike from his mouth to his asshole, jamming it for a few hot licks into the faces worshipping him. Before he could sing another chorus of "I Wanna Eat Your Load," I asked Bryl, "You want to go out for a good smoke?"

We shouldered our way to the door. A Testosterone Case with Popeye forearms stamped our hands as we left. Stepping over the bum and his pals lying in their puke-o-rama, we headed into the alley behind the club. It smelled of piss. We ignored the skag servicing the suit.

"OK, Mr. Creme. What's your real story?"

He looked at me like a naughty cocker spaniel who just shit on the rug and expected the Sunday *Times* across his ass. I reached for his leather lapels. His right hand shot up and grabbed mine. The back of his hand was angry, red, and blistered with fresh cigarette burns.

Terrific. Another creature from Alpha Centauri.

I shook his hand away and slapped him across the face. He went down like shot snot. He knelt in the bum piss and clutched my knees like the Saving Cross and whimpered. I grabbed the shoulder of his jacket, unsnapped the epaulets and using them as handles, forced the punkfucker's shoulders back up against the wall. He grabbed my foot and put the sole of my boot square against his chest. Lordy! Make me a footstool at thy feet! Taking his cue, I crushed him against the wall. His tongue stuck out wet and sticky licking the toe of my boot.

For something in his youth or childhood, he deserved, or thought he deserved, the kind of thing I got to give. I could see a bulge rising in his tight Levi's. My own cock was at fighting stance. (What do authorities mean about sex and violence. Sex is violence. These days.) Outpunking this punk was not a problem. He reached for his fly held closed by six big safety pins. I scraped my boot down, knocking his hand away.

"Mine," I said. "Me. Me. Me. Mine. Asshole!"

With trembling hands he reached up and unlatched my Harley belt. Slowly he popped open my buttons. He lowered my jeans to my knees. Who the fuck wears underwear? My cock sprang out toward his face. I was gonna have me my first genuine certified punk mouth. I slapped him once more, just for the bloody good juice of it. "Not so fast." I spit on him. When in Punkdom, do as the punks do. "We got all night. Go slow. Treat it nice."

Bryl reinvented the blowjob. He had an all-pro tongue. Every few seconds he raised his mournful eyes to check if he was licking me all right. I sneered my best Presley sneer-of-death. Elvis would have liked my version of his style.

Gradually, Bryl worked his way to my roots. He sucked long and steady. I was almost this side of coming when suddenly goddamn coughing came from my left. The soylent green bums had found their way into the alley for more puke time in the old corral. I pulled up my jeans. "Later," I said.

We showed our stamped hands to Mr. Testosterone at the CBGB door. SMEGMA had finished trying and a new group was on stage. A table opened up. We sat thigh to thigh.

"Hey, Fuckers! Meet PLUGG AND THE DRAIN BOYS!"

The crowd managed a cheer. Yay. Yay. Who the fuck are THE DRAIN BOYS? They looked like abortions that got away. The guitar-punk wore a tight dog collar. A safety pin dangled from his ear. The lead singer, Plugg, was meditating, masturbating, waiting his cue, stripped to the waist, ropes of drool hanging from his mouth to his muscular belly. Suddenly he sprang to his dead feet and started the song: "Why do I wanna fuck you Girls when your dog is so mean Girls I don't wanna hold your gland Girls I'm talkin about a plan Girls I don't really want you Girls I need sex Yeah Baby I NEED SEX!" (This shit is copyright 1977 by Plugg Drain Music.)

Bryl and I looked at each other. Suddenly, because everything happens suddenly in the punk world, Plugg threw himself from the stage into the audience, landing on our table. Our two bottles of beer crashed to the floor. We kicked him the shit away just for the fuck of it, and he crawled back onto the stage toward the drums. He stuck his head inside the bass drum to really hear a few hot beats then threw himself onto the floor again, flopping like the beached fish at the end of Fellini's *La Dolce Vita*.

Again, suddenly, another punk from the audience dashed for the stage. Just as suddenly, the vicious-looking DRAIN BOYS drummer rose from behind his drums, and with his sticks in his thick mitts played 12 bars of "Bolero" on the punk's face. The entire CBGB broke into a mass of flailing fists and screams. The punk, who now knew "Bolero" by heart, was hum-wiping his bleeding face across the safety-pinned tits of a tattooed earth-mother punkette. Fan Tan Fanny ran trailing her rear fan along the floor. Behind us, glass shattered.

"You want to blow this joint?" I asked.

"What?"

"Are you ready for your close-up?"

I pulled Bryl to the door.

"Wait a minute," he said. Outside, he dropped his jeans, squatted, parted his cheeks, grunted twice, and dumped a load on the heeby-jeeby sidewalk. Street light showed off bone structure and boner and butt.

We walked east through the meanest part of the Village. Bryl's punk-patrol attitude made anyone we passed choose to think we were invisible. We reached the East River. No problem. I turned to Bryl. "OK," I said. "Now where were we? Oh yeah. Now your little dab'll do me. Do me!"

He stood mute.

I punched him in the stomach as hard as I could. He turned green. I could see that puke-look a guy gets in his crossed eyes, so I grabbed him by his greasy hair and held his head over the water in the dark river below. Why the fuck mess up one more nice city sidewalk? He up-chucked straight beer. This kid was gonna end up back in the Bowery, but right now he was in bloom and hot. "You and the night and the sewage," I said. He sank to his knees, lapping at my crotch like the East River lapped at the cement wall below us. God! I felt poetic. I also felt hard again. "Stop!" I said.

He looked up at me, his mouth still around my cock like a punk choirboy caught on the fourth note of "O Holy Night." I slapped him hard and he let go. "Turn around," I said.

He opened his mouth to speak. I raised my hand. He obeyed. "Drop your jeans."

He reached for his belt and dropped his trousers. "Now, boy, down like a dog." He went down on all fours.

"Bryl," I said, "they should call you 'Doggy.'" I steered my cock straight toward his asshole. Was he ready? Is Flushing in New York? I plunged in. Surprise. He was tighter than I expected. Good. New punk. I pumped him harder. Car lights flashed by. His butthole bloomed. New York rose bright all around us in the dark. His ass had talent a camera would love. His mouth was chanting fuck-me-fuck-me. I pulled out. He thought I was finished. He had another thought to think. I pushed him down further. "OK, Bryl baby, daddy's gonna teach his doggie a new trick."

A shiver ran down his spine. He wagged his butt. Somewhere in the summer night conga music floated on the fucka-fucka air.

I rubbed my hand through the thick Brylcreme in his hair, then held it at his mouth. "Slobber on it," I said.

Without question he slurped my hand. The mix of beerpuke, saliva, and punk grease lubed my fist just fine.

He whined "I can't take that." He nursed a small brown bottle of poppers.

"Don't play Brer Rabbit with me." I pushed my middle finger into his asshole. "Easy," I said. "You're easy." I slipped in my ring finger. "Greasy." Then my index finger. "Sleazy." He moaned. I reached under with my other hand and pulled his butt back to me by his balls. He had a safety pin stuck through his cock. Sirens screamed over the rumble of traffic. My pinky slipped in. "Cheesy." His butthole snapped at my knuckles. I bent my thumb across my palm and drove my fist home to the wrist. The suction of his butt pulled my arm in deeper. I braced my boots.

"What you on?" I said.

He made whining sobs. Music to my ears.

"You underestimate yourself," I said. "Big punks don't cry."

He whined again, but his butt suctioned like a sump and my fist turned a slow 180 to the right and a faster 180 left. Oh yeah. I punchfucked him loose. He liked it. I withdrew my fist and stroked my hard cock, listening to him pleading fuck-me-fuck-me. The night was hot. I spit on my dick and wrapped my fist around it. His butt pucker made little kiss-kiss-kissy sounds flirting with my cock. Like a hand grenade, I jammed my fist, full of my dick, into the ventriloquist lips of his butt. His fruit juicy young hole was punk perfect. His internal heartbeat pulsated around my forearm. I humped away, moving my fist inside his asshole jerking off my dick inside my fist inside his butt. Hell, I even let the guy jerk at himself. And, oh God, how he pulled, his ass-ring tightening down harder on my fist and cock till suddenly we both shot off together, arching up in shouts and juice and rapture into the noise and light of the brilliant New York night that left CBGB down below like a dot on a grid.

God bless participatory journalism.

I kicked him down on the sidewalk. "You been fistfucked, punk."

"It hurt."

"What's your point?"

"I liked it."

"No shit!"

He licked my greasy hand and looked up at me. "You want to go back to CBGB?"

"Fuck that noise."

We cleaned up with a rubber hose at a faucet outside a warehouse. In the lamplight, I figured next day I'd take Bryl back to meet Mapplethorpe at his studio.

"You ever modeled for a photograph?" I asked.

"I can't show my face."

"It ain't about your face, Fist Boy."

On our way back to the West Village, we saw two girls on a stoop. When we passed, they looked up. One of them pointed.

"Mira, Juanita, mira!" she said."Los punks! Los punks!"

About the Authors

Derek Adams is the author of a popular series of detective novels featuring the intrepid Miles Diamond, as well as over 100 short stories which, he insists, are ongoing chapters in his autobiography. Mr. Adams currently lives in Seattle.

Barry Alexander, author of *All the Right Places*, has been published in such gay magazines as *In Touch, Men, BlackMale, Mandate, Honcho,* and *Indulge*. The Iowa writer has also has stories in several anthologies including: *Skinflicks, Casting Couch Confessions, Juniors 2,* and *Friction, Volumes 1 and 2*. When asked what advice he had for aspiring erotic writers, Alexander replied, "I believe in the Teddy Roosevelt approach: Write softly, but carry a big dick."

Jonathan Asche started writing his way out of the closet in 1993 while working as an editor for an Alabama newspaper. "I had all these fantasies and no one to share them with except a word processor," he says. He has since left Alabama, the newspaper business, and the closet. His stories have appeared in several gay men's magazines, including *Torso, Mandate, Inches, In Touch for Men, Indulge,* and *Men*. He now lives in Atlanta.

Jordan Baker is a freelance writer from South Arkansas. His work has appeared in *Hustler* and *Indulge*, as well as several literary magazines. When not writing, he divides his time between collecting swords and practicing yoga.

Michael Cavanaugh has worked as a waiter, a doorman at a luxury hotel, and as a model. He has just recently been employed by a young bachelor who plans to sail around the world in his 120-foot yacht. Michael has met several of his fellow crew members and has said, off the record, that the cruise promises to be memorable.

Dale Chase started out writing for motorcycle magazines, then switched to erotica, which he says is a much better ride. His work has been published in *Men, Freshmen, Indulge,* and *In Touch,* as well as *Cycle World, Cycle,* and *Motorcyclist.* He lives near San Francisco and is at work on a novel.

M. Christian's work can be seen in *Best American Erotica, The Mammoth Books of Erotica* series, *Men For All Seasons, Bar Stories, Quickies 2,* and over 100 other books and magazines. He is the editor of the anthologies *Eros Ex Machina, Midsummer Night's Dreams, Guilty Pleasures,* and, with Simon Sheppard, *Rough Stuff: Tales of Gay Men, Sex, and Power.* A collection of his short stories, entitled *Dirty Words,* is scheduled for publication in the near future. He also writes columns for www.scarletletters.com, www.bone-tree.com, and www.playtime.com. He thinks *way* too much about sex.

R.W. Clinger lives in Pittsburgh where he teaches high school English. R. W. (*rough* and *wet*) is a master at seduction and delivers kisses his life companion calls "intoxicating, long, and blissful." R. W. has a love for spying on lovers, sweaty pumped men, and classic novels. His short stories have appeared in *Blackmale, Indulge, In Touch,* and *Locker Room Tales.*

Grant Foster has contributed short stories to a number of magazines and anthologies. In addition to his fiction, he also writes articles about travel and gay history. When not writing, traveling, or doing historical research, Grant gardens at his home in rural Washington state.

Wendy C. Fries publishes erotica regularly, and has written an outdoors column for *Southwest Adventures,* and one on computers for *California Women.* She is currently working on three books of speculative fiction. Wendy has yet to figure out how to write an erotic story in which jelly-beans play an important part.

Jack Fritscher wrote *Some Dance to Remember* ("The epic gay history: 1970-1982" —*The Advocate*); a memoir of his lover, *Mapplethorpe: Assault with a Deadly Camera*; and the award-winning four-volume series of magazine fiction: *Corporal in Charge of Captain O'Malley, Stand by Your Man,*

Rainbow County, and *Titanic: Forbidden Stories Hollywood Forgot.* Soon after Stonewall, "Fritscher invented the leather prose style." —*Bay Area Reporter.* He has directed 120 erotic videos: www.PalmDriveVideo.com. Research/e-mail: www.JackFritscher.com

T. Hitman is a full-time professional writer who has penned over 500 short stories and articles for major magazines, several books, and episodes of the television series *Star Trek: Voyager.* But it is his love for baseball, hockey, football, and basketball—and other contact sports—that forces him to write gay men's erotica. His novel about the sweat-drenched exploits on and off the field of baseball jocks, *Hardball,* was published in September '99.

Derek Kemp would like you to know that Max the DJ is real. Though some of the elements of "The Hot Nine at 9:00" are fictionalized, most of it is very real. If Max is reading this, he knows Derek's phone number and should call. Derek would very much like to get on with Round Three.

Pierce Lloyd lives in Southern California, where he has too little time and too much fun. He began writing erotica in college because it beat studying for tests.

R.J. March lives in Reading, PA as Robert Warwick. His work, erotic and otherwise, has appeared in *The James White Review, The Mississippi Review, Men,* and *Freshmen,* as well as a number of anthologies. A collection of his stories entitled *Looking for Trouble* was published last Spring.

Roddy Martin's work has appeared in *Friction, Volume 1, Best Gay Erotica, 1998, Advocate Classifieds, Freshmen, In Touch, Indulge, Blackmale,* and in magazines for children and teens.

Alan Mills lives in West Hollywood with a trampy roommate and a neutered cat. He's the editor of *In Touch, Indulge* and *Blackmale,* and is one of this year's GayVN judges. His work is featured in numerous anthologies, including *Friction 2, Skinflicks,* and *Casting Couch Confessions.*

Nick Montgomery is a playwright and novelist living in New Jersey. "Spice Up Your Life" was his first attempt at erotic fiction.

Brent Muller is a journalist and media analyst living in Southern California. He spends his free hours writing, playing hockey, and exploring the great outdoors with his mates.

Lee Alan Ramsay is the pen name of Daddy Bob Allen. Daddy Bob has a 16th century torture grotto carved out of his garage, which at times has been booked as much as six weeks in advance. He has built an international reputation as a leatherman; it has been said that he has forgotten more about S/M than most people will ever know. He has been writing for *The Leather Journal* since its inception in 1987 and is now its news editor. He is also the fiction and photo editor of *Eagle*. He is the author of two books, *The Only Reason I Mention This* and *The Wings of Icarus*.

J.D. Ryan lives in rural South Carolina between a stock car racetrack and a cow pasture, which, along with all the old Westerns on television when he was growing up, probably explains his fascination with the old West. His work has been published in *In Touch, Honcho,* and several anthologies.

Lance Rush is the pen name of L.M. Ross, a poet/playwright living in New York. His work regularly appears in some of today's better stroke publications. In the past year his erotic adventures have appeared in *Bear, Inches, Blackmale, Guys, Indulge, Hombres Latinos, Honcho, Mandate,* and *Torso,* as well as several anthologies. He is currently working on his first erotic novel.

Dominic Santi is a Los Angeles-based freelance writer with stories in the anthologies *Best Gay Erotica 2000, The Mammoth Book of Historical Erotica, Friction, Volume 2, Sex Toy Tales, Hard at Work, Ravish Me, Casting Couch Confessions, The Young and The Hung, Frisky Business, Men for All Seasons,* and *Rough & Ready,* as well as *Indulge, Men, Honcho,* and *FirstHand* magazines. Santi is also the section leader for Alternative Eros in CompuServe's Erotica forum.

Simon Sheppard is the coeditor with M. Christian of *Rough Stuff: Tales of Gay Men, Sex, and Power*. His work has appeared in dozens of anthologies, including *Best American Erotica 2000* and *Best Gay Erotica 2000*. His column, "Sex Talk," appears in queer papers nationwide. For a sadist, he's awfully nice.

Bob Vickery is a regular contributor to *Men* magazine. Stories of his can be found in his two anthologies: *Skin Deep* and *Cock Tales,* and are also included in *Best American Erotica, 2000, Best American Erotica, 1997, Best Gay Erotica, 1999, Friction, Volume 1 and 2,* and *Queer Dharma,* among others. He can be contacted through his web page at www.bobvickery.com.

Alexander Welch, after spending years under the ocean on nuclear submarines for the Navy, claims New Orleans as home, but currently resides on James Island, just outside Charleston, SC. New to the industry, he completed his first gay novel in 1998. He is also a professional truck driver, and discovers many of his story ideas while he travels the highways of America.

Thom Wolf lives and works in the United Kingdom. He has been writing erotica since he was 18 and believes that it is in his blood. His work has appeared in *In Touch, Indulge, Men,* and *Overload.* He likes yoga, sex, and is a fanatical Kylie Minogue fan. He continues to write erotic fiction and dreams of one day producing the ultimate gay sex novel.

Sean Wolfe lives in Denver and is Director of Communications and Public Affairs for a small nonprofit organization. He has written several short stories and three erotic novels, and is working on his first nonerotic novel. He is also a public speaker on gay issues, a Board member of Colorado Business Council (Colorado's gay and lesbian chamber of commerce), and a past Board member of Colorado AIDS Project.

About the Magazines

Bear ("Bear With a Brick"): For subscription information, contact Brush Creek Media at 367 Ninth Street, San Francisco, CA 94103.

Blackmale ("Gorgeous Tits"): For subscription information, write to Blackmale at 13122 Saticoy Street, North Hollywood, CA 91605, call (800) 637-0101.

Bunkhouse ("Line Cabin Fever"): For subscription information, contact Brush Creek Media at 367 Ninth Street, San Francisco, CA 94103.

Dude ("Gustavo: A Love Story"): For subscription information, write to Dude Magazine, c/o Dugent Corporation, 14411 Commerce Way, Suite 420, Miami Lakes, FL 33016.

Firsthand ("For Real"): For subscription information, contact Firsthand Limited at 310 Cedar Lane, Teaneck, NJ 07666.

Freshmen ("The Opportunist," "The All Nighter," "Ready," "Scottie," "Stripped of Inhibitions," "Spice Up Your Life"): For subscription information, call (800) 757-7069.

Honcho ("CBGB 1977"): For subscription information, contact Jiffy Fulfillment at P.O. Box 1102, Cranford, NJ 07016, or at 462 Broadway, 4th Floor, New York, NY 10013.

Inches ("Hot Shave and a Haircut"): For subscription information, contact Jiffy Fulfillment at P.O. Box 1102, Cranford, NJ 07016, or at 462 Broadway, 4th Floor, New York, NY 10013.

Indulge ("Unraveling Hayden," "Santee's Equation," "Smoker," "The Deceivers," "Just a Matter of Time," "Invasion of Privacy"): For subscription information, write to Indulge at 13122 Saticoy Street, North Hollywood, CA 91605, call (800) 637-0101.

In Touch ("Now and Then," "Jacked In," "Joe Pornstar," "Of Monsters and Men"): For subscription information, write to In Touch at 13122 Saticoy Street, North Hollywood, CA 91605, call (800) 637-0101.

Mach ("The Harley," "Getting Even"): For subscription information, contact Brush Creek Media at 367 Ninth Street, San Francisco, CA 94103.

Mandate ("The Wrong Guy"): For subscription information, contact Jiffy Fulfillment at P.O. Box 1102, Cranford, NJ 07016, or at 462 Broadway, 4th Floor, New York, NY 10013.

Manifest Reader ("Firebomber: Cigar Sarge"): For subscription information, contact Alternate Publishing, P.O. Box 14695, San Francisco, CA 94114.

Men ("Basic Training," "Second Chances," "Underway," "Virtual Virgin," "Hunger Takes Over," "Crossing Thresholds," "The Beckoning," "Knowing Johnny," "The Daddy Thing," "Hitchcock," "The Hot Nine at 9:00," "Sharing Jeff," "Out in the Woods," "Peeping Tom"): For subscription information, call (800) 757-7069.

Torso ("Base on Balls"): For subscription information, contact Jiffy Fulfillment at P.O. Box 1102, Cranford, NJ 07016, or at 462 Broadway, 4th Floor, New York, NY 10013.

Vulcan America ("He"): For subscription information, write to Butch Media at P.O. Box 3199, North Hollywood, CA 91609-0199, or call 888-919-0822.